Virtuous Women

ANN GOLTZ

Paperback ISBN: 978-0-9995215-1-9
Ebook ISBN: 978-0-9995215-2-6

Library of Congress Control Number: 2023922023

First paperback edition: March 2024

Cover Art and Interior Formatting by BespokeBookCovers.com

Quiet Publications
131 Daniel Webster Hwy. #876
Nashua, NH 03060
www.quietpublications.com

*For Tom, who believed in me as a writer even when I didn't.
This book wouldn't exist without you.*

Part One

2008 - 2010

Lo, children are an heritage of the Lord: and the fruit of the womb is his reward. As arrows are in the hand of a mighty man, so are children of the youth. Happy is the man that hath his quiver full of them: they shall not be ashamed, but they shall speak with the enemies in the gate.

-Psalm 127:3-5

Chapter One

Hope Wagner had barely settled herself in her usual spot at the end of their family's pew when her two-year-old brother, Benjamin, fought and wiggled his way out of her arms. As he made for the double doors in the back of the church, Hope glanced past her nine other siblings to where her father sat at the opposite end of the pew. He scowled at Benjamin, then at her. She knew that expression. Too well. She launched herself into the center aisle and enveloped the toddler in a bear hug, squeezing him tighter than she needed to, hoping a little pain would help him understand the importance of obedience. Better her bent knees in his back than Papa's belt across it.

"Be quiet," she hissed in his ear. The eyes of the families seated nearby were on her—she could feel them. Some were sympathetic, some amused, some passed judgment. Those were the ones she worried about. She stood up, Benjamin still held tight against her chest.

That's when Hope saw the strange woman standing in the back.

New people didn't just show up at Church of the

Covenant. Sometimes an established family would invite a new person or family to Sunday services, someone they thought would be willing to accept their beliefs. Papa had done that with a couple of the contractors he'd worked with over the years. Both times, he'd met them at the front door and made it clear to everyone they were his invited guests. But no one walked over to welcome this woman. She stood alone, her eyes sweeping across the pews.

The woman's hair was blonde and worked into an intricate braided bun, fancier than usual for church. More importantly, it was uncovered. If anyone had invited her, they hadn't told her about the dress code.

At least she was wearing a dress, though it was unlike any dress Hope had ever seen in real life. It was...the only word Hope could come up with was 'old-fashioned.' Not thrift-shop outdated, like most of the dresses she and her sisters owned, but actually old-fashioned, like something you'd see on the cover of a historical novel at the library. The dress was brown cotton with tiny yellow flowers printed on it, and the tight bodice was buttoned right up to a cameo brooch that was centered between the two flaps of her ivory lace collar. A full skirt hung at her ankles, a pair of black laced boots peeking out beneath it. She reached into her brown drawstring handbag and pulled out a flip phone. She opened it, pressed a button for a few seconds, then returned it to her bag. Papa had just gotten a flip phone, and Hope had seen him turn his off the same way.

Hope realized she was still standing in the middle of the aisle and returned to her seat, Benjamin still struggling in her arms. Pasting a smile on her face in case anyone was watching, she murmured threats in a low, menacing voice. Hope didn't know if Benjamin understood her words yet, but he knew her tone. He stopped trying to escape.

Hope hadn't been the only one to notice the newcomer,

and now almost everyone in the sanctuary was staring at her. The muted conversations that always occurred before the service began had died out, replaced by more furtive whisperings.

The strange woman strode down the center aisle until she found an empty pew a few rows behind Hope's family and slid in, her skirt rustling around her. It was the pew where Hope's Aunt Libby, Uncle Nick, and cousin Jared usually sat.

Hope kept turning around in her seat, pretending to search for someone, glancing at the stranger every time she did. Most of her siblings weren't so subtle. Faith was eight and Joy was nine, plenty old enough to help mind the littles, but both girls were ignoring their charges and sat twisted in their seats, staring at the blonde woman. Beyond them three of the four oldest boys also stared. Only Joshua, who at sixteen was a year younger than Hope, attempted to make his occasional glances toward the pews behind them discreet. Next to him Papa kept his eyes on the large wooden cross hanging at the front of the church, not participating in the spectacle the woman was causing but not discouraging his children from doing so, either. Hope took it as a sign that they weren't doing anything wrong. The service hadn't started yet, and it's not like looking around the church was prohibited.

Between Faith and Joy, the littles were oblivious of the drama around them. They were having a contest to see who could kick higher, three-year-old Grace determined to out-kick her two older brothers. That kind of behavior *was* prohibited. Hope elbowed Faith.

"You're supposed to be watching the kids," Hope whispered.

Faith turned back around with a sigh and told the younger ones to stop kicking. They continued their contest until Hope repeated the order in what Grace always called her "Scary

Hope" voice, the one she'd patterned after Papa. Joy kept watching the newcomer.

Hope peeked back again. The stranger sat tall and stiff, her eyes fixed on the cross in front just like Papa. She must have known she was the center of attention, but she acted like her being there was the most normal thing in the world. For Hope, this was the most exciting thing that had happened in church since Avery McAndrew knocked his knee against the back of the pew and said "shit" loud enough for everyone to hear it.

The door of the church opened again, and even the furtive whispering stopped. Aunt Libby and Uncle Nick walked in, Jared following behind them and greeting everyone he passed with his usual exuberant innocence, his voice booming in the unusual silence. Jared was older than Hope by a few years but acted more like her six-year-old brother, Timothy. Different people in the congregation used different words to describe Jared, from "retarded" or "slow" to "special" or "touched." To Hope her cousin was just a sweet little boy in a big boy's body.

Someone must have told Aunt Libby and Uncle Nick about the newcomer in their pew while they were still in the parking lot because they didn't look surprised to see her sitting there. Aunt Libby whispered something to her husband, and he fell back to walk with Jared. Hope and Joshua gave up all pretense and stared, along with everyone else in the congregation. Even Papa turned to watch his sister approach the stranger.

She smiled down at the newcomer. Aunt Libby was an imposing woman, and that smile didn't make her beautiful. The stranger looked up at her, her expression apprehensive.

How had the woman managed to remain calm for so long? If Hope had been in her shoes, she would have bolted long ago. No, she wouldn't have. She would never have gone to a strange church all by herself to begin with. Even if she'd been allowed to.

"Good morning," Aunt Libby said, her voice carrying in the unusual silence.

"Good morning." The newcomer smiled to match Aunt Libby, but only with her mouth.

"Do you mind if we sit with you? It can be confusing worshiping at a new church. I can show you how we do things here."

The newcomer's smile became real. It lit up her whole face. She was beautiful even when she didn't smile, but the smile made her stunning. Hope felt a small stab of jealousy. No one would ever call her stunning. Or beautiful. Or even pretty. She was just Hope.

"I'd like that."

The strange woman slid gracefully down the pew to make room for Aunt Libby and her family. Muted conversation sprang up in the other pews. Hope's siblings turned back around and stretched necks and shoulders that had become tight with the strain of looking behind them.

"I like her dress," Joy murmured to Faith, who nodded her agreement.

Further down the pew, their fifteen-year-old brother John shook his head and leaned across Samuel and Amos to address his sisters.

"It's indecent," he proclaimed, his voice carrying to the pews around them. "The skirt's fine, but that top could really cause a brother to stumble."

Hope couldn't imagine *anything* causing John to stumble, but she kept her thoughts to herself and hoped Joy would too. She didn't have to worry, though. As if on cue Pastor Kinsley stepped up to the pulpit and began the service.

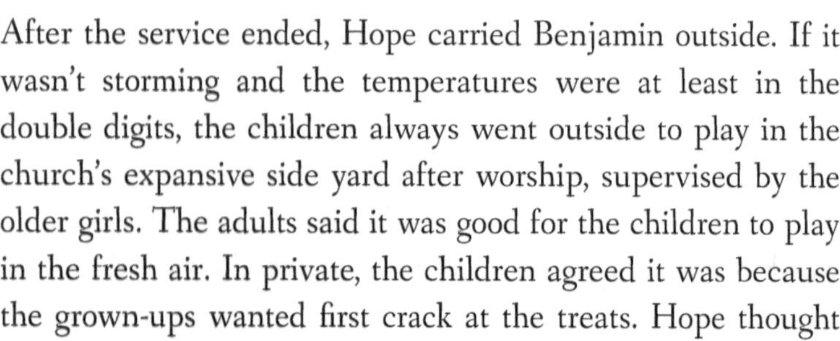

After the service ended, Hope carried Benjamin outside. If it wasn't storming and the temperatures were at least in the double digits, the children always went outside to play in the church's expansive side yard after worship, supervised by the older girls. The adults said it was good for the children to play in the fresh air. In private, the children agreed it was because the grown-ups wanted first crack at the treats. Hope thought both might be right.

She didn't mind the arrangement, especially on days like this when the weather was a perfect combination of cool and sunny. It was halfway through October and the dense greenery of north-central Massachusetts had yielded to orange and gold, shifting and swaying in the breeze and just beginning to carpet the grass. The sun filtered through the foliage, making patterns like lace on the church lawn where the younger children played. The older boys sat in the shade, away from the girls and the younger children, engrossed in whatever boys that age talked about.

Hope sat in her usual place in the sun next to Carolyn and Carolyn's youngest sister, Rebekah. Their families had been friends for years, and their mothers had often been pregnant at the same time. Rebekah was only a few months younger than Benjamin. A late walker, she preferred to sit on the ground, examining fallen leaves and occasionally crawling after bugs, and Benjamin liked to help her find things to discover.

"I wonder if we'll ever see her again," Carolyn mused, watching Benjamin plop down next to her sister.

Hope didn't have to ask who she was talking about. "Probably not. People who just show up without being invited never come back."

She couldn't remember a single uninvited visitor coming back a second time.

"I know," Carolyn said. "It was awkward enough fitting in here with an invitation."

"Who brought you in?" Hope had only vague memories of Carolyn's family being new at Church of the Covenant. She'd been about six when Ted Cook, his wife, Stacy, and their two children arrived.

"The Petersons."

"Joel's family?" As soon as the words were out, Hope regretted them.

Carolyn raised her eyebrows and glanced past the large circle of children playing Brother's Keeper toward the older boys sitting in the shade.

Hope looked across the field as well. Faith stood in the middle of the circle of kids, trying to protect Avery McAndrew, who was more than a foot taller than her, from getting hit with a beanbag being tossed around by those in the circle. She was running around the tall boy, arms wide open, trying to follow the beanbag and keep her body between it and Avery, who was laughing and not doing anything to make himself a smaller target.

Beyond them, under the shadow of the trees lining the church property, sat Joel Peterson. He was older than most of the other boys, older than Hope by three and a half years. Three years, seven months, and twenty-two days, to be exact, though Hope would never admit she knew that. He was tall, with dark brown hair, kind brown eyes, and a gentle mouth filled with crooked teeth. Next to him sat Doug Murphy, who was doing all the talking. Joel nodded politely at what Doug was saying but didn't seem engaged in the conversation. His eyes were on the children playing their game in the middle of the field. He smiled as his sister Hannah threw the beanbag to

Hope's brother Amos, who faked a throw back to Hannah. Faith followed the expected trajectory of the beanbag and left Avery unprotected as Amos hurled the beanbag at him, hitting him on the shoulder. Everyone in the circle howled and Joel laughed, and Hope was sure his eyes moved past the group of children and landed on her. Her cheeks flushed and she looked away, a small smile on her lips.

"You like him," Carolyn said.

Hope couldn't meet her eyes. She had liked Joel since their first conversation a year and a half ago, when he'd helped her park her family's enormous van in the church parking lot, but they hadn't spoken since. He was courting age, and young men and young women weren't supposed to interact without a chaperone.

"That's up to God," Hope said.

"It's up to God whether or not you marry him, but you like him."

"I'm not giving away pieces of my heart."

"I never said you were. But you like him."

"I think he'll make a fine husband to whatever woman God chooses for him," Hope said carefully.

Carolyn grinned. "I think so too."

Hope glanced at her friend and for the first time saw her as a young woman. A pretty young woman, who was kind and nurturing. Carolyn helped her mother care for the six children she'd birthed since arriving at Church of the Covenant eleven years earlier, and, unlike Hope, Carolyn seemed to enjoy it. She was everything a godly young woman was supposed to be, and everything Hope wasn't. If the Petersons brought the Cooks into the church, Carolyn probably got to see Joel often. How could she compete with that?

"Do *you* like him?" she asked, not sure she wanted to hear the answer.

Carolyn laughed and shook her head. "I'm not in danger of giving away pieces of my heart to him. Our families have been friends for a long time, and Joel and Billy got along really well, so I've seen a lot of him." She glanced around and lowered her voice, even though the other girls weren't close enough to over-hear. She leaned closer to Hope. "My parents don't know, and I promised not to tell anyone, but Joel's still in touch with Billy. So, I know he's okay."

"That's great!" Hope said, still wary but happy for her friend. Hope never like Carolyn's older brother—he'd always been moody and rebellious—and she hadn't been surprised when he ran away from home a year ago, shortly after his eigh-teenth birthday. Boys like Billy always left. "Where is he?"

"I promised not to tell," Carolyn said again. "He's okay, though, and he's doing well. And since he's talking to Joel, maybe he'll repent and come home. Joel kind of adopted me as a little sister. You know he has five sisters and only one brother?"

If Joel thought of Carolyn as a little sister, maybe Hope didn't have to worry after all. Relaxing a little she nodded, going along with the change of subject. She knew one of Joel's older sisters was on the men's prayer list. Apparently, Elizabeth Peterson was living in sin with some boy she'd met at college in Oregon. Hope had overheard the men praying about it at a prayer meeting Papa hosted last spring—she had to listen, so she knew when to bring out more coffee. Jack Peterson had taken a lot of flak for sending his daughter so far away from home, especially for college. The fact that it was a Christian college didn't matter. He'd admitted his mistake and they all prayed that Elizabeth would repent and come home, but Hope knew she probably wouldn't. It was hard enough for a boy like Billy to return, but at least he could be seen as a prodigal son, stronger in his faith because of his second chance. If a girl like

Elizabeth returned, the stain of her sin would follow her for the rest of her life.

Hope didn't know if Carolyn knew the truth about Elizabeth. She hadn't been back for a visit since she left for school, and most people assumed she'd met a godly man at that Christian college and married him. Joel's other three older sisters had all married and moved away. His younger siblings, Stephen and Hannah, were still at home.

"Stephen seems like a good person, too," Hope said, trying to cover her interest in Joel.

"He is. And he'll probably make a good husband too. But he's still pretty young, and Joel's a lot closer to ready."

"Stephen's our age!"

Carolyn shrugged and watched Benjamin hand an acorn to Rebekah. She leaned forward to take it away before the little girl could put it in her mouth, causing Benjamin to pound his fist on the ground in frustration. She plucked a clover from the grass and handed it to him, and he promptly made a gift of it to Rebekah. It went straight into her mouth. Carolyn didn't stop her this time. Rebekah made a face and spit it out, and Benjamin laughed. After a moment, so did Rebekah. Carolyn smiled at the two toddlers.

"Girls mature faster than boys," she said. "We're almost ready, Joel's almost ready, and Stephen's not."

Hope was jolted by the idea that she could get married soon. It's what all the girls prepared for, and many of them did marry in their late teens, but to Hope it felt like a big jump to go from helping at home to managing your own home. Even for her.

"Do you feel ready?" she asked.

Carolyn's expression became wistful.

"I don't know. Sometimes I think I know how to run a house and raise children and all that. But I'm not sure I know how to handle a husband. Actually being married. That part scares me a little."

"Me too." Hope was glad she wasn't the only one who felt that way.

Brother's Keeper had broken up, and now the field was a chaotic mass of several dozen children playing Everybody's It Tag. Even some of the young men under the trees joined in. Doug Murphy didn't look happy when Joel got up and ran into the fray, his dark brown hair flying back from his forehead and a broad smile on his face. Hope noticed that Joel chased some of the younger children but always let them escape. More often he made a show of pumping his arms and taking long strides as he tried to outrun the littlest children. His movements were comically slow as he glanced over his shoulder with an exaggerated expression of fear at the small child who would inevitably catch up with him and tag him out. Then he'd walk to the side, touch the beanbag that lay on the ground, and return to the game. Everybody's It Tag only ended when everyone got tired. Or when it was treat time.

Benjamin and Rebekah ran around close to Hope and Carolyn in their waddling little steps, playing their own game of tag. A few toddlers who had been sitting with some of the other girls joined them. Hard experience had taught them they'd be trampled if they tried to join the 'big' kids. Rebekah fell every few steps, her young legs unused to having so much asked of them. Benjamin yelled "Oopsie!" every time she stumbled. The toddlers' laughter blended with the sounds of the other children on the field.

Carolyn didn't take her eyes off Rebekah and Benjamin, a dreamy smile playing on her lips.

"I will miss my brothers and sisters, though, when I get married," she said.

"Me too," Hope said, though she wasn't sure it was as true

for her as it was for Carolyn.

She wasn't watching the children. She was watching Joel. He was walking to the edge of the field away from Grace, who was doing a victory dance for just having tagged him out. Sometimes Hope daydreamed about her Prince Charming coming to save her from all her chores and her siblings' needs and her father's expectations. He'd take her away to his castle where they'd live happily ever after. She knew she'd have to clean that castle, and sooner or later it would be filled with their own children whose needs would dominate her life, but Hope took care to never extend her daydream that far into the future.

She also took care to not imagine her Prince Charming with soft brown eyes and crooked teeth. Joel was a nice person, a brother in Christ helping a sister, like he'd said that day in the parking lot, and there was no more to it than that. And even if there *was* more to it than that, it wouldn't matter. Papa couldn't possibly marry her off right now. Her siblings still needed her. Joy was only nine, not nearly old enough to take over Hope's responsibilities.

Hope wouldn't have to worry about handling a husband for a very long time.

Some of the women came outside and called for the children to come in for treat time. Hope and Carolyn scooped up the toddlers under their care and helped the other girls shepherd the rest of the children to the church, organizing them into an orderly line before they filed inside.

Hope was surprised to see the strange new woman still in the kitchen talking with Aunt Libby and a few of the other women. She was holding a cup of coffee and seemed as relaxed as if she'd known these women for years. Not for the first time, and not for the last, Hope wondered what kind of woman would come to a place like Church of the Covenant alone and uninvited and make herself at home.

Chapter Two

The ride back to Concord took just over an hour, but Jennifer Levine didn't mind. She had a lot to think about. Church this morning had been unsettling. She'd visited over a dozen churches in the past eight months, and she was used to being stared at in the smaller ones—even in some of the larger ones—but she'd never encountered anything like the utter silence that had fallen upon the congregation at her arrival that morning.

The woman who sat in the pew with her had helped. The other women had been friendly to Jennifer when Libby introduced her around after the service, though they'd asked some invasive questions about her background—yes, Levine was a Jewish name, no she hadn't been raised Jewish, more of a non-practicing Methodist like her mother—and they shared their strong opinions about modesty. Regrettably, Jennifer never got to meet any of the men. The women had remained in the kitchen, preparing the refreshments, while the men gathered in pairs and small groups in the fellowship hall. That had been jarring, but it fit with the overall conservative streak she'd noticed in the pastor's sermon. He'd pontificated at length about how Barack Hussein Obama would endanger the Christian foundations of this country if he won the 2008 presidential election. The pastor had even called the Illinois Senator a Muslim terrorist.

Jennifer didn't buy it, but she'd learned early on that the family-oriented churches she preferred tended to be politically conservative. This one appeared to be more family-oriented than any other she'd visited. Insular, even, judging by how she'd been treated so far, but she read that as a positive. They were protective of their own. They valued their families and wanted to keep the church environment safe for them. Jennifer could respect that. It's what she'd been looking for.

They did have strong opinions, though, and Jennifer got the feeling that holding a different opinion was not welcome at Church of the Covenant. Some of what they told her was silly, like when Libby told Jennifer her dress was immodest. How could it be immodest? It went down to her ankles and buttoned up to her throat. No cleavage, no skin showing at all except her face, hands, and neck. But Jennifer had listened politely as a woman named Terri explained that she wanted to mask her figure rather than accentuate it.

In truth she wanted no such thing. Jennifer had a very nice figure, thank you very much. She also liked the style of her dresses just as they were. They made her feel like she was in one of the historical novels she so loved to read, novels that featured strong, dignified women, or the families she admired and were so unlike her own. Her dresses helped her be more like her heroines. The unflappable Jane Eyre, or, if she was feeling a bit sassier, Jo March.

When Jennifer arrived home, both bays of the attached

two-car garage were occupied. Her mouth tightening in annoy-ance, Jennifer pushed the button on the remote in her Prius and opened the door to her designated bay in the detached three-car garage on the opposite side of the wide driveway.

She parked in her bay and strode toward the house, liking the way her skirt swirled around her legs and her boots clumped purposefully on the asphalt. Tall and confident, she chose not to go through the attached garage and into the family room. Instead, she walked the brick path to the front door, unlocked it, and marched in like she owned the place.

Which she didn't.

She could hear the television in the family room but didn't go back there. Closing the door quietly behind her, she climbed the stairs all the way up to her suite on the third floor.

Or, as her mother took great joy in pointing out, the servant's quarters.

As servant's quarters went, it wasn't bad. The door at the top of the stairs opened into a pleasant sitting room. Beyond that was a large, sunny bedroom with an ensuite bathroom. The sitting room had a couch, a rocking chair, and a small wooden dinette. In one corner sat a mini fridge with a microwave on top of it. Next to that was a wardrobe that she'd converted into a small pantry. For anything more, she had to go to the kitchen on the first floor. But Jennifer avoided that as much as she could on her day off. She didn't want to see the family she worked for on the one day she didn't have to. She wished they'd go do something somewhere else on Sundays so she could enjoy the rest of the house in peace, but they never did. So, she hid up here in her room, telling herself she preferred the privacy of her suite.

Jennifer dropped her purse on the dinette and went to the closet in her bedroom. Inside was a large plastic bin with her fabric. She began digging around the neatly folded material, looking for the leftovers from the dresses she'd already made. She had decided to attach a cape overlay to her dresses to make them more acceptable to the women at the church. The cape would hang a little below her waist, covering her curves. It wasn't exactly consistent with the vintage of her style, but it wasn't too far off, either. Some nineteenth century dresses had such embellishments, though they hadn't been included in any of the patterns she'd used. But there was no rule against adding them now.

Jennifer selected the blue striped fabric that matched one of her dresses. There were several yards left over, more than enough for her cape. She spread it out on the craft table in her bedroom and reached for her measuring tape. She had just managed to wrap the tape around her upper arms and torso when there was a knock at her suite door.

It was Hunter, the eight-year-old. His five-year-old sister, Aimi, was right behind him. Jennifer smiled, hiding her irritation. "You know you're not supposed to come up here," she admonished. "This is my private space, and this is my private time."

"Mom sent me to tell you you have a phone call," Hunter said.

"On the house phone?" Jennifer couldn't imagine someone calling her at that number.

Hunter nodded. "She said the cordless doesn't reach up here, so you need to come downstairs."

Aimi tried to sneak past her brother and into the suite. Jennifer caught the little girl and picked her up, enjoying the way her soft, straight black hair felt as it brushed across her cheek.

"How can it not reach up here?" she asked Hunter. "It doesn't have a cord."

Hunter shrugged, and Jennifer knew it was a pointless conversation to have with a child.

"Okay, I'm coming." She stepped out and closed the door firmly behind her before putting Aimi down.

"Can I see your room later?" Aimi asked.

In over two years of being their nanny and living in their house, Jennifer had never allowed the children into her suite. It wasn't for lack of trying on Aimi's part. Or Hunter's.

"No."

Jennifer considered locking the door behind her but figured the kids wouldn't be that bold while she was home. Instead, she insisted they lead her down the stairs all the way to the first floor. Once there, they ran past her and into the family room. A moment later Jennifer heard the TV start back up. Doc Hudson was informing Lightning McQueen that sometimes you have to turn left to go right. She could probably recite that entire movie from memory.

The cordless lay next to its cradle on the kitchen counter. Jennifer picked it up.

"Hello?"

"Jenny, why are you avoiding our calls?"

Jennifer grimaced at her mother's sharp tone and walked into the living room. It was the furthest she could get from both the family room and the home office where Sumiko was most likely working. She settled into the oversized armchair and put her booted feet up on the cream-colored ottoman. The proper young women in her books never sat like this, but they didn't have such comfortable furniture, either.

"I'm not avoiding your calls, Mom. I'm right here. Why didn't you call me on my cell?"

"Your father's been trying to all morning. It goes straight to voicemail every time."

Jennifer sighed. "I turned off my cell phone before church

this morning. I guess I forgot to turn it back on. Why do you always assume the worst?"

"Because the worst is usually true. Your father wants to speak with you."

Jennifer could hear her mother handing the phone over to her father. The fact that her mother didn't even try to converse with her was neither a surprise nor a disappointment. Her father came on the line.

"Jenny, are you okay? I was getting worried when I couldn't reach you."

"I'm fine, Dad. I just forgot to turn my phone back on this morning after church. What's up?"

"I wanted to invite you over for brunch next Sunday. We haven't seen you since August."

Jennifer closed her eyes. Had it been two months since she'd last visited her parents? It didn't seem like it.

"I can't. I'm going to a new church now, and I don't want to miss their service."

"Oh. Well then, how about supper?"

Jennifer hated saying no to her father, but visits with her parents were never pleasant. Her dad tried to be supportive, but he didn't understand her, not really. That lack of understanding came out as a hurt bewilderment that made her feel like she was failing him. Her mother made no effort to be supportive and told Jennifer outright that she was a disappointment.

"I don't think so, Dad. My new church is in Petersham, which is an hour west of here. Driving to Brookline for dinner after that would have me on the road for almost four hours that day."

"But Jenny, Sunday is your only day off! I'm sure there are churches closer to Concord you could go to and still come visit your old parents from time to time."

Even though it was his Judaism she was rejecting, Ira Levine was quite encouraging about Jennifer's search for a church home, even emailing her links to articles he'd found online explaining the differences between denominations. Come to think of it, Jennifer wasn't sure what denomination Church of the Covenant was. She'd have to investigate that.

"I've tried most of the churches close to Concord." She'd tried several of them, anyway. Several others she'd ruled out by looking at their websites. Or by their denomination. Some of her father's links had been helpful. "I really like this one. The people are nice, and they're very family oriented, with lots of kids."

"I'm glad you found a church you like, Jenny, but when will we ever see you? Unless the Whittakers are going to start being reasonable and give you two days off? Your mother and I always managed to give your nannies Saturdays and Sundays. And holidays, too."

Jennifer lowered her voice.

"The Whittakers' situation is different from yours and Mom's. They're both on call a lot even when they're not actually at the hospital, and I've got to be there to watch the kids when they do get called in. They have enough trouble keeping one of them home and not on call every Sunday."

Her father exhaled, irritated. "Even surgeons have days off when they're not on call. There are two of them. They can each take a day to be home and give you a break."

Jennifer glanced at the dining room. Sumiko and Derek's home office was just beyond it. She couldn't see from where she was sitting if the door was open.

"I'm not going to debate my schedule with you, Dad. The Whittakers set it, and I agreed to it."

"You didn't have to, Jenny. You could do so much more."

"You're starting to sound like Mom. I'm sorry I can't come to Brookline next week. It's just too much driving for me now."

"Then we'll come to Concord. We'll take you out to dinner. Will that work?"

At least the visit would be over sooner in a restaurant than if they were at her parents' home.

"Fine," she said. "Six o'clock?"

After agreeing on the time and place, Jennifer pushed the button that would end the call. She leaned her head back and closed her eyes, relaxing into the chair and trying to put her parents out of her mind. Maybe she'd get a book and bring it down to the living room. Hunter and Aimi were busy watching TV. They'd never know she was here.

"Is everything alright Jennifer?"

Jennifer's eyes popped open. She hadn't heard Sumiko enter the room. Hastily she climbed out of the chair, embarrassed to have been caught lounging with her feet up on Sumiko's expensive furniture.

"I'm fine, Sumiko, thank you."

Sumiko smiled. She was almost forty, but her smooth skin and trim figure made her look ten years younger, not much older than Jennifer. "Your mother was very agitated when she couldn't reach you on your cell phone. I was afraid there might be an emergency."

"Any time my mother doesn't get exactly what she wants when she wants it, it's an emergency," Jennifer said.

Sumiko raised an eyebrow but said nothing.

"I'm sorry, that was disrespectful of me. There's no emergency. Everyone's fine."

"Parents love their children," Sumiko said. "Sometimes it seems overbearing, but it comes from love." Her eyes twinkled. "I still endure a very intense love from my parents, and they're all the way in Kyoto."

Jennifer laughed and looked at the phone still in her hand. A thought struck her. "Why couldn't Hunter just bring this upstairs to me?" It would have saved her the discomfort of a conversation with her employer on her only day off.

"If the phone gets too far from the cradle, it doesn't work. It barely works on the second floor, and not at all on the third. The house is too big, I guess."

That made sense. It was a big house. Almost five thousand square feet. Sumiko and Derek had offered to install a private phone line in her suite when she'd first moved in, but she'd felt her cell phone was enough.

Sumiko glanced towards the kitchen.

"I'm afraid I'm not going to be able to cook supper for Hunter and Aimi tonight. I have an article I need to review for the *New England Journal of Medicine,* and I've put it off too long. Are there enough leftovers in the refrigerator for me to heat for them, or should I just order a pizza?"

Jennifer kept her smile on her face, but it was difficult. Sumiko had just been telling her how much parents loved their children, yet she couldn't cook supper for her own the only night of the week she didn't pay someone else to do it? She wasn't even home enough to know what was in her own refrigerator.

"They would probably appreciate the pizza," Jennifer said. "It's so different from the healthy meals I make for them."

Sumiko nodded. "Yes, you are a very good cook. So many interesting meals you make from so many different cultures. Always an education and an experience. My children are fortunate to have you. Pizza will be a nice treat for them. And for you. I'll order for all of us."

Jennifer's cheeks flushed. She had no doubt Sumiko had heard and understood the veiled insult in her words. Not only had she ignored them, but she'd returned the insult with a compliment and an invitation to dinner. The Whittakers didn't go to church, but Sumiko clearly had the whole "turn the other cheek" and "love your neighbor" thing down a lot better than Jennifer.

"That's very generous of you. Thank you."

It was an appropriate atonement for her insult.

Chapter Three

After work on Wednesday, Michael had just enough time to bring Joshua home before heading straight for the Wednesday night men's Bible study. Hope would keep a plate warm for him, and he'd eat before family devotions later that night, if he got home in time. If not, Joshua would lead the devotions, probably with a lot of commentary from John.

The setting sun made the trees behind the church look black against the brilliant orange sky. Long shadows from the tall pines, maples, and oaks conspired with the deep inky blue of the eastern sky to cast both the church and the parking lot in darkness. The headlights from Michael's work truck swept across the other vehicles as he guided his pickup into an empty space way down at the end of the lot, next to the cab of a semi. Ted Cook was usually gone during the week, so Michael was surprised to see his truck here tonight.

The sanctuary windows glowed in the gathering night, but Michael walked past the double front doors that opened into the worship space and headed for the small side door instead. It was unlocked, and he let himself in.

The lights were on downstairs, too, and he could hear the low rumble of men's voices. He went down to join them.

Someone had retrieved two of the old brown folding tables from the storage closet and set them up next to each other, making a large rectangle that could comfortably seat at least sixteen men. There weren't often that many in attendance for the Wednesday night men's Bible study. Some had to work the evening shift or travel during the week like Ted, and a few just didn't bother. Those men would either learn to step up or else find another church.

Michael nodded his greeting to those already assembled and sat down next to Ted. The others were grouped in twos or threes, talking amongst themselves. He made a quick head-count and saw that all but one of the usual attendees were there. They were still waiting on Al Reed, who reliably arrived between five and ten minutes late. Michael didn't understand why Pastor Kinsley didn't just start on time without Al. It might encourage the man to be a bit more prompt. But it was the Pastor's call, not his, so he sat and waited like everyone else. He checked the clock on the wall. 6:30. Right on time.

"Not working this week?" he asked Ted, reaching to the center of the table for the pitcher of water and a paper cup, ignoring the coffee and the cookies. He drank coffee only in the morning and didn't have much of a sweet tooth.

Ted shook his head.

"One of my clients went bankrupt. No warning. Just found out Monday when I went to pick up the load. That route's gone now."

"That's awful," Michael said. "How big was the job?"

Ted bit into a cookie, sprinkling crumbs on his ample belly. He had the classic trucker's physique. "Big. Every four weeks like clockwork. Took the whole week."

Michael winced. His contracting company didn't have any

clients with that kind of stability, but he'd lost several to bankruptcy too, especially in the last year. A quarter of his income without notice, though?

"I know it's not your line, but I've got a build going on that I could use some more hands on. New cul-de-sac in Westminster. I'm trying to finish the exteriors before winter."

Ted brushed the crumbs from his plaid shirt, letting them fall on the floor. "Thanks, Michael, but I'm good. The dispatcher at my old place tossed me a couple of local gigs to help fill the gap while I find a new contract or three. They're always short drivers. They don't pay enough, but it's something. Better than nothing, anyway, and at least I can be with my family every night this week. Besides," he laughed, patting his belly. "I'm not the guy you want to rely on for physical work. The spirit is willing, but the flesh is weak."

Michael chuckled with him. He himself was in excellent shape, often working alongside the men on his crew.

"Well, it's good that you can spend some more time with Stacy. Treasure that, Ted. It's a blessing."

Ted's face grew somber.

"I know, Michael. I thank God every day for my wife and kids. I don't know how you do it."

Michael shrugged. "I do what I have to." He'd learned how to hide the pain that always seized his heart when talk turned to wives. He never let on that the grief he felt was as fresh and bitter as it had been the day Lucy died.

For the first year he'd had a sense of endless waiting. Waiting for the funeral. Waiting to go back to work. Waiting for life to resume its familiar patterns and routines. Waiting for Christmas. Waiting for summer when work would take over his life again. Waiting for the anniversary of Lucy's death. Michael had done all that, gotten through all the 'first-time-we're-doing-this-without-Lucy's,' and then he'd done it again.

The second anniversary of her death had been a month ago. That feeling of waiting had faded away without him noticing, until one day he'd realized it was gone and had been for some time. Michael had known he wouldn't get Lucy back at the end of his waiting, but he'd hoped for something. A lessening of the pain, maybe.

But the pain was just as sharp as it had been two years ago, and the sadness just as crushing. This was his life now. A life without Lucy, and with their eleven children still depending on him, reminding him every day with their presence of what he'd lost. Benjamin was an especially painful reminder. Lucy hadn't lived long enough to know his name or hold him in her arms. Michael had always believed that dying for your family was the greatest sacrifice a person could make. But in his weaker moments, Michael believed Lucy had the easier job. Dying for your family was easy. Living for them, day after day, alone, was much harder.

Ted had fallen into an uncomfortable silence, which he covered by popping another cookie into his mouth. No one liked to talk about Michael's loss. Michael was saved from having to break the silence by the arrival of Al Reed.

The big man strode in without a hint of shame at being late or an apology for making everyone wait. He dropped himself into an empty seat at the end of the table and reached forward to grab a handful of cookies.

"You can start now," he said to the pastor.

Michael shook his head at the man's gall. Even Pastor Kinsley raised an eyebrow at that one.

"I waited for you out of grace and courtesy, Al. Let's begin with a prayer that God will grant us all humility and reverence as we gather this evening to study His Word."

Michael's face was neutral as he bowed his head, but inside he was smirking. Then he turned his heart to the pastor's prayer and realized his own smirk wasn't exactly humble. He prayed for forgiveness and let it go.

After the Bible study was over, Pastor Kinsley asked the elders to remain. Michael wasn't surprised. Ted's presence meant all the elders were here, and such an opportunity was not to be passed up. The elders always had church business to discuss.

The four men who weren't elders made their goodbyes and left. Along with Michael and Ted, Jack Peterson, Scott Payne, and Libby's husband, Nick, remained seated. Al reached forward and positioned the plate with the remaining cookies so it sat in front of him. There weren't many left.

Pastor Kinsley waited until the side door closed behind the last of the departing men.

"Thank you for staying, gentlemen. There are just a few items of note I wanted to bring up. First off, Stan Mullins asks our prayers for Marilyn. She just found out yesterday she's expecting again."

"Expecting another miscarriage," Al muttered.

Michael winced. It may be true, but there was no need for the man to say it out loud.

"Should we pray for them now, Pastor?" he asked.

Pastor Kinsley nodded. "I think an extra, dedicated prayer is in order. Maybe their time of testing is over, and God will finally bless them with a child."

Michael bowed his head and lifted his hands, as did everyone else at the table. His heart was open as he prayed along fervently for a healthy pregnancy and for the expectant parents to remain steadfast in their faith. Lucy had miscarried three times, and he knew the grief that accompanied such a loss. Marilyn Mullins had already lost four pregnancies to miscarriage. At least Michael and Lucy had had other children to comfort them in their pain. Stan and Marilyn had none.

The prayer ended and Michael raised his head, an image of Lucy still occupying his thoughts. Pastor Kinsley was looking straight at him. Michael met his gaze. After several long seconds the others were looking at him, too. Michael's heart sank. He'd known this was coming.

"Michael," the pastor began, his voice much too conversational. "You've been without a wife for, what, about two years now?"

Michael said nothing.

"Have you given any thought to marrying again?"

"I have a wife," he said softly. He wanted to be firm, but he didn't trust his voice not to shake. "I know in my heart God has called me to be husband to one wife and one wife only. She might be with the Lord, but I still have a wife."

"But wouldn't it be better to have a woman to take care of the house and the children?" Scott Payne asked.

Michael's eyes narrowed. Scott had caught onto the pastor's intent too quickly for this to be a spontaneous conversation. His temper rose at the thought of other people discussing his business behind his back.

"Hope's managing," he said.

"But she's just about ready for courtship now," Jack Peterson said. "What will you do if God sends her a husband?"

Michael shrugged off the ridiculous thought.

"Hope's still a young girl. She won't be courting for a few more years."

Ted raised an eyebrow. "Hope's seventeen, just like my Carolyn. God may send her a husband at any time."

Jack nodded his agreement.

Michael worked to keep his face neutral. It was bad enough that Ted was joining in this conversation, but could he be right?

Was Hope seventeen? He tried to think. Michael had never been good with ages and dates. But he had taken her to get her driver's license over a year ago so she could do the weekly grocery shopping. He supposed Hope must be seventeen. How could the endlessly dragging days turn into years that passed so quickly?

"Seventeen's still young. She's got a few more years. Joy will be old enough to take over by then."

"Isn't Joy about the same age as my Rachel?" Ted asked. "Nine? Will she really be ready to manage the house and younger children by herself when she's eleven or twelve? Or even thirteen?"

Michael took a deep breath and let it out slowly. He hadn't given any thought to Hope's eventual courtship and marriage. Just surviving the days without Lucy was hard enough. It had taken Hope ages to figure out a routine that worked despite how well Lucy had prepared her to be a godly woman. They were finally in a good place, with his two eldest sons in apprenticeships and Hope keeping the house and homeschooling the younger children. His life wasn't a happy one, not without Lucy, but it was comfortable and predictable.

But now that Ted put it out there for all the elders to examine, Michael had to admit that Joy wouldn't be ready in three or four years, even with Faith helping. Joy just didn't take to her duties as well as Hope did, and even Hope hadn't been that young when she had to take over for her mother. Freeing Hope for marriage meant disrupting everything. It meant...he knew what it meant, and he didn't want to go there. His head began to ache.

"We'll just have to see what God has in store for us," Michael said carefully.

He thought about the few women of marriageable age in

the congregation. They weren't much older than Hope. His voice took on an edge.

"I'm not going to marry some little girl I've watched grow up, and I'm not going to marry some widow or spinster you've found unless I feel God is calling me to be her husband. And right now, I'm not being called. I appreciate your concern, gentlemen, but I'm the head of my family."

"And your family is part of my flock," Pastor Kinsley reminded him, his own voice sharp and weighty with authority. Even Al sat up straighter. "And as part of my flock, I believe it's time you start thinking of marrying again. The Bible is clear on what families should look like. Genesis two eighteen: 'And the Lord God said, It is not good that the man should be alone; I will make him an help meet for him.' You need a helpmeet, Michael. The other elders agree with me on this."

Fury radiated from Michael in waves. Ted scooted his chair a couple of inches away from him, the loud squeak of worn plastic on linoleum echoing in the otherwise silent room. Michael didn't take his eyes off Pastor Kinsley, but he could see in his peripheral vision that Ted's head was hanging. Good. He should feel guilty for the part he played in this. Ted had known his family for years. He knew how he felt about Lucy. The rest of the elders looked at him calmly, confidently, waiting for him to yield to their authority.

Realization crashed home.

They were church elders, exercising their authority. Michael had been involved in exercising that same authority over other men, too, because that was how God had ordered things. The husband was over his own household, but the church leadership was over the husband, making sure he understood his responsibilities and didn't go astray. Michael had never hesitated to intervene as an elder when a man in the congregation was failing in his responsibilities to his family.

Those men became stronger husbands because of his involvement.

God help him, Michael wasn't even a husband anymore. Not in any way that mattered. He didn't want to marry again. But he hadn't wanted to lose Lucy, either. God demanded obedience. That was a cornerstone of Michael's faith. God demanded obedience, and God would reward the faithful and punish the wicked. He had no choice but to be obedient and faithful.

"And do you and the other elders have anyone in particular in mind?" He tried to blunt the razor edge in his voice and failed.

Pastor Kinsley shrugged as though the tension rolling across the table didn't exist. "Natalie Jacobi is a lovely young woman. Perhaps—"

Michael shook his head. "I remember Natalie when she used to carry around that doll Darlene made for her. No."

"She's not carrying dolls anymore," Al grinned. "She's filled out quite nicely."

"Speak respectfully about Harold's daughter, Al," Pastor Kinsley said.

Al looked insulted by the rebuke. "I was just saying God blessed her with attractive features."

Michael didn't want to listen to the man's disgusting excuses.

"I'm not denying she's pretty. But I knew her when she was a little girl." He could picture Natalie perfectly. 'Pretty' might be a bit of an exaggeration, but that wasn't why he was balking. He would always see her the way she was when the Jacobi family first started attending Church of the Covenant—as a young girl carrying a doll. Michael would submit to the church's authority, but they couldn't ask him to marry a child.

Or someone he saw as a child. "She's got to be closer to my own age. Or at least someone I haven't watched grow up."

"I believe we can accommodate Michael on this."

Everyone stared at Nick, including Michael. Libby's husband rarely spoke in public. But when he did, everyone listened.

Michael gave his brother-in-law a tight smile of gratitude. Nick was considerably older than Libby—he thought maybe as much as twenty years—but at least they'd met as adults.

Nick didn't acknowledge Michael's smile. Nor did he acknowledge Pastor Kinsley's flat stare. He sat straight as a poker in his chair, his arms folded across his thin chest, his face stony. He looked as he always did, as though God had planted him in that spot at the beginning of time and he hadn't moved since. Nor would he, until God chose to move him again. Nothing short of that would make him budge. "Surely between us we can come up with an eligible woman who wouldn't make Michael feel like he was marrying one of his own daughters."

The thought was repulsive, but it summed up Michael's objections perfectly. And it got through to the other men at the table, particularly those with daughters of their own.

"Terri has a cousin," Scott said after a long pause. "Samantha. She's about thirty-five. Divorced, three kids."

"Divorced?" Pastor Kinsley said. "What are you trying to yoke Michael to, Scott?"

Michael wondered the same thing, but let the pastor do his arguing for him.

"Not her fault. Her husband was an adulterer and left her for another woman. Samantha and the kids are living with her parents now. Their church isn't quite as strong in their faith as ours, but they're close enough that I think Samantha could adapt to our ways."

"She was raised in the faith?" Pastor Kinsley asked.

Scott nodded. "Samantha kept the home and home-schooled the children, and they were active in their church. Since the divorce she's had to put the kids in public school and get a job, but I think she'd be happy to get back to a more properly ordered life."

Pastor Kinsley nodded. "It's settled, then. Set up an introduction as soon as possible." He turned to address Michael. "We'll be praying that God will bring you another good woman to care for you and your children. We're all willing to be His vessels and help Him with His work in this."

Michael nodded, numb. "I'll pray about it, and be open to His will," he said woodenly. A divorcee with three children? "I'll let you know where God is leading me."

Chapter Four

Hope loaded the bags of groceries into the back of the fifteen-passenger van, arranging them neatly. She wasn't in any hurry. Her Saturday trip to the grocery store was a welcome respite of solitude, one she looked forward to all week. She didn't have to turn it into a homeschooling lesson for her younger siblings. She didn't have to write up a cleaning schedule for her sisters, or a chore list for her brothers, or supervise all her siblings to make sure they did everything as assigned. She wasn't trapped in the kitchen preparing endless meals. And she wasn't responsible for keeping eight kids between the ages of two and thirteen from murdering each other, destroying the house, getting hurt, or doing anything that Papa would have to deal with when he got home from work. Joshua and John were the only ones who didn't cause her any trouble during the week. Joshua went to work with Papa and John was studying ministry with Pastor Kinsley. They were both gone all day. Very easy to deal with.

Hope placed the last bag in the van and closed and locked the back doors. She returned the shopping cart to the carousel, which was located quite a distance away from her parking spot. Hope didn't mind. Even if she hadn't been trying to extend her time, she'd learned early on that it was much easier to park that behemoth of a vehicle at the back end of the lot where it was less crowded. She managed to get it between the lines, but it filled the space completely and hung out a bit in the back. Hope felt more comfortable when the nearest car was at least three spaces away.

Though if it weren't for the difficulty she'd had parking her family's van in a crowded lot, Hope would never have had her first conversation with Joel. She'd only had a learner's permit then, but Papa had made her drive everyone to church. They'd arrived a few minutes before the service began, and there weren't many empty spaces. Papa needed to meet with Pastor Kinsley before the service, so he'd taken her siblings and gone inside, leaving her to park the van. She'd been just about to panic when Joel arrived with his family, and he'd stayed behind and helped guide her into a spot.

Hope was still grinning at the memory as she climbed into the driver's seat, buckled her seatbelt, started the van, checked her mirrors, and began to back out slowly. Joel had been so encouraging that day, so thoughtful, so...

The van lurched to a stop with a thud, and Hope's head bounced off the headrest as her seatbelt locked. She looked in the rearview mirror again and saw a black car directly behind her. The driver was getting out, already yelling.

"What the fuck, you bitch! Why don't you look where you're going!"

Thoughts of Joel were gone. Hope sat frozen, hands gripping the steering wheel. She'd stomped her foot down on the brake at the moment of impact, and she was still pressing down hard enough that her leg ached. Her heart beat so rapidly she felt lightheaded. She stared with wide eyes at the young man stalking towards the driver-side door of her van.

He pounded his fist on her closed window and pointed back at his car. "Look what you did to my car, you bitch!"

"I'm sorry!" At least that's what she tried to say. Her lips formed the words, but no sound came out.

"What?" He looked even angrier.

"I'm sorry!" The words came out that time, and so did the tears. Sharp tears that burned her eyes even as they blurred her vision.

"Jesus fucking Christ! Get out of the car! Get out!"

He pounded his fist on her window again, and Hope shrank away from it as far as her seatbelt would allow. The man's forearm was covered with tattoos. His dark hair was almost to his shoulders, and he wore a heavy chain around his neck. The nightmare Papa had warned her about was standing inches from her, the van door her only protection. What would he do to her? She wanted to put the van in 'drive' and speed away home. There wasn't a vehicle in front of her, blocking her in. She could do it. She put her hand on the gear shift.

But that would be leaving the scene of an accident. That was much worse than what she'd already done. God was watching. He'd know. Hope grasped the lever and moved it into 'park.' She eased her foot off the brake.

"I said get the fuck out here!" The man tried to open her door, and Hope cringed away again, grateful that Papa had taught her to lock her door as soon as she got in. He'd warned her of situations like this, where someone might try to force their way into her vehicle. She hadn't believed it would really happen, but what did she know?

"Go away!" she cried, burying her face in her hands.

"What's going on here? Is everyone okay? Does that woman need an ambulance?"

Hope looked up at the new voice. A short, heavyset woman in her fifties stood in front of the van. She wore jeans and a baggy sweatshirt, and she was peering through the windshield at Hope.

The angry young man turned his attention to the woman. "No, she doesn't need a fucking ambulance, she needs a fucking clue! She hit my car and now she won't get out!"

The woman studied the young man through narrowed eyes. "I wouldn't get out either, with you yelling like that. Back off and stop scaring her." Despite her height and her age, the woman had a commanding voice. Hope had no trouble hearing her through the closed windows. Even though the man was bigger and stronger, he took a step away from Hope's door. The woman eyed him warily. Commanding voice or not, Hope noticed the woman kept her distance from the man. She looked at Hope through the windshield again.

"Are you okay, Sweetie?"

Hope nodded. She wasn't physically hurt, and she supposed that's what the woman was asking.

"What happened here?"

"She backed into my car! Look!" He pointed to the rear of the van, which rested against the dented side of his car.

The woman glared at him. "I'm asking her." She turned back to Hope. "Tell me what happened, Sweetie."

"I—I looked out my mirrors and didn't see anything, so I backed out. Then we hit." Hope's voice was a whisper.

"I'm sorry, Sweetie, I can't hear you." Her voice still carried easily. "I'm going to walk over to your passenger door. Crack the window a bit so we can talk. Okay?"

Hope nodded, and the woman approached the passenger door. The young man began to walk around the van to join her.

"You stay over there," the woman ordered him, pointing.

"I can't fucking believe this," he muttered, but he remained near the driver's side. Hope felt trapped between them.

The van was tall, and Hope could barely see the woman's face through the passenger window. Papa had cautioned Hope against interacting with worldly people when she was out running errands, but if she had to choose between the two, she'd rather talk to the woman. She pushed the button to lower the window on that side two inches. She was careful to leave the driver's side window all the way up.

"Now, what happened?"

Hope repeated her story.

The woman nodded. "And you're sure you checked all your mirrors? And you looked behind you before you pulled out?"

Hope nodded. She was pretty sure she had. Hadn't she? She wasn't crying any more, but her heart still hammered in her chest, and she felt sick to her stomach.

The short woman raised her voice and looked past Hope to the nightmare standing outside her window. "And how fast were you going? Did you notice this van backing out?"

"I wasn't speeding. She hit me. It's her fault. Anyway, it's none of your business!"

The woman shook her head. "And you think you can handle this by yelling and intimidating a young girl?"

The man threw up his hands. "No. I'm handling this by calling the police." He pulled a cell phone out of his pocket and started dialing.

The police? What was she going to tell the police? What would Papa say when he found out? Her eyes stung again, and her face crumpled.

The woman smiled comfortingly. "This is your first fender bender, isn't it?"

It was more statement than question, but Hope nodded.

"You're not going to get into any trouble. The police are

just going to fill out an accident report for the insurance companies. You'll need to show your license and registration and give them your insurance information. You have all that, right?"

"I think so," Hope whispered. She didn't carry a purse, instead keeping her license in the glove compartment so she wouldn't forget it when she went shopping. There were other important papers in there, too, Papa had said.

"Is there someone you can call? Your mother maybe? Can she come and help you?"

More than ever Hope wished her mother was there to help her. Mama had always dealt with problems and protected Hope and her siblings from the world. So did Papa. In fact, Papa was far more efficient at it than Mama had been. He'd be furious, but he was going to find out anyway. And it would be better for him to talk to the police. Hope had no idea what to say to them.

"My father. But I don't have a phone."

The woman reached into her purse and pulled out a cell phone. "I can't remember the last time I saw a teenager without a phone. Good for your parents. Here. Call your dad."

Hope rolled down the window a bit more, took a deep breath, and reached for the phone.

The drive home was the longest of Hope's life. She thought she was a good driver overall, but she hadn't worked so hard at keeping to the exact speed limit since her driver's test a year and a half ago. Papa's work truck stayed exactly two car lengths behind her the whole way, filling her rearview mirror. Also, it was difficult to drive well when your vision was blurry with tears.

Her siblings were all outside, waiting for her and Papa to

return. Hope didn't know what Papa had told them when he left, but they clearly knew something was going on. She scrubbed at her eyes as she pulled up to the house.

Papa was out of his truck before she'd finished climbing out of the van.

"Samuel and Amos, bring the groceries into the house," he ordered. "Joy and Faith, you put them away. Everyone else, find something to do before I find you something. Hope, upstairs. Now."

Papa strode into the house without waiting to see if his children obeyed him. There was no need to.

Those who had not been named disappeared in a matter of seconds. Paul and Timothy tagged after John and Joshua, and for once the older boys let them. Grace stayed with Faith, who held Benjamin in her arms.

Hope closed the van door and followed her father into the house.

"What happened?" Joy asked as the older girl passed her.

Hope's eyes felt grainy, and her head hurt. "Just put the groceries away," she muttered, and kept walking.

Papa was waiting for her in his bedroom, his belt already in hand.

Hope stood in the doorway and waited for her sentence.

"Your carelessness cost me hundreds of dollars today." His voice was so low it was almost inaudible.

Hope's skin prickled with cold and fear. "Yes, Papa."

"Worse than that, you brought this family to the attention of the authorities."

Hope closed her eyes. "Yes, Papa."

They stood in silence, the weight of those words growing into a physical force that thickened the air around them. Hope couldn't move.

Just getting her license at all had been a nightmare. The

Commonwealth of Massachusetts required that she complete a Driver Education class. Papa had fought that, even trying to get himself declared a certified driving instructor. The State wouldn't allow it. He resented the State telling him what he could and couldn't do, and he'd been uncomfortable enrolling her in a Drivers Ed class with regular teenagers. But he'd been unwilling to wait until she was eighteen, when she could get a license without Drivers Ed. He hated running the errands Mama used to do.

Hope hadn't been very comfortable in that driving school, either. Papa walked her into class every day and was waiting just outside when it was over. None of the students talked to her except when they had to. They dressed differently than she did and talked about things she didn't know about, like music groups and TV shows and movies. They laughed at her clothes behind her back. Hope didn't try to talk to them. She knew Papa would grill her about every class on the ride home, who she talked to and what she said, and she knew she was supposed to keep to herself. Godly people didn't mix with worldly people except when they had to.

She'd mixed with them today.

"The police now know that a seventeen-year-old girl does her family's grocery shopping," Papa said. "That's not what seventeen-year-old girls usually do. They're going to wonder about that. They might want to know how many children are in this house, and where they go to school. They might wonder if you're being properly cared for without a mother. They might ask the Department of Children and Families to open an investigation. All because of your carelessness."

Hope's head hung down in shame. "I'm sorry, Papa."

"Bend over the bed, Hope. You're getting twenty licks. 'Foolishness is bound in the heart of a child, but the rod of correction shall drive it far from him.'"

Twenty! Hope had never gotten more than ten at a time before. But she'd never done anything this terrible before, either.

She did as she was told, grabbing fistfuls of the bright, colorful quilt to brace herself. Hope remembered when Mama had made that quilt. She recognized some of the fabric. There was a piece of khaki that had once been pants. One of her brothers—Amos maybe?—had ripped a hole big enough that Mama couldn't repair it, and the pants had become quilting material. Hope pressed her cheek against the fabric as she had pressed her cheek against Mama's chest so many times. It felt like such a long time ago.

The thick corduroy of her skirt helped blunt the first few blows, but it wasn't much protection against the worn leather of the belt wielded by Papa's strong construction worker arm. She counted the licks aloud as they landed, each number coming out a tortured gasp. By twenty her bottom was on fire. But there was no blood.

She deserved much worse.

"From now on either Joshua or John will accompany you on all your errands," Papa said, threading his belt back through the loops on his trousers. "You are not to leave this house without one of them. Do you understand?" It wasn't a question.

"Yes, Papa," Hope choked.

"Good. Now go wash your face, pray for forgiveness and that God will protect this family from unbelievers, then go downstairs and do your chores." He closed his eyes and his mouth twisted as though he'd bit into something sour. "Don't forget that I'm having supper at the Payne's house tonight, so it will be just you and your siblings. I don't expect to be late."

Hope nodded and shuffled out of the room, her head down. She couldn't stop her tears, and Papa got mad when she and her sisters cried. He called it manipulation.

She went into the bathroom, soaked a washcloth with cold water, and rubbed her eyes and cheeks. The sound of Papa's heavy footsteps was loud on the stairs. He would probably spend the day in his workshop, building furniture. He liked to work with his hands. He also seemed to like not being in the house. That suited Hope.

With her face cool but her eyes still leaking, Hope went into her bedroom. Benjamin's crib was against one wall, her dresser and Mama's sewing machine against another. Her narrow bed jutted out from the third wall, and Mama's nursing chair sat in the corner. As always, Hope's eyes went to the large piece of framed needlework that dominated the wall above her bed. *Who can find a virtuous woman? For her price is far above rubies. The heart of her husband doth safely trust in her, so that he shall have no need of spoil. She will do him good and not evil all the days of her life.* It went on, describing the deeds of a virtuous woman, and concluded, *Favour is deceitful, and beauty is vain: but a woman that feareth the* LORD, *she shall be praised. Give her the fruit of her hands; and let her own works praise her in the gates. Proverbs 31:10-31.*

Mama had made that for Hope when she was nine. She'd been resentful that she had so many household chores, including taking care of her younger siblings. Faith had just been born, Mama's third baby in as many years. Samuel was just out of diapers, and John and Joshua needed constant supervision. Mama had told her she was preparing Hope to be the Proverbs 31 Virtuous Woman, which is what all women should strive for. It had made Hope feel special.

At Mama's funeral Pastor Kinsley read Proverbs 31:10-31 and said Papa had been blessed to find such a woman. He'd also said Mama's work would continue through her children as they honored her memory through obedience to their father and by committing themselves to the tasks God had ordained for them.

Hope knew what God had ordained for her. Aunt Libby had told her when she'd put Benjamin into her arms only minutes after he'd been born, only minutes after Mama had died. Hope was to be mother to him and to all her siblings, raising them to be arrows for Christ, fighting to establish God's Kingdom on Earth, as Mama had. But she was only fifteen! Days earlier Hope had been an arrow in her father's quiver. At the funeral she realized she'd been shot into the battle, the speed of her trajectory as terrifying as it was inevitable.

Hope had been failing to live up to her mother's example ever since.

She walked over to the dresser, picked up her nail clippers, and pushed her left sleeve up above her elbow. The underside of her forearm was covered in scars and scabs, some healed, some relatively fresh. Hope found a spot near her elbow where the skin had mostly healed, dug the clippers into the soft flesh, and began to pray.

Please God, please help me be a better person. Please fix whatever's wrong with me and help me to joyfully serve You. Blood began to bead, and she clipped off a little piece of skin. Hope pushed the corner of her clippers into the wound and pressed them closed again. The pain in her arm muted the pain in her backside, and she began to feel a little better. *Forgive me, Lord. Forgive me for not being good enough, for being selfish, for being careless. Forgive me for being me, Lord, and help me be someone else. Protect my family from my mistakes. Help me be good. Amen.*

Hope took a tissue and wiped the blood off the nail clippers, then held the bloody tissue to her arm. She didn't expect God to answer her prayers. He never did.

Chapter Five

When Jennifer walked into Church of the Covenant on Sunday, she was prepared for the stares. The cape overlay came out better than she'd hoped, and she'd sectioned it so she could move her arms without uncovering the front of her dress. She'd added a band of navy-blue at the bottom, nicely contrasting with the light blue and white stripes of her dress and cape, and had added an identical band to the bottom of her skirt. That band also matched the navy-blue head covering that now rested on the top of her head. Jennifer had opted for a style she'd seen on some of the younger women—a wide headband that extended over the crown of her head. The kerchief style most of the older women wore was too frumpy for Jennifer's tastes.

Some people did stare at her, though not the way they had the week before. People seemed merely surprised that she'd returned, rather than shocked she was there at all. At least this time the church didn't go silent. She saw a few people she recognized. That was Terri sitting next to a tall, handsome man in his late thirties. Five perfectly groomed children sat in the pew next to them, all girls except for the youngest, who was wearing an adorable sailor suit. Terri's husband turned to look at Jennifer, taking his time studying her. Jennifer met his eye, challenging him to find fault. He scowled and turned back around in his seat. He must have said something to his wife because Terri twisted around to give Jennifer an appraising look. She turned back without so much as a smile.

Jennifer's resolve began to slip. Terri hadn't been unfriendly when they'd met the week before, not exactly, but she hadn't been friendly, either. Jennifer had gotten the sense that Terri was one of those women who considered life a competitive sport, and Jennifer was competition. She had hoped there wouldn't be people like that in a church of all places, but apparently there were.

Stacy had also noticed Jennifer's arrival, and her smile was warm as she waved. Jennifer waved back. She considered joining her, but Stacy's pew was already full with her large husband and seven children. The pews could hold more than nine people, but she'd seen how closely everyone had to sit to make that work, the children jammed in next to each other, practically—and sometimes literally—sitting on each other's laps. Jennifer didn't think they'd appreciate that level of intimacy with her. She wasn't sure she'd appreciate it, either. Not with a family that wasn't her own.

There was plenty of room in Libby's pew, and she had invited Jennifer to come back. Making up her mind, she strode to the same pew she'd sat in the week before and slid to the middle, leaving space for Libby and her family when they arrived.

While she waited, Jennifer toyed with the cover of her Bible. Last week she'd had to look on with Libby. Everyone brought their own to the service. Fortunately, she already owned one. She'd bought it when she first started visiting churches and had been reading it on her own at home. It had taken her a while to figure out the structure, and she found the New Testament to be an easier read than the Old Testament, but she still struggled with the fact that it wasn't linear. Jennifer had been embarrassed when she finally figured out that the four gospels were four versions of the same story, and not to be read straight through like a novel. She felt like she should have known that. But Jennifer's religious upbringing had been limited to being baptized in a Methodist church as an infant and occasionally attending Christmas Eve and Easter morning services. She'd never gone to Sunday School or been in a Christmas pageant.

Right now, though, Jennifer was just grateful that her Bible looked like a book that had been opened more than a few times. These people seemed pretty serious about their Bibles.

"Hi Jennifer! You came back!"

Jennifer was jerked out of her thoughts by Jared's booming voice next to her. She smiled at the young man and greeted him in return. Libby gently pulled her son back.

"Let me sit next to Jennifer, Jared. You can sit on the other side of Dad."

Jared looked confused for a moment, then his face brightened. "New seats! We have new seats! I get to sit on the aisle now!"

Libby looked at Jennifer's head covering, cape overlay, and the Bible in her hand. "Yes, Jared," she said, still looking at Jennifer. "I think these are going to be our new seats for a while."

A thrill shot through Jennifer. Libby, obviously a woman of importance here, had given her stamp of approval! Adding a head covering and cape hadn't been so hard. Becoming a fixture here and seeing if this congregation could give her what she wanted should be easy now.

Libby settled down next to Jennifer. "I'm glad to see you took my advice," she said. She reached out a hand for Jennifer's Bible. "May I?"

Jennifer gave it to her.

"Leather cover, very nice. They last much longer than the paperbacks." Libby opened it and flipped through. "I don't see any highlighting or underlining of favorite verses."

Jennifer felt her cheeks redden. "I'm still new at this. And I didn't think you were supposed to write in Bibles."

"It's fine to write in Bibles, as long as it's helping you to understand God's will." She handed Jennifer's Bible back to her. "It's just as well you didn't write in it. It's the wrong one."

"How can it be the wrong one? There's only one Bible."

Libby pointed to the print at the bottom of the cover. "New International Version. A bad translation. Not as bad as some of the others, but it's still theologically biased and inaccurate. The King James Version is the only truly faithful translation there is."

Jennifer nodded. She'd noticed last week that Libby's Bible, and the one Pastor What's-His-Name read from, was more poetic than she remembered her own being. Now she knew why.

So, she'd get another Bible. No big deal.

Jennifer had always been good with remembering names, and she was glad for that talent after the service. As before, Libby brought her to the kitchen with the other women of the church. Most of them greeted her with a bright exclamation of "You came back!" Jennifer heard the unspoken "We didn't think you would."

But she had, and she was able to greet most of the women

by name, which impressed them as much as her new cape and head covering did. There were a few she hadn't met the previous week, women who had been at the other end of the kitchen, older women who seemed to supervise everyone else.

"Louise, this is Jennifer Levine. She's been trying to find a new church home, and she thinks Church of the Covenant might be what she's been looking for. Jennifer, this is Louise Kinsley, the pastor's wife."

Jennifer smiled. "It's a pleasure to meet you, Louise."

Louise studied her the way Terri's husband had, especially her head covering and cape. "You took Libby's advice. Good. Being open to receiving guidance and direction is an important part of Church of the Covenant. If you're going to become one of us, you have to understand what we believe. Christ is over all of us, and He gives the church authority over its members. The church guides men to be strong heads of their families, and to protect and provide for their wives and children. Women are to be helpmeets and mothers. Traditional gender roles. I'm putting this out there now because a lot of women today aren't willing to accept that, and I'd rather you know right from the start who we are and what we expect. Are you willing to submit to the husband God chooses for you?"

And Jennifer had thought Libby was blunt.

In theory she liked the idea of traditional gender roles, but inwardly she cringed at the word 'submit.' She'd never been very submissive. Jennifer preferred to think of herself as a fighter. She'd always had to fight for what she wanted, and her outspokenness and tenacity had brought her a lot further than submission ever would have.

But wasn't that what she was trying to get away from? Having to fight all the time? Hadn't Jennifer been looking for a place where she might find a man with traditional family values, who would want children as much as she did and agree that she should stay home and be a good mother to them, just like the women in the books she loved? Didn't it stand to reason that traditional gender roles would be a part of that? All her nineteenth century literary heroines lived in a patriarchal world and still managed to be women Jennifer admired. And these women here in this kitchen! They were real, contemporary women who had lots of children and were able to dedicate themselves to them full time just like the families in her beloved novels. They trusted their husbands to provide for them and support them as wives and mothers. Those were traditional gender roles, and they came with rules she hadn't been taught. Submission was one of them. Jennifer had never been submissive, but that wasn't surprising, considering who raised her. Her mother was aggressive and strong and sharp as a tack, and those traits had made her one of the most sought-after attorneys in Boston. But it also made her a terrible mother who paid strangers to raise her only child.

All Jennifer wanted was to be a good mother, one who was there for her kids whenever they needed her. She wanted them to feel loved and accepted. She wanted them to know they were important. That wasn't how she was raised.

It's something she was going to have to learn.

Jennifer took a deep breath and looked Louise in the eye. "If God chooses a husband for me, I will gladly submit to his authority," she said.

Chapter Six

The men were crammed around the table in Al Reed's tiny kitchen. Michael preferred anyone's house to Al's, but they all took turns hosting these early morning Saturday prayer breakfasts. Morgan Reed had prepared endless stacks of pancakes for them, but no sausages or bacon. Michael took some margarine from the large tub in the middle of the table, smeared it on his pancakes, and squirted the store-brand maple syrup to flavor it. He was pretty sure "maple syrup" would not appear on the ingredients list if he looked, but he ate to be polite to Morgan. She stood off to the side, wearing her head covering even at home, anxiously watching to make sure the men had everything they needed. Michael pitied her. It couldn't be easy, being married to Al.

Michael realized the uncharitable path his thoughts were taking, checking off his list of Al's many faults, and reminded himself that God called people to follow Him in different ways, with different challenges. Al wasn't blessed with a successful business, like Michael was. He worked long hours as a custodian at a hospital, a job that was messy and grueling and paid little. Yet he managed to keep a roof over his family's head and food on their table. Morgan was attentive and obedient, and Al always volunteered his boys for whatever work Pastor Kinsley needed done around the church. Al was a strong believer in the Bible and, despite his perpetual tardiness, never actually missed a meeting. Only Michael and Pastor Kinsley could say the same.

The house was small and in poor repair, the cold November air seeping through the thin walls and old windows, but the residual heat of the stove and the crowd of bodies in the tiny room kept the kitchen warm enough.

Pastor Kinsley gestured with his fork. "A little more coffee for me, Morgan, and then we'll get started."

Al's wife darted to the coffee pot on the counter and topped off the pastor's large, chipped mug. She kept her eyes on the table as she circled around it, pouring more coffee into each man's cup. Michael put his hand over his, declining her offer. The coffee was weak, little more than brown water. It would be enough of a chore to drink what he had.

"Go wait in the living room, Morgan," Al said. "We don't need you in here anymore."

If she was hurt by Al's dismissive tone, Morgan didn't show it. She merely put the coffee pot back on the counter and left, not looking at anyone.

Pastor Kinsley nodded in approval. "We'll discuss business while we eat, and then we'll pray."

They talked for a few minutes about some repairs needed on the church building which Michael would oversee. He didn't mind. Maintaining that building was a point of personal pride and a service to God.

Next, they discussed the financial situations of some of the church families. None were represented at the table, of course.

A couple of women had told Louise they were concerned about their families' wellbeing and were considering applying for heating aid and food stamps from the State.

"Obviously their husbands need to be told," Scott said. "Wives shouldn't be gossiping about a man's ability to provide for his family."

Al nodded. "And those women need to be disciplined."

"Is there a way we can help those families, so they're not tempted to go to the State?" Michael asked.

"I've already told the men involved," Pastor Kinsley said. "And I've told them to make sure their wives understand their place. I also reminded those men they have a responsibility to provide for their families, without assistance from the government or anyone else. These aren't men like Ted here, who fell on temporary hard times."

"I never asked for any help, Pastor." Ted's voice was tight.

Pastor Kinsley nodded. "I know you didn't, Ted. You're a strong leader for your family and you did what you had to to provide for them. If you had asked for help, you would have received it because we all know what kind of man you are. But some of these men are chronic cases. They need to step up and take care of their families better, and rewarding them for their weakness by giving them a handout isn't going to do them any favors."

That settled, they moved on to prayer requests from specific church members. After that list was completed, Pastor Kinsley threw one more out that made Michael's shoulders tense.

"And we need to pray for our newest member, that God will find her a husband."

Scott frowned. "Isn't this a little quick, Pastor? Jennifer Levine's only been attending Church of the Covenant for a few weeks."

"Jennifer's been meeting with Louise and me every Sunday afternoon, and she's been very receptive to the instruction we've given her. She's eager to learn and follow the way of Christ. She reads the books Louise gives her on being a help-meet and a keeper of the home, and she insists that's the kind of family she's always wanted. The Lord has called her to be among us, and we have an obligation to help her fulfill her calling as wife and mother." Pastor Kinsley was very careful not to look at Michael when he said this, but Michael knew what he was thinking.

Michael's introduction to Terri's cousin had been a disaster. Samantha was a timid, needy woman who exuded a sense of helplessness. Her three children had been out of control at supper, and it was Terri who spoke sharply to them and Scott who brought them upstairs one at a time for character training. Samantha had tried to stop the discipline, making excuses for their behavior rather than condemning it. Even Scott had agreed that she wasn't a good match for Michael, and a second meeting was unnecessary.

None of the elders had been able to come up with any other potential wives for Michael, and he'd been living in a state of perpetual dread ever since the pastor and his wife began meeting with the strange newcomer. Michael knew exactly where that would lead, and he'd taken pains to be as bristly and unapproachable on the subject as possible. He had no desire to yoke himself to someone as bold and unconventional as Jennifer Levine appeared to be.

He understood the elders' problem, though. Jennifer needed a husband to lead her in the way of Christ, but it was difficult to find a husband for a woman her age. At twenty-seven she was older than most of the men considering courtship, and the men her own age or a few years older were already married. The elders would not consider yoking her with a younger man—she might suffer from a false sense of superiority over her younger husband, and a woman not raised in the faith would need to be under the authority of a stronger, more experienced man, but the few older men without wives were too advanced in years. They were no longer able to support a growing family, and many of them lived under the care of one of their adult children.

Michael was the notable exception.

But Pastor Kinsley didn't press the issue directly. Instead, he led them in prayer, including a prayer that God would join together women and men who needed the support and comfort that marriage alone could provide. He also prayed that Jennifer Levine and Michael Wagner would be led to the spouses God had chosen for them.

Not subtle, but indirect enough that Michael could say "Amen" and be done with it. He left the prayer meeting as quickly as possible.

The pastor prayed that same prayer at every Saturday morning meeting, but no one raised the subject with Michael, and his heightened state of alarm gradually subsided. So, he was caught off guard when the pastor ambushed him on a Sunday afternoon in late November.

He arrived at the church office at two-thirty, as requested. The door was open, and he was halfway through it before he saw her. Jennifer was sitting in front of Pastor Kinsley's desk, with Mrs. Kinsley seated next to her. They all looked at him as he entered.

"I'm sorry for interrupting," Michael said. He kept his gaze on the pastor. "You asked me to stop by to look at the windows in the sanctuary?"

Pastor Kinsley stood, smiling. "Yes, yes, of course." He gestured to the ladies. "Michael, have you met Jennifer Levine?"

Jennifer and Louise both stood, and Michael had no choice but to look at the strange newcomer to their church. Today she wore a dress the color of bricks, with a short cape hanging down around her torso. Her blonde hair was decently covered by a matching kerchief. Her blue eyes were wide as she looked at him, and she smiled as she reached out her hand as if to shake.

Louise touched Jennifer's extended arm and whispered something to her, and she quickly returned her hand to her side. Her cheeks were as red as her dress.

"It's nice to meet you," Michael said, grateful the pastor's wife had saved him from having to correct the woman's behavior.

"It's a pleasure to meet you, too." Her voice was husky and musical. Michael thought it would be nice to listen to her read aloud.

They stood in awkward silence. Michael knew the pastor expected him to engage this woman in friendly conversation, but he was too resentful of the obvious set-up. "The windows?" he prompted the pastor.

Pastor Kinsley nodded. "Yes, the windows in the sanctuary have been letting in quite a draft. I was hoping you'd be able to fix that." He turned his attention to Jennifer. "Michael's a general contractor. He restored this old building when we established Church of the Covenant here sixteen years ago. He and his wife, may she rest in peace, were founding members. He's been a real blessing to us all."

Jennifer's eyes never left Michael's face. "I'm sure he has," she murmured.

He didn't like the way she was looking at him. Her gaze was much too appraising, and he fought the sudden urge to tell her he wasn't for sale. He had to remind himself that it wasn't her fault. Pastor Kinsley had set this up, and Jennifer was nothing more than an innocent young woman looking for guidance from her pastor.

Only she didn't look innocent. She'd seemed unsurprised by his arrival in the pastor's office, and the pleasure in her expression when Pastor Kinsley introduced them was unmistakable. His mouth tightened.

"Will you show me which windows, Pastor, or do you want me to look at them all?"

Pastor Kinsley sighed. "I'll show you. Louise, will you continue with Jennifer?"

The two women took their seats again and the pastor followed Michael into the hallway.

"She's a lovely young woman," Pastor Kinsley observed as they walked toward the sanctuary.

Michael didn't answer.

"You really should consider getting to know her. I think Jennifer would make a fine wife for you."

"She's too bold," Michael said, his voice low and contained. "And she has too much to learn. I have enough on my plate without teaching a worldly woman how to follow our ways. Did you see her try to shake my hand?"

"Louise took care of that. Jennifer learns quickly. And she's not intimidated by the idea of marrying a man with eleven children already. That alone is worth something."

They entered the sanctuary, and Michael felt calmed by the peace of the place. He shook his head and made his voice softer, both in volume and in tone. "That only shows how naïve she is. She doesn't know what she doesn't know."

"So teach her. Be her head."

"I'm not called to be her head."

"Maybe you're just not listening."

Michael stopped and glared at the pastor. "That's going a bit far, isn't it?"

"Is it?" Pastor Kinsley asked.

The two men stood in the middle aisle, staring at each other. The pastor's question bounced around in Michael's head, demanding an answer. The sanctuary didn't feel as peaceful as it had.

"The window's over here." Pastor Kinsley ended the confrontation and led Michael to the nearest window.

Michael followed and stood before it. He put his hand up to feel around the edges. It was a windy day outside, but he felt nothing seeping through. He said as much to the pastor.

"I guess I must have been mistaken, then," Pastor Kinsley said. He turned away and headed back toward his office. "Sorry to interrupt your family time, Michael. You'd better get home to those blessings God has given you. And think about what I said."

He was around the corner and out of sight before Michael could reply.

Michael did think about what Pastor Kinsley had said. Thought about it, and dismissed it. Jennifer was too bold, too naïve, and too much work for him to consider courting. He was prepared to proclaim his decision and defend it to the pastor and to the elders the next time any of them brought it up.

Except none of them did. Several more weeks went by, and when the issue was broached again, it was Libby who sprang it on him.

She walked with him to his van as they were leaving church one cold Sunday morning in mid-December and, without preamble, she hit him with it. "You have to consider courting Jennifer."

"I do? Are you an elder now? I wasn't aware."

His older sister, several inches shorter than he, gave him the look that had cowed him since they were children. Michael stood taller. She wasn't going to cow him this time. Not on this. He held her gaze with an effort.

"You need a wife." She jerked her chin at his van, and he turned to look. Hope was trying to buckle a squirming Benjamin into his car seat. "It's not fair to Hope. You know that."

Of all the arguments for why Michael needed a wife, this was the one he couldn't counter. Like Jennifer, Hope was also called to be a helpmeet, a proper wife and mother, and it was his responsibility to see her married to a godly young man. By keeping her home to run his own household, he was failing in his responsibility as her father. As much as he hated to admit it, Ted was right. Joy wouldn't be ready to take over managing his household for several more years. If he waited until then Hope would be nearly the same age Jennifer was now, and he'd have just as much trouble finding a husband for her as the elders were for Jennifer.

No. He was comfortable with things as they were. There was no need to disrupt his household with a bold young woman in strange clothing. Surely God wasn't leading him to her.

"Jennifer's too young. She's not much older than Hope." 'Too young' had ruled out all the other women in the church the elders had wanted to match him with. It was as good an excuse as any.

"Jennifer's twenty-seven, ten years older than Hope. And it's not like she's someone you knew as a little girl and watched grow up." She smirked at Michael's outraged expression. "Yes, Nick told me. Don't act like you never told Lucy what happened at the men's meetings. Anyway, you're only fifteen years older than Jennifer. That's nothing. Nick's eighteen years older than me." Her face softened, as much as his sister's face ever softened. She wasn't a soft woman. "Jennifer needs a stronger, wiser man to instruct her in the ways of godly living.

She's been in the world her whole life, and she's become set in some habits and mindsets that need to be changed, but she's eager to leave all that behind. You could show her the way."

Libby's words invoked a memory, causing Michael to grow rigid. She couldn't be going there.

Her voice became gentle, almost wistful. "In some ways Jennifer reminds me of Lucy. They share a lot of the same challenges. You did so well with Lucy, maybe God is sending you another woman to rescue and bring into the fold."

The ever-present melancholy that Michael worked so hard to keep buried rose to the surface, and he struggled to shove it back down. Lucy had known nothing about God when they first met, but after her chaotic childhood, she'd been eager to learn. When Michael offered his authority, his guidance, and his love, she'd embraced the opportunity and flourished in her new role. Gratitude was in her eyes whenever she looked at him, even after a decade and a half of marriage, and Michael saw her as a blessing and reward from God, granted to him for rescuing such a vulnerable young woman and bringing her to Christ. Now she was gone, and here was another vulnerable young woman in need of a godly husband to show her the way.

He watched as Hope finished securing Benjamin in his car seat and checked to make sure all her other siblings were safely buckled before climbing into the front passenger seat. She would need a husband soon. As much as Michael didn't want to disrupt his life, God had called him to lead his family in holiness and obedience. How could he do that if he put his own comfort and preferences before God's will? *It is not good that the man should be alone.* It had grated on him when Pastor Kinsley quoted that at him, but it was God's Word. And Michael was alone, as his pastor, the other church elders, and now his own sister kept reminding him. And if he didn't act soon his daughter would be alone, too, because of his own self-ishness.

He sighed, defeated. "Invite Jennifer to Christmas dinner at my house," he told Libby. "I'm not promising anything, but we'll see."

Chapter Seven

Jennifer cursed out loud as she drove down the dark street for the fifth time. Where was the frigging house? She was supposed to be there at five-thirty, and now it was almost six. Her car crept along as she peered into the woods that engulfed one side of the road. Jennifer had checked the number on every other house on the street, and none of them was right. It had to be somewhere in these damn trees.

She craned her neck and saw a twinkle of light peek out briefly from behind the thick trunks of leafless maples. Jennifer stopped her car, pulled a small flashlight from the glove compartment, and opened her window to the sharp winter air. The weak beam sweeping along the tree trunks gave the impression that the forest was moving, and Jennifer's frustration began to give way to fear. Her childhood in Brookline, Massachusetts had not prepared her to be alone on a dark road surrounded by forest. Hell, even idyllic Concord hadn't prepared her for this.

She shook off her fear and told herself she was being ridiculous. This was a residential neighborhood. If she screamed, somebody would hear her. Wouldn't they?

The flashlight beam caught a dark mailbox next to a narrow break in the trees. She couldn't see a name or number in the faint light, but this had to be it.

Still nervous that she was in the wrong place, Jennifer maneuvered her Prius down the winding gravel driveway. She sighed with relief when she came upon Libby's familiar minivan parked alongside a heavy-duty pickup and one of those large vans that was so ubiquitous at Church of the Covenant. She parked behind it and got out, hunching inside her homemade black wool cloak. Her ski parka would have kept her warmer, but she liked the way the cloak complimented her dress.

No lights illuminated the front walk, so Jennifer picked her way along the rocky path to the front door. Aware of how late she was, she jabbed her finger at the doorbell.

The teenage girl who sat at the end of her family's pew and took such good care of her siblings opened the door. She jumped out of the way as Jennifer strode past her into the house and towards the three adults who stood to meet her. Several small children played at their feet along with Libby's adult son Jared, who was just as engaged in the toy cars as his much younger cousins. The older children were in two groups, the boys playing a board game and the girls working on a puzzle.

Jennifer planted herself in front of the attractive middle-aged man she had come all this way to meet and wagged a finger in his face, unconsciously defaulting to the nanny-nagging-her-charge posture she spent so much of her weekdays assuming. "I have been driving up and down this street for half an hour! I found your neighbors without a problem, but your driveway is practically invisible! You really need to put a reflector on your mailbox or something. A floodlight on your house would be a good idea, too. Nobody can find you back here!"

The man's face was expressionless as he stared at her past the finger she still had pointed at him. He didn't say anything.

Jennifer's cheeks heated under his gaze. She remembered why she was there, what Libby and Louise and the other women had told her about the role of women, and her hand dropped to her side. But she continued to meet his eye.

The children watched from the floor as the silence dragged on. The older children's games and conversations had ceased with Jennifer's tirade. Their full attention was on her. Only Jared continued to zoom cars around the coffee table legs.

Finally, Michael broke the silence. "That's the point."

Jennifer's cheeks grew hotter, and she dropped her eyes to the floor. "I'm sorry. I wanted so much to make a good impression, and arriving late wasn't how I intended to do it."

Michael didn't reply. Jennifer began to feel like a child being chastised by her grown-ups. She glanced at Libby for help.

"My brother values his privacy and prefers his home not be disturbed by strangers," Libby said, shooting the man a hard look. "Guests, however, usually receive better treatment."

The young woman who had opened the door closed it, and Libby's brother took a deep breath before speaking. "I'm sorry," he said. "Maybe we can all start over. It's nice to see you again, Jennifer. May I take your...cloak?"

"Thank you." Jennifer undid the clasp and swung the cloak off her shoulders with a flourish, revealing her new dress underneath. She'd made it special for this dinner, a red, white, and green plaid with white lace trim. She'd adapted her pattern to make the bodice looser, accommodating the modesty standards of the church. Jennifer preferred the original design—it was much more authentic to the Victorian era—but she was tired of capes.

Michael cocked an eyebrow at her outfit but said nothing as he took her cloak and carried it out of the room. He returned a moment later empty-handed and, with a sweeping gesture of his arm, introduced his family.

"Libby and Nick you know," he said, and Jennifer nodded graciously at the couple who had been so welcoming to her at Church of the Covenant. "And you know Jared." Michael smiled at his nephew, who was too busy causing a multi-matchbox pileup to notice. "Those are my three youngest sons. Boys, tell Miss Levine your names and how old you are."

The oldest of the three looked down shyly. "I'm Timothy. I'm six."

The next boy grinned. "I'm Paul. I just turned five on December twenty-second. I'm almost a Christmas baby, like Jesus!"

Jennifer grinned back. "Well, happy birthday a few days late, Paul."

There was a brief silence as the toddler just stared at Jennifer, his mouth slightly ajar.

"That's Benjamin," Paul volunteered. "He's only two, so he doesn't talk much yet."

"I see," Jennifer said. She squatted down so she was almost eye level with the boy. He had the most adorable brown curls. "It's very nice to meet you, Benjamin."

He closed his mouth and smiled, holding out a tiny Corvette. "Cah," he said.

Jennifer nodded. "Yes, car. It's a yellow car."

Benjamin pulled his arm back and studied the toy wonderingly. "Weh-wo cah," he repeated.

Michael cleared his throat, and Jennifer stood.

"Behind you is my eldest daughter, Hope."

Jennifer turned and smiled at the young woman who still stood by the front door. "I'm glad to meet you, Hope."

The girl barely glanced at her before returning her eyes to the floor. "I'm glad to meet you, too." Her eyes darted to her father, then back at Jennifer. It seemed an effort for the girl to look at her face. "I'm seventeen."

Before Jennifer could comment, one of the teenage boys sitting on the floor playing Monopoly spoke up. "I'm Joshua. I'm sixteen."

"And I'm John," said the boy next to him. "I'm fifteen."

The introductions continued around the game board. "I'm Amos. I'm eleven."

"I'm Samuel. I'm thirteen."

"I'm glad to meet you all." Jennifer turned her attention to the group of girls. A half-finished puzzle of a vibrant garden scene was on the floor between them. Jennifer guessed it to have about five hundred pieces. Impressive, for children so young.

"I'm Faith. I'm nine."

"I'm Joy. I'm ten. I love your dress!"

Jennifer beamed. "Thank you, Joy. Yours is very pretty, too." In truth it was rather drab, a shapeless, dingy yellow frock, but Jennifer could be charitable. Joy smirked as though she knew exactly what Jennifer was thinking.

The other girl—Faith—leaned over and whispered in the ear of her youngest sister. The little girl stood up, walked over to Jennifer, and curtsied like a princess.

"I'm Grace," she said in a clear voice. "I'm four, and I'm very pleased to meet you!" She spoiled it a little by looking back at Joy. The older girl was holding her stomach, laughing silently.

Faith looked flabbergasted. "I didn't tell her to do *that*," she muttered.

Jennifer held in her own laughter and returned a perfect princess curtsy of her own. "I'm very pleased to make your acquaintance, Miss Grace."

"Just Grace," the little girl said.

"Just Grace, then," Jennifer agreed.

Michael cleared his throat again. "Hope, is there something you need to be doing right now?" he asked.

Hope disappeared into the kitchen, and Michael gestured to the couch. "Please join us," he said.

By the time Jennifer was seated next to Libby, the little boys had resumed their noisy play and the older children had turned their attention back to their activities. The room, which had been nearly silent since Jennifer had lectured Michael—she still winced at that—was suddenly quite loud.

The adults tried to make conversation, but their difficulty hearing each other over the noise was only one of the problems. Jennifer wasn't sure what to say, and Michael seemed disinclined to take the lead. Libby made a few attempts to get everyone talking, but each topic petered out after a few brief exchanges. Jennifer knew Nick to be a man of few words, and he had none at all this evening. She was relieved when Hope came out of the kitchen to announce that dinner was ready.

Jennifer followed Libby into a surprisingly large kitchen. Michael sat at the head of the table, Nick took the chair to his right, and Libby guided Jennifer to the seat at his left before sitting down next to her husband. Jared sat next to his mother. The rest of the Wagner children arranged themselves more or less according to age, with Joy and Faith positioned near the littler ones in case they needed help. Hope was at the opposite end of the table from her father, Benjamin's high chair pulled next to her. For a moment Jennifer envied the little ones, surrounded by such familial love even in the absence of a mother. Libby had told her the family's story, of course. She was sure the children had been devastated when their mother died, but they all loved and cared for each other so well that they were thriving regardless. She'd never felt that loved or cared for as a child, and she was raised by both her parents. Well, nannies. One must not forget the nannies.

"Let us thank the Lord for His abundant blessings," Michael said.

Jennifer smiled as everyone bowed their heads and folded their hands on their laps. They could be a Norman Rockwell painting! "This all looks so lovely," Jennifer said when the table grace ended and everyone began to fill their plates.

"Help yourself." Michael didn't look up as he heaped slices of turkey onto his plate and began drowning them in gravy. "I don't know how you're used to doing it, but we do it family style here."

Jennifer accepted a bowl of mashed potatoes from the oldest boy and put a small spoonful on her plate before passing it to Michael. "Family style works for me."

Dinner continued with little conversation as everyone ate their fill. Jennifer noted with satisfaction that the food was simple and traditional, without any of the elegant affectations her mother had added over the years. There were no toasted brioche rounds with crème fraîce and caviar, and the chicken liver pâté with white truffles would have been woefully out of place on this table. Instead, they feasted on turkey with homemade gravy, stuffing, cranberry sauce, mashed potatoes, peas, winter squash, and dozens of large pinwheel rolls. No two rolls were the same size, and some barely resembled pinwheels. Jennifer could picture the little girls giggling with flour on their cheeks and the tips of their noses as they shaped the dough by hand, and she smiled. She'd much rather be here than at her parents' annual catered affair. She didn't feel the slightest bit guilty about lying to her parents about having to work today.

Her mother had complained and made yet another dig about Jennifer's chosen profession, but it wasn't anything Jennifer hadn't heard before. Tuning out her mother's criticism was second nature.

She sampled a little of everything but didn't load her plate the way everyone else did, as though such fare was a rare treat to be consumed before it was gone. She was the first one finished, and she sat back in her chair, observing everyone else at the table. Michael didn't look in her direction as he moved food from his plate to his mouth, and Jennifer remembered Pastor Kinsley's warning that Michael might take a while to warm up to her. The children were all clean and well-behaved. But everyone was busily shoveling food into their mouths, and the lack of conversation did not fit her idea of what a family Christmas dinner should be like. Jennifer decided it was up to her to fix that.

"That was delicious. My compliments to the chef!"

No one responded.

Jennifer's gaze shifted away from the table to the rest of the kitchen. Her eyes widened when she noticed the stove had ten burners and dual ovens. "I've never seen a stove like that in a house before!"

"It's an industrial grade stove, the kind you find in restaurants," Michael said.

"And the refrigerator, too?"

Michael nodded.

"Is one side the freezer?"

"No, both sides are refrigerator. Our freezer is in the basement."

"Is that industrial grade, too?" Jennifer asked, smiling.

Michael nodded again, and bit into the roll he'd just finished buttering.

"I guess it makes sense, seeing as you have an industrial-sized family." She tittered at her own joke, but no one else laughed. Jennifer cleared her throat, pretending she hadn't laughed, either. Hope had a hint of pity in her expression, and Jennifer wasn't sure if she should be ashamed that she was the object of pity or grateful that at least someone at this table wasn't hostile towards her. Libby wouldn't look up from the meal in front of her. Michael continued to move food from his plate to his mouth, his fork steady and methodical, fueling his body. He wasn't going to make this easy for her.

"Did you have to do much remodeling on the kitchen in order to get those to fit? They're so much larger than most appliances, but they fit the counters and the cabinets perfectly."

"I built this kitchen to accommodate them. They're original to the house."

"You built this house?"

"Yes."

Another blockade. Jennifer looked again at Libby, who finally met her eye. Libby smiled a little and shrugged her shoulders. The message was clear. Libby got Jennifer here; whether anything came of it was up to Jennifer. And Jennifer wanted something to come of it. Despite the awkwardness, this man was impressive. He was mature, responsible, successful, and dedicated to his family. He was a wonderful father, judging by the behavior of his motherless children. She glanced at him again and added 'handsome' to the list. His brown hair had hints of grey, and his face still held the last vestiges of a tan even in late December. She couldn't help but notice how fit he was. He was everything she'd ever dreamed of in a husband.

But he was staring at his plate, not at her. Time for a new strategy.

"That's right. I knew you were in construction. I've heard your eldest son works for you, too." Jennifer smiled at the young man sitting next to her, so like his father in appearance. "Joshua, is it?"

"Yes, Ma'am."

"Do you like working for your father?"

"Yes, Ma'am." So like his father in conversational skills, too.

"Of course, you're going to say that when I ask you in front of everyone."

She'd meant to be playful, but Joshua apparently didn't take it that way. Her words broke him out of his rigid imitation of his father's eating style. "I really do like working for him. He's a great mentor, and I've always wanted to learn his trade."

She'd said the wrong thing. Again. "I was only teasing. What do you like best about working in construction?"

Everyone looked at Joshua, even Michael, and Jennifer wondered if anyone had ever asked him that before.

Joshua thought for a few seconds, choosing his words. "I like seeing the way everything comes together. The way everything depends on everything else to work right. If you cut corners on the small stuff no one sees or thinks about, the whole structure is weak, no matter how well-built the rest of it is. It reminds me of the Body of Christ, and how we all have a job to do, and none of those jobs are small or unimportant. I like being reminded of that while I work. It encourages me to take care with everything, because everything I do glorifies God. Even the small stuff."

Jennifer was impressed, and she wasn't the only one. Everyone had stopped eating except Benjamin, who was meticulously smashing peas into his mashed potatoes, and Jared, who was unrolling his pinwheel roll into a long, doughy cord. Nick was nodding, and Michael looked at his eldest son with admiration, the first real emotional response Jennifer had seen from him. "Well said, son," he murmured, and again Jennifer was touched by this man's love for his family.

Joshua dropped his eyes to his plate and scooped up some stuffing, not looking at anyone. His cheeks flamed red.

"That was beautiful." Jennifer turned to Michael. "You should be proud."

"I am."

"You've raised them well."

Michael's gaze returned to his plate. "I had help."

The silence spread across the table as every thought turned to Lucy.

Jennifer wanted to kick herself. But like it or not, Lucy's memory was a fact she was going to have to contend with. Libby had been clear about that. "She must have been an amazing woman."

"She was."

Jennifer took a deep breath. "Everyone speaks so highly of your wife. I wish I could have met her. I've been inspired by the way she was able to leave her worldly upbringing behind and become a godly woman with a godly family. Her story gives me hope."

The silence grew heavier, and Jennifer was afraid she'd gone too far.

Michael glanced at Libby, who raised an eyebrow at him. Michael sighed and looked back at Jennifer.

"It takes a lot of commitment." His voice took on a lecturing tone, but at least he was talking. "The world teaches a woman's worth is in what she does. The Bible teaches a woman's worth is in what she is. It's difficult for a lot of women to give up the ideals of worldly achievement and embrace being a wife and mother, submitting to the authority of her husband."

Jennifer had heard enough about the rewards of submission that she no longer cringed at the word. Submission could give her the simple, family-oriented life she wanted. "I'd like to make that commitment," she said, her heart pounding as she put it all out there. "If God would send me a loving husband I could submit to."

The older children exchanged startled glances with each other.

Libby continued to look at Michael with an eyebrow raised.

Michael studied his fork. It rested on his empty plate, a small clump of mashed potato stuck between two of the tines. There was nothing about it to warrant such scrutiny.

Jennifer stood, holding her own empty plate in her hand. "Let me take that for you," she said to Michael, reaching for his plate. "Is anyone else done?"

"My daughters can do that."

"Let them enjoy their Christmas. They prepared this wonderful meal. The least I can do is clean up."

The three oldest girls grinned at each other, and Jennifer knew she'd made three allies.

Jennifer's enthusiasm for doing the dishes faded when she discovered there wasn't an industrial sized dishwasher to go along with the stove and refrigerator. There was only a giant, two-basin sink. Jennifer filled one side with hot, soapy water and Hope took up drying duty next to her as everyone else left the kitchen. Faith led Benjamin out by the hand.

"Why don't you have a dishwasher?" Jennifer asked as Hope showed her the scraps bin for the compost pile.

"There wasn't one big enough to do the job that would fit in a normal kitchen, and it would take too long. It really is quicker to do by hand."

Jennifer doubted that but said nothing as she loaded a pile of plates into the steaming water and began to scrub. For a few minutes they stood in silence as she washed and rinsed, and

Hope dried and put away. She could hear the children playing in the living room, though their overfull bellies encouraged slower, more subdued car races than they'd had earlier. Michael, Nick, and Libby were in there as well, their voices drowned out by the children. Jennifer would have given anything to know what they were saying.

Despite the shared work, the silence in the kitchen was becoming awkward. "I noticed you don't have a Christmas tree or any Christmas decorations."

"Christmas trees are pagan. We have a crèche."

"Is that where you put your stockings and presents? Next to the crèche?"

The young woman stopped drying the glass she was holding and stared at Jennifer. "You really are worldly, aren't you?"

Jennifer's mouth tightened, though she pretended it was because of the stubborn film of mashed potato she was scrubbing off a plate. It was an effort to keep her voice light. "What do you mean?"

"Christmas is Jesus's birthday, not ours. We don't do secular Christmas with all that greed and stuff. We have the big dinner because Jesus's birthday is worth a special meal."

"I know I'm worldly, Hope. I wasn't raised the way you were. I always liked Christmas with the decorations and gift-giving, but I can see how it's been taken too far, and the focus has moved away from what's important. I think I can adapt."

"Why do you want to adapt so much?" Hope put down her dish towel and leaned against the counter, facing Jennifer, arms crossed. She was much bolder and more direct when she wasn't in a room full of people. A little too bold and direct for Jennifer's comfort. "We all know why you're here. You don't even know Papa. Why do you want him to court you?"

Jennifer's face flushed a deep red. "Am I that obvious?"

Hope nodded, and Jennifer played with the sponge under the warm, soapy water, ignoring the pile of dishes that still towered next to the sink. How could she explain her actions to a sheltered teenager who had no frame of reference? How could Jennifer make someone who had always lived in a loving, close-knit family understand the debilitating loneliness of someone who was born only to feed her parents' egos and be nothing more than a bragging point for them? What could Hope know about the need to live up to constantly changing—and sometimes contradicting—societal expectations, none clearly defined but all required to function in a world Hope had never had to deal with? Jennifer hoped this young woman would never experience the frustration of trying to be everything to everyone, changing herself to suit the differing and often competing needs of parents, employers, friends, and lovers. Hope didn't know how lucky she was to live a life where she was loved and protected, her role defined and valued. Hope lived a life Jennifer had only read about in books, the life Jennifer wanted more than anything else, and she didn't even know how enviable her position was.

"Yes, Hope, I want your father to court me, even though I don't know him very well. But historically, arranged marriages have done better than when people date and try to marry for love. I think that's because the roles are predetermined and both parties understand they're in a partnership, with the husband having his responsibilities, the wife having hers, and with God as the ultimate authority. It's so simple, and that's what I want. You have what's important. You have a close family you can depend on who will protect you. You have a belief system that informs your choices and tells you what to expect. So, you have to live without some conveniences and frills, like a dishwasher and Christmas trees. But your future is set and secure. I'd like mine to be, too."

Hope looked thoughtful as she picked up her towel and began drying again, but she said nothing.

Jennifer resumed her washing, and they continued their work in silence. As Jennifer refilled the basin with clean rinsing water for the third time, she asked, "Is your father a good man?"

"Yes," Hope said without hesitation.

Jennifer felt a loosening in her chest. "Do you think I'm crazy?"

Hope took longer to answer this time. "No," she said finally. "I think what you say makes sense."

They finished the dishes, each woman lost in her own thoughts. After Hope put the last utensil away, she gave Jennifer a sidelong glance. "The apple pie is his favorite," she said casually. "Warmed up in the oven, with a big scoop of vanilla ice cream on top."

Jennifer squeezed the teenager's shoulder. "Thank you, Hope."

Chapter Eight

A few days after Christmas, Michael received a handwritten note in the mail.

Dear Michael,

I wanted to thank you for a lovely Christmas. It was such a blessing to share the anniversary of our Savior's birth with you and your delightful children. Your family is a true testament to God's faithfulness to His people.

Your sister in Christ,

Jennifer

Jennifer's words were on his mind when he opened his Bible to lead family devotions that evening. They were going through Proverbs again, Michael's favorite book, and he picked up where he had left off the night before. "'Trust in the LORD with all thine heart; and lean not unto thine own understanding. In all thy ways acknowledge him, and he shall direct thy paths. Be not wise in thine own eyes: fear the LORD, and depart from evil. It shall be health to thy navel, and marrow to thy bones.'"

Michael's face was blank as he closed his Bible. It couldn't be a coincidence. His thoughts were a tangle as his children looked at him expectantly, waiting for him to expound on the text and tell them what it meant for their lives.

"I think we should just meditate on these words tonight."

No one commented on the change in routine. They sat in silence for several long minutes. Michael's eyes were open, but he barely noticed when the little ones began to fidget and Hope gave them stern looks and silent warnings to keep still. He was deep in prayer, trying to discern God's will. He'd asked Hope what she and Jennifer had talked about while they were doing the dishes, and her report confirmed what he'd suspected about the woman's motives. But what else was a woman like her supposed to do? She had no proper male authority, and she needed one. Michael had been insisting he didn't need to marry again, but was he confusing his wants with his needs? More importantly, was confusing his wants with God's will? Words from the text swirled in his head. *Lean not unto thine own understanding. Be not wise in thine own eyes. Trust in the Lord.*

Finally, Michael broke the silence. "I've been wise in my own eyes, and I've leaned on my own understanding. God has spoken to me through Pastor Kinsley, the elders, Aunt Libby, and now through His own holy Word. They've all told me it's time for me to marry again, and I've been proud and stubborn and have ignored their counsel. It's time I trust in the Lord with all my heart and let Him direct my path. And it seems He is leading my path towards Jennifer." He paused and looked at each of his children. The older ones kept their expressions neutral. The middle ones stared at him with eyes wide and mouths open. The youngest ones looked back at him blankly. Michael's gaze lingered on Hope a moment longer than the others, and he made his decision. He needed to secure her future, not hold her back. "I'm going to court her. This is a courtship, not an engagement. God may reveal we're not meant to be together. But we'll just have to wait and find out."

Jennifer was the last to find out about her courtship. After Michael announced his decision to Pastor Kinsley and the elders at the next prayer meeting, he invited her over for dinner again, this time without Libby's family. He told her his intentions when they'd finished eating and Hope was wiping spaghetti sauce from Benjamin's face and hands.

Jennifer's eyes darted around to all the faces staring at her, as though she couldn't believe he'd told her this in front of everyone. Then she broke into a wide smile as she looked back at Michael. "I'd like that," she said, reaching for his hand.

Michael jerked his own hand away and put it on his lap. "No physical contact during courtship," he said. He could feel his hand tingling where the tips of her fingers had brushed his skin. He wasn't sure if he liked the sensation or not.

"Of course." Jennifer's cheeks were aflame, and she stared down at the table.

Michael cursed himself for his reaction. "I'm sorry." His voice was soft and gentle, a tone he hadn't used since Lucy was there to hear it. She was the last one to touch his hand. It had tingled then, too. "You don't know our ways. Courtship is a time for talking and getting to know each other, and we shouldn't allow ourselves to rush into anything because of temptations of the flesh." He hoped his children were listening to this, because his words were for their ears as much as Jennifer's.

Jennifer nodded, still staring at her plate. "I understand." But her cheeks were still red, her eyes bright.

This was going to be harder than he'd thought. "Hope, Joshua, take everyone into the living room. Joy, you and Faith can do the dishes later."

Once the children had left the room, he reached out a hand and placed it on Jennifer's shoulder. It wasn't allowed, strictly speaking, especially alone, but he wanted to make her feel comfortable. "I haven't done this in a long time, Jennifer, and, honestly, I wasn't very good at it back then. Lucy was very patient with me, and I hope you will be, too."

Jennifer smiled and touched the hand on her shoulder.

Fire sprang up at the points of contact and burned its way through his blood and into all his extremities. Yes, there was a reason this wasn't allowed. The touch was brief, though its effect on him lingered. She folded her hands on the table in front of her.

"I will be, Michael. And I hope you'll be patient with me."

Over the next several weeks Michael had plenty of opportunities to be patient. Jennifer tried to abide by the rules of courtship and godly living, but certain behavioral codes—like how inappropriate it was for her to grab his children in a sudden hug, including his older sons—weren't as obvious to her as they were to him. Michael corrected Jennifer as gently as he could, and Joshua, John, Samuel, and Amos all learned to keep out of her reach, but Jennifer's ignorance continued to embarrass them all.

As they got to know each other better, Michael couldn't help but compare Jennifer's background with Lucy's. There were similarities, but there were also striking differences. Both women were neglected by their own parents, but where Lucy was born out of wedlock to an unprepared sixteen-year-old mother and never knew her father, Jennifer was born to highly educated professionals. Lucy had learned to take care of herself at an early age, while Jennifer was pampered with private schools and nannies. Jennifer spent her childhood reading books about families that stuck together and worked to get through hard times, and the hard times always brought them closer, but her actual family never had hard times. Lucy had known nothing but hard times since the day she was born, though they hadn't brought her family any closer. Lucy had left college during her second year to marry Michael, and never worked outside the home other than a few after-school jobs when she was young. Jennifer had supported herself since she finished her graduate degree, first as a high school English teacher, then as a live-in nanny. Neither had the support of their families and found themselves alone, with no one to help or guide them.

And both women wanted to escape the failures and the shortcomings of the world and seek refuge in a godly family, headed by a godly man.

Michael began to understand Jennifer's persistence at sticking with Church of the Covenant and courtship, despite the fact that it was all so foreign to her. The world had left her with a terrible emptiness and a longing for what God had ordained as right and proper. He felt the first stirrings of protectiveness toward this strange new woman, and he prayed that God would help him show her the way towards becoming a helpmeet and mother.

As the weeks turned into months, God seemed to answer his prayers. Jennifer was learning. Most of the time she corrected her own behavior after being told only once. She was good with the children and was always quick to help with the dishes when she joined them for Sunday dinner. Pastor Kinsley and his wife, Louise, continued to instruct her, and they helped her to reject her mother's liberal Methodism as well as her father's secular Judaism and instead embrace the true Christian faith.

Once the snow melted in late March, Michael showed Jennifer around his property. She'd seen the house and the driveway but had never more than peeked through the kitchen window at the backyard. He showed her the chicken coop, the backyard garden, the new, additional garden Samuel and Amos had planted along the side of the house, and the goat pen deeper back in the trees. They continued on to the far end of his property line, the woods so dense that all signs of habitation were hidden, then walked around the perimeter of his property.

"When I bought this land, the neighborhood was nothing more than a plan on some town official's drafting board. They'd just cut the road, and they divided the woods on either side into two-acre plots. I bought three of them before any utilities had been run along the street, when they were still cheap. I left most of it wooded, and just cleared this center portion for the house and everything. I've cleared more as I've needed it, but I like having the buffer of woods between me and everyone else."

Jennifer's eyes sparkled. "I remember how hard it was to find this place on Christmas. But now I understand why you went to so much trouble. It's like your own little world back here. I love how you have your own chickens and goats and apple trees. And the gardens are huge! It's like a little farm!"

Michael laughed. "Not even close. I was raised on a farm. These are gardens and a few backyard animals. The gardens are bigger than they used to be, and we have more chickens than we need. Samuel and Amos are interested in farming, so they've expanded things and sell what we don't need at the farmer's market. My brother, Joseph, gives them advice, and I take them to his farm sometimes so he can work with them and show them how to do things."

"Your brother's a farmer, too?"

Michael nodded. "He took over my parents' farm, a little west of Springfield. My mother lives there with him and his wife, Linda. My father died while I was still in high school."

Jennifer went to take his hand, but caught herself and clasped her own hands together in front of her. "Michael, I'm so sorry."

Michael shrugged. "It was a long time ago. He was a good man. Everything he did was for his family. There were nine of us, and he worked hard to keep us fed and clothed. It wasn't an easy life, but it was a good one. It's what I'm trying to do with my own family."

Jennifer gave him a curious look. "I didn't know you had eight brothers and sisters. Until today I only knew about Libby."

The tour concluded when they arrived back at the house. Michael sat on the porch steps, the kitchen door behind him. Jennifer sat next to him, smoothing her long, old-fashioned skirt under her legs. She wore pink today, still in that strange, antique style she favored. She sat close, but not too close. He smiled. She really was trying.

"Libby's the oldest, Joseph is second, and I'm the baby of the family. I don't see the others anymore."

Jennifer nodded in understanding. "A falling out?"

"Yes," he said. "They kept trying to bring worldly influences into my home. Electronic games and videos and things like that. They wouldn't respect that I'm raising my children according to God's Word, so I had to cut ties to protect my family." He sighed and examined his calloused hands. He didn't like talking about this, but Jennifer had a right to know.

"Momma wasn't happy. I haven't cut ties with her, but I have had to limit how much influence she has here. She doesn't see things the way I do, either."

Jennifer's eyebrows furrowed. "You didn't get your religious beliefs from her?"

"No, not really. I mean, I went to a good, Bible-believing church when I was growing up. At least it was good at first. But over the years it got more liberal, and started picking and choosing what parts of the Bible to follow and what parts it could ignore. Pastor Kinsley was a member there before he was a pastor, and he tried to reform them after he got back from Bible college, but the leadership wouldn't listen. He left to plant Church of the Covenant as an independent church, and I followed. So did Libby and Nick. Momma and Joseph still go to the old church near Springfield, but it's really watered down from what it used to be. I'm afraid for their souls, but I can't force them to see the light. At least Joseph has respected my wishes and not challenged me on how I'm raising my children."

They sat in silence for a few minutes. They could hear Samuel and Amos in the garden next to the house, preparing it for their spring planting. The other children were inside.

"Well, I can't blame you for choosing this life. It's simple and focused, just the way God intended."

Michael glanced at the woman on the step beside him. Her dress, though old-fashioned, was homemade and modest. She still wore her hair in a fancy braided bun, but he'd talk to her about that. Most importantly, she looked at him with longing and admiration, not only for him, but for the life he'd built.

"Just the way God intended," he repeated, and had to restrain himself from taking her soft hand in his rough one.

～

Hope was surprised when Papa brought Joshua home early from the construction site, showered, changed his clothes, and left after informing her that Joshua would lead family devotions that evening.

"I won't be late," he said as he hurried out the kitchen door to his truck, its engine still warm from the drive home. Papa didn't explain himself, and Hope didn't expect him to.

"I wonder if he'll do it at the table, or take her for a walk after dinner," Joshua mused as their father's truck disappeared down the driveway.

Hope brought the wall calendar that she used for meal planning and the shopping list into the living room so she could look it over while keeping an eye on Grace, who was keeping an eye on Benjamin. "Do what?" she asked, only half listening to her brothers. Amos's birthday was coming up, and Mama's practice had been to make the birthday kid's favorite meal for supper, with homemade birthday cake for dessert. She also sewed a new outfit as a birthday present. Hope had done her best to keep up with that tradition, but Faith had taken over the sewing after only a few months. Even at seven Faith had been a better seamstress than Hope. Hope still made the suppers happen, though, so she added shredded mozzarella and pepperoni to the list. There was sauce in the freezer made from last year's tomatoes, and she could make the pizza dough herself.

"Ask Jennifer to marry him," Joshua said.

That got her attention. "He's seeing her tonight?"

Joshua nodded.

Hope put down her pen. "That doesn't mean he's going to propose." She couldn't imagine Papa doing that, even if the courtship was going well. Or was it that she didn't want Papa to propose? She'd felt off balance ever since Christmas, not sure how to respond to this new development in their lives. It wasn't like she could do anything about it, though, so she'd mostly tried not to think about it.

Faith and Joy looked up from their game of checkers, and John closed the Jonathan Edwards biography he was reading. Grace was supervising Benjamin as he scribbled in his coloring book, neither of them paying any attention to their siblings. Paul and Timothy were having matchbox car races in the kitchen, and Samuel and Amos were outside, expanding the chicken coop yet again in the fading daylight. They wanted to add more fresh eggs and roasters to their table at the farmer's market.

"Think about it, Hope." Joshua spoke with an exaggerated patience she resented. "It's Thursday night. When has Papa ever seen Jennifer on a Thursday night? When has Papa ever taken her to a restaurant?"

"It would be a bad precedent to set," John said. "It would raise her expectations to beyond reasonable, unless it's for a special occasion. I think Joshua's right. He's going to propose tonight."

"I wonder if she'll say yes," Joy said. Hope's sister adored Jennifer, mostly for the behaviors Papa hated, like her boisterous laughter and copious hugs, which Hope knew Jennifer continued to give when Papa wasn't looking.

"Of course she'll say yes," John said. "She's been throwing herself at Papa for months."

"That's Papa's business, not yours," Joshua said. "If Papa does marry Jennifer, she'll be your stepmother and you'll have to honor her like she was your real mother."

"I'll honor her as my father's wife," John said quietly. "But she won't be my mother."

Joshua and John began to argue. Hope didn't want to hear it, so she left Faith and Joy in charge of Grace and Benjamin and banished Paul and Timothy from the kitchen so she could get started on supper. A small ball of worry grew in her stomach. She liked Jennifer well enough, but Hope was finally at a place where she was comfortable managing the house and caring for her siblings. It had taken her a long time to get there, and Papa marrying Jennifer would change everything. How could she go back to being just a sister to her siblings, not the stand-in for their mother? What was she, if not the carer of children and keeper of the home? As the eldest she'd always had more responsibilities than the younger kids, even when Mama was alive, but she'd still been just a daughter, only one of Papa's many children. Hope couldn't imagine going back to that now. She couldn't even remember what it had been like.

Everyone except Hope, Joshua, and John were in bed when Papa returned.

"What are you three still doing up?" he asked, shrugging out of his coat.

Hope rose from the couch where she was correcting Timothy's workbook pages and took it from him. She hung it on its hook and returned to her seat. The couch was near the wood stove, which provided welcome heat in the cold house. Papa refused to turn the thermostat up any higher than 58 degrees, and the warmer days of April were still punctuated with cold nights.

"We want to know what she said," Joshua said, grinning.

Papa glanced at his oldest son, a slight smile playing on his lips. "'She' has a name. And why would Jennifer's conversation tonight be of particular interest to you?"

John wasn't joining in the fun. "Are you going to have a new wife?"

"Yes."

The single word hung in the air between them, charging the room with its promise of change and disruption. Hope could almost see the sparks in the air.

Joshua walked over to his father and stuck out his hand. "Congratulations, Papa."

Papa shook it and looked at John. "Any more questions?" The smile was gone.

"No, Papa," John said. He got up and extended his hand, too. "Congratulations."

Hope stayed where she was but added her congratulations to her brothers'. She knew Papa's marriage had nothing to do with her, but she couldn't help but feel like she was being demoted in some way.

It was as though Papa could read her thoughts. "I know this is going to be an adjustment," he said. "For all of us. But I believe God has brought Jennifer to us for a reason. You need a mother." John's face tightened, and though he said nothing, Papa noticed. His voice softened. "I know she's no replacement for your mother, and she never will be. But this household needs a woman to run it."

Shame flooded Hope. Clearly, she wasn't managing the household as well as she'd thought, and Papa was tired of all her failures and mistakes. They marched through her mind in a parade, the most egregious one leading with horns and drums. Even though nothing had come of her car accident in October —there had been no social workers, no investigation—there could have been. And she'd made plenty of other mistakes, aside from that one. Suppers served late because she couldn't manage her time. Disciplinary issues with her siblings that Papa had to handle because she couldn't control their behavior well enough. Papa had decided she'd never fill her mother's shoes. Hope knew she never could, but it hurt that he was giving up on her. She took comfort in the knowledge that her nail clippers were waiting for her upstairs, ready to provide their sharp relief.

Joshua must have heard the same thing Hope did. "Hope's doing okay, Papa. Nothing's getting missed."

All three turned to look at her. Their attention weighed on Hope like a lead blanket. She stared at the floor, afraid if they looked at her face they'd see her shame and sadness and anger and fear and all the other un-Christ-like feelings she was hiding. She shoved those forbidden feelings even deeper and tried to keep her expression neutral.

"Yes, Hope has been doing very well," Papa said. "I didn't mean to suggest she wasn't. But as I've been reminded recently, Hope's eighteen now, and ready to think about starting her own family."

Wait, what? Hope was rooted to the spot, the worn carpet filling her vision.

Papa walked over to her, put a finger under her chin, and raised her head so she had to look him in the eyes. All he'd see right now was confusion, and she didn't think that was inappropriate to the circumstances. "I've been approached about a courtship for you," he said softly.

Blood rushed into her cheeks, and she felt dizzy. "Really? Who?" Her voice wasn't capable of anything stronger than a whisper.

"We don't need to talk about that now," Papa said, letting go of Hope's face.

Hope disagreed but didn't dare voice her objection. She was too busy trying to remain upright.

"But that's part of the reason why I decided to go ahead and propose to Jennifer. I can't be selfish. I have to do what's best for my family, and you are all getting older. You three in particular are close to the time when you'll need to move on with your own adult lives. You can stop smirking at your sister, Joshua, because you're not all that far away from starting your own family, either."

His words had the desired effect, and a look of terror replaced Joshua's smirk. Hope couldn't enjoy his discomfort, though. Someone had approached Papa about a courtship for her? *Who?* She tried not to get her hopes up about Joel and failed. What if it wasn't him? What if it was?

Joshua cleared his throat and changed the subject. "What did Jennifer say when you asked her?"

Now it was Papa's turn to smirk. "She started to describe what kind of engagement ring she wanted. A 'classic diamond solitaire with a yellow gold band,' is what she said."

Hope laughed along with her brothers.

"She expected you to buy her a diamond ring?" John said, disbelief stamped on his face. Papa nodded, and John shook his head. "She's got a lot to learn, doesn't she?"

"She does," Papa said. "But your mother had almost as much to learn, and I think Jennifer is just as eager to do what she needs in order to be the woman God intended her to be."

"But she doesn't have any idea what that is!"

"Then I'll teach her." Papa's voice was low and cold.

John dropped his eyes to the floor. The boys didn't usually look down meekly, but John had gone too far, and they all knew it. "Yes, Papa."

"Go to bed, all of you. The wedding's in a little more than a month, so things are going to get pretty busy around here. I'll tell the others tomorrow night at dinner. You three keep quiet about it."

Joshua and John said goodnight and went upstairs. Hope lingered, her amusement at the diamond ring gone. Papa's voice wasn't as cold as it had been, but it wasn't warm, either. But she had to know.

"What is it, Hope?"

Her eyes stung with the tears she tried to hold in, and her voice trembled as she begged, "Papa, please tell me who?"

She expected him to be angry. Papa didn't like begging, and he didn't like to be pestered for a different answer than the one he'd already given. And he *hated* tears. But he wasn't angry. He pulled her into a gentle, protective hug that took her by surprise. Hope couldn't remember the last time Papa touched her with anything but his belt, and a few tears escaped.

"Joel Peterson," he said, and Hope let out a sigh.

She wouldn't need her nail clippers after all.

Chapter Nine

J ennifer was surprised the wedding would happen so quickly, but Libby assured her the timing was normal and adequate. If a couple decided to turn their courtship into an engagement, there was no reason to wait, and godly weddings were simple affairs. There would be a ceremony in the church, of course, followed by a reception dinner in the church basement. The women of the church would plan among themselves who would bring what dishes, as well as make the bouquets from their own flower gardens. Jack Peterson's wife, Janine, was a decent photographer and would take pictures. Since dancing was forbidden, there was no need for a band or DJ. The groom, his best man, and her bridesmaids wouldn't waste money on formal attire they'd never wear again, and would instead be dressed in the nicest clothes they already owned. Jennifer's only concern would be her own wedding dress, which should also be simple and modest.

It wasn't the wedding Jennifer had dreamed of, but she couldn't help but admire its simplicity. And simplicity was the point, wasn't it?

Jennifer chose Hope as her maid of honor, and Joy and Faith as bridesmaids. Grace would be the flower girl. Jennifer did have a few friends from college she'd kept in touch with, but they didn't have much in common anymore, and she hadn't seen them in months anyway. She'd decided a clean break from her past was best. She also quit her job with the Whittakers, giving them a week's notice. With only a month to prepare for her wedding and her own new family, she didn't have time to manage the Whittaker household. Aimi was devastated to learn she wouldn't be the flower girl, and Sumiko and Derek were so angry about the short notice that Jennifer decided it was best to not invite them to the wedding at all.

She hadn't had a chance to spend much time alone with her future stepdaughters, so Jennifer made an occasion out of the great unveiling of their dresses. She asked them to figure out what they'd wear for her wedding, and brought tea and cookies up to the girls' room on Sunday so they could have a party while they showed them to her.

The only comfortable place to sit was on Grace's twin bed, across the room from the bunk beds Faith and Joy shared. Jennifer settled herself on the bed as the three younger girls plopped themselves down on the floor. The nice tea set Jennifer had brought with her rested on its tray, also on the hardwood floor. The plate of cookies sat within easy reach of Joy's, Faith's, and Grace's fingers.

Hope carried her dress in from the bedroom she shared with Benjamin across the hall, and Jennifer struggled to keep the smile on her face as the teenager proudly held up a faded red frock covered in tiny white flowers.

"It's nice," Jennifer said after a moment. "Though it's a little frayed and worn out. It's also a much larger size than you need, I think."

Hope hugged the dress to herself. "It was my mother's.

Papa bought it for her new as a birthday present. She'd already had six children by then, and her figure wasn't perfect."

The last thing Jennifer wanted was for Hope to be defensive. "I know your mother was very beautiful, and I'm sure that dress was quite flattering on her. But you don't have the shape of someone who's birthed six babies."

Hope continued to hug the dress to her bosom, and Jennifer couldn't think of anything she could say that wouldn't make the situation worse. Faith and Joy continued to sip their tea and take too many cookies. Grace was too interested in the cookies to touch her cup of heavily sugared tea.

Jennifer smiled at Hope and tried to put her at ease. "Maybe if I see it on you," she said.

Before Hope could reply Grace jumped up, nearly knocking over her teacup. "I want to wear mine now, too. Hope, can I change in your room?"

Hope nodded, and Grace raced to the dresser. She pulled something out of the bottom drawer, and Jennifer saw a flash of bright pink before Grace darted into the hallway.

"I'll put it on so you can see it's a nice dress," Hope said stiffly, following the little girl.

Faith brushed the cookie crumbs off her hands, got up, and went to the closet. Joy sighed and went with her.

Faith pulled out a navy-blue dress covered in giant purple, yellow, pink, and aqua flowers. "Here's mine," she said, holding the hanger that held it high. The large, square lace collar framing the neck was something Jennifer hadn't seen in well over a decade. She was still searching for words when Joy pulled out her own dress.

"This is what I've got," she said, something orange gripped in her fist.

Jennifer joined them in front of the closet and touched the

fabric. Just as she'd feared: heavy polyester. She held it up and examined it. The style made Faith's dress look fashionable.

"I see."

They stood there in silence for a few minutes while Jennifer kept her smile pasted on and continued to examine the dresses, looking for something redeeming in them. Joy was properly disgusted by the rag she'd selected, but Faith looked as though she couldn't understand what the problem was.

Jennifer had nothing against vintage clothing. Her own style of dress hardly adhered to contemporary fashion trends. But at least she had a style. Her homemade designs were an intentional choice, part of how she chose to present herself to the world. The clothing her future stepdaughters held were thrift store discards, purchased only because they fit, sort of, and were cheap.

Grace burst through the door and spun wildly in the middle of the room. The ruffled skirt of her bright pink dress twirled around her. Jennifer caught the little girl when she stumbled and studied the dress. The fit was a little loose, providing her room to grow, and the stitches were only slightly uneven. Jennifer had seen enough of the girls' clothing to recognize Faith's handiwork, and she guessed Grace was wearing her most recent birthday dress.

Hope walked in behind her, wearing the faded red frock. As Jennifer expected, it was at least three sizes too big for the girl.

She looked at her future wedding party and their ugly, mismatched, worn-out garments. Hope had her arms wrapped around herself, as though hugging the woman who had once worn that dress. This was dangerous territory. Jennifer returned the orange polyester thing to Joy, sat back on Grace's bed, and sipped her tea. Words eluded her. She didn't want to be insulting.

"Are these really the best dresses you have?" she finally asked, trying and failing to keep her voice light. She couldn't remember seeing them wear anything better, but she hadn't been evaluating their wardrobe with her wedding in mind, either.

The girls nodded.

Jennifer pictured them standing next to her on her wedding day, their atrocities next to her lace. She'd given up on her dream wedding, but she wasn't going to compromise on this. "I think we can do better," she said.

Hope recoiled as if struck. "What's wrong with it?"

Grace's face fell. "I can't wear my pink twirly dress?"

Diplomacy was more important than truth right now, and Jennifer applied tact where she could. "All that's wrong with your dress, Hope, is that it's too big for you, and it's a bit worn out. If that were all, I could live with it. And Grace, your dress is adorable. But your pink and Hope's red just do not work together. And that orange, and those flowers..." There was nothing tactful she could say about those. "Do you two like those dresses?"

Faith shrugged, and Joy burst out with an emphatic "No!"

"Is it really a sin for you to get new dresses for a wedding?"

"It's not a sin to get new dresses," Hope said. "But it is expensive."

"You're not poor." Jennifer knew Michael could afford to buy the girls new dresses. They didn't even have to be formal bridesmaid's gowns. They just needed to be nice dresses that looked good together.

"No, we're not poor. But it takes a lot of money to keep a family as big as ours going." There was a slight edge to Hope's voice, and Jennifer knew she was going to have to work hard to make up the ground she'd lost with the girl.

Hope took on a lecturing tone. "We're lucky because Papa's

got a successful business, but his company doesn't do as well in winter, and we're in a big recession right now. He makes up some of the difference with snowplowing, but he can't do anything about the recession. We have a lot of lean times, and the only way we get through is by being as frugal as we can during the good times so we have something to fall back on."

The girl was no doubt repeating something her father had drilled into her, but Jennifer had endured plenty of lectures from Michael already about their way of life. He had lost a lot of clients because of the housing crash, but he'd also told her his company could ride this out. He'd laid off most of his employees, and he, Joshua, and two other men had spent the winter doing all the interior work on a cul-de-sac in Westminster. With only four of them it took months longer than he would have liked, but people weren't lining up to buy new houses right now. And with so few workers to pay, Michael had managed to make a tidy sum on the job despite the recession.

"That makes good fiscal sense as a general rule," she said. "But this is a wedding! Your father's wedding. *My* wedding!" She stopped, an idea forming. "So, the only problem is that your father doesn't want to spend the money?"

"'It's a wasteful extravagance,'" Faith quoted.

Jennifer could imagine Michael saying those exact words. "Then we'll say no more about it. What are your sizes?"

Joy's eyes grew wide. "What are you going to do?"

"Ask me no questions, and I'll tell you no lies."

"I really think you should ask Papa about whatever it is you're planning," Hope cautioned.

Jennifer smiled. "Sometimes it's better to ask forgiveness than permission."

The girls looked at her, stunned. Apparently, that was a philosophy they'd never heard before.

Chapter Ten

The wedding was on a Saturday, and Hope wondered if Jennifer somehow managed to order the weather. The sun was high and bright, but not too hot. A few wispy clouds accented the blue sky and a light breeze, not strong enough to be called a wind, moved the air without being a nuisance to clothing or hair.

Jennifer had shown up unannounced two days before with homemade dresses for the girls. Papa was angry, but Jennifer convinced him she had misunderstood his intent. Eventually he'd agreed that it would be a shame to waste the dresses and consented to the girls wearing them for the wedding.

Hope and her sisters knew Jennifer was lying, but none of them told Papa. Hope didn't know why Faith and Grace kept quiet, though it was clear that Joy wanted a new dress. Maybe the younger two didn't want to see Papa's wrath fall upon Jennifer for such a crime. That was why Hope didn't say anything. She still wasn't sure how she felt about their marriage, but despite her strange ways and her missteps, Hope liked Jennifer and didn't want to see her get hurt. And knowing that her own future included a courtship with Joel made Hope less worried about her role in the house.

Jennifer also lied about the fabric not being expensive. It was light and cool and soft against her skin. Hope had never seen silk before, but she was certain that's what the dresses were. And they were all different colors, so Jennifer hadn't bought in bulk, either. She had anticipated what flowers would be used for the bouquets and bought the silk with that in mind. Faith's dress matched the lilacs perfectly, and Joy's was the deep purple of irises. Grace's dress was the vibrant pink of azaleas, and Hope's pale pink was reminiscent of early roses.

Jennifer's parents arrived at the church half an hour before the wedding began, surprising Hope and nearly everyone else. Jennifer had implied that she had nothing to do with them anymore, yet she greeted them warmly when they walked into Pastor Kinsley's office where Aunt Libby and Mrs. Kinsley were fussing over Jennifer, Hope, and the rest of the Wagner girls.

"Mom, Dad! I'm so glad you came!" Jennifer's smile was brilliant.

Jennifer's father wore a tuxedo and had thin white hair and a close-trimmed white beard. He stood a head shorter than the woman next to him. Jennifer's mother would have been tall even without her black high-heeled shoes. Her dress was a deep royal blue that showed her knees, the tiny beads on it shining and reflecting the light. Gold and pearl jewelry sparkled from her ears, throat, and wrist. She wore make-up, and her short blonde hair was uncovered and meticulously styled.

"What else could we do?" her mother asked. "You told us you were getting married and said you wanted us to be part of it. So, we're here."

"You could act like you're even a little happy for me," Jennifer said, her smile fading.

"I think you're making the biggest mistake of your life. I'm not going to pretend otherwise."

Aunt Libby and Mrs. Kinsley looked at each other, worry and disapproval etched on their faces. The younger girls shrank against the wall, afraid of this imposing woman in high heels and short dress. Not wanting to be noticed, Hope tried to look anywhere except at the scene before her, but the office was small and there wasn't anywhere else to look. She studied the floor instead, peeking up occasionally so she could follow the conversation. Hope didn't want to be part of it, but she didn't want to miss it, either. She'd never imagined Jennifer as having parents. Jennifer was a grown woman, a worldly woman. Hope had never thought about her being a daughter before.

"Are you going to try and ruin my day, too?" Jennifer asked her father.

His voice was kind and sad, not accusatory like his wife's. "I don't understand why you want to do this. But if it makes you happy, then it's what I want for you."

"This is what I want."

Hope heard movement and peeked at the man. He was walking over to Jennifer, and he embraced her in a gentle hug, being careful not to muss her dress or hair. "Then I'm happy for you."

"So where is this new family you're marrying into?" Jennifer's mother asked. "I want to meet them."

"The girls are right here." Jennifer stepped out of her father's embrace and introduced them. Her mother's gaze penetrated their skins and their souls as she studied them one by one.

"How adorable," Mrs. Levine said, her tone making it clear she found them anything but. "How old are you?" she barked at Hope.

"Eighteen," Hope whispered.

Mrs. Levine snorted and turned to her daughter. "You're going to try to mother someone who's just nine years younger than you?"

"Stop it, Mom." Her voice was just as confident and commanding as her mother's. Hope had never heard Jennifer speak like that before.

"It's a big deal, parenting children. And you're inheriting four of them? At least they're all girls. You always did want your life to be just like *Little Women*."

Jennifer's face flushed a deep red and Hope realized she hadn't told her mother how many children her husband-to-be had.

Mrs. Levine's eyes narrowed and she turned back to Hope, who dropped her gaze to the floor again.

"Do you have any brothers?"

Hope nodded, still looking at the floor, not wanting to see the sharp, disapproving features of Jennifer's mother. Suddenly her vision was filled with an older, angrier version of Jennifer as Mrs. Levine crouched down and stuck her face right under Hope's.

"How many?"

Frightened by the woman's proximity, Hope opened her mouth, but no words came out.

Mrs. Levine asked again, her words slow and drawn out, as though speaking to someone who was stupid, or who didn't understand English. "How many brothers do you have?"

Jennifer marched across the room and put a protective arm around Hope, who was happy to hide herself in the soft, silken lace of Jennifer's dress.

"Stop it, Mom. This isn't a courtroom, and Hope isn't a witness for the prosecution. She has seven brothers, okay? There are eleven children. And I'm going to be their mother."

For once Hope wasn't offended by the idea of Jennifer

trying to take her mother's place. After so many years of having to protect her siblings, it was nice having someone else stand up and protect her. Jennifer's mother was everything Papa told her the world expected women to be, and she was terrifying.

Mrs. Levine straightened from her crouched position and stared at her daughter. "Eleven," she said flatly.

Mr. Levine came and stood by his wife's side. "Jenny, that's a lot of, uh, responsibility. Are you sure you're..."

"Dad, I'm getting married in twenty minutes. It's a little late to try to talk me out of it."

"You didn't give us any other chances, did you?"

Jennifer's voice lost some of its forcefulness. "This is what I want. Just be happy for me."

"I love you and I'm concerned about you," he said. "That's the best I can do right now. Just promise me, you do have—you are on—birth control?"

Now everyone in the room was embarrassed except for Jennifer's mother. She was standing close to Jennifer, trying to overpower her with her presence. Hope didn't think anything could embarrass her.

Jennifer stood taller, though her mother's high heels gave the older woman a slight advantage. "We don't believe in birth control," she said. "We believe God will give us as many children as He wants us to have." Aunt Libby and Mrs. Kinsley nodded their approval from their place in front of the pastor's bookshelves.

Mrs. Levine opened her mouth, but Mr. Levine put his hand on his wife's shoulder. "She's made up her mind," he said gently. "And she's just as stubborn as you are. Let's not make this a battle."

Mrs. Levine pressed her lips together in a tight line and nodded.

Mr. Levine looked at Jennifer. "We wish you the best," he told her, and began to guide his wife out of the room.

Hope felt the tension leaving with them.

As they reached the door, Jennifer's mother stopped and looked back at the four young girls in silk dresses. "Hope. Joy. Faith. Grace," she said. Her eyes shifted back to Jennifer. "Your stepdaughters are expected to be virtues, not people. Every woman I've seen here defers to some man. They even wear head coverings. You do understand the socio-historical significance of that, don't you? You'll be your husband's property and a baby factory and nothing else." She gave her daughter a withering stare that Hope felt just standing next to its target. "You're an insult to every woman who fought to give you the choices and opportunities you so casually reject, and you have no idea what you're getting yourself into." She turned and strode out of the room, her head high, her shoulders squared.

Jennifer's father sighed. "*I* wish you the best."

"Daddy?" Jennifer's voice was small and scared, almost like Grace's when she woke from a nightmare.

"Yes, Jenny?"

"Will you walk me down the aisle?"

Mr. Levine looked at the women scattered around the room. Jennifer's protective arm was still around Hope's shoulders. Grace huddled against Faith, who tried to comfort her, and Joy looked thoughtfully at the door Mrs. Levine just exited. Aunt Libby and Mrs. Kinsley still watched from the side of the room, observing but not participating in this little family drama. Mrs. Kinsley had tugged her head covering closer to her forehead, making it more prominent.

"Tradition is important to you," he said. "Yes, I will. Let me just get your mother settled, and I'll be back to escort you."

Hope doubted Mrs. Levine needed help with anything, but she kept that thought to herself.

"Your father seems like a nice enough man," Mrs. Kinsley said once he'd left the room. "For a Jew."

Hope forgot all about the scene in Pastor Kinsley's office as she walked down the aisle behind Joy. Faith was already waiting in her place up front and to the left. Pastor Kinsley was in the middle, with Papa and Joshua standing on his other side.

Hope knew she was supposed to keep her eyes straight ahead, but she couldn't help glancing at the people sitting in the pews. They were all staring at her. People only stared at her when she did something wrong, and even though she hadn't done anything—at least, nothing they knew about—she wanted to lower her head in shame and hide the sin that dwelt behind her eyes.

Carolyn, rocking Rebekah on her lap, smiled at Hope and nodded.

Hope risked a small smile back.

Three rows down she saw Joel sitting with his family. He stared at Hope wide-eyed, his mouth slightly open. When he saw her looking at him, his mouth slid into a grin. Hope's cheeks flushed and her eyes snapped forward, but she found it easier to walk the rest of the way with her back straight and her head held high. The silk dress caressed her flesh as it flowed around her. For the first time in her life, she felt beautiful, and she didn't care who saw it. God created beauty, and people glorified Him when they appreciated it. Hope had heard Jennifer say that to her sisters once.

She took her place next to Joy, and Grace stepped into the empty aisle, holding her bouquet. With deliberate consideration she put her right foot forward, then assiduously brought her left foot up next to it. She stood still for a full second, then slid her left foot forward with the same care. In this way she inched to the front of the church, concentrating so hard she forgot to smile, not realizing how much time she was taking as she did her best to walk the way Jennifer had shown her. The congregation smiled at her earnestness, and even Papa's face softened as he watched his youngest daughter.

Grace finally reached the end of the aisle and took her place in front of Hope, beaming as she saw all the smiles directed at her.

Then the music changed, and no one was looking at Grace anymore. Every head turned to the back of the church, where the shapes of Jennifer and Mr. Levine were silhouetted against the square of sunlight streaming through the open doors, the bride several inches taller than her father. They stepped forward as one, as though they'd practiced a hundred times, and with each step deeper into the church their appearances grew more distinct.

Hope had already seen Jennifer in her wedding dress— she'd been wearing it in the Pastor's office earlier—but the dress had more power in the middle of the sanctuary. Jennifer was stunning, draped in miles of pure white lace. Lace from her high collar down to the train that dragged three feet behind her. Lace flowing down her arms to her wrists. Lace covering her bodice and full skirt. A veil of thin lace covered her face, her intricately braided blonde hair, and her back. There was no way Jennifer had made this dress in the last month. Hope suspected Jennifer had been working on her wedding dress since Christmas. Maybe longer.

She glided down the aisle on Mr. Levine's arm, her eyes locked with Michael's, and stood before Pastor Kinsley. She was a vision out of a classic novel. She was also a violation of every part of 1 Timothy 2:9. *In like manner also, that women adorn themselves in modest apparel, with shamefacedness and sobriety; not with broided hair, or gold, or pearls, or costly array.* The dress was modest in the sense that it didn't reveal much flesh, and the sheer amount of material served to mask her figure. But it certainly qualified as 'costly array,' and there was nothing shamefaced about Jennifer's demeanor. Light glinted off the gold attached to her earlobes, a small circle of it surrounding a single pearl.

Hope had noticed the holes in Jennifer's earlobes months earlier, but she'd never seen her wear earrings before. She hadn't been wearing them in Pastor Kinsley's office, and Hope recognized another application of 'it's better to ask forgiveness than permission.' Hope wondered how many times Jennifer would get away with that before she discovered there was a limit to the number of times Papa would forgive.

Papa's face revealed nothing as he stepped forward to take Jennifer's hand. Mr. Levine stepped back and sat down next to his wife, and Pastor Kinsley raised his eyebrows. He gave Mr. Levine a hard look.

"Who gives this woman?" It was more of a demand than a question.

Mr. Levine met the pastor's glower. "She gives herself."

Jennifer turned and looked at him with pleading eyes.

"Her mother and I do," he sighed.

Mrs. Levine gave a little snort.

Pastor Kinsley nodded and turned back to the bride and groom, dismissing Mr. Levine and ignoring Mrs. Levine as he continued the service.

The worst part of being maid of honor was having to sit at the head table. Papa and Jennifer sat in the center. Grandma and Uncle Joseph sat next to Papa, with Joshua seated next to

Uncle Joseph. Mr. Levine placed himself between his daughter and his wife, leaving Hope seated at the far end of the table next to Mrs. Levine. Her younger siblings sat at various tables with guests, and Hope wished she had Benjamin with her, just so she'd have something to focus on. She tried not to look in the direction of the Petersons. She could feel Joel's eyes on her, though, and she wondered how ridiculous she looked, perched at the end of the table being ignored.

Hope glanced at Mrs. Levine, who stared at her plate and picked at the homemade food, and was surprised to see she wasn't wearing earrings. Hadn't she worn a pair in Pastor Kinsley's office? Hope thought she remembered seeing them. Everything else about her was perfectly put together, from her chin-length blonde hair to her matching gold-and-pearl bracelet and necklace, but her earlobes were empty save for the small holes that indicated earrings once resided there. Hope thought of the earrings Jennifer now wore. Her mother must have given her the earrings out of her own ears. Why would she do that? She didn't seem like the kind of person to do anything nice for her daughter, especially at a wedding she didn't approve of. Even now she sat in stony silence, radiating anger and disapproval and something else Hope couldn't quite name. Disappointment, maybe?

Jennifer was the exact opposite of her mother. She was vivacious and excited, talking to her father and her new husband nonstop, barely pausing to sample her food. Mr. Levine nodded and tried to converse with her, though she gave him little opportunity to say anything. Papa's demeanor mirrored Mrs. Levine's. He used the food on his plate to fuel his body, enjoying his wedding feast no more or less than he enjoyed any other meal. He wore his best suit, which he'd worn on many regular Sundays. Aside from the lavishly attired woman sitting beside him, he could have been at any ordinary church function.

Grandma didn't seem to mind Papa's silence. The simple act of eating took all her concentration and effort. Grandma had been a big part of Hope's life when she was little, when Papa still let her come over to the house a lot. Those visits had lessened as Hope got older, and they'd stopped entirely after Mama died. Now Hope only saw her grandmother when she brought Samuel and Amos over to Uncle Joseph's farm. The last few times, Grandma had to be reminded of everyone's name. She was still kind to her grandchildren, but it was more of a generic, absentminded kindness.

Hope tried to avoid her grandmother on those visits and hated herself for it. But it was too painful to be around someone who didn't remember all the times Hope had sat in her lap when Mama's lap didn't have room for her anymore, all the hugs she'd given, all the secrets they'd shared. Those experiences with Grandma, like so many others, were part of a childhood long left behind. Hope could only deal with the present.

After the cake was served and eaten—Papa had objected to making a big performance of the bride and groom cutting and feeding the first pieces to each other—people began to get up and wander around, visiting other tables. As much as Hope wanted to go talk to Carolyn, or her sisters, or anyone, she wasn't allowed to leave her seat. Being at the head table had more disadvantages than having to sit next to Mrs. Levine. Guests came up to congratulate Jennifer and Papa, and sometimes said a few words to Grandma or Uncle Joseph or Joshua. No one wanted to talk to Jennifer's parents, so they skipped Hope's end of the table.

Finally, Mr. Levine leaned over and murmured something to his wife, and they both got up and switched seats. Mrs.

Levine sat stiffly next to her daughter, ignoring her and the people congratulating her. Everyone appreciated her silence.

Mr. Levine smiled at Hope. "So, you're Grace, right?"

Hope jumped at the sudden acknowledgment of her existence. "No, Grace is the flower girl. I'm Hope."

"Ira Levine. It's nice to meet you, Hope." He stuck out his hand for her to shake. Hope looked at it, not sure what to do. How to shake hands with a man was not something she'd been taught. She glanced at Papa, not sure if she should try to shake back, but he was still looking down at his plate. Hope put her hand in Mr. Levine's briefly, then jerked it away and put it back in her lap. If that was the wrong thing to do, Mr. Levine was kind enough to not say so.

"I wish I'd had the chance to meet you all before this," he said. "Jenny never mentioned you until she called to tell us about the wedding a couple of weeks ago. No formal invitations, even!" He sounded bewildered at the lack of etiquette.

Hope didn't know what to say, so she said nothing.

Mr. Levine continued as though she was holding up her end of the conversation. "Judy and I were shocked, to say the least. We talk on the phone a few times a month, and we meet her for dinner when we can work out our schedules, but she never told us she was dating anyone. You can imagine how surprised we were to hear our baby was getting married!"

"I can imagine," Hope mumbled, though in truth she couldn't imagine anything about these people.

Mr. Levine nodded, then turned it into a shake of his head.

Hope wondered how he kept from getting dizzy.

"Five or six times a year is all we see her now. You'd think she lived hours away! But Brookline isn't that far from Concord. Just about an hour, if you go on the weekend and avoid rush hour traffic. But the Whittakers, that family she worked for, made her work Saturdays. I guess I can understand

Jenny wanting to relax on Sundays and not make the drive. We always gave Jenny's nanny the entire weekend off. Sometimes Judy or I had to work, but we always made sure one of us was home, or at least able to bring her with us." Mr. Levine sat back in his chair and smiled, reminiscing. "I'm not sure which she enjoyed more. Coming with me to the bank where she could draw all over the whiteboard in the conference room or going to the law library with Judy. Jenny loved it when Judy would give her something to look up. It was like she was on a treasure hunt. She'd come back with the information, so proud of herself, and Judy would copy it down on her legal pad as though it were critical for the case she was working on. It had nothing to do with her case, of course. She just wanted to keep Jenny busy, and Jenny wanted to be helpful."

Hope listened with interest. This wasn't at all how Jennifer described her childhood.

"You know, now that I think about it, I think she liked the law library better. More opportunities to learn new things than at the bank. She always loved learning new things."

Finally Hope thought of something she could say. "You're a banker? I thought Jennifer said you did something with computers."

Mr. Levine's smiled broadened, showing straight white teeth. He really did have a kind face. His thin white hair was slightly disheveled, giving him a mischievous look, and the lines on his face made his eyes smile. His close-cropped white beard covered the bottom half of his face and rose and fell with his lips. Smiling seemed to be his natural expression, and it fit him well. "So, she did tell you about us!" he exclaimed. "I was beginning to wonder if Jenny even admitted she had parents before today."

Hope wasn't about to tell him what Jennifer had said about her parents, how they were self-centered and neglectful, so she waited for him to continue. Based on how the conversation had gone so far, she had no doubt he would. She wasn't wrong.

"Yes, I do something with computers. Specifically, I'm a software engineer, doing more consulting these days than anything else. But back in the eighties there weren't many people who did things with computers, so I was one of the guys who plugged in and networked the banks. I could go into more detail if you'd like, but most people's eyes glaze over at this point, so I usually leave it at that." He peered into Hope's eyes. "Yup, I can see the glaze already!"

Hope giggled, and Mr. Levine laughed, too. It was a nice sound. Then his expression grew serious, and he peered at her again. "Are there really eleven of you?"

"Yes." Hope wondered why that was so hard for people to believe. Large families were the norm only a generation or two ago. Grandma had seven brothers and sisters who lived to adulthood, and then went on to have nine children of her own. Hope's family wasn't strange; people had just forgotten how much the world had changed.

"That's going to be quite an adjustment for Jenny. She's our one and only, and she's always liked her space. She even complained about the Whittakers, how they never went out on her day off, so if she wanted to be alone, she had to leave the house. I don't imagine she'll get a lot of alone time in a house with eleven children. Plus however many she has of her own. She's still young enough she could have quite a few."

Color rose on Hope's cheeks, and he noticed.

"But I shouldn't be talking about such things with you. Tell me a little about yourself. What's your favorite subject in school? What do you like to do for fun?"

Hope didn't know how to answer those questions. She looked around for inspiration, and her heart fluttered when she saw Joel working his way up the table. He was going against the traffic, having started with Joshua, then moving on to Uncle Joseph and Grandma, then Papa and Jennifer. He exchanged a few brief words with each before moving on.

Still waiting for an answer, Mr. Levine turned to see what had captured her attention.

Joel planted himself on the other side of the table from Jennifer's parents, the first to address either of them.

Mrs. Levine looked at him in surprise.

"Mr. and Mrs. Levine, I want to congratulate you on the marriage of your daughter," Joel said. His words had the sound of something he'd rehearsed, but they also sounded sincere. "Jennifer—uh, Mrs. Wagner—has worked hard to fit into our community, and I'm sure she and Mr. Wagner will be very happy together."

Mrs. Levine grunted her thanks, and Mr. Levine stuck out his hand for Joel to shake.

Hope watched as Joel grasped the offered hand firmly, pumped it up and down twice, and let go.

"Thank you, uh..."

"Joel," he said absently, his attention already on Hope. "Joel Peterson."

"Thank you, Joel."

There was a silence as Hope stared at Joel, so close, almost as close as they'd been the day he'd helped her. That time there had only been a van door between them. This time it was the width of a table. The table seemed less, somehow.

Next to her, Mr. Levine turned to his wife. "Judy, I'd like to go out and get some air. Come with me."

The meager politeness Joel had startled out of her was gone. "Why should I come with you?"

"Because you're miserable here, you need a break, I enjoy your company, and I want to give these two young people as much privacy as I can manage in this crowded room."

Hope looked down and Joel looked away, both mortified. Joel didn't leave, though. "I appreciate that," he mumbled to Mr. Levine.

A ghost of a smile flitted across Mrs. Levine's face. "It's a wedding," she said. "And love is in the air, apparently." She stood up. "Some fresh air would be nice."

Jennifer's parents left, and Joel remained on the other side of the table from Hope. She risked a glance at his face but looked down quickly. Even though Papa had told her about Joel's courtship request a month ago, the courtship still hadn't been announced, and Papa had told her to act as though she didn't know about it until he announced it. Hope prayed that Joel hadn't changed his mind.

"Uh, congratulations on your father's marriage," he said.

"Thank you."

He leaned over the table to get a little closer to Hope, and her heart fluttered again. "Your father said he told you about my wanting to court you. You're okay with the idea?" His voice shook with nervousness, and that made Hope feel a little better.

"Yes," she murmured, and the muscles in his face relaxed.

"Good. Your father said we should wait a few weeks until Jennif—uh, your stepmother—gets settled before we make it public or do anything to move it forward."

"He told me the same thing."

Joel flashed his smile at her, the one that electrified her down to her toes. His teeth weren't as straight as Mr. Levine's, but Hope didn't care. "I can't wait to start spending more time with you," he said.

Hope smiled back, a little more confidently this time, and his grin broadened in return. "Me too."

She felt someone's eyes on her—not Joel's—and looked around. Papa was leaning forward, looking past Jennifer and straight at the two of them, ignoring Carolyn's father standing in front of him. Carolyn and her mother were there, too. Carolyn was still holding Rebekah. Her mother had dark circles under her eyes, and her smile looked forced. They all turned to see what Papa was staring at.

Hope recognized her father's demeanor and felt a chill.

Joel must have understood what that expression meant, too, because he jerked erect. "Congratulations again," he said loudly.

"Thank you." Hope's voice was just as loud. Nothing to see here. Nothing but ordinary congratulations to the groom's daughter.

Papa looked away, and Joel leaned forward again. "By the way, you look beautiful." He straightened up and was gone.

Was she electrified before? That was nothing compared to this.

Hope barely noticed as Carolyn's parents came to her end of the table and congratulated her, then they were gone, too.

Carolyn remained in front of her. "Congratulations," she said. Not waiting for an acknowledgment, she added, "Do you have something to tell me?"

Hope grinned and chose her words with care. "Nothing I'm free to talk about at this time."

Carolyn grinned back. "Then congratulations again. I'm really happy for you."

Hope wanted to stand and hug her best friend, but Papa was looking at her again. "Thank you," she said.

Hope watched Carolyn join her parents at their table. Now that she didn't have to engage with anyone, Mrs. Cook stared into space. If Hope had to name her expression, it would be despair. She wondered why and hoped everything was okay with her friend's family.

When Jennifer's parents returned, Mr. Levine announced it was time for them to go. "It really was a delight meeting you," he said to Hope. He glanced over at the Petersons' table, and Joel began studying the wall next to him, pretending he hadn't been admiring the maid of honor. "And good luck with everything," he added conspiratorially.

"Thank you," Hope said, blushing again. She couldn't understand why Jennifer spoke so negatively about her father.

"Good luck, Jennifer," Mrs. Levine said. "You're going to need it."

Hope had no problem understanding why Jennifer spoke so negatively about her mother.

"Please keep in touch," Mr. Levine said to his daughter. His eyes were misty. "I just sprouted a son-in-law and eleven grandchildren. I would like to be a part of your lives."

Jennifer blinked her own tears away. "I'd like that, Daddy."

Papa stepped in front of Jennifer and stuck out his hand.

Mr. Levine shook it.

"I'll take good care of her," Papa said. He didn't acknowledge Mr. Levine's statement. Hope didn't know if Mr. Levine understood what Papa was really saying, but Hope did. Papa was responsible for Jennifer now, and he'd decide who would be in her life. And Hope didn't think Jennifer would see much of her parents after today.

Chapter Eleven

The Bed and Breakfast was secluded on its own forty acres of well-maintained lawns and gardens, a small mountain range lining the northern horizon. Nothing was visible between the restored antique farmhouse and the mountains but trees and a lake, and Jennifer found it easy to convince herself she'd been transported back to a day when her many homemade dresses were the height of fashion.

Dusk was falling when Jennifer and Michael stepped into their room. A pastel quilt covered the queen-sized brass bed. The small table by the window sported an antique lamp sitting on a lace tablecloth, and fresh flowers adorned the mantle over the decorative fireplace. Michael went straight to the windows and pulled the shades.

"Oh, Michael, it's beautiful! Thank you for finding this place."

Michael shrugged. "Libby recommended it. She thought you'd like it."

"Libby was right," she said. She glided over to her new husband, still wearing her lace gown, though she'd removed the veil from her hair. Her train dragged across the polished wood floor. Jennifer put her arms around Michael's neck and was pleased to feel his large, calloused hands rest on her hips. "I loved having our first kiss at the altar today," she murmured. "But now I'd like to see how you kiss without a hundred people watching."

Michael hesitated for a moment, then lowered his lips to hers. He was cautious at first, but as Jennifer kissed him back, he responded in kind. His mouth opened, and he groaned when her tongue found his. His hands slid up her back while she ran her fingers through his salt and pepper hair.

"Jennifer..." Michael pulled away, sighing her name. His face was flushed, and he was more off balance than Jennifer had ever seen him. She put a finger to his lips and smiled seductively.

"Why don't you get in bed, and I'll meet you there in a minute." She turned her back to him. "Would you be so kind as to unbutton me first?"

Michael drew a line with his finger from the bottom of her upswept hair down the back of her neck to the first button, opened it, and continued to trail his finger to the next button, and the next, until her entire back was exposed to him. Jennifer shivered with delight and tossed a smile over her shoulder at him. "Thank you," she said. She glided to her overnight bag, which Michael had left near the decorative fireplace.

"Where are you going?"

"Just to freshen up. I'll only be a minute." Jennifer walked into the small ensuite bathroom and closed the door behind her.

Once in the privacy of the bathroom, she removed a hanger from her bag, slid out of her wedding gown, and hung it on a hook. She admired it for a moment, savoring the fact that she was married to her own Mr. Rochester. Jennifer would give the children a classical education just like Jane Eyre and spend the rest of her time making her house a true home, filled with love and simple pleasures. She didn't care what her mother said. Women were crazy for wanting anything other than this.

That reminded her. She removed the earrings her father had given her just before he'd walked her down the aisle. "From your mother," he'd said. "Something borrowed." She slipped them into her toiletries bag and resolved to return them at the first opportunity. They had been perfect.

She reached into her bag again and pulled out a small package wrapped in pink tissue paper. If a kiss and a bare back could get Michael so turned on, wait until he saw her in this.

Jennifer peeled off her bra and panties and stepped into the lingerie. It was white silk in some places, lace in others, suggesting and tantalizing, but not actually revealing. She removed the multitude of bobby pins holding up her hair and brushed out the braids, letting her long flaxen locks curl down her back. She pulled them over one shoulder and studied herself in the mirror. Yes, Michael should be pleased with his new wife. Very pleased. Jennifer's breath quickened at the thought, and she hurried to open the bathroom door.

Full dark had descended outside, and Michael had turned on one of the bedside lamps to brighten the gloom. He wasn't in bed as she'd instructed but sat perched on the edge of it, still dressed except for his jacket and tie. Jennifer floated across the area rug to pose at the foot of the bed, letting him drink in the sight of her. She tingled with anticipation.

"What do you think you're doing?" Michael's voice was low and controlled, the voice she'd come to associate with him being angry. Her eyes flew to his face.

Michael's jaw was tight. His earlier lust had turned into something else. Fury? Disgust? A little of both? Jennifer's arms twitched as she wrapped them around herself, trying to cover her almost-nudity.

"What's wrong? I thought you'd like it?" Embarrassment turned her statement into a question. Didn't he find her attractive?

"Like it?" he asked through clenched teeth. "Why would I like my wife looking like a whore?"

"Michael!" Humiliation and shame battled her own fury as she digested his words. Fury won. "How dare you say that! I bought this for you, for our wedding night."

"I expected to spend my wedding night with my chaste bride, schooling her in the ways of godly marital love." He rose from the bed and stood in front of Jennifer. She was tall, but he still towered over her, and it took all her willpower not to cower. "Are you chaste, my bride?" His words dripped with scorn.

Jennifer was still furious. "No more than you are."

Michael took a step back. "I was married." His voice was hard and unyielding. "Don't pretend you didn't know that. My wife and I discovered the physical side of love together on our wedding night, and I've never been with anyone else. What's your excuse?"

Jennifer's fury wavered as a new onslaught of shame flooded her body. What was her excuse? She claimed to be devoted to old-fashioned, biblical values, but she'd given away her virginity long ago. And she'd had other lovers as well, none of whom she wanted to marry, not that any had asked. She remembered her sessions with the Kinsleys, remembered the words they'd used to describe worldly women like her. Fornicator. Sinner. She hadn't associated those words with herself in those sessions because that wasn't who she was anymore.

"I've made some mistakes," she conceded quietly.

"That would explain how quickly you heated things up.

You've had practice. How much practice? How many men have already used what's mine?"

Jennifer's head dropped in humiliation. "You're not really asking me that."

"I want to know how many men you've violated our marriage bed with."

"I didn't violate our marriage bed! I didn't even know you back then!"

"That doesn't matter!" he roared. "You should have been saving yourself for me!" Michael closed his eyes and took a deep breath. "How many?" he repeated, his voice again quiet and in control.

He wasn't going to let this go. "Five or six," Jennifer said, not looking at him.

Michael grabbed her chin and forced her to face him. His own face was white with rage and Jennifer cringed, bracing herself for his blow.

Only his words hit her. "Was it five? Or was it six?" His voice was barely audible, each word chiseled to sharpness and heavy as marble. "Or don't you even know?"

"Five!"

"Name them."

"Michael, please. Let's not do this. It's in the past, and I'm sorry." Her voice broke and hot tears leaked from her eyes. "I'm so sorry."

"I want to know the names of the men you'll be comparing me to."

"I won't compare! I just want to be your wife. I don't want anyone else."

"Their names."

Jennifer's jaw ached from the pressure of his fingers. "Tyler," she sobbed. "Chris. Neil. Shawn. And...Robert." Tears ran down her cheeks, and she prayed Michael didn't notice her hesitation on the last name. There had actually been a Rob and a Bobby, but there was no way she was admitting to six lovers now. "Please, Michael. They were years ago. Before I knew better. Before I repented."

Michael let go of her face, and Jennifer fell to the floor. He grabbed the quilt from the bed and flung it at her. "Cover yourself up," he said in disgust.

Jennifer did, wrapping the soft cotton around every inch of exposed flesh below her chin. The quilt was thick enough to absorb her tears as they continued to fall, but it didn't stop her shaking.

Michael sat on the bed, his elbows on his knees, his face in his hands. He was quiet while Jennifer cried out her shame and humiliation.

"Did you repent?" he asked when her sobs began to taper off.

"Yes. Yes! I'm so sorry for what I did!" Much to her own amazement, Jennifer realized she was. She wanted this new life with Michael. She believed what Pastor Kinsley had told her about God's design for the family. She'd longed for a family like this her whole life, yet she never questioned the easy sexuality she'd enjoyed since late high school. Her weekly conversations with Pastor Kinsley had gone over how evil the world was and how those who lived according to the Bible could be saved, but they'd spent far more time discussing the characteristics of a godly woman than dwelling on Jennifer's past transgressions. She'd always planned to be faithful in marriage, but it never occurred to her that her past promiscuity might impact relations with her future husband. She'd always assumed his sexual history would be similar to her own, if not longer.

Jennifer had never thought of herself as promiscuous, but she had to admit that the word fit. Tyler, Chris, and Bobby had been long-term relationships only if you considered two to six months long-term. Neil and Shawn were more 'friends with benefits.' There was no getting around the fact that Rob was a one-night stand. Fresh tears welled in her eyes.

Michael slid off the bed and knelt beside her.

Jennifer pulled the quilt tighter around herself.

"I believe you," Michael said. "You're not what I expected. I knew you were raised by sinners according to the world's standards, and I thought I understood what that meant." His face took on a faraway look.

He was thinking of Lucy. She had been raised by sinners according to the world's standards, too, but she must not have strayed as far off the path as Jennifer. Michael might worry about being compared to Jennifer's previous lovers, but she would always be compared to Michael's first wife, and she knew she would never measure up.

Michael shook his head as if to clear it and continued. "Let's pray together now, that God will give us new hearts and guide our marriage."

Jennifer pulled herself up on her knees and faced her new husband. He reached out to her, and she snaked a hand from under the quilt to grasp his, her other hand holding her covering in place. He bowed his head, and she mirrored him.

"Almighty God, we pray that You will forgive this fallen woman her sins and wash her clean with the blood of Your Son. Remove from her the stain of fornication and grant her true repentance. Cleanse her from all her past unrighteousness, and give her a new heart, one that is open and obedient to Your will and my authority. Help me to teach her Your ways and correct her faults, that I may form her into the woman You intend her to be. In Jesus's name, amen."

"Amen," Jennifer repeated.

"Have you said the Sinner's Prayer?"

Jennifer nodded. "Pastor Kinsley led me in it."

"I think you need to say it again."

Jennifer thought back to the day she'd said the Sinner's Prayer in the pastor's office. She'd said the words, but she hadn't *prayed* them. She hadn't really thought about what they meant. It was something she'd had to check off the list before she could take the next step towards her new, uncomplicated life.

"I think you're right," Jennifer agreed. "But I don't remember all the words exactly."

"Repeat after me."

Jennifer followed his guidance and prayed the prayer again. The words weren't identical to the ones Pastor Kinsley used, but the sentiment was the same. Having accepted Jesus Christ as her personal Lord and Savior and invited God to take over her heart and her life, she felt as though a weight had been lifted from her shoulders as she opened her eyes and looked at her new husband, waiting for him to tell her what to do next. Following her own mind certainly hadn't done her any good.

"Go into the bathroom, wash your face, brush your hair, throw that tasteless garment in the trash where it belongs, and change into something more appropriate."

Jennifer's cheeks flamed, and the tears threatened again. "I —I didn't bring anything else." Michael was silent, and Jennifer continued in a rush. "It's our wedding night...I didn't think I'd —need—anything else."

The silence continued for half of eternity before Michael spoke again. "It is our wedding night," he conceded. "And I did rent this room for a reason. Go throw that thing away and come to bed. Stay wrapped in the quilt. It's indecent to be walking around naked, even if we're alone."

Jennifer did not spend Sunday strolling the idyllic grounds on the arm of her new husband as she'd planned. Immediately after breakfast they checked out of the B&B and went to the extended-stay hotel where she'd been living since she quit her job with the Whittakers. Michael watched as Jennifer unpacked all the clothes she'd already folded into her luggage, and then he examined each article to determine whether it was modest enough to remain in her wardrobe. The pile of rejects was alarmingly high. Every pair of pants she owned went into that pile, including her comfy sweats and her favorite blue jeans. All her shorts, t-shirts, tank tops, and even her short-sleeved blouses joined the pants. Not a single nightie or pair of pajamas made the cut, either. They either showed too much skin, or else the pant bottoms made them too manly. Michael rejected her lacy bras and panties, though he allowed her to keep her sports bra and the few plain cotton underpants she owned. Jennifer was relieved to see at least all her homemade dresses were allowed to stay. Other than those, however, she didn't have much left.

"I just realized that, until this week, I've never seen you except on a Sunday. I didn't know you dressed differently for church than you do the rest of the time." Was that a hint of accusation in his voice?

"Sometimes I wear those dresses on weekdays, like I did the night you proposed. But sometimes they're just not practical for what I'm doing. Or they're too fancy." The word her mother used to describe them popped into her mind, and for the first time Jennifer was able to see her point. "They are a little costumey."

Michael put a comforting arm around her. After she'd thrown away the lingerie, he'd made an effort to be kinder and gentler to her. When she came to bed he'd turned away, allowing her to drop the quilt and scurry under the sheets unobserved. He'd held her in his arms, not moving, giving them both time to get used to the feel of the other. After a while he'd begun to rub against her, and Jennifer had frozen. His body felt good against hers, but she didn't feel particularly sexual after her humiliation. Michael's hands had moved over her body, exploring, fondling her so she'd be wet enough to allow him entry, then he'd climbed on top of her. She spread her legs to give him access but was too afraid to respond or fondle him in return. Jennifer didn't want to do anything to remind him of her previous experience. Her lack of enthusiasm hadn't seemed to bother him, though, and when he was finished, he'd held her until he fell asleep. Jennifer had lain awake for a long time, not daring to move, feeling his semen soak into the sheet beneath her and dry on her skin. In the morning he'd been gallant and polite, carrying her bag, opening doors for her, holding her chair at the breakfast table. And now ensuring she would be modestly dressed at all times. Jennifer was grateful she'd packed one of her costumey dresses to wear that day. She wasn't sure what Michael would have done if she'd put on a pair of pants.

Michael surveyed the small collection of dresses that would go back into her suitcase. "You do seem to have a lot of 'Sunday best,' and not much in the way of everyday clothes." He smiled benevolently. "How would you like it if I took you shopping?"

"Now?"

Michael nodded. "You can make some new, functional clothes for yourself when we get home, but that's going to take some time. We'll get you a few items now to hold you over until they're ready."

"I'd like that," Jennifer lied. Shopping for functional clothes was not at all how she wanted to spend the last and only day of her honeymoon. But he was trying, and she would too.

She hid her horror when Michael drove past the mall and

took her to a thrift store in a run-down part of town, where Jennifer was able to find some jumpers, loose-fitting long-sleeved shirts, and long skirts. She rejected quite a bit of what Michael suggested, remembering with a twinge of guilt the harsh comments she'd made to the girls about the dresses they'd selected for her wedding. If this was where they shopped, she had no trouble believing they'd produced the very best they had.

Jennifer insisted on buying new pajamas and undergarments and held her peace when Michael took her to Walmart. Jennifer had never shopped at Walmart in her life, and she'd certainly never considered buying clothes there. But at least the clothes were new, and she walked out with two modest bras, a package of cotton panties, and two long nightgowns. The next stop was the fabric store so Jennifer could buy what she needed to make some more clothes for herself. She intended to wear those thrift store rags for as brief a time as possible.

"You're spending an awful lot of money," Michael said. "You don't need that many outfits. We do have a washing machine, you know."

Jennifer smiled sweetly at her husband. She'd already closed her checking and savings accounts and put the entire amount into a cashier's check written out to Michael. Later this week she'd sign her Prius over to him to sell. It wasn't practical for her new life. She wasn't wild about giving him all her money, but Pastor Kinsley insisted it was God's will that the man be the provider, and any resources she had must be given to her husband. She'd thought of the Bennet daughters and their meager dowries in *Pride and Prejudice*, and how she would soon, like them, be completely dependent upon her husband's ability to provide for her. She'd agreed that giving up her bank accounts and car was a small price to pay for the future she was getting. But the amount she was spending on clothes and fabric was a tiny fraction of the dowry she'd given him. They could afford this, even with the recession.

"Just a few more things to get me started. I have hardly a week's worth of regular clothes."

Michael conceded, and Jennifer selected as many fabrics as she could until Michael protested again. Afterward they grabbed a quick supper as the last outing of their honeymoon and hurried to make it home in time for family devotions.

"I want us to pray together as a complete family tonight," he explained.

"Of course," Jennifer agreed, ready for this disaster of a honeymoon to be over. She walked with her husband into her new home where she would assume her long-coveted role as traditional wife and mother, ignoring the nagging voice of her own mother's warnings echoing in her head.

Chapter Twelve

At Papa's bidding, Hope sent her siblings outside to play while she walked Jennifer through the daily routine, explaining what needed to be done and when, who was responsible for which chores, how the family calendar and the shopping list worked together, etc. Jennifer nodded and followed along, commenting that everything seemed well organized and efficient. Hope stifled a sinful sense of pride at hearing that.

"I don't think I'll have any trouble managing this," Jennifer said. "What about schooling for you and your siblings?"

Hope led her to the schoolroom, a long, narrow room off the living room, with its big table and two tall bookcases against the back wall. Jennifer's smile faltered, and Hope tried to look at the space through her stepmother's eyes. Her pride withered and died. Only two shelves in one of the bookcases held books; the rest were filled with board games, coloring books, pads of drawing and construction paper, crayons, boxes with scraps of fabric, needles and thread for quilting, a bin full of wooden blocks, another full of dolls, and two more filled with toy cars. One shelf held some of Papa's old trade journals, another Amos and Samuel's seed catalogs, cash box, and farm ledger. Hope doubted real classrooms looked like this.

"What curricula do you use?" Jennifer asked. Hope showed her the workbooks, which Jennifer flipped through with a distasteful twist to her mouth. "No science? No history? No geography? No *literature*?" That last seemed to offend her the most.

Hope gestured to the McGuffey Readers. "We get a lot of history and literature from those," she explained, as Jennifer thumbed through some of the larger volumes.

"But these are only excerpts."

"We used to go to the library once a week, and Mama would get us the original sources if we asked for them. She also got us other books when we asked questions or were curious about something. We still go to the library sometimes, and I check out a lot of the original sources for Joy. She's the only one who asks for them."

Jennifer returned her attention to the workbooks. "Well, I guess that's something," she murmured, flipping through them again. "Samuel and Amos are less than halfway through their workbooks, and Faith's only a little further along. Timothy's about where he should be at this point in the school year, and Joy's already finished. Why the differences? And what about the rest of you? Joshua I can understand, but what about John? What about the little kids? What about you?"

Hope studied the carpet as the onslaught of words washed over her. Her cheeks burned, and she rubbed her forearms under her sleeves. She hadn't used her nail clippers in a while and had no scabs to comfort her. "I did the best I could," she mumbled. Until today, she'd been rather proud of her homeschooling.

Jennifer set the workbooks on the table and pulled her stepdaughter into a hug. Hope stiffened at the contact. "I'm sorry,

Hope. I didn't mean to disparage your efforts. You did very well under very difficult circumstances. I have a Master of Arts in Teaching from Smith College, and I taught high school English for two years before I became a nanny. I see things a little differently, that's all. I just want you all to get the best education you possibly can."

Hope endured the embrace. She was grateful when Jennifer released her, though her shame remained. Her third year of homeschooling her siblings was going better than her second, which had gone much better than her first, but she could still imagine how inadequate it must look to a real teacher.

Jennifer guided her to a chair and sat down next to her. "Now, first explain to me why you, John, and the little kids don't have workbooks."

"Benjamin's too young for anything. Grace and Paul are learning their letters and numbers through games and puzzles. They're not ready for workbooks, though Paul should get one next year. John's studying ministry with Pastor Kinsley, and he gives him books to read. Sometimes he has him write reports or something. I don't have anything to do with that."

"And you?"

"I—I teach the others and manage the house." The workbook Mama had ordered for her just before she died still sat untouched on the shelf.

"I was afraid of that. What do you tell the school district? You have to get your curriculum approved by them each year, don't you?"

Hope squirmed in her seat and studied her hands.

Jennifer's eyes narrowed. "You do notify your local district that you're homeschooling, don't you? It's the law in Massachusetts. I checked."

Hope's voice was barely audible. "Papa says it's a stupid

law. It's every parent's right to educate their children as they see fit, and it's none of the government's business what we do."

"Really." Jennifer's tone was flat, and Hope's heart sank as she imagined the scene to come.

"Don't cross him on this, Jennifer," she begged. "Please? He hates how much he has to allow government interference in his business. He keeps it out of his home as much as he can."

Jennifer was quiet for a minute. "I didn't know that. What else does he do to keep the government out of his home?"

Hope resumed her study of the carpet. Papa also hated having people talk about his private affairs. If he'd wanted Jennifer to know these things, he would have told her himself.

"It's not my place to tell you," she said.

Jennifer took her hand. "Hope, I've learned a few things about your father in the last few days that I hadn't realized before." Her face darkened, and Hope wondered exactly what happened on their honeymoon. The Jennifer who joined them for family devotions last night was very different from the Jennifer who oozed giddy exuberance at the reception on Saturday. "And he's learned a few things about me. One of the things we've both learned is that—is that I still have a lot to learn. A lot." Her eyes began to glisten. "There are things your father assumes I understand, when in truth it never occurred to me to think that way." One tear broke free and ran down her cheek. Hope stared at it in fascination before Jennifer brushed it away. "I want to understand," she said, her voice trembling. "I don't like the way I've lived before this, and I want to do it your way. Please help me."

Hope was stunned. During the courtship Jennifer always seemed so relaxed and self-assured. What had Papa done to her?

"He mostly keeps people away from us," Hope said. "We don't go to doctors or dentists or anything. Aunt Libby gives us advice and herbal remedies if we're sick. If the doorbell rings during the day when Papa's not home, we don't answer it. We only go to the library in the afternoons when public school is out or on Saturdays, so no one knows we're homeschooled."

Jennifer smiled and wiped the remaining moisture from her eyes. "Okay, I don't have to talk to the school system. But I still plan to design a more comprehensive curriculum for all of you. Are Faith, Samuel, and Amos struggling with their work? Is that why they're so far behind?"

Hope explained about her brothers' interests in farming and their table at the farm stand. She also admitted that Faith spent more of her time keeping Timothy on track and playing phonics games with Paul and Grace than doing her own work.

"I hadn't realized their interest in farming was more than a hobby. I can customize their work to build on that," Jennifer mused. "And don't worry about Faith being behind. Or you. Teaching someone else is the best way to cement your own understanding. You're both a little behind grade level, but I think you'll be able to catch up in no time. Give me a year, and I'll have you ready for college!"

The change in her stepmother's demeanor startled Hope. How could Jennifer switch between uncertainty and determination so quickly? And *college?*

"I'm not going to college," she said. "I might be married in a year." Her face flushed, from embarrassment or pleasure she wasn't sure. It felt risky to say it out loud, like it was a dream that might not come true if she told anyone.

Jennifer's smile was indulgent. "Yes, that's theoretically possible. But let's focus on your studies for now, and worry about Mr. Right when he presents himself."

"No, really! I'm going to start my courtship in a couple of weeks, once you get settled. Papa already gave Joel his permission."

Jennifer's eyebrows arched toward her hairline. "What are you talking about, Hope? You're only eighteen."

Hope shrugged. Courtship at eighteen must be one of those things that was foreign to Jennifer but normal to everyone else. Some of them started at seventeen. "Joel Peterson asked Papa if he could court me, and Papa said yes." She remembered her father's admission that Joel's request played a part in his decision to propose to Jennifer and thought it best to keep that information to herself. "You've been through a courtship," Hope said instead. "You know how quickly things can move. Papa wants to make sure you're settled before we announce it or start anything."

That goofy grin was on her face again. She hoped things would move quickly. Marrying Joel was her happily-ever-after. Her power struggles with her siblings would be over and she'd be done caring for little kids. At least, she'd be done until she started having kids of her own, but that would take the better part of a year, at least, and then it would only be one at a time. And they'd be her own children—hers and Joel's—not siblings. That was an important difference.

"Joel asked your father if he could court you, and your father said yes," Jennifer repeated, as though trying to make sense of a complicated set of instructions.

Hope nodded.

"Did anyone bother to ask you, Hope? Do you like this Joel? Do you even know him? What if you said you didn't want to be courted, that you're not ready?"

Hope decided the goofy grin could stay where it was. It wasn't like she could do anything about it anyway. And it was kind of funny how Jennifer had just been through a courtship of her own, but she didn't seem to know the first thing about it. Hope supposed Jennifer's had been a little different, being a newcomer and old and all that.

"I could have told Papa I'm not ready, but that would be a lie. I am ready. And I do like Joel. I've liked him for a long time." Her grin grew wider, nearly splitting her face. "When Papa told me someone asked to court me, I prayed it was him, and it was! God actually answered my prayer this time! And yes," she added, noticing Jennifer's look of disapproval. "Joel did ask me, at your wedding. He's nice like that."

Jennifer sighed and squeezed the hand she was still holding. "I'm happy for you, Hope. Just don't rush into anything. A courtship isn't a marriage agreement, right? You can still change your mind? It's important to get to know someone really well before you marry them. If you decide Joel's not the right man for you after all, you don't have to marry him, right?"

Hope remembered the conversation she'd had with Jennifer while washing dishes together after Christmas dinner, a little more than four months ago. Jennifer had been so eager to be courted by Papa, even while admitting that she didn't know him at all. *Is your father a good man*, was all she'd asked. Now, after two days of marriage, she was urging caution and discernment? Hope wondered again what her father had done to Jennifer on their honeymoon, and she withdrew her hand. She didn't want to think about that. And she didn't want to think about her courtship failing.

"No, they don't always end in marriage. But there needs to be a really good reason for ending the courtship. And even if there is, it's usually a strike against the people involved. Especially the girl."

"Why especially the girl?"

"Because girls are so emotional, and we're a lot more likely to give away pieces of our heart than boys are. And once we've given away pieces of our heart, there's no getting them back, and we'll have denied that part of ourselves to our future husband."

Jennifer shivered and closed her eyes. "Yes, that would be bad," she said. "I'm glad you're being courted by someone you already know you like."

"Don't tell anyone, okay? I don't want people to think I've already given Joel pieces of my heart. I haven't, you know." Hope willed Jennifer to believe her. "I've been careful not to think about him too much." Daydreaming didn't count as thinking.

Jennifer smiled. "I'm sure you have been." They sat for a few moments, each lost in her own thoughts. Finally, Jennifer broke the reverie. "Tell me how I can help you prepare for marriage."

Hope's smile was back. "Get settled into the routine here, so Papa will let Joel start courting me."

Jennifer stood. "Well, then, why don't you show me the laundry room?"

When Hope went downstairs to make breakfast the next morning, she found the coffee brewed and Jennifer following Mama's old recipe for biscuits. Jennifer assigned the chores and taught the lessons, taking over nearly all of Hope's usual responsibilities, and she continued to do so day after day. Hope still took care of Benjamin, though, and she now had school-work of her own to complete. Jennifer had developed a learning plan for Hope as well as her younger siblings.

And then there were the questions.

Jennifer cornered Hope at least once or twice a day. "How does apprenticeship work with the boys?" "Is your father involved at all with homeschooling?" "Do you celebrate any holidays besides Christmas?" "Do you ever go on field trips?" "Is there a set time for going out to buy new clothes?" "What's the best way to ask your father for money?" "Does your father allow you girls to wear your hair in ponytails, or does it always have to be a bun?" "Do you ever meet up with other home-schoolers?"

Hope told her what she could, though she wasn't comfort-able answering some of the questions about her father. "Why don't you ask Papa?" she suggested once.

Jennifer laughed nervously. "Oh, he's got enough to worry about. I don't want to bother him with these little things."

Halfway through her second week, Jennifer took over Benjamin's care. Hope had mixed feelings about that. Jennifer hadn't given Hope any of Faith or Joy's chores and taking care of Benjamin was the only contribution Hope was making to the household. On the other hand, it would be nice not having a toddler tagging along with her all the time. She'd begun working on a quilt for her marriage bed, and it would be easier to focus on her schoolwork without him. Hope also wanted to do well on the assignments Jennifer was giving her, even if she didn't think they were important. Benjamin distracted her from both her quilting and her schoolwork.

With all her other duties being seen to by Jennifer, Hope had a lot more attention to give to the toddler. Benjamin seemed to love having her all to himself. When Jennifer took over his care from Hope, Benjamin rejected this arrangement with ferocious energy.

That night at supper, Jennifer slid Benjamin's highchair next to her own seat instead of Hope's after she'd buckled him into it.

"No!" Benjamin screamed. He threw his plate on the floor. The plastic disk bounced harmlessly before skidding to a stop next to the counter.

Jennifer and Hope both went to calm him down.

As they reached the furious child, Papa stepped in. "Don't touch him," he ordered in his calm, dangerous voice.

Hope and Jennifer both froze.

Papa loomed over his shrieking son. "Stop screaming now, Benjamin."

"Sit with Hope! I want Hope!" the boy cried, banging his fist on his plastic tray.

Papa unbuckled his belt and removed Benjamin from his chair. Right there in the kitchen he yanked down Benjamin's pants, unpinned one side of his diaper so there would be nothing to cushion the blows, and spanked his bottom once. The crack of the worn leather striking bare skin echoed through the silent kitchen. Everyone from Hope to Grace stood stock still, not watching their father discipline their youngest brother. Only Jennifer looked on, her face a mask of horror.

"Stop screaming now, Benjamin," Papa said, still in that same quiet voice.

Benjamin hollered in pain and rage. Papa spanked him again. "Stop screaming now, Benjamin."

Benjamin continued to howl.

Papa spanked him again.

Benjamin's bottom was turning an angry red.

"Stop screaming now, Benjamin." Papa's voice never changed.

This went on for several repetitions before Benjamin finally realized that Papa was bigger, stronger, and unrelenting, and there would be no rescue from Hope or Jennifer. His wails tapered off into choking sobs of betrayal.

Papa recognized that sobbing was not screaming. He stood up and handed Benjamin to Jennifer, who looked stricken.

"I think he needs a new diaper," Papa said conversationally, as though he'd been playing with the boy and just noticed an unpleasant smell. Then he put his face inches from his terrified son's. "Jennifer is going to change your diaper, and then you are going to sit next to Jennifer at supper from now on. Do you understand?"

Benjamin buried his face in Jennifer's neck.

Hope felt a surprising stab of jealousy. Comforting Benjamin was her job. At least, it used to be.

Papa grabbed a handful of Benjamin's thick brown hair and yanked his head back. "Do you understand?"

"Ya!" Benjamin gasped.

Papa let go of Benjamin's head.

Jennifer's hand went straight to the mussed-up curls and began rubbing with small, gentle strokes. Hope could almost feel the soft locks under her own fingers.

"Change him but don't comfort him," Papa told Jennifer as he threaded his belt back through the loops on his pants. "He needs to understand he deserved that."

Jennifer looked like she wanted to protest but didn't. "Yes, Michael."

She had to learn sometime, Hope thought. *They both did.*

As Jennifer carried the sobbing child out of the room, Papa sat down in his chair, a signal that everyone else could move, too. They took their seats silently, Hope pausing first to retrieve Benjamin's plate and place it back on his highchair's built-in plastic tray.

"What was that about, Hope?" Papa asked.

She explained about Jennifer taking over Benjamin's care. "Why?"

Hope considered her words before speaking. Joshua and John knew about her courtship, though not who, but Papa wanted to keep it from the rest of her siblings until he made it public. "Jennifer wants to be fully responsible for the care of the family for when...for if...things...change."

Papa stared at her, and Hope knew she hadn't chosen her words carefully enough.

"I can see some wisdom in that," he said. "What are you doing with your time if Jennifer's taken over all your responsibilities? Idle hands are the devil's workshop."

"I've been spending more time reading my Bible," Hope said truthfully. Twenty minutes a day was twenty minutes more than she'd spent reading her Bible before Jennifer took over all her chores. "Jennifer's given me some schoolwork to do, and I've started making a quilt."

"That's it?"

Hope's heart sank. "I was taking care of Benjamin until today. I was hoping..." she hesitated, not sure what Papa's mood was, or if this was a good time. She could still hear the crack of his belt striking Benjamin's bottom.

"You were hoping what?"

He seemed more curious than angry, so Hope ventured forward. "I was hoping that, once I don't have to care for Benjamin all day, I might be able to get back to studying midwifery with Aunt Libby." She'd begun her studies during her mother's last pregnancy, but all that had ended with Mama's death. There hadn't been time for them after that.

Papa's eyes bored into her, examining her, searching her soul for hidden sins. She studied her plate, hoping she'd buried them deep enough that he wouldn't find them.

Across the table Samuel stared at his empty plate, too, as though he might be able to make food appear on it by the force of his will. Next to him Amos craned his neck, trying to see what was in the pans on the stove. Jennifer's meals were quite different from what they were used to, and the pungent smell coming from the pans promised tonight's meal would be another culinary adventure. Neither said anything, though.

They would eat when Papa said they could eat, and complaining would only cause more delay. And pain.

"How's Jennifer been doing?"

Hope knew better than to push her father for an answer he wasn't ready to give and went with the abrupt change in conversation.

"She's doing good, Papa."

Papa looked at the rest of his children. "Do you agree, Samuel? Amos? Has your stepmother been managing the household chores, your schooling, and your behavior well?"

Samuel shrugged. "I guess so. Everything's been getting done. But she's making us do more workbook work and written assignments."

"At the expense of your farming?"

Amos joined in. "No, she's been really interested in that."

Samuel nodded. "She's making us read articles on things like supply and demand and subsidy plans. She says she wants us to understand farming on a marco level."

"Macro level," Hope corrected automatically.

Everyone looked at her, and she resumed studying her empty plate.

"Have any of you been giving her any trouble?" Papa asked.

"No, Papa," Joy volunteered with wide-eyed innocence.

Hope's mouth tightened, but she said nothing. Technically Joy was telling the truth. She liked Jennifer and hadn't given her any trouble at all. But she'd plagued Hope with snide remarks about her lack of chores when no one was around to hear.

Papa considered this, and everyone waited in silence until the sound of Jennifer's footsteps on the stairs floated into the kitchen. She appeared, carrying a red-eyed Benjamin in her arms.

"I hope you weren't waiting for me," she said as she gently

placed Benjamin into his highchair. He winced but made no sound.

"We eat together as a family," Papa said.

"Of course." Jennifer took her own seat as soon as Benjamin was buckled.

"Let us pray."

The meal was a silent one, the only noise being the scraping of forks on plates, quiet chewing, and frequent requests for more milk or bread. Tonight's dish—something Jennifer called 'lamb vindaloo'—was spicy, and Hope wasn't sure what she thought of it. She finished in record time, though, not having to feed Benjamin in addition to herself. Jennifer took longer, cutting Benjamin's meat into bite-sized pieces and trying to get him to eat his rice with a spoon instead of his fingers. None of the younger children liked spicy food. Hope had been cooking for them long enough to know that. But they all ate without complaint. The memory of Benjamin's punishment was an effective motivator.

As the meal wound down, Papa cleared his throat. "I have an announcement to make."

"You're getting married," Samuel piped up, invoking the last time Papa uttered those words at supper. Everyone laughed, easing the tension that had settled over the table like a shroud.

"Don't be a wise guy," Papa said, though there was no hint of threat in his voice. "Although it does have to do with marriage, God willing."

Hope reddened, and Jennifer gave her an encouraging smile.

"I have given Joel Peterson permission to court Hope. I asked him to wait until Jennifer settled in, but I think it's time now." Papa looked at Hope. "I pray you will conduct yourself as a Christian lady should, bringing honor to your mother and me."

"I will, Papa."

"I'm so happy for you!" Faith exclaimed. She glanced at Joy, who silently glared at her plate.

A moment later Joy jumped as though she'd been kicked. She scowled at Faith, who looked much too innocent.

"Congratulations," Joy grumbled.

"You're leaving?" Grace appeared ready to cry.

"Not yet," Hope said, although she could already feel the distance growing between her and her siblings. She wasn't their caretaker anymore. For the youngest ones, like Grace, that was an experience outside of memory. For Hope, it was a weight lifted.

"Only if Joel doesn't run screaming once he gets to know her," Samuel said.

Hope shot him a withering look.

"Samuel," Papa warned.

"Sorry," Samuel mumbled.

"Joel's a good man," John said, and Joshua nodded in agreement.

"Congratulations, Hope," Jennifer said from her spot next to Papa. "I truly hope it all works out the way you want."

"Thank you, Jennifer." Hope was touched by her stepmother's sincerity.

"It will all work out according to God's plan," Papa said, and everyone nodded at his sage words. "Oh, and Jennifer?"

"Yes?"

Papa picked up his empty plate. "Don't make this again. Ask Hope to show you Lucy's recipe box and start making normal meals."

After devotions that night Papa appeared to be in a good mood, so Hope approached him again.

"Midwifery?" she asked.

Papa took her hand in a rare display of affection. "That's not my decision to make anymore. I'll have to see what Joel thinks about it. I'll call him tomorrow and tell him he can begin courting you. I'll ask him about midwifery then."

"Thank you, Papa. Good night." Hope went upstairs to her room, her insides still fluttering. She didn't think Joel would object, but how could she know? How well did she know him, really? This wasn't a daydream. This was real.

Hope didn't sleep much that night, for the first time considering the possibility that the real Joel might not match up with the Joel of her dreams, and she might not be the girl of his. And what then?

Chapter Thirteen

Jennifer used the top of a plastic cup to cut disks out of the rolled dough on the counter. Homemade biscuits and fresh eggs from the backyard chickens for breakfast every morning had been homey and quaint at first, but making the same thing day after day became monotonous. The pancakes she made for the kids' birthdays and on Sunday mornings were a welcome change, but they, too, were losing their charm. Everything took so long to prepare. Jennifer missed the simplicity of cereal. Or toast! But toast meant bread, which was something Michael insisted had to be baked at home from scratch, and without the assistance of a bread machine. She made enough loaves to keep Michael, Joshua, and John supplied with sandwiches in their lunch boxes, plus a few more to bulk up supper from time to time, but biscuits were much quicker and easier to make for breakfast.

She gathered the ribbons of leftover dough, worked them into a ball, and slapped the ball back down on the counter with more force than necessary before rolling it to half-inch thickness, smaller in diameter than the original piece. Hardened bits of dried dough stuck to the rim of the plastic cup, marring the perfect roundness of the disks she cut. Jennifer didn't care. No one studied her biscuits before cramming them into their mouths. They only noticed if there weren't enough.

Michael wouldn't allow cereal because it was too expensive. She had bought a few large boxes of Cheerios once anyway, just to prove him wrong. Aside from the fact that Cheerios didn't taste right with goat milk, the cereal was gone within three days. Michael had given her a piece of paper and watched her calculate how much flour she could have purchased with the money she'd spent on cereal, and how many biscuits she could have made for the same amount. It was no contest. Keeping a family of thirteen fed was expensive, and it made sense to economize.

Jennifer's hand rubbed the small bump of her tummy and she smiled. Soon they'd be a family of fourteen. She marveled at that. Married less than five months and she was about to begin her second trimester, as near as Libby could figure. Jennifer would have preferred an OB/GYN, but Michael was adamant that Christians didn't need medical care, only God. And Libby was no help on that one. She'd personally 'caught' dozens of babies, and she was sure she could comfort and coach Jennifer through this natural process better than any doctor. No one talked about the fact that at least one mother didn't survive despite Libby's comfort and coaching. Jennifer often wondered if a real doctor could have saved Lucy. She also wondered if there had been others who shared Lucy's fate.

Her smile gone, Jennifer returned her hand to the dough. A few more turns with the rolling pin and the biscuits would be ready for the oven. Then she could scramble the eggs. Her stomach lurched at the thought.

A few weeks after discovering her pregnancy, Jennifer had developed an aversion to anything related to poultry. It was easy enough to keep the chicken down to a minimum at supper —they did a lot with rice and beans, and meats were usually cheaper cuts like ground beef and sausage, but there was no avoiding eggs for breakfast six days a week. She tried to get Michael to let her cook oatmeal instead. That could be purchased in bulk, and she could make it with water instead of milk, but he insisted that as long as they had eggs, they were going to eat them. Jennifer could supplement their biscuits with oatmeal in the wintertime when the chickens weren't laying as much, but until then he expected scrambled eggs every morning.

And once Michael made a decision, all discussion on the subject was closed.

Jennifer was putting the sheets of biscuits in the oven when Hope entered the kitchen. She headed straight for the coffee pot. "Morning."

"Good morning," Jennifer replied.

Jennifer regretted that she'd been so successful at convincing the teenager she didn't need any help. Hope never offered anymore, and Jennifer was too proud to ask. Besides, Hope's courtship seemed to be going well, and Jennifer expected her to be married off soon. Jennifer's own courtship turned into an engagement after a little more than three months. If that was the norm, Hope should be getting engaged any day now.

Hope stirred milk and sugar into her coffee and took it into the living room without another word. Gone was the timid and insecure child Jennifer had met almost a year ago. In her place was a serene young woman who was comfortable in her own skin, perhaps for the first time in her life. Jennifer didn't have to wonder what caused the change—she'd chaperoned Hope and Joel a few times when they sat talking after Sunday dinner. The boy was smitten with Hope and didn't miss an opportunity to praise or compliment her. From the family dynamics Jennifer had observed both prior to her own marriage and after it, Hope had never been treated that way before. It made her more confident and relaxed.

She hadn't even complained when she'd lost her bedroom, an unintended consequence of Jennifer taking over Benjamin's care. Jennifer had planned to transition Benjamin into the boys' bedroom and give Hope some privacy, but Michael objected. With seven boys crammed into a single room, Hope had no business having a bedroom to herself. Instead, Michael removed Benjamin's crib, put a mattress on the floor for him, and moved Hope's bed into the room her sisters shared. Michael had built all the beds himself, and he'd designed them so they could be stand-alone twins or stacked as bunks. Hope now slept above Grace, who loved the new, cave-like quality of her own bed. Paul's and Timothy's beds were in with Benjamin's.

Jennifer opened the refrigerator and removed a knobby piece of ginger root. She wanted an antacid, but Michael didn't believe in pharmaceuticals, either. Raw ginger root tasted terrible, but it did help with her nausea. Too bad none of the natural substitutes for Tylenol Libby had recommended had any effect on her headaches.

She cut a thin slice off the edge and began to chew it. She'd make tea after breakfast. Ginger didn't taste quite as bad when it was brewed with lemon and sweetened with honey, but she didn't have time right now. The piece in her mouth should enable her to scramble the eggs, at least.

Michael had his faults. He took frugality to an extreme, and he didn't understand that women might have interests other than housework and childcare. But however high a standard he held her to, he held himself to one just as high. Jennifer resented having to cook all their meals from scratch, but

Michael made all their furniture from scratch. He also wore clothes that were homemade or purchased from thrift stores, no better than anyone else in the family. Hope hadn't lied; Michael was a good man. A difficult one to live with at times, but good, nonetheless.

Jennifer tried to focus on that as she cracked egg after egg into a large bowl, ignoring the churning in her stomach. Michael had never misrepresented himself or his expectations. He was a religious patriarch who took his responsibilities as husband, father, and church elder seriously. He expected his wife to be submissive and his children to be obedient; in return he saw to his family's spiritual and material needs and led by example. Unlike many of the men in the church, he took care not to abuse his position of authority.

As Jennifer had become friendlier with some of the women at Church of the Covenant, she'd realized there was a darker side to this system she admired. Despite their wives' attempts to keep such things quiet, she knew some of the men didn't live up to their responsibilities. More than a few were on some kind of public assistance, unable to support their large families. Most would never admit it, though, as they nodded in agreement when Pastor Kinsley preached against the evils of the liberal socialist government and emphasized the biblical command to be self-sufficient. He'd even convinced some men who should have been on public assistance to not accept it.

Shannon Murphy had let it slip that her heat had been shut off early last spring, and she didn't know what they were going to do when the weather turned cold again. Ted Cook kept his family housed, clothed, and fed without relying on public assistance, but he did it by working as a regional truck driver. He was gone all week, which meant he had no connection to his family and no involvement at all in raising their children. Jennifer doubted Ted realized how little involvement Stacy had in their children's care, either. Stacy was bright and cheerful at church on Sundays, but during the week she stayed in her bed most days, rousing herself only to go grocery shopping twice a week. That activity usually took her six or seven hours. Her eldest daughter Carolyn managed the household much the way Hope had after her mother's death. Except on the weekends when Ted was home. Then she only "helped" her mother. The cookies Stacy always brought to church were Carolyn's work. Ted knew none of this, of course. He managed to be home almost every weekend, and he expected his family to treat him like a king, rewarding him for his hard work. He also expected Stacy to perform her wifely duties with enthusiasm whenever he was able to sleep in his own bed. She pretended to be happy about God blessing her with so many children, but in truth she was horrified by her own fertility. She'd discovered she was pregnant with her ninth child just before Jennifer's wedding and was due to give birth a few weeks before Jennifer would.

Jennifer rubbed her protruding belly again. It could be worse. Marilyn Mullins and her husband Stan had been married for six years and still hadn't been blessed with children. Marilyn had no trouble getting pregnant; she just couldn't stay that way for long. The women at church counseled her on her diet, and Pastor Kinsley urged her to trust God and confess her sins, but nothing worked. Stan wasn't permitted to be an elder, and the women kept Marilyn at arm's length. If God didn't trust her with children, there must be something wrong with her soul.

Other women deferred entirely to their husbands, unable to make a simple decision without their input or approval. Terri Payne bragged about the list of chores her husband gave her to do each day, which he checked for completion as soon as he got home from work. She claimed it proved he cared. Morgan Reed looked fearful every time her husband came near, and her children cringed when they were in their father's presence. Scott Payne and Al Reed were both elders.

Jennifer knew she was lucky to have married Michael. She disagreed with how he disciplined the children, but at least he was consistent about it. The kids knew what infractions would earn them a whipping—no, a *spanking* is what he called it—and what behavior would keep them clear of his belt. And he'd never used his belt on Jennifer. She was certain some of the women at church had received spousal discipline from their husbands. Some, like Morgan Reed, on a regular basis.

She pushed the eggs around the pan with a spatula, squeezing the ginger root between her teeth and sucking the bitter juice. Michael would be down soon to preside over breakfast with his family. Jennifer's heart beat a little faster and her stomach roiled a little harder, and she firmly reminded herself how lucky she was.

Hope sat in the living room, her Bible open on her lap, aware of the sounds of breakfast being prepared but not really listening. She was rereading the Gospels for the fourth time since Jennifer had taken over her duties. The Gospels portrayed Jesus differently than she was used to. Papa and Pastor Kinsley usually quoted Paul when they warned about a strict, holy Jesus who would judge her for her deeds and be angry if she sinned in any way, but the Jesus of the Gospels was much kinder and more understanding of people's faults and weaknesses. Idly, Hope wondered why she didn't hear more about that side of Jesus. She didn't think too much about it, though. Her husband, her father, and her pastor were responsible for making sure she understood what was important in the Bible. Hope had to trust them to guide her faith.

She read the words on the page in front of her, unaware of the smile that played on her lips. She'd already begun to think of Joel as her husband. He was nothing like she'd expected and more wonderful than she'd imagined. Joel saw her as someone strong and capable, and told her how impressed he was with how she kept her family together after her mother died. He said he was the lucky one in their relationship, because he got to be with someone as amazing as her.

Hope tried to see herself through Joel's eyes, but she couldn't. She did what her family needed her to do, nothing more. Anyone would have done the same. Papa would have made sure of it. And she knew she was far from amazing.

She didn't argue with Joel when he said such things, though, because she didn't really want to win that argument. Hope liked the version of herself that Joel saw. She hoped that maybe, if he kept seeing her like that, she might become that person.

The sound of retching jolted Hope out of her reverie. She sprang from her seat and raced into the kitchen, where she found Jennifer bent over the sink, emptying the contents of her stomach. The eggs were still on the stove, beginning to turn brown. Hope turned off the burner, pushed the eggs around the pan with the spatula, and returned to her stepmother.

"It's those eggs!" Jennifer sobbed. "I just can't handle those frigging eggs!"

Hope winced at the profanity. It was a habit Jennifer hadn't been able to break, no matter how many times Papa spoke to her about it. "Why don't you try some ginger?" Hope suggested.

Jennifer snorted and gestured to the fouled sink. "I did. It's in there, along with last night's supper. It didn't help."

Hope knew morning sickness and food aversions were common among pregnant women, but Aunt Libby said they could be overcome with a positive attitude. Jennifer was making good progress toward becoming a proper wife and mother, but the further along her pregnancy advanced, the more ground she lost in cultivating a joyful spirit. Hope was torn between wanting to tell her to stop being so self-centered and wanting to make things easier for her. She knew her aunt would choose the former, citing the historical precedent of women's fortitude amid difficult and unpleasant circumstances. Hope also knew her own mother spent much of the last five years of her life in bed, coping with or recovering from pregnancies. Jennifer's pale face, the dark circles under her eyes, and her shaking hands reminded Hope of all the times in the past few years when she herself had been sick and had to cook the meals and do her chores anyway, because there was no one to help Hope the way she'd helped Mama. Joel's words echoed in her head. *You're strong and smart, and I like that. You don't wait to be told what to do. You see something that needs to be done, and you do it.*

Hope got a tissue from the box on the counter and handed it to Jennifer. "Go back upstairs and lie down for a while," she said. "I'll finish breakfast. How long have the biscuits been in?"

"I have to do this. Your father—"

"Wants his breakfast," Hope interrupted. "And you're in no condition to get it for him."

Jennifer backed away from the sink and collapsed into a chair. Her eyes filled with tears. "I can't do it," she said. "It's too hard."

Hope turned on the faucet and rinsed the vomit down the drain. "You can do it. You are doing it. You're just sick and tired." She glanced back at Jennifer's hunched form and red-rimmed eyes. "And hormonal," she added.

Jennifer started to protest, but Hope cut her off again. "Even worldly women get hormonal when they're pregnant,

Jennifer. You are a pregnant woman, so accept that you're hormonal and go back to bed. I've got this."

Jennifer sat for a moment, her head in her hands.

Hope ignored her.

Finally, Jennifer pulled herself up, one hand on the table supporting her until she got her balance again, and staggered out of the kitchen. "The biscuits should be ready in about five minutes," she muttered as she left.

Once alone in the kitchen, Hope opened the oven door. Jennifer didn't exactly burn the biscuits, but she did tend to leave them in the oven a bit too long, making them drier and harder than everyone liked. As expected, the tops were just beginning to brown. Hope took them out and shut off the oven, then reignited the burner under the eggs. Parts were slightly brown and other parts still gooey, so she broke up the pieces and moved them around the pan until they, too, were done.

Papa came into the kitchen as Hope was setting the table. She paused what she was doing so she could retrieve his favorite mug and pour him a cup of coffee.

"Jennifer told me you sent her back to bed," he said, taking a sip. "What's going on?"

"Morning sickness. She threw up in the sink."

"That never stopped your mother."

It had, but Papa had a selective memory when it came to Hope's mother. Also, Mama took great pains to hide her discomfort from her husband. Hope had covered for her many times.

"Women's bodies respond to pregnancies differently. Jennifer's morning sickness seems to be pretty bad, especially with eggs. Maybe I should take over breakfast for a while."

Papa sipped his coffee, considering. "How old is Joy?"

"Ten."

"That's old enough. You were cooking at ten, weren't you?"

Hope couldn't keep the pride out of her voice as she put the last plates on the table. "Mama started teaching me when I was eight."

"Then it's time you start teaching your sisters. It's clear Jennifer isn't up to the task, and I know things are going well with you and Joel."

Hope blushed, grinned, and looked down at her feet. "They are."

"He's working hard to save money and prove himself financially stable enough to support a family. From my conversations with him and his father, I think he should be ready to provide a home for you in a few more months. I'd like you to stay around here until after the baby's born, so we don't have too many things going on at once."

Hope's heart leaped in her chest. A home with Joel after the baby was born! It looked like there would be another spring wedding for the Wagner family. "Yes, Papa."

The sky was darkening just enough that Michael had to switch on his headlights as he guided his truck down the winding, tree-lined streets. The leaves were beginning to turn and fall, bringing to his mind thoughts of death. He used to like autumn, but now it reminded him of how much he'd lost when he lost Lucy. She'd understood his heavy burden of responsibility, and she'd lent him her quiet strength and capable hands, becoming his partner in life. She gave him what he needed, and in return he gave her everything he was and everything he had. The two had become one, and it was good.

And it was gone.

His new wife was unhappy, and Michael didn't know how to fix it. Jennifer was more set in her worldly ways than he'd realized and wasn't adjusting well. Michael didn't understand how Lucy and Jennifer could both come from worldly backgrounds and have such different reactions to salvation. Lucy embraced her role and was fulfilled by it. Jennifer had claimed she wanted this life, but now that he'd given it to her, she seemed to resent it. Neither of Michael's wives had known Christ before meeting him. Lucy had accepted Him into her heart with joy and thanksgiving, allowing Him to enrich her daily activities with blessedness. Jennifer participated in the rituals at home and at church, but Michael doubted she understood what Jesus had to do with laundry.

And she certainly didn't understand why it was so important to raise the children to be godly.

His children were arrows in his quiver, his sons future warriors in the battle to bring America and the world back to Christ. They and others like them would need the support of their women to keep the home and raise the next generation of warriors. For all that Jennifer bemoaned the sorry lack of parental involvement and guidance in her own home and in the homes of her former charges and students, she didn't seem to grasp that such involvement required the complete attention of the mother. If girls weren't raised to understand the importance of Christian motherhood, they would abandon their families and be deceived by the lies of feminism and worldly self-fulfillment. Their husbands and children would suffer, and the war would be lost.

The intersection with the right turn that would lead him home was coming up, but Michael continued to drive straight. One of his contractors had given Joshua a ride home earlier, and dinner wouldn't be on the table for another half hour. He wasn't ready to go home yet. He had to figure out what to do about Jennifer.

Everything with her was a battle. Accommodating her

wishes usually required some compromise on a basic principle, and he couldn't compromise any further. Earlier that day Jennifer had protested when he told her to use school time to teach the girls how to follow recipes instead of doing busywork in their workbooks. She'd refused, telling him Joy had the potential to go to college—*college!*—and her time would be better spent preparing for that.

This latest thing with the girls' schooling was their biggest point of contention to date, and it was crucial in determining the dynamics of their relationship going forward. Jennifer had demonstrated beyond a doubt that she wasn't a follower, but Michael couldn't allow her to take the lead.

He drove through the small Massachusetts town that had been his home for almost two decades until he reached the sign that bordered the next town, then turned around and drove through it again. Back and forth he drove, passing by the turn that would lead him home, now on the left, now on the right, now on the left again, dread building each time he approached it only to be replaced by guilt each time he passed it. He was late for supper, and that added to his guilt.

Finally, he pulled to the side of the otherwise empty road and turned off his engine. Full dark had descended, and the chill of the late September evening crept into the cab of his truck. He closed his eyes and prayed.

Forty minutes later he started his truck up again, calm, cold, and resolved. He switched off the heater before it could blast to life, preferring the sharp, invigorating air.

Lucy married him because she loved him, and the rest fell into place. Jennifer married him because she wanted to be supported as a wife and mother, and she thought he would do that for her. He couldn't blame her. He never loved her, either. He'd married her because he needed a helpmeet, and she was willing to step into that role. It was better when he had a wife he loved, but love was not a requirement for a successful marriage. Clearly defined roles, responsibilities, and expectations were far more important. He would call a family meeting and remind everyone of their duties to God and to each other, and he would enforce compliance.

In his efforts to make Jennifer happy he'd compromised too much, and that had been a mistake. It was time for him to step up and be the leader his family needed him to be, and his family, including his wife, would follow.

He'd make sure of it.

Chapter Fourteen

"You're quiet today," Joel said, casting a worried look at Hope. "Is everything okay?"

"I'm fine." Hope tried to keep her voice light. "Just thinking."

"About what?"

Hope shrugged. "Nothing."

They were walking down Joel's street, his younger brother and sister trailing in their wake as chaperones. There was no sidewalk. Cars drove by at irregular intervals, just frequently enough to keep them close to the tree line. Joel stooped to pick up a narrow stick lying on the ground.

"You sure are giving nothing a lot of thought," he said, shaking the dirt off the stick.

A ghost of a smile haunted her lips and was gone.

"Come on, Hope. I really want to know what you're thinking."

"It's family stuff. I can't talk about it."

Joel extended one end of the stick to Hope. "Take this."

She considered it, then grasped the proffered branch.

Joel didn't let go of the other end. "Now we're holding hands," he said.

Hope looked down at the stick that connected them. Two feet of bark-covered wood separated their hands. She swung her end forward a little, and Joel let his arm swing along with it. Hope squeezed her end and imagined the pressure of his fingers on hers when she saw him tighten his hand in a squeeze of his own. Her smile returned. Stephen and Hannah could honestly report to their parents that Joel and Hope never touched each other.

"I'm your family," Joel said softly.

"Not yet. I still answer to Papa."

Joel's hand tightened on the branch again, and Hope could feel his frustration charging through the dead wood. "You're eighteen. I just turned twenty-two. Don't you think it's kind of stupid that we're legal adults, but we have to answer to our parents?"

"You have more freedom in that than I do," Hope said. "Men always do."

"That's not true in my family." Bitterness twisted his mouth. "Do you know about my sister?"

"Which one?" Hope asked, careful to keep her voice neutral.

"Beth. Elizabeth," he amended when he saw Hope's baffled look. "Everyone here calls her Elizabeth, but she prefers Beth."

Hope decided to be honest. This was Joel, after all, and it was clearly a painful topic for him. And it was keeping him from asking about her family issues. "I overheard something once, when the elders were meeting at my house."

"What did you overhear?"

Hope took a deep breath, not wanting to level the accusation but not wanting to lie to him, either. "That she's living in sin with some man in Oregon."

Joel's eyes burned with intensity, and Hope wondered if she should have lied after all.

"When was this?"

"Spring of last year, I think."

His whole body relaxed, and the stick seemed lighter in her hand. It wasn't the response she was expecting. "Good, they don't know," he murmured.

"Joel, what?"

He didn't answer until a string of four cars sped by. "Beth and Mark moved to Seattle two years ago. And they got married there. Justice of the Peace, not a church wedding. Beth doesn't want anyone back here to know. I'm the only one she still talks to." His eyes darted to the right, indicating his younger siblings behind them. "Stephen and Hannah would tell."

"You're good at keeping secrets." Hope wasn't sure how she felt about that. "Carolyn said you know where Billy is."

"Yes."

Hope waited for a few moments as the silence stretched on. "Are you going to tell me?"

"No."

"So, you'll keep secrets from me, too." Hope let go of her end of the stick. Her mood had been low all day, and it wasn't getting better.

"Hope, no. It's just that—Billy's not part of my story, and he has nothing to do with us. I told Carolyn because I knew she was worried, and I knew she wouldn't tell her parents. I trusted you with Beth. You could make her life, and mine, really difficult if you told anyone what you know. But I didn't keep it from you."

"Why not?" Hope ignored the end of the stick that he still held out to her.

"Because she's important to us, for what I want to tell you."

He scrubbed his free hand through his thick, wavy hair. "I'll understand if you want to call things off, but I have to tell you."

Call things off? Hope's heart plummeted. This day couldn't get any worse. "Tell me what? Joel, what are you talking about?"

"Keep your voice down!" He took a deep breath. "Sorry, but I can't trust Stephen and Hannah. Hope, I'm a Christian. I really am. I want you to understand that."

Hope was having trouble understanding anything right now. "Of course you are," she said.

"But I don't think everything Pastor Kinsley says is right. I don't think it's all about rules and authority and morality. I don't think people like Beth and Billy are damned for wanting to live their own lives and make their own choices. There's so much more to the world than we were told, and God created all of it. I think—I think we could do things differently and still be acceptable to Him."

Shock filled Hope. No one questioned Pastor Kinsley, and Pastor Kinsley was clear that it *was* all about rules and authority and morality. "What things?" she croaked.

"I want to go to school. College. Working in a computer repair shop and maybe owning my own someday isn't enough. I want to study computer science and be an engineer. I want my wife to follow her dreams, even if that means school and a career. I want kids, but not a whole bunch. Two or three. Maybe four at the most. I want us to serve God with the gifts we have, not the way our parents and the church tell us we have to." He began chewing the nails on his left hand, the stick hanging forlornly from his right, the tip dragging on the ground. "Beth is smart. Smarter than Mark. And he's fine with that. They both do what they're good at, and it works out. They're partners, and that's the kind of marriage I want us to have."

Hope tried to disentangle her jumbled emotions. She'd

known Joel was different, but this? Him going to college and becoming an engineer wasn't out of the question. Some of the men at church had college degrees. But the rest? Possibilities exploded in her mind, boundless potentials terrifying in their breadth. Only two or three kids? Four at the most? "Are you serious?" she whispered.

"Yes," came the strangled, miserable reply.

"Why haven't you left already?"

"Because I'm waiting for you. If you still want me."

They walked in silence as Hope wrestled with Joel's revelation, and his implied question. Did she still want him? What would this mean for their family? For their future? *Her* future? She'd always known what her life would look like because there had only ever been one option, and she'd accepted that without question even though there were parts she didn't like. But here was Joel, the man Papa had approved to court her, telling her things could be different. She felt as though she was falling through an abyss, with nothing to anchor her or direct her to what was right.

Hope kept her eyes on the ground in front of her. Several cars went by on the other side. A few brownish-orange leaves had fallen from the trees, but the road they walked was still lined with a brilliant canopy of color, probably bringing out the leaf-peepers and creating the high volume of traffic.

She could see Joel's scuffed work boots as he stepped alongside her, the stick swinging by his side. She wasn't alone in that abyss. She did have a direction. She did have an anchor. Hope reached down and grasped the other end of the stick. "Okay," she said.

Joel's coffee-brown eyes were wide and hopeful. "Really?"

Hope smiled and nodded.

Joel swung the stick in a wide arc. "Will you marry me?" he asked.

Hope's breath caught in her throat. "You asked Papa?"

"No, and I won't until I have your answer. I don't care what he thinks. I'm asking you, Hope. Will you marry me?"

"Yes!" The forbidden, dangerous word was out of her mouth before she could stop it. And then she realized she didn't want to stop it. She wanted it out there, if not for the world to hear yet, then for Joel.

Abruptly Joel reversed direction. Hope followed him as he approached his brother and sister. "We're turning around," he told them. Hannah and Stephen stepped into the road to allow them to pass, but several oncoming cars kept them from stepping too far. They were crowded in a little knot, and Joel positioned himself between his siblings and his fiancé, taking advantage of his broad shoulders and height to block their view. For the briefest of moments, he had the privacy to squeeze Hope's shoulder. She gasped and hesitated in surprise. He placed his hand against the small of her back to gently guide her forward. The electricity of his touch sizzled through her veins.

"Watch your step," he said. "There are a lot of rocks to trip over." He removed his hand before his siblings could see where it was.

"You're crazy!" Hope giggled when they were a few yards ahead again.

"Are you mad at me?"

Hope shook her head, grinning. "No. You just surprised me. I liked it, though." She glanced down at the stick that still swung between them. "I wish I could hold your hand for real," she ventured, feeling bold.

"So do I. I'll try to figure something out. But I don't want you to be afraid of me, Hope. If I ever do something you don't like, just tell me and I'll stop."

Hope thought about her future with this man, a future

where she wouldn't be trapped in a house full of kids, a future where she was free to pursue midwifery or whatever else she wanted. A future in which she would be an equal partner. She was afraid of that unfamiliar life, but...

"I'm not afraid of you," she said.

"I'm glad." His voice sobered. "So, what's going on at home? I could tell it was really bothering you."

Hope shrugged. It didn't seem as important now as it had before. "Papa ran out of patience with Jennifer. They had an argument a few days ago about what Jennifer should be teaching my sisters and how we should be spending our time, and she wouldn't back down. Papa came home late from work that night, so we had to hold supper for over an hour waiting for him. Then he called a family meeting where he reminded us of our responsibilities and said he would do whatever it takes to make sure we're prepared for our God-given callings." She thought back to her father's words, and knew he'd end her courtship immediately if he found out what Joel wanted for them. "He's started giving Jennifer a chore list for herself and all us girls each day, and he checks it every night to make sure it all gets done. He told her that we should spend our home-schooling time on homemaking skills instead of academics. Paul and Timothy will still get workbook assignments, but Samuel and Amos should focus on their farming and us girls should focus on being helpmeets. Jennifer told Papa we have too much potential to waste it scrambling eggs every day. It was bad."

Joel winced. "Jennifer didn't know what she was getting into, did she?"

"I don't think she did. A couple of months ago she had me read one of her favorite books. It's called *An Old Fashioned Girl* by Louisa May Alcott. Papa said it was okay for me to read because McGuffey has an excerpt. It's all about how important family and a simple lifestyle are, and I think that's what

Jennifer thought we'd be like. But the people in that book aren't godly Christians. It was written like a hundred and fifty years ago, and that's just the way things were back then. I think if Papa actually read the whole book, he'd ban it. Polly, the main character, goes away from her family and stays for several months with a friend in the city, then when she gets older, she moves to the city permanently. She has her own place and supports herself by working as a teacher. All with her family's blessing. But it talks about old-fashioned family values, and I think that's what Jennifer wanted."

Joel whistled. "She had no idea."

They walked along the road in silence, Joel's house growing larger as they drew closer. Stephen and Hannah kept their distance behind the couple, ensuring no physical contact occurred between them. Even Polly would have been allowed to hold Sydney's or Tom's arm when out walking with them.

"Papa says he wants me to stay home until the baby's born, sometime in March."

Joel's eyes narrowed. "He didn't tell me that. My bank account should reach the right amount in early December. That's what my father's been waiting for."

"The right amount?"

Joel chuckled. "The right amount of money that will convince him and everyone else that I'm financially stable enough to support a wife and growing family. I've saved every penny I've earned for the last five years, and I've been working extra hours for the last few months. By December I'll have enough to pay cash for a fixer-upper and fund the work it needs."

Hope's eyes grew dreamy as she imagined living in a house alone with Joel. "Have you found one yet? What's it like?"

"Hope, that's my father's plan. I told you; I have different ideas about how I want to live my life." They reached Joel's parents' house and began to walk up the driveway. "Does your father listen in on another phone when I call you?"

"No, he took the phone out of his bedroom so Jennifer couldn't use it. The only phone in the house now is in his office. He used to sit in there with me when you called, but he stopped doing that a few weeks ago."

"Good. I'll tell you more on Wednesday night. Just don't say or do anything that will tip your father off!"

Autumn's transition to winter was interminable to Hope. Joel planned for them to move to Seattle where his sister Beth and her husband Mark could help them get established. They'd both attend college, and then stay in the Seattle area after graduation. They'd never be able to live the lives they wanted if their parents were close enough to interfere.

Joel was concerned about what this would do to Hope's relationship with her family. He would have his sister, and he thought his parents might eventually come around, but neither he nor Hope believed Michael would ever accept his daughter as a college graduate, possible career woman, and mother of few.

Hope wasn't concerned at all. She looked forward to her escape. She'd miss her siblings a little, but it hadn't been the same with them since Mama died. Hope hadn't been able to reclaim her role as merely a sister after Jennifer arrived, and she didn't really have a place in her family. She was more than ready to reinvent herself as Joel's wife and Beth's sister, and the loss of her own family was a small price to pay for that.

Not that she had a clear idea of what her new life would be like. Hope read the college brochures Joel gave her from cover to cover, but she had no idea what she wanted to study. She'd been learning midwifery from Aunt Libby, but mostly because that was the only option open to her, and even that would be limited by her duties as wife and mother. Now she had dozens —no, *hundreds!*—of possibilities to choose from, and she couldn't begin to narrow it down.

Joel had told her not to worry about it. "If you try something and it doesn't work out, you can just try something else," he'd told her. Hope marveled at how he could accept failure as a learning experience. Not getting something right the first time meant shame and humiliation for her and disappointment for those who were counting on her. It was another way in which her life with Joel would be different from anything she'd experienced. Even Mama had had little patience for mistakes made more than once, and she'd admonished that many of those could be avoided by paying careful attention the first time.

All Hope needed now was for Jennifer to give birth. Once that happened, she could marry Joel and start a whole new life with him.

Chapter Fifteen

If Jennifer could have had her baby sooner, she would have. Libby had told her most morning sickness went away after the first trimester, but hers, stubbornly, remained. She referred to it as all-day-every-day sickness whenever Libby, Hope, or Michael downplayed its impact.

Michael and Hope had never experienced pregnancy, so Jennifer could forgive them their callousness. But Libby had, and the older woman's betrayal was sharp. Where she had once given Jennifer advice and gentle guidance on matters of religious and home life, Libby now gave her orders and directives. She referred Jennifer back to the books she'd been given during her early meetings with Pastor Kinsley and his wife, books describing a woman's role as helpmeet to her husband and producer of children. Apparently, Jennifer was to know and obey those books better than the Bible itself.

Jennifer wanted to be like the women in those books. The promise of a large, close-knit family was enticing, and the books more than suggested that such a family was hers for the making if she could only be submissive enough to Michael and joyful enough in her household duties. Jennifer tried to be joyful as she got up early to cook the same breakfast every morning. She tried to control her food aversions with cheerful thoughts of good nutrition and her family's health and growth. She tried to recognize the endless laundry and cleaning and childcare and meal preparation as the structure necessary for her family's wellbeing. She gave herself willingly and with forced enthusiasm to Michael whenever he wanted her, but sex was uncomfortable now and her libido nonexistent, and it was hard to be joyful when her husband didn't seem to care about her comfort or satisfaction at all. At the end of the day, all her hard work resulted in the house looking exactly the way it had that morning, and Michael only noticed her efforts when they failed to meet his expectations. Far from the happy, love-filled home of those books and her dreams, Jennifer existed in a nightmare of invisibility and inadequacy. And Michael and Libby—and even Hope—reinforced that view when they minimized or dismissed her struggles.

She wanted an OB/GYN to make sure the persistent morning sickness was nothing to worry about, but Libby was deeply offended by the suggestion that her services were insufficient. Michael would go into a long diatribe about how much the medical profession *didn't* know, and how doctors were nothing but snake-oil salesmen who only wanted to prescribe expensive toxic chemicals that would help the government control the population. Jennifer could only shake her head in disbelief when Michael made such pronouncements. He was such a logical, intelligent man in most other ways, but his ideas about medicine and government were beyond the pale.

By the eighth month of her pregnancy, Jennifer decided Stacy Cook had the right idea after all. One morning she simply stayed in bed. She told the girls to do their chores, watch Benjamin, help the younger boys with their workbook pages, and prepare the meals. The only time she got up was when she went to retrieve a book from the school room. She had trouble finding anything she wanted to read. All of the novels were historical, and they all depicted the happy, close-knit families Jennifer had always longed for. The one she still longed for. She'd spent her whole life comparing her family to the characters in books, and real life never came close to measuring up. Those books had once shown Jennifer her dreams, and she'd vowed to make them her reality. Now they were quaint stories that no longer spoke to her. She selected *Jane Eyre*, because at least Jane refused to compromise who she was for anyone. Jane only married Rochester when she could do so on her own terms.

Unfortunately, unlike Stacy Cook, Jennifer was not blessed with a husband who was away all week. When Michael came home from work and found her still in bed, he was livid. He ordered her to do the dishes after supper that night—usually Faith's job—and put Samuel in charge of making sure Jennifer did her assigned chores while he was at work.

Day after miserable day Jennifer dragged her sore, heavy body out of bed and did the minimum she could to satisfy Michael. Samuel was inattentive enough that she got away with outsourcing most of her chores to the girls. Amos noticed, but for reasons Jennifer didn't understand he kept his observations to himself. He'd grown quiet in the past year, waging his own private war with puberty in silence, and maybe he understood better than his brother that it wasn't always possible to force your body to do what you wanted it to. She hated that Samuel was supposed to spy on her for her husband and she had to sneak around the fifteen-year-old to take breaks or hand something off to the girls. It wasn't like she was doing something sinister or contrary to her marriage vows. She only needed some extra help with the housework during her last weeks of pregnancy. What was so sinful about that?

Jennifer was reclining on the couch, napping lightly as most of the kids did pages in their workbooks near the warmth of the wood stove and Benjamin scribbled in a coloring book, when she felt a sudden wetness in her underpants and under her bottom. She stood up and turned to look at the large dark spot on the worn cushions. Warm liquid ran down her legs, soaking the bloomers she wore under her second-hand denim jumper. The kids looked up from their workbooks and stared.

"Did you have a potty accident?" Grace asked, her eyes wide.

Jennifer faltered. She wasn't sure what was happening.

"No, silly," Joy told her sister. "Her water broke. It's time for the baby to come out." She turned to Jennifer. "I'll get Hope. You go upstairs and lie down. Me and Faith will clean this up."

Jennifer nodded, both embarrassed and grateful that her eleven-year-old stepdaughter was able to assess and manage the situation and tell her what to do.

Hope met Jennifer in her room and helped her change into a clean nightgown.

"Were you teaching school when your water broke?" she asked.

Jennifer nodded, sliding under the covers of her bed. It felt so warm and comforting when Michael wasn't filling it with his judgment and expectations.

"Then you should go back downstairs and keep doing that. After that, do your regular chores."

"What? But I'm in labor!"

Hope smiled, pulled the covers away, and drew Jennifer to a sitting position. "You're in early labor. You'll start having contractions soon, but they'll be mild and pretty far apart. It's best for you to keep moving. Drink lots of water and eat small snacks. When your contractions get stronger and closer together, then maybe we can talk about you getting into bed."

Jennifer didn't understand how Hope could be so dense. "But I'm in labor," she explained, as patiently as she could.

"I know you're in labor, and I'm telling you what's best for you and your baby."

"I want to talk to Libby!"

Hope shrugged. "Go ahead, but she'll tell you the same thing I did."

Jennifer hated it when Hope was right. She stood in Michael's office, one of Benjamin's diapers shoved inside her underpants like a giant maxi-pad, listening to Libby lecture her over the phone about the importance of movement and focusing on her regular routine. She hung up, distraught. What was wrong with these people? Didn't they realize she was *in labor*? She picked up the phone again to call Michael's cell but hesitated before she dialed. Michael had proved himself to be less concerned about her comfort and wellbeing than Libby. He wouldn't countermand his sister's orders. He wouldn't even come home to hold her hand and keep her company. Eyes stinging with frustrated tears, Jennifer cradled the phone again and went back to the living room where the kids were still doing pages in their workbooks. Had it only been twenty minutes since her water broke?

Time continued its unnatural slow pace. It seemed as though the few workbook pages she'd assigned took all morning, but when they were finally completed, Jennifer found she still had over an hour before she needed to start preparing lunch. She glanced at her chore schedule and saw that today she was supposed to deep clean the living room. Great.

Every few minutes Jennifer went back upstairs to replace the sopping diaper with a clean one. After her fourth change she decided she'd better launder the diapers before they ran out. Soon her own child would need them. For once this thought filled her with fear rather than the sweet tenderness it usually inspired.

The contractions began an hour later. At first, they were mild, like menstrual cramps. Jennifer dusted the tables and vacuumed the carpet, couches, and chairs. Benjamin ran his toy cars around her feet and the vacuum cleaner, making motor sounds as he pushed his little vehicles across the floor and crashed them into the leg of the coffee table.

"Benjamin, please, go play!" Jennifer cried, exasperated.

Benjamin held up his toy car, the same yellow Corvette he'd shown her that first Christmas. It seemed so long ago. "I am playing," he said.

"Play somewhere else."

"Where? It's yucky outside."

Jennifer's abdomen clenched painfully, and she threw the vacuum cleaner attachment on the floor. It landed less than a foot from the boy. "Just go!"

Benjamin ran upstairs, bawling, and Jennifer collapsed on the couch, choking on her sobs. She hadn't meant to scare him. She hadn't meant to throw the vacuum cleaner at him. Had she? She couldn't think. This was not how she'd imagined giving birth to her first child, laboring alone on the couch she'd just vacuumed, with no one around who cared. Not for the first time in recent months, she wished for her parents. Michael forbade her from contacting them, pointing out—correctly— that they would try to entice her back to their worldly ways and away from her God-given duties. They'd called her several times, but Michael only allowed her to speak to them once, after her mother threatened to call the police and report her daughter as a missing person. Michael had stood over her as she'd assured them that she was healthy and happy, and she would prefer if they would not call again. Michael then removed the phone from their bedroom, reducing the chance that Jennifer would call her parents or answer should they try to call back. She wasn't allowed in his office, except in emergencies.

She never told her parents about her pregnancy.

Jennifer was still sobbing on the couch when Hope came downstairs, carrying a red-faced Benjamin in her arms.

"Are you okay?"

Jennifer glared at her. "What do you think?"

"Do you want this baby to be born healthy and without complications?"

"You know I do."

"Then you need to move around. The human body isn't meant to be still during the day. You need to do your regular routine to keep your muscles and joints working and strong, so your body can help your baby get into position and come out. If you just lie around, the baby has no way to know which way is out."

Jennifer wiped the tears from her cheeks with her hands, then wiped her hands on her nightgown. "Why didn't you tell me that before?"

"I did."

"No, you didn't. You told me to do my chores. You told me it was bad for me to lie down, but you didn't tell me why. You didn't tell me *anything*. I have no idea what to expect!" Fresh tears dampened her cheeks.

Hope put Benjamin down on the floor, where he grabbed his abandoned cars and vroomed them around the living room again. She sat next to her stepmother and took her hand.

"I thought Libby explained it to you."

Jennifer shook her head. "You've both told me what to do and not to worry, but you won't tell me why. You won't tell me what's normal, except when I come to you with a concern. Then you brush me off and say, 'It's normal,' like I'm supposed to know that. I've never done this before. I don't know what's coming. I don't know what to do." Her eyes pleaded with Hope through tears. "And don't tell me to do my chores!"

Hope took her stepmother in her arms and held her while Jennifer cried on her shoulder. She'd become more comfortable with hugging in the last few months. When Jennifer's sobs subsided, Hope explained the three stages of labor.

"How long will I be in early labor?" Jennifer asked.

"It varies. It could be up to eight or twelve hours."

Jennifer's heart dropped. "I don't think I can do that," she whispered.

Hope squeezed her hand. "At this point, you don't have a choice. That's another reason why you should just do what you normally do. It will distract you from the labor and make the time go faster."

"That's the first thing you've said that makes sense." Her mouth tightened as another contraction came and went. They were still no stronger than bad menstrual cramps, but they were hard to ignore. "Will you stay with me? I don't want to do this alone."

Jennifer was still in early labor when Michael, Joshua, and John returned home that evening, but her contractions were much stronger and closer together. She excused herself from the dinner table after eating only a few bites of the meal she'd helped Hope prepare. Hope gave her permission to go upstairs and lie down, but stayed at the table to finish her own meal.

Jennifer curled up under the covers and tried to be thankful that she was giving birth and cheerful about the process, but all she felt was exhaustion, pain, and fear. She was breathing through a contraction when Michael arrived at her side. With practiced movements he began to massage her lower back.

"How are you doing?" he asked.

Tears leaked from the corners of Jennifer's eyes, though she couldn't tell if they were from pain, fear, joy, or sadness. This was the first time in months Michael had touched her in a way that was about her comfort rather than his pleasure.

"I'm scared," she whispered, praying desperately that he would understand how much of an understatement that was.

"You'll be fine. Giving birth is the most natural thing in the world."

She should have known better than to hope. "So I've heard."

Michael didn't comment on her sarcasm. Instead, he asked, "Have you given any thought to what you want to name the baby?"

Jennifer smiled despite the pain. She had given this a lot of thought. She'd always like the names Dylan and Alexandra, but she knew Michael would insist on biblical names. "Adam if it's a boy, Abigail if it's a girl."

Michael was quiet for a moment, and Jennifer went rigid as another contraction gripped her. His fingers dug deeper into her lower back until her breathing slowed again.

"Those are both good, biblical names," he said. "But I've always given thought to what a person did before I'll use his namesake. Adam rebelled against God by listening to his wife's counsel. That's not the model I want for my son's life. Abigail helped King David and eventually became his wife, but she disobeyed and disrespected her first husband. And I've always wanted my daughters to embody biblical virtues."

Your stepdaughters are expected to be virtues, not people.

Jennifer pushed the memory of her mother's words away. "What did you have in mind?"

"Lucy and I had considered some other names before Benjamin was born. Benjamin wasn't on the list, but it seemed appropriate to name him after Jacob's twelfth son, whose mother died while birthing him. There's Gabriel, the bringer of good news. Any of the other three Gospel writers. Jacob. Noah. We could think of more if you don't like any of those."

"What about girls?"

"Mercy? Prudence? Charity?"

Jennifer tried to blink back her tears, but too many had already found their way out, and it was impossible to stop them now.

"What about Mary? Elizabeth? Sarah? Rebekah? Rachel? They were all good examples."

"They're not virtues."

No, they're people. The expectation that your life would be patterned after someone else's was better than being an idea devoid of personhood.

They sat in silence until they heard the doorbell ring downstairs, and Libby's voice as Hope opened the door. Michael stood.

"God has seen fit to give me more boys than girls," he said. "Maybe He'll do so again, and this won't be an issue this time."

Jennifer was grateful for the contraction that saved her from having to reply as he left the room.

Hope had always wanted to assist her aunt with a birth, but now that she had that chance, she found herself wishing she could hide in her room with her sisters until it was over.

The contractions were very close together now, and

Jennifer cried and panted in the brief pauses between them. "Please," she sobbed. "I can't take it. I can't do this. Please take me to the hospital."

"It would hurt just as much in a hospital as it does here," Aunt Libby snapped. "This is the way God intended for children to come into the world. 'Unto the woman he said, I will greatly multiply thy sorrow and thy conception; in sorrow thou shalt bring forth children; and thy desire shall be to thy husband, and he shall rule over thee.'"

Jennifer gasped as another contraction seized her, then screamed in pain.

Hope took the sweaty hand that gripped the covers and held it in her own. She was used to seeing Aunt Libby put people at ease, but she realized now that her aunt only encouraged the efforts of those who were trying to do what they were supposed to do. Amid her travails, Jennifer had abandoned her attempts at submission and self-sacrifice, and Aunt Libby had no patience for Jennifer's fear and doubts. Hope could imagine being in her stepmother's position and tried to give her the comfort and understanding that she herself would want to receive.

Jennifer squeezed her hand hard enough that Hope almost cried out herself, but she clamped her mouth shut and wiped her stepmother's forehead with a cool, damp washcloth instead. After a minute or two Jennifer's screams subsided, and she went back to panting and sobbing. Before she could catch her breath, however, she gasped and cried out, "Oh, God, not again!"

Aunt Libby nodded. "It's time to push." She and Hope slid Jennifer up on the bed and propped several pillows behind her back.

"When I say 'push,' you push. If I say 'stop,' you stop. Do you think you can do that much at least?"

Even understanding her impatience with Jennifer, Hope thought her aunt was being harsh. She couldn't confront her, but she could offer a little more support to her stepmother.

"Jennifer, look at me," she said gently.

Jennifer turned frightened, pleading eyes toward the kind voice.

"Your body is going to want to push, and you should do what your body wants. You might want to hold your breath so you can push harder, but don't. If you're not getting any oxygen, neither is your baby, so make sure you breathe. There's a chance the umbilical cord might get wrapped or compressed, or your baby might not be in the right position to come out. If that happens, Aunt Libby will tell you not to push and it's very important that you listen to her, no matter what your body wants. If everything goes like it should, you can push your baby all the way out, no problem. But if she tells you to stop, you need to let her fix whatever's wrong, and she can't do that if you're still pushing. Understand?"

Jennifer nodded and grasped her hand again. "Thank you," she said.

"Push!" Aunt Libby ordered.

The next half hour passed with Aunt Libby barking "Push!" Hope encouraging her stepmother to "Breathe!" and Jennifer groaning and panting. Finally, a fourth voice joined the cacophony—the thin, outraged voice of an infant forced into a cold, bright, unfamiliar world.

"What is it?" Jennifer cried. "Is it a boy or a girl?"

Aunt Libby took her time cleaning the tiny, wriggling form and didn't answer right away.

Hope couldn't see much of what her aunt was doing. She whispered to Jennifer, "It seems healthy."

"What is it?" Jennifer gasped.

Aunt Libby finished wrapping the tiny baby in a clean

blanket and, with a tight mouth, handed the bundle to Jennifer. "Meet your daughter," she said.

Jennifer took the bundle into her arms as tears leaked from her eyes and dripped off her chin. "My daughter," she whispered. Her body shook as she cried harder, until Aunt Libby snapped for her to be still so she could deliver the afterbirth.

"We're not finished yet. At some point you're going to have to bear down. If you can't do that while holding the baby, then give her to Hope."

Hope helped Jennifer brace herself, but the new mother was in no hurry to hand over her infant. She held the child to her breast and smiled through her tears as the baby found a nipple and began to suck. Hope murmured encouragement in a low voice as Aunt Libby made sure nothing was left in Jennifer's uterus.

Eventually she announced she was done.

"Your life is going to be a lot different from now on," Aunt Libby told Jennifer. She rubbed her eyes, which were red from exhaustion. "Your comfort, your health, even your life isn't worth as much as that precious child God has seen fit to give you. She's a gift and a responsibility. It's up to you and Michael to raise this child for the Lord. You must teach her her place in the world and her duty for God's kingdom. Not just with your words, but with your actions. She will learn from you, for better or for worse." The baby was sleeping now, and Aunt Libby's voice became uncharacteristically gentle. "I know it's been a difficult transition, Jennifer. I know it's been hard for you to adjust to this life. But it's not just your own soul at stake now, but your daughter's. For the sake of her eternal soul, give up your selfishness and rebellion. Submit to Michael and be the wife and mother God expects you to be."

Jennifer took a deep breath and looked at Aunt Libby. Her

voice was firm as she said, "I will do whatever it takes to help my daughter become the person she was born to be."

Aunt Libby nodded, satisfied.

Hope couldn't stop staring at the new mother holding her child. She'd seen her own mother holding her siblings when they were only a few minutes old, but she'd been a child herself then. Now she was very nearly engaged—with the baby born, Joel could formally propose—and she knew she might hold an infant of her own in as little as a year, depending on when the wedding was. She already knew about the sleepless nights and the constant exhaustion that would dominate Jennifer's life for the next few months—the endless diapers and spit-up and laundry, all while keeping up with the housework and meal preparation and homeschooling—and suddenly her own eyes glistened as much as her stepmother's.

Aunt Libby noticed Hope's expression and put a gentle hand on her shoulder. "Soon it will be you," she promised, misunderstanding the cause of her niece's unshed tears.

Hope nodded, not trusting her voice. It was four o'clock Wednesday morning. Tonight was her weekly telephone call with Joel, and she needed to talk with him. She needed to know if he meant what he'd said about waiting to start a family, and about keeping it small. Despite all their conversations and planning, until now she'd only ever been able to imagine the life she'd always prepared for. But now she knew. She didn't want that life. Her future involved college, Seattle, a career, and Joel, who would make it all possible.

Chapter Sixteen

The only birth Michael had ever attended was Benjamin's, and the memory was painful enough that he chose to spend the night on a cot in his office rather than stay with Jennifer. He told himself she didn't need him, that Lucy gave birth to ten children without him by her side, and he would only be in Libby's way.

Michael met his new daughter for the first time before he left for work the next morning. He held the sleeping infant in gentle arms, ignoring the wary looks Jennifer shot him from the bed. She was a minefield that could explode at any moment, and he was in the mood for neither an explosion nor a careful negotiation. Instead, he studied his new daughter's tiny features.

The light fuzz on the top of her head was blonde like Jennifer's. Her eyes were closed, and she was wrapped in a soft, quilted blanket pieced together from older blankets that had become ragged with age. He recalled Faith showing it to him a few weeks ago when she'd finished stitching it together. The well-worn fabric was as soft and velvety as the newborn skin it enfolded.

"God is merciful," he murmured.

Jennifer was silent.

"I think we should name her Mercy."

Still no word from the bed. Michael dragged his eyes away from his daughter and to his wife.

Jennifer was sitting up, studying him with an unreadable expression.

"Are you leaving this up to me?" he asked. "I'm willing to hear your opinion." He braced himself for a quarrel. He'd counter her argumentativeness with strength.

"You can call her what you want." Her voice was flat and expressionless.

Michael smiled at this small victory. The exhaustion of childbirth must have worn her down. He hoped her submission would last. "Then Mercy she is."

As he handed his daughter back to her mother, he kissed Jennifer on the cheek and nuzzled her ear. "You did well."

Jennifer sat stone-like on the bed, and he withdrew, chalking up her unresponsiveness to tiredness. She was up all night birthing a baby, he reminded himself.

"Hope can see to things today," he offered magnanimously. "But I'm sure Libby told you how important it is for you to get up and start moving around as soon as possible. So don't stay in bed, and tomorrow I want you to start doing simple chores."

Jennifer didn't answer. She stared at the baby in her arms as though Michael didn't exist, and he had to remind himself again that, for all she'd been taking care of his children for nearly a year, she was, after all, a new mother. Maybe he'd give her an extra day or two to get used to her new role.

Hope moved more slowly than usual, but no one complained when she canceled school and focused on getting the minimum amount of housework done. She was tired, but she knew she was in better shape than Jennifer, who wouldn't leave her room. The older woman allowed Joy, Faith, and Grace to visit the baby for only a few minutes before asking them to leave, and she never permitted them to hold her. The only time she left her room was to go to the bathroom, and she brought Mercy in with her while she took a bath.

When Papa came home that evening, he ordered Jennifer downstairs to eat the supper Hope and Joy had cooked, but she picked at her food in silence until her husband let her be excused from the table.

Jennifer joined them for breakfast the next morning as well but excused herself right after Papa, Joshua, and John left for work. The rest of the boys went outside to help Samuel and Amos prepare for the spring planting, now that they were sure all the frost had left the ground for the season. That counted as school for the boys, but the girls still needed something to do.

Hope put Faith and Grace in charge of dishes and Joy in charge of laundry while she scoured the bookshelves to see what she could piece together for a lesson. Jennifer had procured quite an array of interesting resources, and Hope didn't want them to go to waste.

It was still chilly, so Hope brought a few books to the couch near the wood stove. She was flipping through a grammar book when the door to Papa's office opened and Jennifer emerged, eyes red. She froze when she saw Hope.

"You're not supposed to be in there alone," Hope said.

"I—I needed to look something up on the computer. About babies."

"You can ask me or Aunt Libby if you have a question about babies."

Jennifer's eyes dropped to the floor, but she said nothing.

"Did you get your question answered?"

"Uh, yeah, I did." Her voice was low and husky, as though she might start crying again. Hope waited, but Jennifer didn't expand on her answer. Instead, she fidgeted with a ruffle on the front of her bulbous nightgown.

"What was it?"

"What was what?"

Hope struggled to keep her patience. Jennifer gave birth a day and a half ago, true, but that was no reason to be this scatterbrained.

"What was your question? The one you had to look up on the computer?"

Jennifer's eyes darted from side to side, and she licked her chapped lips. At that moment, they both heard the pitiful wail of a newborn coming from above. "I have to go!" Jennifer cried, fleeing up the stairs.

Hope shook her head and resumed looking through the grammar book. Infants could go a few minutes without getting immediate attention, and it was good practice for them. Jennifer had a lot to learn about being a mother.

After school and chores were finished, Hope climbed up on her bunk and retrieved the college brochures Joel had given her. Last night when they'd talked, he'd reassured her that they could wait to have children, and they could stop after two. Hope didn't want to think about the mechanics of that—she was knowledgeable about delivering babies, but she'd been taught very little about how babies were made. She knew sex caused conception, and Aunt Libby finally explained what sex was, but Hope couldn't quite imagine how that worked. She'd changed plenty of her brothers' diapers and she knew what boy parts looked like, but how they managed to insert those floppy little things into a woman's special place was beyond her. She only knew that any interference with the natural course of conception was an affront to God. Hope had no idea what kind of interference there could be, other than some pill that caused abortions. Maybe Joel was more informed on this subject than she was, but she certainly couldn't ask him about such things. Once they reached Seattle she could talk to his sister Beth about it. She and Mark didn't have any children. Joel never came out and said it, but Hope had the impression that Beth was childless because she wanted to be, not because God had cursed her.

She thought about how she'd felt the one time Joel kissed her, when Jennifer was chaperoning and had left them alone in the kitchen for a few minutes. Warmth had flooded her body, and she'd tingled all over. Especially *down there*. Maybe God designed men's and women's bodies to know what to do. Certainly no one had taught her how to kiss, but she and Joel had figured it out without much difficulty.

Blushing, she returned to her college brochures. There was a program for certified nurse midwives that looked interesting. They received a lot more training than Aunt Libby had, and they worked with doctors in hospitals in case something went wrong. Hope couldn't help but wonder if Mama might have survived if she'd been brought to a hospital. Everyone always said it was God's will, but hadn't God given people the wisdom to build hospitals and the ability to do amazing things with medicine? Why would God allow such advances in technology if He didn't intend for His people to use them?

Michael arrived in the kitchen Saturday morning after the early morning prayer breakfast and was pleased to find Jennifer up, dressed, and cooking breakfast for the children. She hadn't done that the day before. He gave his wife a peck on the cheek before grabbing his mug.

Jennifer didn't smile or even acknowledge her husband. Instead, she snatched Mercy from her basket on the table and held her close, setting the table one handed. Once everyone else had come to the table, Jennifer served the eggs and biscuits the same way.

"Aren't you eating anything?" Michael asked, noting Jennifer didn't set a plate for herself.

"I'm not hungry."

Michael smiled indulgently. Once she realized he understood what she was feeling, maybe she'd stop being so prickly. "I know you want to lose the baby weight, but you do need to eat."

Jennifer's eyes narrowed, and she took a deep breath before answering. "I had a biscuit right after they came out of the oven. They're best when they're hot."

Michael's smile disappeared. Fine. He could be prickly too. "You should wait for everyone to come down before you eat. We're a family, and we eat together."

"I'll remember that."

The rest of the meal passed in silence, the children sensing the tension between their father and stepmother.

Michael studied his wife, who sat stiffly, not looking at anyone, staring instead at the table or at the infant cradled in her arms. He understood her desire to spend time with her new baby—Lucy had been the same way with each new addition to their family. But since Mercy was born, Jennifer had completely ignored the other children she was supposed to be raising. She barely acknowledged the husband she'd vowed to honor and obey. She certainly had no interest in the house she was supposed to be keeping. Mercy took all her time, attention, and affection. Michael believed every child was a blessing, and Mercy was not the only blessing in the house. It was his responsibility as husband and father to help Jennifer recognize Mercy's place in the family and remind her of her own.

"Jennifer," he said, breaking the uncomfortable silence. He was mindful that everyone had turned to look at him, not just Jennifer, and he needed to set an example for how husbands ought to treat their wives. "I'm glad to see you getting back to your routine. The girls can do the dishes. You'll finalize the grocery list and do the shopping today, and you'll leave Mercy here. Joy and Faith need to learn how to take care of an infant, and Hope will begin to teach them while you're out."

Jennifer clutched the quilt-wrapped bundle to her chest. She glanced at her stepdaughters and, for some reason, at the clock before returning her gaze to her husband. Her detached expression was gone. "I—I can't. I'm—not ready."

"You can, and you will. It was a normal birth, and you've had three full days to recover. I'll assign the girls the more physically demanding bits of housework for a week or two, but you've lounged around enough, and you're spoiling Mercy with all that attention."

"She's a baby. She needs the attention."

"She needs attention," Michael agreed. "But it doesn't have to be from you."

"I'm her mother!"

"And you're stepmother to eleven other children who also need your attention!" He stopped and took a breath to calm himself. He never used to raise his voice. "And it's important for Joy and Faith to learn how to care for infants. They were too young to help much with Benjamin. They need to learn how to take care of Mercy, and you need to learn how to split your attention. There's too much for you to do to lose yourself in caring for one baby girl. Joy and Faith will see to most of her needs during the day—except nursing, of course—and you will keep up with your other responsibilities."

Jennifer's face turned white. Michael took it as shame, though no tears glistened in her large blue eyes. She stole another glance at the clock.

"Why do you care so much about the time all of a sudden?" Michael demanded to know.

Forks scraped across plates with hardly a sound as the children tried to avoid being noticed.

Jennifer forced her gaze back to Michael and took a deep, shaking breath of her own. "I'm trying to figure out how to fit grocery shopping into the baby's feeding schedule, alright? I need to nurse her again in about two hours, so I'll go after that."

Michael shook his head. She'd chosen to make this a battle, and he would not back down until he'd won it. "You can be there and back in two hours."

"No, I have to finalize the grocery list, like you said. And... and you were right. I need to eat something else. I need some eggs and another biscuit."

"There are no more eggs."

"Oatmeal then. I'm feeling weak, and I need to eat."

Michael could feel his rage building. He had told her to eat something. How could she make obeying him into an act of rebellion? "Eat quickly. You're holding us all up. We eat together as a family, and now we all have to sit here until you're done." He looked around at his sons and daughters. "No one leaves this table until Jennifer is finished." It was a rule he usually enforced at supper, not breakfast.

His children nodded. Samuel reached for another biscuit. After a moment's hesitation, seeing that Michael didn't object, Amos did the same.

Jennifer rose gracefully, still holding Mercy, and retrieved the tub of oatmeal from the pantry. "Does anyone else want any? There weren't many eggs this morning. The chickens still aren't producing much."

Michael spoke before anyone else could answer. "We've all had plenty. Just make your own breakfast."

Jennifer shrugged, and Michael caught his sons' eyes. *No more*, he mouthed. They nodded, stuffed the biscuits in their mouths, sat with their hands folded, and waited for Jennifer.

It took nearly fifteen minutes before the oatmeal was done. Michael doubted it needed that much time to cook, but Jennifer insisted she had to keep the heat low to avoid scorching the pan. He knew nothing about such things, so he looked at Hope, one eyebrow raised in question. She shrugged, then nodded. Maybe it did take that much time.

He kept a tight grip on his patience as Jennifer brought the bowl of mush to the table and spooned small bites into her mouth, chewing slowly, taking a sip of water between every bite. For some reason she was stretching this out as long as possible. Was there no end to her rebellion?

She kept her gaze on the table next to her bowl, and Michael was sure she could feel the stares of twelve sets of eyes as she made a show of eating her breakfast. Benjamin and Grace began to fidget, and for once Michael welcomed it. The more discomfort he could cause Jennifer, the better. He didn't know what she was playing at, but she would learn that he was the authority in this family. She would honor and obey him.

Jennifer looked up and dared to smile at him. "Are you sure you don't want any?"

Michael ground his teeth. "No. And you're done."

"I still have a little oatmeal left, and I haven't had a biscuit yet."

"You're done."

She glanced at the clock again. The hands showed it was almost nine o'clock.

"Fine," Jennifer said, rising. "I'll start on the dishes."

Michael rose, too. "Joy and Faith will do the dishes. You will go to the grocery store. Now." His voice was low and dangerous.

Joy froze in the act of pushing her chair away from the table.

No one else moved.

Jennifer's voice was equally low. "Then I'll finalize the grocery list."

"It's fine as it is."

Jennifer walked to the counter where the pad of paper was kept. The big family calendar hung on the pantry door next to it. She laughed; it was a harsh, mirthless sound in the otherwise silent kitchen. "No one's written out the meals for next week, and the grocery list only says rice and flour." She looked up at Michael, who had crossed the room to stand next to her. "You expect me—"

Michael slapped her, and her head whipped to the side. The *crack* of the strike woke Mercy, who had been sleeping in her mother's arms. Eleven sets of eyes averted to the table, not wanting to see their father's anger or their stepmother's shame.

"You are being rebellious and disrespectful to me. I will not tolerate such an attitude in my wife, and I will not permit you to model such behavior in front of my children." His voice was barely audible over Mercy's crying, but he didn't raise it. He had no doubt that everyone in the room caught his intent, whether or not they heard his actual words.

Jennifer kept a tight grip on her daughter as her free hand rubbed her cheek. Michael's handprint burned an angry red on her skin, and Jennifer's nostrils flared as she controlled her tears. Or was it her temper? Michael wasn't sure which, and he didn't care.

"Okay," she said, drawing a shaking breath. "You've hit me.

Now what?"

Michael struck her again, this time hard enough to make her cry out. He reached for Mercy.

Jennifer drew back, clutching the baby to her chest, her forearms forming a protective cage around the wailing infant.

"Give me the baby."

"No."

Michael stared at his wife's defiant face. What would it take for her to learn proper respect? He'd always believed wives could be corrected and guided without physical discipline. He'd never had much respect for men like Al Reed, who solved every problem in his family with his fists. There was a place for displays of strength and power, but a well-disciplined home shouldn't require many of them. And grown women should know better than to flaunt their disobedience and reject their husbands' authority.

"Give me the baby."

"I said no. You'll have to beat me to a bloody pulp before I let you touch my daughter."

Michael wasn't sure if he was more shocked by her words or her tone. He glanced at the table behind him. Most of the children were staring at their empty plates, Joy's chair still half-pushed away from the table. He wished none of them had seen any of this. It was fine for them to witness him disciplining one of their siblings—it served as a lesson for all of them. But Michael had always tried to model the best behavior of a husband and father. It was easy with Lucy, who was naturally an obedient wife and supportive mother. But Jennifer was intent on modeling rebellion and defiance. He had to show his daughters how evil that behavior was, and he had to show his sons that a man must never allow himself to be controlled by a woman. He turned back to Jennifer, committed.

"If that's really the way you want it," he said softly. "I can make that happen."

Jennifer hunched herself around Mercy and Michael took a step toward her.

The doorbell rang.

Jennifer's head snapped toward the living room. She looked relieved, as though she believed the doorbell had saved her from his discipline.

"Nobody move," Michael said. "We're not going to answer that."

Jennifer whirled around to face him, and he was caught off guard when, instead of protesting, she shoved him away from her. He stumbled back and tripped over Joy's chair, knocking it over and sending them both crashing to the floor. Jennifer ran into the living room and whipped open the front door. Michael was just getting to his feet when he heard her cry out, "Thank God!"

He stormed into the living room to tell whoever it was to leave and stopped cold when he saw Jennifer's parents standing in the doorway.

"Jenny, what happened to your face?" His mother-in-law's glare was menacing and contemptuous as she shifted her focus to Michael. "You assaulted my daughter."

"This does not concern you," he said, fighting to keep his voice calm.

Jennifer sobbed openly, her cheek still crimson where Michael struck her.

Her parents didn't seem at all surprised to see Jennifer holding a newborn. She must have called and told them, never mind the fact that he'd forbidden her to contact them. "I did not invite you into my home. Leave now."

Judy Levine took two deliberate steps into the living room toward him.

Ira Levine slithered past his wife and wrapped his arms around his weeping daughter.

Jennifer melted into her father's embrace, her breast heaving and her breath coming in gasps. "I'm sorry Daddy. I'm so sorry."

"It's all right, sweetheart. We're here now." He put his hand on Mercy's head, and Jennifer shifted her arms to give him better access to the baby. She hadn't let anyone else touch her since she was born.

Michael bristled and took a step toward them.

Judy planted herself in front of him. "You and I have some matters to attend to, Mr. Wagner."

Michael regarded the woman standing in his way. Her short blonde hair was perfectly styled, just as it had been on his wedding day. Make-up evened out her skin tone and accentuated her large blue eyes. It was an attractive face, the face Jennifer would have in thirty years, but there was also a hardness there that didn't come from maturity alone. In her long black wool coat and high heels, she was almost as tall as he was. His mouth twisted in distaste.

"We have nothing to discuss." He turned his attention to Ira, who was cooing at Mercy. Michael's youngest child had stopped crying and was staring at this new face in front of her. "Mr. Levine, please take your wife and leave my home."

Ira didn't glance up. "I suggest you listen to what Judy has to say." He blew out his cheeks and made a ridiculous face. Mercy stared, uncomprehending, but Jennifer chuckled, no longer weeping.

Michael couldn't believe the gall of these people. His fury rose when Jennifer's mother removed her scarf and coat. She laid them on the back of his chair before settling herself into it. For the first time he noticed her black leather briefcase.

"Put your coat back on, Mrs. Levine. You are not staying."

"Don't growl at me, Mr. Wagner. I won't be intimidated. And you will not even consider assaulting me. I suspected domestic violence, but I chose to come here without the police. If you threaten me in any way, I will call them." She smiled, and Michael was reminded of a vulture examining its prey. "Trust me. You don't want them here to witness this."

Michael's heart pounded as he wrestled with his rage and confusion. No, he didn't want the police in his house. He'd always been careful to keep them out of his personal business.

He ignored the woman perched on his chair and walked over to Ira and Jennifer. Jennifer recoiled, and Ira pulled her closer.

"If there are matters to be discussed, then let's discuss them, father to father," Michael said to the older man.

Ira laughed in disbelief. "You're talking to the wrong person," he said. "And if I were you, I wouldn't antagonize Judy any more than you already have. You'll only make it harder on yourself." He turned his face back to his daughter. "Let me help you gather your things."

"What things?" Michael didn't understand any of this. "Jennifer, what is going on here?"

"Sit down, Mr. Wagner," Judy commanded from her chair. "And I will tell you what's going on here."

Michael resented being ordered about by a woman, but it was clear he wasn't going to get anywhere with Ira. The man had given up his authority and allowed his wife to rule over him. No wonder Jennifer had such a difficult time adjusting to a properly ordered marriage.

He sat himself on the couch opposite Judy's chair—no, his chair!—and focused his gaze on a point above her head.

She snorted. "Fine, don't look me in the eye. You can still hear me, and I suggest you listen closely. Your marriage to my daughter is over. She called me a few days ago, and I had my firm draw up the divorce papers. You will sign them."

His breakfast turned rancid in his stomach. His arms broke out in gooseflesh, and his hands began to shake. His wife wanted to divorce him? The urge to jump out of his seat and break something was almost overwhelming, but he reminded himself that he was the leader of his family and he needed to remain in control. "I will sign nothing of the kind."

"Yes, you will. You'll find the terms more than reasonable. Jenny isn't asking for any alimony from you or any part of your business holdings. Against my advice she isn't asking you to return the money she gave you from her personal checking and savings accounts when you were married. I understand that totaled more than eighteen thousand dollars. Plus, she signed over ownership of her 2005 Toyota Prius."

Michael grunted. He'd traded in Jennifer's car and used her money to buy a new truck for work. His old one was twenty years old, and the rust was taking over. Vehicles didn't last forever with these New England winters. "I'm not signing any divorce papers," he repeated.

Judy ignored him, pulling two brown folders from her briefcase. "The other matter is child support. You won't have to pay that, either, because you're going to terminate your parental rights to my granddaughter."

Michael exploded out of his seat. "Get out!" he shouted. "Take your papers and get out of my house! You have no right to come here and threaten my family! Stay away from me, stay away from my wife, and stay away from my daughter! Get *out!*"

Judy regarded him calmly from the chair. "Would you like to hit me, Mr. Wagner? By all means, give me a nice, fresh bruise that I can use to demonstrate your violent temper."

His gaze found Jennifer cowering behind her father near the door. She hadn't gone to pack any bags, but she was wearing her coat. Mercy was still snugly wrapped in the soft pastel quilt, sleeping peacefully in Ira's arms, oblivious of the drama going on around her.

"You made a promise before God," Michael said, bitterness heavy in his voice. "You vowed to honor and obey me, until death do us part. God won't stand for being lied to. He will punish you and Mercy. Do you really want to condemn that innocent soul to hell?"

"No," Jennifer said.

Judy's head whipped around, and hope sprang in Michael's chest.

"Jenny—" Mrs. Levine began, but Jennifer cut her off.

"Mom, don't. Let me." Jennifer took a breath and fresh tears welled in the corners of her eyes. Her voice was steady, though she sounded as tired as she looked. "I don't want to condemn my daughter to hell. That's why I'm taking her out of here. This house is hell. My life here is hell. Your belief system is hell. I'm not afraid of your God's wrath because I don't believe your God exists, or at least he doesn't behave the way you think he does. Now please sign my mother's papers so my daughter and I can leave your hell."

His wife was lost. Stunned, Michael turned back to Judy. Her cold smile was back, and again he had to fight the urge to hit something. Or someone. Preferably a face with blue eyes, framed by blonde hair. At this point he didn't care if that face was mature and made-up or clean and unlined. Either would do.

Both folders were open on the coffee table. Judy offered him an expensive-looking silver pen. Michael grabbed it out of her hand and sat back down, but he didn't pull the folders toward him. If Jennifer's parents hadn't gotten involved, he could have solved this. He could have shown his wife how dependent she was on him and used that to train her to be obedient and submissive. He knew now that he'd been much too easy on her. She'd manipulated him with her tears and shows of helplessness, and he'd given her too much leeway with her chores and especially with her attitude. And now, with her parents here to take her away and keep him from her, there was nothing he could do to teach her the error of her ways. He'd made a terrible mistake, and they were denying him the opportunity to correct it.

"If my wife wants to sin against God and face eternal damnation, that's her business. You won't let me save her from herself. I'll sign the divorce papers. But she gets nothing of mine, including my daughter. Mercy stays."

Judy shook her head, still smiling. "Mr. Wagner, you seem to be laboring under the delusion that this is a negotiation. It isn't. You will sign the divorce papers, and you will terminate your parental rights to the child you call Mercy."

"You can't make me." Michael cringed at the petulance in his voice.

His mother-in-law's smile grew wider as she leaned toward him, very much the vulture, and Michael felt a chill. The faint scent of her perfume was foreign to his nose, and it didn't help the churning in his stomach. He told himself this woman didn't intimidate him, even as he drew back from her.

"I believe I can," she said. "You see, all I have to do is bring my daughter to the police station where that mark you put on her face will be photographed and documented, and you will be charged with domestic violence. While she is there, she will give a statement detailing instances of child abuse perpetrated by you in this house. She has described for me how you use your belt to whip your children. She has described to me instances of medical neglect, including refusing to provide her any prenatal care or bring her to a hospital to deliver her baby when she begged you to do so. I understand none of your children has ever been seen by a doctor or a dentist. I'm sure the authorities would be very interested in that. I'm sure they'd also be very interested to hear about your children's education. You failed to notify your local school district of your plan to home educate. You failed to request approval of their homeschooling plan. That is a violation of Massachusetts state law. I'm sure the school district will be quite eager to review the curricula you use and evaluate whether or not it constitutes an adequate education. I think we both know how they'll answer that question." Her smile disappeared, and the vulture was ready to strike. "If it were up to me, I'd report you anyway. But all Jenny wants is to leave with her daughter, so that is my priority. I am not a mandated reporter. Sign these papers, and we'll leave you to ruin the rest of your children in peace. Don't sign these papers, and I'll have the police and the Department of Children and Families crawling up your ass before lunch."

She wasn't bluffing. A lot of the allegations Jennifer could make against him were he-said/she-said and would eventually amount to nothing, but only after several invasive investigations. Michael imagined social workers coming to talk to his children, interviewing them without him present, questioning them about discipline, quizzing them on things like religions of the world and evolutionary science. He imagined them being taken away from him, sent to foster homes where strangers would get paid to do unspeakable things to them. He was their father, and he had to protect them. But he was Mercy's father, too. It was an impossible choice.

He thought of Abraham being told to sacrifice his son Isaac as a burnt offering. He thought of Jacob being told wild beasts had killed his beloved Joseph and being given his son's ripped and bloody coat as proof. True, God spared Isaac at the last minute and Joseph's death was faked, but their fathers experienced their losses nonetheless. And of course, there was God Himself, sacrificing His only Son on the cross for the sake of the world.

Fathers couldn't always save their children. Sometimes they even had to sacrifice one.

He looked again at Jennifer, the anguish in his heart visible on his face. "You said you wanted this life. You wanted a family-centered life with traditional values. Isn't that what I gave you?"

"It is," she said quietly. "But it didn't turn out the way I thought it would. I'm sorry. I never meant to hurt you." The tears that had been quivering in the corners of her eyes grew large and spilled over, running down her cheeks. The red mark on her cheekbone was deepening to purple, a bruise that would last for days.

Michael felt a pang of guilt, and his strength began to crumble. What did he do to cause his family to be broken in this way? He'd only ever tried to serve God, leading his family by command and example, putting his trust in God's ways over the world's ways, and now he'd lost two wives and a daughter because of it.

His eyes rested on the two brown folders, still lying open on the coffee table. Folders filled with papers that said he was no longer married and no longer had a daughter. But he knew he was married, and Mercy would always be his child. No piece of paper could change that. God wasn't tearing his family apart, the world was. The world with its perfectly styled blonde hair and large blue eyes. He remembered the intricate braids Jennifer wore when she first attended church and her old-fashioned dresses that were a parody of modesty. He remembered her carefully crafted story about being estranged from her worldly parents and wanting nothing more than a husband who would provide her a hearth and home. A passage from Proverbs jumped into his mind. *With her much fair speech she caused him to yield, with the flattering of her lips she forced him. He goeth after her straightway, as an ox goeth to slaughter, or as a fool to the correction of the stocks; Till a dart strike through his liver; as a bird hasteth to the snare, and knoweth not that it is for his life.*

Michael's only sin was relaxing his vigilance against the devil, and the devil found a way into his home. All Michael could do now was cast the devil out and work harder to protect his remaining children.

He gripped the silver pen in his hand and scrawled his name next to all the little yellow SIGN HERE arrows. When he had signed the last page in the second folder, he shoved everything back towards Judy.

"Take your papers, take your imp of Satan, take my daughter as a blood sacrifice, and get out of my home."

Judy picked up the papers and flipped through them, making sure he hadn't missed any of the yellow arrows. Satisfied, she put them back into her briefcase and rose. "Jenny, do you have everything?"

Jennifer was watching Michael, sorrow etched on her pretty face. He felt bile rise in his throat at her show of emotion. She glanced at the door to the kitchen, then away, cheeks flaring red without any assistance from him. Was that shame? Finally? Michael turned to see what affected her so, and was horrified to see his children standing in the doorway, watching the scene in the living room.

Jennifer gestured to the infant in her father's arms. "Just her. Nothing else here is mine." Michael was still looking at the shocked faces of his children when their stepmother took their sister and left, closing the door behind her without saying goodbye.

Chapter Seventeen

Hope held Benjamin in her arms, his face buried in her neck as she tried to quiet his sobs. Grace was crying into Faith's skirt. Faith and Joy both had tears running down their cheeks and dripping off their chins. Hope's eyes were dry, but she was shaken. Judging by their expressions, so were Joshua and John. The rest of her brothers looked frightened, and Hope couldn't blame them.

Papa stood in the center of the living room, staring at them. His face was white, and his fists were clenched at his side. All the tension that Jennifer and her parents had built up remained, and continued to grow as though it were alive. Hope could feel it in the air and could see her father buckling under its weight.

"Satan found his way into our home," he told them. "He's gone now, but we have to purge this house of any trace of him. Samuel and Amos, go clear a spot outside for a fire pit. Everyone else, go find anything that belonged to *that woman* and put it in a pile outside. We're going to destroy everything she brought or made here!"

It took a moment for everyone to get their feet moving, but they broke their paralysis when he shouted, "Go!" and took a step towards them. Samuel and Amos grabbed their coats and headed outside through the kitchen, Timothy and Paul right behind them.

"You two go in the woods and gather sticks for the fire," Amos told them, his voice a hoarse whisper. Hope envied him and Samuel their escape, and she didn't blame her younger brothers for wanting the same.

Papa stormed up the stairs, and a moment later his bedroom door slammed.

Joshua moved through the living room and removed the few samplers Jennifer had made from the wall, leaving empty nails in their place. Hope put Benjamin down after telling him to go to his room, and he scampered up the stairs while she grabbed the only quilt Jennifer had managed to finish off the couch.

John went to the schoolroom and began picking books off the shelf. Faith and Joy were with him, Joy's eyes brimming as John's arms filled with the books and lesson plans that had opened up her world. She rubbed her shoulder absently, massaging where her father had fallen on her.

"I—I think some of those were in the McGuffeys," she said. "Can't we keep those?"

"The McGuffeys aren't infallible," he told her. "Papa said to gather everything she brought into the house. Do you want to ask him if you can keep her books?"

They could hear their father upstairs storming around his bedroom, slamming doors and drawers.

Joy's face paled. "No," she said in a small voice.

Hope felt her sister's despair as John removed all the Louisa May Alcotts, the Brontë sisters, even the *Anne of Green Gables* series from the shelf, but she knew better than to interfere. Instead, she knelt down to examine the contents of the lower shelves. When John began tipping the *Little House on the Prairie* books into his overfull arms, Joy squeaked.

"Those were Mama's!" she cried.

"I don't remember them."

"They were Mama's! Hope, tell him!"

Hope looked up from where she was kneeling, the crafting supplies on the shelf before her. She wasn't sure if she was supposed to get rid of consumables that Jennifer had replenished, or just new items she had introduced.

"The *Little House* books were Mama's," she said tiredly. "I read them when I was eight."

John looked at his older sister, suspicion darkening his face. "I know you two were taken in by *her*," he said. "We can't allow any of Satan's influence to remain in this house."

Joshua had come in from the living room as well. "Ease up, John," he told his brother. "I remember the *Little House* books. Mama gave me the first one to read, and I told her it was boring. *Little House, Elsie Dinsmore*, and two or three by Jane Austen were all we had besides the McGuffeys. Books to teach the girls how to be good and proper. Everything else goes."

John nodded, accepting his brother's testimony. Hope felt a flash of irritation and turned back to the crafting shelf. Consumables could stay, she decided.

Michael sat on the edge of his bed, his head cradled in his hands, still smelling of wood smoke. The closet door was ajar, half his clothes piled on the floor where they'd fallen when he ripped Jennifer's dresses off their hangers. The dresser drawers were open, their contents spilling over the sides. The bed was stripped, its covering consumed by the backyard blaze. He'd made love to *that woman* in this bed. Michael had burned all his sheets and blankets, except for the quilts his beloved Lucy had made. He'd sleep wrapped in the fruits of his real wife's care and industry until he could buy new bedding.

Mercy's crib mocked him from the corner.

They'd gathered every trace they could find of *that woman* —every book she'd added to the library, every lesson plan she'd incorporated into their homeschool, every stitch of clothing she'd worn or made—and burned it all. Michael had led his family in prayer around the bonfire, asking God's forgiveness for his waywardness with the temptress, begging for guidance as they moved forward in God's light and truth. He said a few words in memory of his infant daughter, dead to them now. Michael had only held her once, and he tried to forget the feel of her slight, soft weight wrapped in the patchwork quilt Faith had made from old baby blankets. He regretted letting *that woman* take the quilt, but there was nothing he could do about it now. It was yet another thing that was out of his control, and for that he hated her even more.

A soft knock at his door pulled Michael from his reverie. "Come in," he called from between his fingers.

Hope walked in, her steps hesitating as she surveyed the mess around her.

Michael winced. This room showed his weakness, and he had to be strong. He had to be in control. "What is it, Hope?" At least his voice didn't shake. He only sounded tired, and that was to be expected.

"Papa, I wanted to ask your permission to call Joel and tell him what happened. I know I'll see him tomorrow at church, but I think he should know before anyone else."

Dread filled Michael. Church tomorrow. Telling people about what happened. He hadn't thought about that, but people were going to find out. Everyone would know how he failed to keep his family together, how he failed to protect his children. Everyone would know he committed the sin of divorce. It didn't matter that a shrew with short blonde hair blackmailed him into it. He was the head of his household, and it was his responsibility. Michael had failed to keep order in his own home, and everyone would know it.

Hope stood with her back straight, radiating confidence and the serene presence that was so characteristic of her mother. The rest of the house was back in order because Hope saw to it after the bonfire. She'd planned the week's meals and gone grocery shopping. She'd cooked supper and injected a degree of normalcy and stability into the chaos *that woman's* leaving had created. She would make a fine, capable wife, just like her mother before her.

But when Joel took Hope as his wife, Michael would have to do without her. Joy wasn't a decent cook yet. Faith was a little better, but they were both much too young, and they lacked the maturity to run the household. It wouldn't work. That was part of the reason he'd married the temptress in the first place. He'd needed a woman to run his household so Hope could marry at the customary age.

He understood now that God had other plans.

"Hope, I agree Joel should know. I'll call him and tell him myself. But you have to realize, that woman doing what she did has changed things."

Hope crossed her arms in front of her, a gesture reminiscent of Jennifer when she was being stubborn. Michael was going to have to stamp that out, and soon.

"What do you mean?"

"I mean it doesn't appear to be God's will that you get engaged right now. Your duty to this family comes first, and this family needs you now more than Joel does. I'm not going to end the courtship, but I am going to suspend it."

Tears welled in his daughter's eyes, and Michael struggled to hold his anger in check. He was getting tired of looking at women's tears.

"For how long?"

Michael thought about that. Hope stepped into her mother's shoes quite well at fifteen, but Lucy had instructed her and led by example for Hope's entire life. Joy had been much younger when her mother died, and she'd never been as diligent a student as Hope. Joy was stubborn and rebellious, and he expected it would be a long time before she learned the error of her ways. Especially now that he had to deal with the damage that temptress had caused. Joy admired her stepmother and tried to emulate her. It was going to take a lot of work to undo that.

"Seven years," Michael decided. "Joel is going to have to wait for you for seven years." He thought of Laban making the same pronouncement to Jacob regarding his daughter Rachel. It felt right.

Hope's face lost all color. "Seven years?"

"It'll go by fast."

"But what if he won't wait that long?"

"If Joel's not willing to wait on God's time, then he's not a man worth marrying."

Hope shook her head.

Michael felt his patience slip further. "Don't shake your head at me, Hope. I won't tolerate defiance in my own daughter."

"No," Hope said.

The rage Michael had been battling to suppress all day rose to the surface. He stood to face his daughter, using his greater size to tower over her. "Did you say 'no' to me? Did you *dare* say 'no' to me?" He was losing control, but the rage gave him energy and strength, and he welcomed it over the exhaustion he'd felt since the bonfire.

Hope took a deep breath. "I said no." Her back straightened even more. She was still much shorter than he but his looming over her didn't have the shrinking effect it usually did. "I'm nineteen, Papa, and I can get married whenever I want to. Joel's already asked me, and I said yes."

Michael couldn't believe what he was hearing. "You gave your heart away without my permission? Joel had no right to ask you, and you don't have the authority to accept his proposal! The engagement never happened, and the courtship is off!"

Incredulous, he watched as she shook her head again, denying his pronouncement. Her eyes flashed, and that's when he saw it. Her eyes were brown, not blue, but they had the same rebellion and defiance he'd seen in Jennifer's. He hadn't managed to burn all traces of the demon today. The demon had entered his eldest daughter.

"You can't make me—"

His fist planted directly in her left eye, cutting off her blasphemous speech as she sprawled on the ground.

He reached for his belt and unbuckled it. "Bend over the bed, Hope. 'Foolishness is bound in the heart of a child, but the rod of correction shall drive it far from him!'"

Hope remained on the floor, her hands covering her injured eye. "I'm not a child!" she screamed. "I'm a grown woman, and I'm going to marry Joel!"

Michael could almost see her brown hair turn blonde, her brown eyes turn blue. *That woman* had often complained that he treated her as a child instead of an adult. She'd never understood that he was responsible for every member of his household, and her behavior determined the kind of treatment she received. He would correct foolishness in his children and his wife alike, just as he would break the rebellious spirit of anyone who dared defy him.

His belt was clenched in his fist, and he brought it down upon his daughter. The square buckle struck her shoulder, and she cried out in pain. Michael lifted his arm and brought his belt down again on her back. And on her buttocks. And on her arm. Next it hit the back of her head and snagged in her hair. He ripped it free.

Hope climbed to her knees and tried to crawl toward the bed. He followed her, not caring to find out if she planned to bend over it as instructed or hide under it. He continued to rain blows down on her arms, back, buttocks, and legs even after she stopped crawling and lay motionless on the floor. Her screams of pain tapered off to whimpers, which faded to nothing, and Michael didn't hear his own screams of fury echoing in the room. That demon had already taken so much from him. He had to get it out. He had to save his daughter!

Suddenly his arm was stopped in midair. Michael was aware of pressure on his wrist as he heard Joshua's voice in his ear. "I think she's had enough, Papa."

Michael whirled to face his eldest son. John stood in the doorway, watching. "Let go of me!" Michael growled. He tried to pull his arm away, but his son's grip was surprisingly strong. Joshua had been carrying lumber, knocking down walls, and installing drywall for Michael for three and a half years. For the first time Michael realized his son was stronger than he was. Michael's face turned white with fury.

Joshua's eyes were full of fear. His voice shook as he told his father to let go of the belt. "Please, Papa. Don't do this."

Michael made a fist with his free hand and brandished it at his son. "I am the man of this house! It's my duty to correct my children when they defy God's will!"

Joshua caught Michael's fist and held it. "Not like this, Papa. You'll kill her."

"I'm saving her! The demon's in her, and I have to save her!"

Joshua never raised his voice. He possessed all the self-control Michael used to display and model for his sons. Still holding his father's hands, almost like they were dancing, he slowly turned the older man around so he could see Hope. The belt dangled from Michael's right hand, the buckle bouncing harmlessly off Joshua's shoulder. "Look at her, Papa. Is that how you correct your children? Is that how you save them?"

Michael looked down at his daughter, expecting to see a demon grinning up at him. Instead, he saw a silent form clad in a blue corduroy jumper and oversized grey sweater, curled up like a baby. Her thick brown hair had escaped her bun and was splayed around her in a tangle on the floor, a few strands pasted on her cheek and neck. Hope's arms, which she'd held up to protect her face, had fallen to the side, revealing a swollen eye with a cut at the edge of the eyebrow. Her jaw was slack, her eyes closed, and her face was wet with useless tears. The only sign she was still alive was the slow rising and falling of her chest.

The belt dropped from his hand and fell to the uncarpeted floor with a loud clang. Joshua let go of his wrists, but Michael didn't notice and kept them raised, his muscles locked. "What have I done?" he whispered.

Joshua took his father's arm again and guided him to the naked bed. John came in and sat next to him. "It's okay, Papa. God can forgive you. 'Let all bitterness, and wrath, and anger, and clamour, and evil speaking, be put away from you, with all malice. And be ye kind to one another, tenderhearted, forgiving one another, even as God for Christ's sake hath forgiven you.'"

With a mix of humiliation and relief, Michael let John

minister to him while Joshua gathered his unconscious sister in his arms and carried her from the room.

The first thing Hope was aware of was the cold. She floated in blackness, not thinking and not feeling, but the cold seeped into her awareness. And under the cold, pain.

She struggled to remain in the comforting blackness. It was safe, and she knew leaving would be dangerous, but the cold was pulling her out. She could hear sounds now, murmured voices, and someone was sobbing. And that oppressive cold was all around. The black acquired a tinge of red, and she tried to open her eyes, but only the right one obeyed. She wished it hadn't. She closed it against the harsh light, and against the pain that was becoming stronger than the cold. There were two people sobbing now, and Hope realized she was one of them.

"Wake up, Hope." Hope knew that voice, but it didn't belong in her room. "You're going to be just fine."

No, she wasn't going to be just fine. She remembered the belt with its buckle and the terrible expression on Papa's face as he struck her with it again and again. And he was taking Joel away from her! That knowledge hurt more than her body. She wanted to sink back into the blackness where no thoughts or feelings could touch her.

The cold on her body lessened, though it still weighed heavily on her skull. "Joy, go put these to soak in the ice water again and bring me the towels that are in there now. Remember, wring them out just enough so they don't drip too much." It was that voice again. Where had she heard it last? Hope struggled to place it. Babies. It had something to do with babies.

"What can I do, Aunt Libby?" Faith's voice was instantly recognizable, giving Hope the answer she sought. Aunt Libby was the owner of the voice that didn't belong in her room. She was the closest thing they had to a doctor. Hope's sobs increased, causing her more pain. She missed the cold that encompassed her body.

"Keep Grace calm. She's upsetting Hope."

Grace was the source of the other sobs. Hope didn't want to upset her little sister. She tried to control her own moans, but she couldn't do anything about the tears that streamed from her eyes. One of her eyes, anyway. The other one wouldn't open under its cold weight, and Hope didn't want to think about why. Despite her best efforts, her sobs increased.

"Calm down, Hope. It's not that bad." Aunt Libby's voice was gentle but stern. "Just some bruising. Nothing's broken. You'll be sore for a few days, but there's no permanent damage."

She heard Joy return and suddenly the cold was back, more intense than before. As the ice-water-soaked towels were laid on her bare back and legs she gasped and tried to push herself off the bed.

Aunt Libby's hand rested on the back of her head, and the light pressure of her aunt's fingers was enough to pin her in place. "Lie still. This will help with the pain and swelling."

Hope opened her one eye. It took a minute to focus on her aunt, and on the room behind her. She was in her own room, as she'd guessed, but not in her own bed. She could see her bed high up on the other side of the room, above Grace's bed, where Faith sat with the little girl on her lap. Joy stood beside them. Hope must be on Faith's lower bunk, beneath Joy's. She was lying on her stomach, her right, unmarred cheek on Faith's pillow, her arms alongside her body. One large, wet towel was tucked with its end around her neck just under her hairline and covered her shoulders, arms, and back, its other end stopping midway down her buttocks. A second towel started at her waist and stretched all the way down her legs, covering her feet. She realized she was naked. Tears of shame and pain continued to leak out her right eye, sliding across her head toward her ear, soaking Faith's pillow.

The towels arranged, Aunt Libby knelt on the floor so her head was level with Hope's. "Your father told me what happened, Hope." There was no pity in her voice. Only accusation. "You should never have provoked him like that. Doesn't he have enough to deal with, without you going off and giving your heart away and making promises you have no business making? Pastor Kinsley's downstairs with him now. He wants to speak with you, too. I'll let him know you'll be down shortly." She got to her feet and exited the room, leaving Hope still weeping her silent tears on the bed.

Once the door closed behind Aunt Libby, Hope's sisters rushed to her, Faith sliding the last two feet on her knees through her long denim skirt. Grace tried to throw her arms around Hope's neck but only succeeded in knocking the ice pack off her face, causing her older sister to wince at the pressure on her bruised shoulder.

Joy pulled her back. "Don't touch her," she scolded, replacing the fallen ice pack with uncommon gentleness.

"It's okay," Hope mumbled, snaking her hand out from under the cold, damp towel. Grace clutched it with both fists, trapping Hope's fingers. Hope didn't mind. Her sister's desperate grasp was the only warmth she felt.

Faith knelt next to Grace, her lips trembling. Hope's pain, despair, and shame made room for the guilt that appeared and demanded acknowledgment.

"I'm making your bed all wet," Hope said. "I'm sorry. I don't know why they didn't put me in my own bed. I didn't mean to ruin yours."

"Your bed is too high. We wouldn't be able to reach you up

there, and it's going to be a while before you can climb up and down yourself. I'll sleep in your bed for now, and you sleep in mine."

Hope nodded and wished she hadn't. Her head throbbed.

Joy knelt next to Faith. Her trademark anger was in her eyes, but for once it wasn't directed at Hope. "They're all saying you provoked Papa into disciplining you, and you kept provoking him so he couldn't stop." She paused as a haunted look floated across her features. "We could hear you screaming, Hope. We heard you saying 'no' and 'stop' and 'please.' He was just yelling sounds, not making any sense." Joy looked intently at her sister, her eyes much older than her eleven years. "What really happened?"

Joy's description brought the whole, terrifying event back to Hope. She closed her eyes against the memory, but it was even more vivid in the red-tinged darkness.

"I don't want to talk about it." Fresh tears traveled the well-worn path to Faith's pillow.

Faith gave Joy a meaningful look and Joy dropped the subject. Grace let go of her sister's hand, raced across the room to her own bed, and returned holding a battered brown teddy bear. She placed it on the pillow, above Hope's head. "Here," she said. "Bear-Bear will make you feel better."

Hope had to smile at the little girl's earnestness. "Thank you, Grace." But the only thing that would make her feel better would be Joel coming to take her away from this place, and she'd ensured Papa would never allow that to happen. Not even in seven years.

Pastor Kinsley sat on the chair where Judy Levine had held court earlier in the day. Papa sat on the couch, Joshua and John on his left, Aunt Libby on his right. Hope stood in the middle of the room, dressed in an oversized flannel nightgown with her shapeless polyester robe zippered all the way up. She wore thick woolen socks on her feet that covered her legs to her knees, though both the nightgown and the robe reached her ankles. She hoped no one would ask her to sit. She'd made it down the stairs and to the center of the room, but Hope's entire back throbbed. The cold from the towels had seeped into her bones, and gooseflesh covered her arms. Her head pounded from the effort of not shivering.

Pastor Kinsley studied her in silence, and everyone else waited for him to speak.

Hope risked a quick glance at her family on the couch. Her brothers and aunt were staring at her. Papa sat rigidly, his head down and his folded hands resting against his forehead in a position of prayer. Hope looked back at the pastor, then down at the floor when she saw his stern expression. She could feel the four sets of eyes boring into her, looking into her soul, and she closed her own eyes against the scrutiny. The eyes are windows to the soul, so maybe if they couldn't see her eyes they wouldn't see how sin-stained her soul really was.

"You did a job on her face alright," Pastor Kinsley said finally.

Hope flinched at the pastor's booming voice and tried not to grimace in pain.

Papa put his hands on his lap and glanced up at his daughter. His face was impassive, but Hope thought she could see a hint of sorrow in his eyes. A tiny ember of hope ignited in her breast.

"I guess I did."

"You'll have to keep her home until that heals. No need to cause tongues to go wagging any more than they're going to already. Say she took Jennifer's leaving hard and is too distraught to leave the house. They were close, weren't they?"

Papa hesitated, having no idea what went on in the house when he wasn't there, but John stepped into the breach. "Yes, they were close. Hope guided Jennifer in running the house, and I think Jennifer was preparing Hope for married life."

Hope pursed her lips as she restrained herself from correcting her brother. The first part was true enough in the beginning, but Jennifer hadn't done anything to prepare Hope for married life.

Pastor Kinsley wasn't looking at Hope's lips, however. He was looking at John, his protégé, nodding at the sage wisdom coming from the boy's mouth. "Yes, I can see that. An unfortunate role model for Hope." He shifted his gaze back to her and scowled. "She wasn't here very long, but she caused a lot of damage. Hope, I understand you and Joel Peterson have been doing things that aren't appropriate for young people to be doing."

Color rose in Hope's cheeks. Why did he have to put it like that? It wasn't like they had a physical relationship, other than the few times he'd managed to hold her hand, and that one kiss. "We were courting," she croaked. Her throat was still raw from screaming, and she didn't have much voice left.

"There are rules for courtship. You and Joel violated those rules and violated the purity of your hearts."

Hope reminded herself that he didn't know about the hand-holding and the kiss. "The courtship was going well, and Papa said he'd give permission to make it an engagement as soon as Jennifer's baby was born."

Papa made a small sound, but when Hope looked at him, he wore the same impassive expression. The ember of hope in her chest flickered but held.

"Is this true, Michael?" the pastor asked.

"That was the plan. But then God showed me He has other plans. I had to alter mine to conform to His will."

Pastor Kinsley smiled. "It takes humility and courage to recognize when we're not conforming to His will, and strength to be more obedient." He turned back to Hope. "You do understand your father is answerable to God, and that he must ensure God's will is done by all under his authority."

It wasn't a question, but Hope knew she was expected to answer anyway. "Yes, Pastor Kinsley."

"Yet you and Joel promised to marry each other, without permission and without considering whether it was what God intended."

The pain in Hope's back was building, and her head felt like it was caught in a vise. The heat from the wood stove bathed those on the furniture in its warmth but didn't touch her. Why was she on trial when her father was the one who lost his temper and sinned? Joel had permission to court her, and everyone knew courtships were supposed to lead to marriage. What did they do that was so wrong?

But she knew. Joel's vision for their life together was outside the bounds of what their families and the church expected. It was sinful. They'd planned to deceive their families and move to Seattle under false pretenses, where she would circumvent God's will regarding the size of her own family, study modern medicine, and encourage women to trust man instead of God. Pastor Kinsley didn't know any of this, but God did. And God wasn't pleased.

"The courtship was going well," Hope repeated, the tears threatening. "Papa promised. We—we love each other, Joel and me." There was that, too. It wasn't just a new and different life she wanted; it was life with Joel himself. She'd be happy with Joel no matter what their life was like, no matter how many children they had, no matter where they lived. She liked the way she felt when she was with him, and she wanted more of that. A single tear slipped down her cheek.

"You're just a young girl who didn't guard her heart properly," Pastor Kinsley said. "You're infatuated, not in love. Joel should have known better, but I won't be able to talk with the Petersons until tomorrow after church. It's too late for me to go over tonight, but I'll explain to them tomorrow why the courtship has to end." He sighed, the weight of his office heavy upon his shoulders. "Michael, you are going through a trial. Read Job, remain steadfast, and don't give the devil a foothold."

Papa folded his hands against his forehead again, ostensibly praying.

"Joshua, you did well in helping your father tonight. He's clearly raised you to understand a father's responsibilities to his family. Just remember that despite his momentary lapse of judgment, he's still your father, and you are not his equal."

Joshua nodded, exhaling in his relief that he wouldn't be called out for interfering with Papa's discipline.

"John, you did the right thing by calling me. This home needed some extra spiritual support. Libby, thank you for your help, as always. Michael might need a little more support in the coming weeks and months as he works through this trial."

"I'm always happy to help however I can."

Pastor Kinsley turned his attention to Hope, and his voice grew harder. "Young lady, I hope now you understand the folly of provoking your father to anger. He's being tried, and he needs his family to help him, not try him more. I know you're disappointed your courtship is over, but this is God's will. Your place is here with your family. If and when God chooses to send you a husband, your father will recognize the signs and see that it happens. Until then, you are under his authority and must obey him as you would God Himself. Disobedience to your father is the same as disobedience to God, and rebelling against Him will doom your soul to eternal damnation. Do you understand?"

Hope's heart hurt almost as much as her head. Everyone in the room except Papa was staring at her, waiting for her declaration of submission or rebellion. If she tried to defend her engagement, they'd gang up on her until she gave in. She wouldn't put it past Pastor Kinsley to beat her himself. She'd heard rumors.

She mumbled her affirmation, and the tiny ember of hope inside her gutted and died. Something else died, too, she didn't know what, but she could feel herself detaching from the pain that engulfed her entire being. It was a relief to feel nothing, and she embraced it.

Pastor Kinsley didn't notice or didn't care, now that everything was settled. "That's a good girl. And remember, 'Let not the sun go down upon your wrath; neither give place to the devil.' Any anger or resentment you feel toward your father right now is misplaced. You have a stiff neck, and an evil woman has been influencing you. It's going to take a while for the remnants of her time here to lose their power. You must be vigilant." He turned his head to include everyone in the room. "You must all be vigilant."

The occupants of the couch all nodded in solemn agreement, even Papa.

Pastor Kinsley rose from his chair. "Let's pray."

The pastor left after his prayer, and Papa saw him to the door. Her brothers headed upstairs, Joshua pausing to look at Hope in sympathy. He said nothing, and neither did she, though Joy had told her how Joshua stopped the beating. Now she wished he hadn't. He followed John up to the room they shared with Samuel and Amos, who had no doubt been hiding at the top of the stairs, listening. Joy was probably with them.

Hope remained standing in the middle of the living room as

Aunt Libby exchanged a few words with Papa before following Pastor Kinsley into the night-shrouded driveway. She hadn't been dismissed yet, and Hope wasn't sure if she should follow her brothers upstairs or remain where she was. She wasn't crying anymore. Tears weren't even threatening. She was numb. She'd brought this on herself. This was her punishment for plotting with Joel. The tempting life he'd offered was too good to be true, like all the devil's promises, and she'd been taken in. Pastor Kinsley was right. She was under Papa's authority until he gave her to a husband. Papa had punished her severely, but he'd had a very good reason.

Everything was her fault.

The door closed behind her aunt, and Papa's shoulders slumped as he turned. He started when he saw Hope still standing in the living room. "I thought you'd gone back up," he said.

"Do you want me to?" Her voice was as hollow as she felt.

"Yes."

Hope turned and made her way up the stairs, each step causing her to wince in pain. She welcomed the pain, though. She deserved that pain.

She didn't see her father take a step after her and then stop himself. She didn't see the guilt and sorrow on his face as he watched the empty shell of his daughter walk away from him. She didn't see him grab his Bible from the table or see him collapse into his chair to pray some more.

Hope was looking ahead to her future, and she didn't see anything at all.

Part Two

2016 - 2023

Train up a child in the way he should go: and when he is
old, he will not depart from it.
-Proverbs 22:6

Chapter Eighteen

Hope handed her sister the tissue-wrapped box. "Happy birthday, Joy."

Joy took the box without enthusiasm. "Thank you, Hope." They went through this ritual as they did for every birthday, pretending Hope made the gift inside instead of Faith. This year, for Joy's eighteenth birthday, Faith had knitted a purple sweater and paired it with a long tan linen skirt. She'd learned to knit from Joshua's wife, Megan, and had picked it up with the same ease as she did everything related to handicraft. Hope had tried to learn as well but couldn't quite get the hang of it. It didn't matter. She didn't care about knitting anyway.

Papa drained the rest of his coffee and stood up. "I'll be in my workshop." His face was lined, his skin sallow, and only a few strands of brown stood out on his grey head. He shrugged into his heavy sheepskin coat and left without acknowledging his daughter's birthday, signaling it was time for the girls to do their Saturday morning chores.

Joy exited the kitchen to begin her laundry duties without a word, and Hope watched her leave with growing unease. What was she planning?

She forced her attention back to the calendar. Paul was turning thirteen in a few weeks. With two birthdays and Christmas this month, she'd need to be especially frugal with the grocery budget. Samuel and Amos would bring a turkey from Uncle Joseph's farm, but Hope would still need to provide everything else for the family feast. Fortunately, the boys had culled the flock for her when they came home for a visit in October, and she had half a dozen stew birds in the freezer.

In addition to the ever-present rice and beans, Hope added some root vegetables that weren't too expensive this time of year, flour for bread, boxes of pasta, sausages, and ground beef to the grocery list. That done, she walked through the house, making sure her sisters were doing their chores and seeing if anything else needed to be assigned. The woodpile in the living room was getting low, and Hope made a mental note to ask Paul and Benjamin to bring in more wood from the shed. Grace was almost finished with the downstairs half-bath, using her bucket of bleach water to disinfect everything she'd already scrubbed with vinegar and baking soda. All that was left was the floor, and then she'd tackle the two full bathrooms upstairs.

Hope found Joy in the boys' bedroom, stripping the sheets from Benjamin's bed. "You should do the blankets, too," she said.

Joy glared at her and pointedly stepped over a blanket lying in a heap on the floor.

"I'll tell Papa if you don't."

Joy turned her back on her and pulled the sheets and blankets off Timothy's top bunk. "Of course you will." She balled the sheets up and tossed them into the laundry basket. The blankets joined the heap on the floor.

"Don't do this, Joy." And then, before she could stop herself, she asked, "What are you planning?"

Joy froze, her face unreadable. "What makes you think I'm planning anything?"

"Because I know you. You've been talking for years about going out on your own as soon as you turned eighteen. You might have fooled Papa into thinking you've seen the light, but you haven't fooled me."

Joy's cheeks lost a little of their color. "What did you tell Papa?"

"Nothing. I haven't told Papa anything because I know what he'll do to you." Hope's expression was pleading. "I don't want you to get hurt, Joy. I'm trying to protect you. Do as you're told, don't be rebellious, and everything will work out."

"Like it did for you?"

Hope winced, her sister's blow landing a direct hit. "I know my place," she said. "Papa might still find a husband for me. You're old enough now to manage this house, and the kids are practically raising themselves." It was true. Timothy was directing his own education in computers in a way that met with Papa's approval, and Paul and Benjamin kept themselves out of trouble and did the workbooks John sent for their home-schooling from his college alma mater's publishing house. Faith and Grace did their workbooks as well, though Faith only did them because Joy made her. Grace tried a little harder, but like Faith she preferred domestic duties to schoolwork.

"Papa's more likely to find a husband for me," Joy said. "He doesn't trust me to take over for you. He told me he's not going to teach me to drive because he doesn't want me to get—how did he put it? 'An inflated sense of independence.' He's going to leave it up to my husband to decide if I get a license. Speaking of which, shouldn't you be off at the grocery store enjoying your weekly dose of alone time?"

Hope would not be distracted. "What are you planning?"

Joy's grin was more of a sneer. "I'm planning to launder these sheets *and* blankets, like a good little slave."

Hope turned to leave but stopped at the door and turned back. "Whatever you're thinking of doing, Joy, don't. For your sake, just don't."

"Go to the store, Hope, and mind your own business."

"You are my business," Hope said, stepping into the hallway. "You and the others are why I'm here."

Joy ignored her, and Hope wandered into her own room to pray for her sister's soul. She didn't expect God to answer. He never did. But prayer was a habit Papa had beaten into her, so Hope prayed out of obedience, if nothing else.

She no longer used her nail clippers to pray. She hadn't needed them when Joel was courting her, but she began to use them again once her bruises stopped hurting. The little cuts didn't help, though, so she began to get reckless when handling knives. She wasn't trying to kill herself; she was just being careless. That's what she kept telling herself. Hope reasoned if it was God's will that she died then so be it. But she wasn't doing anything to *make* it happen. Nevertheless, after Joel sneaked into the backyard to talk to her when she went to collect the morning eggs, after he begged her to run away with him and she begged him to get right with the Lord and be obedient to his parents, after he said his last goodbye and wished her well, she began to drag the blades along her skin, pressing down just hard enough to make scratches that barely bled. And then on that terrible Sunday a few weeks later when Carolyn told Hope that Joel was gone and his parents suspected he'd run away to join his sister in Oregon, Hope pressed harder.

Grace had been drying the dishes and putting them away. Hope stood still, her arms submerged in the warm, soapy water up to her elbows.

"What's wrong, Hope? Why did you stop?" And then, her voice rising, "Why is the water turning red?"

Hope was dizzy and slid to the floor as she heard her youngest sister shriek, "Papa! Hope's got blood! Papa, help! Hope's got *a lot* of blood!"

Papa, Joshua, and John had come running, and Hope mumbled something about the knife slipping. Papa chose to believe her story even though a knife slipping while being washed was unlikely to slash both wrists so deeply. They patched her up and sent her to bed for a few days to heal. Papa never spoke of it again, and most of her siblings followed his lead. John lectured her about the sinfulness of despair and gave her some Bible verses to read. Joshua sat with her for a few minutes every night, praying aloud that God would heal her body and soul. His prayers affected her no more than John's Bible verses did. Joy and Faith seemed afraid of her, and Grace wouldn't leave her side.

None of it touched Hope. God hadn't wanted her to die, so she was going to have to continue in this life. She stopped playing with knives, stopped using her nail clippers for anything but keeping her nails trimmed, and accepted that God's punishment for her was to manage her father's house and raise her siblings, and do it without the joy He had promised to those who served Him. Such joy was beyond her own ability to generate, and it was clear God didn't find her worthy of such a gift.

She'd done her best to fulfill her duty to her family anyway, year after year, for the seven years Papa had told her Joel would have to wait to marry her. But at the end of those seven years Joel hadn't returned home, and Hope's youngest siblings still needed her guidance on their path to righteousness, the path she had somehow missed herself.

Her greatest fear was that Joy was missing it as well. And

Hope didn't know what to do about that except pray to an absent God.

The frigid, lifeless winter yielded to early spring, with its cold rains washing the dirty snow away and its pungent air causing Hope's nose to clog and eyes to itch. Summer came with its heat, making the second floor of the house almost unbearable despite the trees that sheltered it from the sun and shielded it from peering eyes. Autumn was a welcome change, with its cool breezes and brilliant leaves which fell until the trees were bare, and then the fallen leaves turned brown, coating the ground with their rot until they were covered by winter's snow. Eventually the cold rains came again, the seasons marking the passage of time. It all meant nothing to Hope. Whatever the season, her life was always the same. The only thing that changed was how many layers of clothing she wore.

Hope sat at the school room table waiting for her siblings to finish the workbook pages she'd assigned when the telephone in Papa's office rang. Joy gave Hope a pleading look, and the older girl shook her head. Only Hope was allowed to answer incoming calls. No one was permitted to call out unless it was an emergency and they had to reach Papa.

She picked up on the fifth ring. It was Joshua.

"Hope, I need you to come get Cassandra and Christina and bring them home with you for a little while."

The panic in her brother's voice brought gooseflesh to Hope's arms. "Why? What's going on?"

"It's Megan. There's something wrong with her. She's been getting sicker and sicker since she lost the baby."

"Did you call Aunt Libby?" Hope knew about Megan's recent miscarriage. Aunt Libby helped with the aftermath.

"No, and I'm not going to. Hope, just come." His voice broke. "She's acting really strange, like she doesn't even realize we're here. She's feverish, and her breathing doesn't sound right. I'm taking her to the hospital. I can't lose Megan."

"I'm on my way." Hope hung up the phone so she wouldn't have to hear her brother cry.

~

Papa was in his workshop, so Hope answered when Joshua called back later that evening. Megan had been transferred by helicopter from the small hospital in Gardner to UMass Medical Center in Worcester and was now in the Intensive Care Unit. She didn't hear from him again until two days later, Saturday, when he finally left the hospital to get a shower and a change of clothes. Hair still damp, he arrived at his childhood home and embraced his daughters in a hug the girls had to wiggle out of when he wouldn't let go.

Hope watched, a small part of her envying her nieces the relationship they had with their father. Joshua never learned that from Papa. It must have been Mama's influence.

"Daddy, why are you crying?" Cassandra asked, spreading his tears around his cheek with her small finger. He grabbed her hand and gently kissed it.

"Because I've missed you, and I'm so happy to see you," Joshua said, his voice thick.

"Where's Mommy?"

Hope, Papa, and the rest of the Wagner children stood back, watching the reunion, the tension in the air palpable as they all waited to hear the answer.

"Mommy is in the hospital. She's still really sick, but she's getting better."

Hope felt a loosening in her chest and was able to breathe again.

"Why don't you two go with Aunt Grace and let Daddy talk to Grandpa for a little while." He looked up at Hope. "Could you fix me something to eat? I haven't had anything but hospital cafeteria food in days."

"Sure. Eggs okay?"

"That would be great. And some biscuits?"

Hope shrugged her assent. Joshua had eaten scrambled eggs and biscuits nearly every day of his life, and Hope couldn't believe he wasn't sick of them yet. She hated them.

Much to her surprise, Joshua followed her into the kitchen. She'd assumed he'd talk to Papa in Papa's office, but both men took their usual seats at the table while she preheated the oven and gathered the necessary ingredients to make breakfast for the second time that day. "Papa, do you want me to make you some eggs, too?"

"No, but I'll have some of those biscuits when they're ready."

"Me too," Joy said, walking in.

"You're not a part of this conversation," Papa informed her.

"But I want to know how Megan's doing!"

"I'll tell you what you need to know later. Now go find something to do somewhere else."

Joy planted herself in her chair. "I've already finished my chores for the day."

"Hope," Papa said. "When's the last time the chicken coop was cleaned out?"

"About a week and a half ago," Hope muttered, reluctant to tell the truth but not willing to lie.

Joy shot daggers at her older sister as Papa sent her out to clean the chicken coop. Hope was going to pay for that later. Joy would make sure of it.

"I didn't mind if she stayed, Papa," Joshua said.

"She needs to be reminded that she's still under my authority. She had no right to walk in here and insert herself into the conversation."

Hope went back to making biscuits. She didn't know if she was part of the conversation or if she just happened to be in the same room where Papa and Joshua were talking. To be safe, she assumed the latter.

"How's Megan really?" Papa asked.

"She's getting better. I wouldn't lie to the girls about that."

"I didn't say you did."

Joshua took a deep breath and let it out slowly. "Sorry, Papa. It's been a rough couple of days."

"I can imagine. Hospitals aren't good places." There was no mistaking the disapproval in his tone.

Hope cut the butter into the flour, salt, and baking powder mixture with slow, deliberate strokes, taking care to make as little noise as possible.

Joshua sat up in his chair and looked at his father levelly. "That hospital saved her life. It's a miracle she didn't die a week ago."

Papa didn't flinch under his son's gaze. "What was wrong with her?"

"Septic shock."

"I don't speak medical jargon."

"She had an infection that spread throughout her body and damaged some of her organs. They think they've got it under control now, but she's going to be in the hospital for at least another week." His voice shook. "If I'd gotten her treatment sooner, it wouldn't have been so bad. But I didn't. I waited until it was almost too late."

Papa waved a hand dismissively. "Doctors always say things like that. They want you to come to them at the first sign of illness so they can make you dependent on their drugs and squeeze more money out of you. As it is, this is going to cost you a fortune."

"I know this is going to be expensive, Papa. Am I supposed to put a price on my wife's life? Is she worth ten thousand dollars but not fifty thousand? A hundred thousand? What would you have paid to save Mama?"

The words hung in the air as the two men stared at each other across the corner of the table, Papa at its head, Joshua to his right. Hope stood frozen with a round piece of dough in her hand, shocked that her brother would invoke their mother. It didn't matter that everyone was thinking about her. It was one of those things you just didn't say out loud. Especially to Papa.

Papa's voice was deadly quiet. "I wouldn't have sold my soul. If it's God's will to take someone, you don't stand in His way. Your mother knew that, and so do I."

"Not everyone at church believes modern medicine is evil, Papa."

Hope's eyes widened in surprise. This was news to her.

Joshua continued. "Some of us believe life is precious enough that we should do everything within reason to save it."

"Within reason," Papa repeated.

"People disagree about what that means. But man can't create something from nothing. Only God can do that. These medicines, they come from things God created. These treatments and surgeries, they come from people understanding how the human body works, but they don't create new life. They're all tools that can be used or misused, but they're not evil."

Hope went back to cutting circles out of the rolled dough. She'd had similar thoughts about modern medicine, once. God punished her for those thoughts. She wondered how God was going to punish Joshua.

"That's a slippery slope you're on, son. Once you start making religious arguments to justify substituting your own will for God's, you'll find the road to hell is broad and well-traveled."

"We're going to have to agree to disagree on this one, Papa. I'm the head of my house and my family, and I make the decisions for them. I made this decision, and I stand by it. I would appreciate it if you wouldn't attack me because you disagree. Now, do you want to know about Megan or not?"

"You already told me about her. She had an infection, she's getting better, and she'll be home in a week."

"Don't you want to know why she's going to be there that long, or what caused the infection?"

"Joshua, those are things I can't control, so I leave them in God's hands. I don't see the point of dwelling on it."

Joshua stared at his father, his mouth ajar. His eyes shone.

Hope prayed her brother wouldn't start crying in front of Papa.

Joshua blinked and cleared his throat. "So you don't want to know."

"No, I don't."

They sat, unspeaking, eyes locked.

The biscuits were ready to go into the oven, but Hope was afraid the men might notice her if she moved, and she didn't think they'd appreciate her eavesdropping.

The oven beeped, announcing it had reached 425 degrees. Both men looked at her, and she opened the oven and placed the cookie sheet on the top rack. They were still looking at her when she closed the oven door. Eyes downcast, Hope shuffled to the refrigerator to retrieve the eggs.

Papa stood. "Hope, I'll be in my workshop. When they're ready, bring me two biscuits fresh from the oven. Buttered."

"Yes, Papa."

She stole a glance at her brother as the door closed behind their father, then turned her back on him and hurried to the counter so she wouldn't see his silent tears. Before this week she'd never seen her brother cry, not even when their mother died. Now a lifetime's worth of tears refused to be ignored.

Joshua got up and retrieved a tissue from the box on the counter while she whisked the eggs. He sat back down after he'd wiped his face.

Hope poured the eggs into a pan and began pushing them around with a spatula. "What caused the infection?" she asked when he was in control of himself again.

A relieved smile played on Joshua's lips, and Hope realized he needed to talk about this. He wanted it to be with his father, but he'd settle for her.

"When Megan lost the baby, not everything...came out. What was left got infected, and then the infection spread." A shadow crossed his face. "It was bad, Hope. Really bad. They were surprised she was still alive when I told them she'd miscarried over a week ago and had been sick for several days. Most people who have this and don't get treatment right away die from it. Megan is young, strong, and otherwise healthy, and they think that's why she survived."

Hope continued to push the eggs around in the pan. "So she's going to be okay? After a week the infection will be healed, and she'll be back to normal?"

Joshua's head dropped. "Mostly. There was some damage to her kidneys, but they think that will get better in time, though she'll have to watch her diet. Not too much protein, that sort of thing. But the infection was so bad it destroyed her—her inside lady parts." They avoided each other's eyes, embarrassed. Men didn't talk about these things. "They did surgery to take everything out. She can't have any more children."

Hope thought about Megan. She came from a large family

as well, and she and Joshua had been looking forward to having a house full of children. But Cassandra and Christina were all they'd ever have. This was how God was going to punish Joshua. His trust in modern medicine saved his wife's life, but it also made her incapable of giving her husband a proper quiver-full of children. He'd only have his two girls. He'd never have a son to carry on his name. He'd never have the opportunity to teach a boy how to be a man.

"I'm so sorry, Joshua."

"Thanks." Joshua ran a hand through his hair. "Megan doesn't know yet. She's still pretty out of it. I'll tell her in a few days when they move her out of the ICU. She's not going to be happy, but I hope she'll understand."

Hope turned off the burner, dumped the eggs on a plate, and set it before her brother. "She's going to say she was willing to risk death in order to help God bring forth a new life." Bearing children was the most important job a woman had. All girls knew that.

Joshua didn't speak for a minute while he shoveled eggs into his mouth.

Hope went to the oven and removed the golden-brown biscuits.

"There was no new life to save," he said. "She already lost the baby. She probably would have died if I hadn't authorized the surgery. If I hadn't, and if she'd managed to survive anyway, she wouldn't be able to carry another child to term, and she'd have a higher risk of getting another infection that would probably kill her." Hope wasn't sure if he was trying to convince her or himself. "This way, even though I closed the door on future children, she'll live to raise the ones we already have." His voice was pleading, wanting affirmation that he'd done the right thing. For the first time in years Hope felt like Joshua's older sister, not a female subordinate, subject to his authority. "That's just as important as bringing new life into the world, isn't it Hope? Being around to raise our girls?"

In the living room Hope could hear Faith and Grace playing with Cassandra and Christina. Joshua's daughters squealed with delight as their aunts pretended to scold their dollies. She knew Timothy, Paul, and Benjamin were somewhere in the woods around the house, possibly teasing Joy as she cleaned out the chicken coop. She thought of how eager Samuel and Amos had been to take refuge at their uncle's farm under the guise of furthering their education. She thought of how John didn't hesitate to leave the family and go to a Bible college in Florida, and how he never came back after graduation. Instead, he'd married and established a new life for himself down south. She thought of Papa, hiding in his workshop as he always did because he couldn't bear to be around his children. She allowed herself to notice her own body and felt the ever-present throbbing of her head, the heaviness of her limbs, the emptiness of her soul. Everything would have been so different if Mama had lived. Hope would be happily married and raising her own children, Joy wouldn't be so rebellious, the rest of her siblings would have been better behaved and more rooted in the family, and Papa would be happy. Despite her best efforts, Hope had failed to be the mother her siblings needed.

She looked away from her brother and wished she still had tears to cry. "Children need their mother," she murmured.

"I knew you'd understand," Joshua said, his whole face relaxing.

Hope grabbed a plate. "I'd better bring Papa his biscuits while they're still hot."

Chapter Nineteen

Megan was released from the hospital six days later, though she was still shaky on her feet and tired easily. Wanting to know if his second daughter was ready for courtship, Michael sent Joy over to help tend Joshua's house and manage the children for a few weeks, allowing Megan to ease back into her duties.

He wanted Joy married as soon as possible. She wasn't as rebellious as she used to be, but she was still strong-willed, and he didn't want to take any chances. More than any of her sisters, Joy needed to be under authority at all times. Al Reed had a son a few years older than Joy, and though Michael didn't like the man's methods, he couldn't deny their effectiveness. At any rate, Al would never tolerate a weak son, and Joy needed someone with a strong force of will to make her learn and accept her place in life.

Surprisingly, Joy didn't complain about being sent to her brother's house. She only asked if she could call home every other night to talk to Faith. Michael didn't see the harm in it.

Faith was much better at homemaking than Joy was, and if Joy had any problems or questions, Faith could answer them.

Joy returned home a month later, in early May, and Joshua reported she'd been a great help to Megan despite the amount of time she'd spent on his computer. She did an excellent job keeping the house clean, cared for Cassandra and Christina tolerably well, and most of her meals were edible. Michael decided it was time to talk to Al about a courtship between Joy and Jimmy.

"Yeah, it's probably time my Jimmy got himself a wife," Al said the next Sunday after church. "It would be good for him. Might settle him down some."

"He is working, isn't he?"

"He's got a job. He's been working security for the last year, and he likes it. Lets him be tough. He's just a little restless. You know what boys are like at that age."

Michael knew what he'd been like at that age, and he'd been nothing like Jimmy Reed. But Joy was nothing like Lucy had been, either.

"I'll talk to him about Joy. See if he's game." Al frowned. "But hey, this isn't going to be a repeat of that Peterson business, is it?"

"That was an unusual situation," Michael said flatly.

"Yeah, and it ruined the Peterson boy. Running away and getting into who knows what? I don't want the same thing happening to my Jimmy."

Michael took a deep breath. Did he really want to be connected to this man through marriage? "Joel Peterson had some—unfortunate—ideas about life, and I'm just glad my daughter got out of that situation before it was too late. He would have ruined her. You know his sister went bad years before his courtship with my daughter ever started. We had nothing to do with what happened to him afterwards."

Al rubbed his knuckles on the stubble of his chin. "Maybe. I'd forgotten about his sister being a whore."

"Look, if you're that concerned, we can forget the whole thing." As much as Michael wanted to marry Joy off, a part of him hoped Al would refuse.

"No, Jimmy has to marry somebody. It may as well be Joy. I guess she's pretty enough. At least she's local. Long distance courtships are a hassle."

"Talk to Jimmy and see what he says. If he doesn't want to court Joy, that's fine. Just let me know either way."

Al grinned. "He'll say yes."

"As long as it's his decision. This is a lifetime commitment he's considering."

"My kids always make their own decisions," Al protested, still grinning. "It's my duty as their father to make sure they're the right ones."

Later that evening Jimmy called and formally asked Michael for permission to court Joy. His polite manner surprised Michael, and he reminded himself that Jimmy was not Al. He asked Jimmy about his faith, work, and vision for his family, and was impressed by the young man's answers. Jimmy had indeed been working as a security guard for the past year, though his assignment location changed according to the needs of the company's clients. He didn't mind, though, and his supervisor was giving him more responsibility. Jimmy thought he might be on track to be a supervisor himself before too long.

Michael knew it would be a struggle for Jimmy to support a family working as a security guard, but he was encouraged by the young man's confidence that he was moving up the ranks.

And his daughters knew how to economize. Joy would make the best of it.

"You have my permission," Michael said. "I'll talk to Joy. She might want a few days to think about it, so expect to hear from her Wednesday night. For the duration of your courtship, there will be no physical contact of any kind. You can talk on the phone on Wednesday nights, and you can visit each other's homes after church on Sunday afternoons. You are to have chaperones with you at all times."

"I understand the rules, sir. And I guarantee I will keep your daughter safe and pure."

Michael announced Jimmy's intent after devotions that night when he had all his children together.

He was prepared for reluctance. He was prepared for rebellion. He was prepared for outbursts of anger and excuses that she wasn't ready. He was also prepared for the possibility that his daughter really had embraced her role and would be happy at the news of her courtship.

Joy didn't respond in any of those ways. Instead, she looked at him in horror as she repeated her intended's name.

"Jimmy Reed? *Jimmy Reed?*" She looked at Faith, who grasped Grace's hand. Then Joy burst into tears.

Michael was stunned. Had he ever seen his daughter cry? He didn't think so, not even when he disciplined her with his belt.

Timothy, Paul, and Benjamin backed towards the stairs and made their way up to the second floor with uncharacteristic silence.

"What's this about, Joy?" Michael could feel his patience wearing thin already.

"I'm not ready! I need more time!"

"You're ready," he said. "There's nothing left for you to learn here. You know how to cook, clean, sew, and care for children. Once you're married, your husband will teach you the rest."

"I'm not good at any of those things," Joy muttered.

"Then make sure you get plenty of practice before your wedding. Now, there's to be no more crying. Wash your face and start thinking about what you might want to say to Jimmy when he calls you on Wednesday."

"Wednesday," Joy repeated, looking at Faith. Their expressions mirrored each other, though Michael couldn't identify it. He'd never been good at reading emotions. It couldn't be fear. Faith's chin dropped a hair, and then she raised it back up again, her lips tight.

"I'll be in my workshop," he said, irritated. If he left it up to Joy, she'd probably go out on her own, get a job, and never get married. Girls were too emotional to make their own decisions. He left his daughters standing in the living room and his sons hiding in their bedrooms upstairs.

Hope's sisters were in the same room they'd always shared, though Hope now had the bedroom next door all to herself. Once the four oldest boys moved out, Papa gave Hope their empty room for her own, with the admonishment that she was to use the privacy to deepen her prayer life. Hope prayed out of obedience, not faith, but Papa couldn't tell the difference. She didn't expect God to answer, and He didn't.

She walked into the girls' room without knocking. The curtains were drawn, but enough early-morning light filtered through the heavy pink fabric for her to see thirteen-year-old Grace curled up on her bed against the far wall. Faith's bed was neatly made, and Joy's top bunk was a tangled mess of sheets and quilts. Confused, Hope stepped back into the hallway.

Neither bathroom was in use, and she'd been alone downstairs when she started breakfast a few minutes ago. She entered her sisters' room again and switched on the light.

"Grace, wake up." Hope shook her youngest sister. "Where did they go? Where did they go, Grace? Wake up!"

She groaned and pulled away. "Where did who go?"

"Faith and Joy are gone, Grace. Where are they?"

Grace sat up, blinking. "What are you talking about?"

Exasperated and more than a little panicked, Hope stormed over to her sisters' empty beds. She put a hand on Joy's mattress and found it cold. Hope ducked down to study the lower bunk. Faith's sheets and quilt were smoothed and tucked in without a wrinkle. The pillow was perfectly centered, the corners of the pillowcase sharp.

Hope looked at the pillowcase again. Even with the overhead light on, Faith's lower bunk was always in shadow. Trembling, Hope reached out and touched the folded piece of white paper that was almost invisible against the bleached pillowcase. She sat down on the patchwork quilt—the first one Faith made, she remembered—and began to read, stooping her shoulders so she wouldn't bump her head on the wooden frame above.

Dear Hope,

I'm sorry to say goodbye like this, but there isn't time for any other way. Joy has wanted to leave for a long time and she wanted me to go with her, but I wasn't sure if I wanted to go but now I do. Joy doesn't want to marry Jimmy Reed and she knows Papa won't listen. I want to see other things and other places, just to see what they're like, but I know Papa will never let me. Godly people live in other places, so it can't be all sinful. Joy made a friend on the computer who is helping us get set up, so we're already not alone. I promise we'll be

good, and I'll call you when I can. Give my love to everyone,
especially Grace, and please try to understand.

    Love, Faith

Hope sat, stunned, gripping the paper.

Grace sat next to her. "What does it say?"

Numb, Hope handed her sister the note.

Grace read it, her eyes growing larger and her jaw slackening as she reached the bottom of the page. "They're gone?" Her eyes shone with tears. "They just left?"

"It looks that way." Hope wasn't surprised Joy ran away. If anything, she was astonished her sister had waited so long. But Faith? Faith was so helpful and obedient. She was good at everything girls were supposed to be good at, like Carolyn was, and she'd always seemed content with the way things were. How did Joy manage to pull Faith away from everything that was familiar and comfortable?

Grace was crying. Hope hugged her, and Grace wet her collar with her tears just as she had when she was a frightened toddler.

Hope pulled away before the darkness and grief overwhelmed her. "I have to tell Papa."

Chapter Twenty

Hope had thought the scandal was bad when Jennifer left and Papa ended her courtship with Joel, but that was nothing compared to the church's reaction to her runaway sisters. At least Jennifer had been an outsider, and people in the congregation could pity Papa for falling prey to her lies and deceit. The other elders wouldn't even accept Papa's resignation when he announced his divorce. The situation between Hope and Joel had been regrettable but understandable, given the circumstances, and the congregation aimed most of the vitriol at the absent traitor.

This time the blame rested squarely on the Wagner family.

As patriarch, Papa bore the brunt of the responsibility, though Hope knew it was her fault. He'd failed to train his daughters in the way they should go, which meant he'd probably failed to train the rest of his children, as well. This time Papa was forced to step down as an elder, and all his remaining children were ostracized. Hope had never seen her father look so beaten, and her guilt compelled her to make him his favorite meals and keep the house clean and quiet for him. She made sure her remaining siblings acted shamefaced and repentant at church, hoping their behavior would prove Papa was a good Christian father and godly leader. But everyone except Joshua and Megan continued to shun them all. Even Aunt Libby and Uncle Nick kept their distance, though Aunt Libby had been doing that since Joshua took Megan to the hospital.

Most of the women had theories about why the girls went bad, some blaming Papa for not paying enough attention to his children, more blaming Hope. They'd all seen the signs that Joy was a rebel and a bad influence, and why hadn't Hope stepped in to rescue Faith from such pressure? Hope had no defense against their accusations and endured them silently as she waited for something else to knock her family out of the spotlight. Something always did. Talk of Papa's divorce and her failed courtship had waned when Jack Peterson announced his son Stephen's courtship to Hope's friend Carolyn a few months later. Megan's sterility had been the topic of conversation until Hope's runaway sisters grabbed the women's attention. It was only a matter of time before something else would happen and cause the gossip to shift again.

It took four months, but Carolyn came to the rescue again. After eight years of marriage, Carolyn was proving to be just as fertile as her mother. She went into labor the first week of August, four weeks earlier than expected, and Aunt Libby was there to catch her fifth child.

By fall things were back to normal at church, though Aunt Libby didn't show any inclination to forgive Joshua for not calling her when Megan was ill. She was certain she would have been able to heal Megan and save her fertility. Joshua was just as happy to ignore his aunt, and Megan learned to ignore her occasional jibes. Al Reed never missed an opportunity to mention how a courtship with a Wagner girl ruined a young man. "First the Peterson boy and now my poor Jimmy!" he lamented whenever he had an audience. Jimmy, who'd never exchanged two words with the girl who ruined him, didn't seem particularly aggrieved.

At home they achieved a new normal, one that required little adjustment for Papa and the boys but demanded an entirely new routine for Hope and Grace. All the chores were now split two ways instead of four. Homeschooling wouldn't happen at all were it not for John continuing to send workbooks published by his alma mater to his brothers. Hope checked occasionally to make sure the boys were doing their work, and that was the extent of it. Grace insisted she knew enough reading and consumer math to function as a wife and mother and wanted to focus more of her time on domestic pursuits. Hope didn't argue with her. Maybe she could help one of her sisters turn out right, at least.

Hope managed to make Benjamin a new shirt for his birthday in September and put a lot of effort into the dress she gave Grace when she turned fourteen in November. It had been a while since Hope had sewn, with Faith making everyone's gifts for so long. Faith had even made her own birthday presents for the last several years, ensuring she got something nice that was well made. But Hope wanted to do something special for her youngest sister and bought a new pattern and material in Grace's favorite shade of pink.

Christmas was subdued and tense. For the first time in Hope's memory, Aunt Libby and Uncle Nick declined Papa's invitation. They and Jared were going to spend Christmas in Virginia with their eldest son Jake and his family. That still left fourteen people to feed, though. In addition to Papa and the five Wagner children that still lived at home, Joshua and Megan were there with Cassandra and Christina, and Samuel and Amos brought Uncle Joseph and Aunt Linda from the farm, whose own children lived too far away to have Christmas dinner with their parents. Hope and Grace scrambled to make the day go smoothly with only half the usual number of hands to help. Megan offered her assistance but had barely finished tying on Joy's apron when her daughters came in demanding her attention. They were shy around all the people, and they wanted Mommy, not Daddy. Still wearing the apron, Megan shrugged apologetically and herded her children out of the kitchen.

No one mentioned Joy or Faith, but their absence overshadowed the festivities. The guests left early, Papa went out to his workshop, the boys played a board game in the living room, and Hope and Grace cleaned the kitchen. They collapsed in their chairs after the last dish had been put away.

"Is this what Christmas has always been like for you?" Grace asked.

"Pretty much."

Grace pulled herself up and hugged her sister. "I'm sorry. I should have helped more."

Hope hugged her sister back. After so many years of wanting recognition for her efforts, she was uncomfortable now that someone had noticed. "It's okay. You were a huge help today."

They stayed that way for a few minutes, Hope seated and Grace standing behind her chair, her arms wrapped around her sister's shoulders.

"Do you think they're okay?" Grace whispered.

There was no need to ask who 'they' were. Hope kept her own voice low, though her brothers were making a lot of noise in the living room and Papa couldn't possibly hear them from his workshop. "I don't know. I hope so."

"I wish they'd call or write."

"Me too."

"I'm worried."

The prolonged contact was getting to be too much, and Hope shrugged her sister off. "So am I, Grace. But there's nothing we can do."

Grace released her sister and sat back down. "I know. It's in God's hands."

"That's right."

"I pray for them every day."

"That's good. I do, too." Hope didn't mention that she doubted God cared enough to listen to her prayers. Maybe He'd listen to Grace.

On January fifth, Hope stumbled downstairs in the early morning darkness to find Grace already in the kitchen brewing coffee and preparing to cook breakfast. "What are you doing up?" Hope yawned. "And what's with the pancake batter?"

Grace smiled and told her sister to sit down. "They're your birthday pancakes."

"My what?"

"I'll be right back." Grace disappeared into the living room and returned a moment later holding a tissue-paper wrapped box. "Happy Birthday!"

Hope stared at her sister in disbelief. It had been thirteen years since anyone in her family had said those words to her. Mama had been the last one. "How did you know?"

Grace grinned, enormously pleased with herself. "I asked Carolyn. Why don't you ever put your birthday on the calendar? I knew you were fourteen years older than me, but I never knew when your birthday was."

It had seemed wrong to make her own birthday pancakes and cake after Mama died, so she hadn't bothered to mark it. No one had ever noticed the omission. "It wasn't important. Carolyn always wishes me a happy birthday on the Sunday closest. How did you think to ask her?"

"I figured if anyone knew, it would be her." Neither of

them commented on the fact that Grace hadn't bothered to ask Papa. "Open your present!"

With great care, Hope separated the tape from the paper and unwrapped the tattered box underneath, removed the lid, and admired the fabric within. It was dark green cotton, covered by a chaotic array of lighter green dots. She lifted it up and found it was a long, full skirt. "Thank you, Grace. It's beautiful!"

Grace was bouncing excitedly next to her. "There's more. Look!"

Hope had been so focused on the skirt that she hadn't noticed what it covered. She draped the garment over the back of the chair next to her and reached into the box again. Her hand emerged holding a soft knitted sweater the exact shade of green as the skirt's small dots. "When did you get so good at knitting?"

"Megan taught me last year, and I've been practicing. And she got me the yarn and the fabric. I wanted to keep it a secret, so I've been making it at night after everyone was in bed. Do you like it?"

Hope dropped the sweater back in the box and hugged her sister hard. Her eyes stung, and it took her a moment to realize she was still capable of tears after all. "I love it!" When was the last time she'd gotten new clothes? There had been a few trips to the secondhand store over the years, but the last time she'd been given something especially for her was when Jennifer had presented them all with dresses for her wedding. The pale pink silk had gone into the bonfire, along with the rest of Jennifer's things.

A thought struck Hope. "But the sewing machine is in my room. How did you—"

Grace stepped back, a mischievous grin on her face. "I hand sewed it."

"You didn't! That must have taken forever!" She picked up the skirt again and studied the small, even stitches. "Grace, this is amazing work! But you shouldn't have gone through all the trouble."

"It was worth it," Grace said, folding the used paper carefully so it could be put back in the supply cabinet. "You're worth it."

Bleakness settled on Hope's heart, dampening her joy. "No, I'm not."

Grace knelt next to her sister's chair, putting herself in Hope's line of vision. Her oversized bathrobe, a hand-me-down of Hope's, puddled on the kitchen floor around her. "Yes, you are," she said, taking Hope's hands in her own. "I never realized how much you do, how much you've always done."

The discomfort at being recognized made Hope want to disappear. "You and Faith and Joy helped a lot," she deflected. "I didn't do it all."

"You did most of it, and you took care of us." Her eyes glistened. "You're the only mother I've ever known."

Hope shook her head, denying the falsehood. "I'm your sister, not your mother. Mama was a wonderful person who loved you very much and took great care of all of us."

"But I don't remember her. I only remember you. And you're a wonderful person, too."

Hope didn't want to argue anymore. Grace would never understand how depraved she was anyway, and for that Hope was grateful.

Chapter Twenty-One

Michael held his Bible in front of him as he read aloud from the second chapter of Jeremiah. Once he finished, he paused to let the meaning of the words sink in. His children sat around him, the heat from the wood stove putting a flush in their cheeks. They kept their eyes on the floor, waiting for him to continue. He struggled to find the words.

What could Michael tell them? He hadn't felt God's presence in a long time. His faith was based on the idea that God punished the wicked and rewarded the faithful, but that didn't seem to hold true in his own life. He'd always been faithful, but that faithfulness lost him two wives and three daughters. And even during those trials his faith never failed. Had God failed?

If God failed, then Michael's entire life had been a lie. His children's lives wasted. His wife's life needlessly lost. As confused as Michael felt, he couldn't accept that. Lucy's death was not needless. He must honor her sacrifice and remain faithful, especially in the face of doubt.

His children waited for him to open their minds to the

Scriptures. Michael still didn't feel God's presence, but the truth that God rewarded the faithful and punished the wicked was engraved on his soul, and he would engrave it on his children's souls, too. Renewing his resolve, Michael launched into his explanation of the text's relevance to their lives. "Even though God plants you and gives you the advantage of His Word from the time you were born, you can still stray from His way. He saved you from bondage and sin, and you owe Him everything. But if your heart isn't pure, God will know. No matter what you do to make yourself look clean, God will see your filth."

Hope shifted, catching Michael's attention. He knew she'd suffered a lot since Joy and Faith ran away, but he didn't know how to acknowledge it beyond comforting her with God's Word. "But remember that God is merciful and forgiving. If you pray and ask Him for a clean heart, He will give you one. If you repent of your sins and turn to Him, He will accept you. But you must truly repent, or He'll have nothing to do with you."

Hope didn't seem comforted by these words, and Michael wondered what she'd done to have such a guilty conscience. Before he could ask, the phone in his office rang and Hope jumped to her feet.

"I'll get it."

"Sit down, Hope. Whoever it is can wait while we finish our devotions to God. No one is more important than Him."

Chastened, Hope sank back onto the couch. The phone continued to ring.

"Take a moment and examine your hearts," Michael said. "Admit your wrongdoings to God and ask His forgiveness. Don't hold anything back because He'll know. You can't hide anything from Him."

He bowed his head to show that God's commandments applied to him, too, and his children followed suit. Michael couldn't focus on his heart, though, because the phone was still ringing. He kept his head bowed anyway.

"That's twelve rings," Timothy muttered.

"Thirteen," Benjamin corrected a moment later.

Michael exhaled in irritation. "Stop counting the rings and examine your hearts," he growled. The phone rang again. *Fourteen*, he thought. *Fifteen.*

"People usually give up after ten," Timothy said. "It might be important."

Michael was about to berate his son for not giving enough attention to his devotion but stopped when he realized he wasn't doing any better. He couldn't hold his children to a higher standard than he himself could maintain. That would be hypocrisy.

"Keep examining your hearts and pray that God will focus your thoughts," he ordered, getting up from his chair and striding into his office. He picked up the phone on the nineteenth ring, annoyed that he'd been keeping count.

"Hello!" he barked into the receiver.

There was no response at first, but the line wasn't silent, either. Whoever was calling was in a public place, and a noisy one at that. Then he heard a sob. "Papa?"

Michael felt himself grow cold as a mix of emotions flooded through him. Hurt. Fear. Sorrow. Anger. Anger won out. "I have nothing to say to you, Faith."

"Papa, don't hang up, please?"

God must have led him to that chapter in Jeremiah. "I can't support your choices. Unless you repent, I will have nothing to do with you."

He could hear her weeping, and Michael fought within

himself. He missed his daughters with a fierceness he hadn't felt since Lucy died, but they'd rejected his authority. They'd rejected him, and by extension, God. Michael wanted them home, but it had to be on his terms. Anything less and he'd be leading them to hell. Steeling himself against her emotional manipulation, he said, "Goodbye, Faith."

"Papa, I repent!"

Relief filled him, but he kept his voice stern. "Do you really?"

"Yes," Faith choked. "Papa, please come get me. I want to come home."

"Where are you?"

"Worcester. The bus station."

"I'm on my way."

It was almost ten when Michael parked his truck alongside the curb in front of the Peter Pan bus terminal in Worcester, Massachusetts. There were signs labeling it a no parking zone, so he kept the engine running and rolled down his window, searching for his daughter in the bright artificial light. The sidewalk was littered with fast food wrappers, cigarette butts, beer bottles, and homeless men. The sound of sirens pierced the night, and the stench of rotting garbage and old urine wafted into his truck. Not for the first time since they'd left, Michael feared for his daughters' physical safety as well as their souls. Faith had been waiting for over an hour in this horrible place. He hoped he wasn't too late.

A figure at the far end of the terminal walked toward him with small, hesitant steps. Faith's hair was unbound and cut to her shoulders, and she wore a denim jacket not nearly warm enough for the frigid February air. The shape of her legs was on display for all to see beneath her tight blue jeans, and her feet were clad in low-heeled, impractical leather boots. As she got closer Michael could see black streaks under her eyes. Make-up that couldn't withstand her tears.

But underneath all that, it was Faith. He stepped out of his truck to meet her.

They stood before each other, Michael studying his daughter without expression, Faith hanging her head in shame. A brown leather purse that matched her boots hung from her shoulder, but she had no other luggage.

"Where's Joy?" His words made a cloud of mist in the cold night air.

"She's not coming," Faith said softly, and Michael's heart sank. He'd guessed he wouldn't get both his daughters back this night, but he'd hoped.

"Where is she?"

Faith began sobbing again. "She wouldn't—she's at home. In our apartment. We had a fight."

Michael took her arm, and she gasped in pain and surprise. "Get in the truck." He pushed her in the direction of the passenger side, and she climbed in, buckling her seatbelt.

Michael sat behind the wheel for a moment, trying to decide what to do. The apartment must not be far for Faith to have made her way here by herself. He could make her tell him where it was, and he could drive over there and—what? Knock on the door and let his wayward daughter decide whether to let him in or not? Michael wanted to beat some sense into her and make her come home. He wanted to protect her from herself and the world and never let her come to any harm. He wanted to see her again.

He reminded himself that he couldn't have anything to do

with her until she saw the error of her ways, repented, and asked his forgiveness. His chest tight, Michael silently relinquished his second daughter into God's hands, put his truck in gear, and headed home.

For nearly an hour they listened to the sound of the truck's engine rumbling through the cab, joined occasionally by the *whish* of a passing car. Faith had stopped sobbing, for which Michael was grateful. Whenever he glanced over at the passenger seat, he could see her head turned away from him, staring out her window, hands resting on her denim-clad thighs.

"As soon as you get home you're going to put on some decent clothes," he said.

"Yes, Papa."

"I assume you don't have anything with you? Not much can fit inside that silly little purse of yours."

"No, Papa. Nothing I had in the apartment was...appropriate."

Michael shook his head and turned off the state highway. "You're lucky we didn't burn your clothes when you left. They're all still in your closet."

"Thank you, Papa."

They rode the rest of the way in silence. As Michael steered the truck down the long, dark driveway he said, "Go in, get dressed, do not wake up Grace, and come to my room. We're going to discuss your repentance."

Faith closed her eyes and took a deep breath. "Yes, Papa."

Michael could see the fear on his daughter's face, and he softened his voice. "You did the right thing calling me, Faith. I'm glad you're home."

A hint of a smile touched her lips before disappearing. "Me too, Papa."

He killed the engine. "Go in and get changed now. Then come to my room. I want to know everything you've been up

to." And then he'd figure out how much to tell his other children without giving them ideas.

Papa called Pastor Kinsley with the news of Faith's return, so no one at Church of the Covenant was surprised to see six children instead of five spill out of the minivan on Sunday. The decaying fifteen-passenger van had finally quit for good the previous autumn, and with fewer children at home, Papa hadn't seen the need to replace it with an equally large vehicle.

A few women—Megan and Carolyn among them—told Hope how relieved they were that Faith was back home, safe and sound. The rest, however, wanted to know just how far her sister had fallen. Telling them Papa didn't want Faith to talk about it only launched them into speculation. The more generous supposed she'd been living in sin, while a few were convinced she'd been working as a prostitute. All agreed she was damaged goods, and no decent young man would marry her now.

Hope wanted to be outraged at these accusations, but she couldn't be. Girls who did what Faith did *were* damaged goods. Hope didn't believe the rest, but even she had to agree that Faith was different now. She wasn't the easygoing girl Hope remembered. She'd always done her chores diligently, but now she did them with a vengeance. She obsessed about every detail, frantically working until the job was done perfectly. Faith no longer chatted with her sisters as they crossed paths during the day, focusing instead on each speck of dust on the furniture and every inch of unpolished floor. Hope and Grace didn't know what to say to her. Faith was forbidden from talking about her time away, and whatever had passed for conversation between them before was now forgotten. Hope and Grace continued to talk and enjoy each other's company, but Faith remained an outsider. Their months of having no sisters but each other had brought them closer than Hope had ever been with any of her siblings, and she found herself unable to open that bond up to a third, even if that third was Faith.

But the gossip continued, growing more sordid with each passing week, and after three months Hope couldn't stand to hear any more. She cornered Faith while she was scrubbing the downstairs bathroom.

"What were you and Joy doing in Worcester?"

Faith's shoulders tensed and she turned her back on the older girl. "Papa told me not to talk about it."

"Papa doesn't know the women all think you're a prostitute who had a baby and sent it off somewhere."

"What?" Faith spun around, her eyes wide and horrified. "That's not true!"

"I believe you, Faith. But I can't tell them the truth, so they're filling in the blanks for themselves."

"Hope, it was nothing like that, I swear! But Papa told me I can't talk about it." Her face crumpled. "They really think that of me?"

"Yes, they do."

Faith sank to the floor and leaned her back against the toilet. "We shared a studio apartment. I worked at Walmart, and Joy was a waitress at a place called Damien's. We drank soda and tried beer and watched TV and stuff. But mostly we worked to pay the rent." Her cheeks flushed. "We had boyfriends, but I never let him do more than kiss me. I shouldn't have let him do that and I'm not proud of it, but I never did what they think I did." She put her head in her hands. "If Papa finds out I told he'll kill me."

Hope sat on the floor next to her sister, but Faith slid a few inches away from her. The distance between them felt like an impassable chasm. "He might be mad, but he'd be furious if he knew what the women at church are saying. Let me tell them the truth. Maybe then they'll stop gossiping."

"Whatever," Faith said, her voice as wooden as her expression.

Most of the women accepted Hope's testimony. A few grumbled that they still hadn't heard the full story, but for the most part comments about Faith faded into the background. They ceased entirely when Tabitha Payne began a courtship with a young man in Vermont whose family she and her mother met at a homeschooling convention. After all, weddings and pregnancies were always the favorite topic of conversation among the women at Church of the Covenant. It was what they lived for.

As weddings always did, Tabitha Payne's brought with it romantic speculation about who would be next. Al Reed, desperate to get his oldest son out of the house, insisted loudly and to everyone too polite to tell him to be quiet that Papa owed him a daughter. Hope hadn't given much thought to Jimmy Reed when Papa had arranged Joy's courtship because that courtship never even began. But now she couldn't help but wonder what kind of husband a man raised by Al Reed would be. She didn't know Jimmy personally, but she'd heard the women say he was a little wild. Joy might have found that appealing, but she didn't think Faith would.

Papa apparently felt the same way. He deflected Al's outbursts and calmly told him his daughters weren't inter-changeable.

But Faith was nineteen, and the sooner she was married the better. Most girls married between the ages of eighteen and twenty-three. At twenty-eight, Hope was a lost cause. Papa never even tried to find another courtship for her after her seven years of waiting were over. It was too late for her. But it wasn't too late for Faith.

Papa tried to find a suitable young man to court her, but the limited number of men of courtship age at Church of the Covenant were put off by her 'past indiscretions.' Even if she wasn't a prostitute who hid a baby away, Faith was still damaged goods. And Jimmy Reed was as desperate to get out of his father's house as Al was desperate to get him out. He was the only one willing to court Faith.

Reluctantly, Papa had to admit that Faith's only hope of living down her past was to become a respectable wife and mother. Whatever else he was, Jimmy was the son of a church elder, groomed to be a Christian patriarch just like his father and therefore able to be a proper authority over his wife. Faith was lucky to get that offer, and she wasn't likely to get another.

Faith agreed to the courtship with a bright and grateful smile. She'd put more effort into her interactions with others since she found out what people were saying about her. She was always the first to volunteer for the lowliest of tasks, the embodiment of joyful service. She approached her courtship with Jimmy the same way.

But Hope noticed the brief moments of hollowness before Faith sprang into action with chores or a conversation, as though she was gathering her strength for what she was about to do. Hope suspected her sister donned her exuberance as she did her dress, putting it on in the morning and taking it off again when the day was done, month after month, for the fifteen months it took Jimmy to save enough money for the down payment on a house. And Hope knew exactly where Faith had learned to do that.

The church was always stifling in the summer months, but

this particular Saturday in August was worse than usual. Though the thunderstorms of the past few days had passed, the air remained heavy and wet. Hope's cotton dress stuck to her skin, and the frizzled tendrils of hair that stood out around Grace's bun mirrored her own. She was grateful for the loose three-quarter sleeves of her dress and felt bad for Faith in her heavy white satin.

Samuel and Amos managed to escape the farm for Faith's wedding. During the reception they talked excitedly about the parcel of land they'd purchased and were turning into an organic farm.

"Will you actually be able to make a living with that?" Papa asked them. "Why don't you go after the same kind of contracts that Uncle Joseph gets?"

"Uncle Joseph's been earning less and less money from those contracts each year," Amos explained. "He'd be operating at a loss if it weren't for his Social Security. And there's a huge demand for locally grown organic produce and grass-fed, free-range meat, especially since Covid shut everything down. With the supply chains so messed up, people are starting to realize their food doesn't actually come from the grocery store. The margins are smaller, but the demand is huge, and you have a lot more control than if you get big company contracts."

Hope could tell Papa wasn't wild about this plan, but his boys were adults and had been living with and learning from Uncle Joseph for almost a decade. And Papa had other concerns about them besides their plan for an organic farm.

Samuel had brought his girlfriend, who was a surprise to everyone. Jodi was from a conservative Christian family, but they didn't follow the courtship model. Hope had to smile when Samuel assured Papa he was behaving as though they were courting, and his intentions were honorable. She saw the way Samuel and Jodi looked at each other. Samuel's intentions probably were honorable, but their relationship clearly involved more freedom than the courtship model allowed. Papa wasn't happy about that, and he was even less happy when he asked Amos about his prospects for a family. Amos turned red and mumbled that he didn't have time for anything but the farm. At twenty-three, Amos should have been starting a family.

John and Ashley had driven up from Tennessee for the occasion, along with their three children. It was the first time John's family had been to Massachusetts, and the first time Hope got to meet her nephews and niece. It was also the first time the entire family had been together since John moved to Florida to attend college.

Almost the entire family. No one mentioned Joy, but their silence couldn't erase her memory. If anything, it made her absence more noticeable.

The reception was short-lived because of the uncomfortable heat and humidity. The food was eaten quickly, and the newlyweds didn't linger before leaving for the cooler air of New Hampshire's White Mountains. Jimmy had been lucky to get a campsite reservation for their honeymoon. Since the whole country had shut down because of the pandemic in March, it seemed like everybody wanted to go camping now.

The pandemic hadn't impacted Hope much. She had to wear a mask at the grocery store, and some of her usual staples weren't always available, but that was it. The Massachusetts governor had outlawed church services, but Pastor Kinsley had kept Church of the Covenant open anyway. He'd preached against the persecution of Christians, and denounced Covid-19 as an elaborate hoax. None of his faithful flock turned him in, and they were so out of the way that no one else noticed or cared.

Hope felt lighter as she helped return the church hall to its normal state. She'd missed Faith when she and Joy left, but her return hadn't erased anyone's loss. The girl who returned wasn't the same girl who had run away, and it had been difficult for Hope to pretend that she was. Now Faith was safely and respectably married, and Hope could stop pretending. She had found contentment in her friendship with Grace, and she was eager to get back to it.

Chapter Twenty-Two

It was one of those rare evenings when neither Timothy nor Paul had to work, and both were home for dinner. They were feasting on pork chops courtesy of Samuel and Amos. The boys had been running their organic farm for two years, and their predictions about the demand for locally sourced food lasting beyond the initial supply-chain disruptions of the pandemic had proved correct. Hope could see why. She'd rarely bought pork chops from the grocery store because they were too expensive, but she'd done it a few times if they were on sale. The ones her brothers supplied were worlds better. Grace served them up with her homemade applesauce and early green beans from the boys' greenhouse.

Papa surprised his daughters by asking them about their day. He often asked Timothy and Paul how things were going at work, but this was the first time in years he'd shown an interest in his girls' lives.

"It was just like any other day, Papa," Hope said.

"And what's that like? What do you two do all day?"

Hope shifted and glanced at her younger sister, who was

studying her plate. Since Timothy and Paul started working and Benjamin began his apprenticeship with Papa and Joshua, there hadn't been much for the girls to do. They finished their chores in no time, and then spent hours on end doing handcrafts. They often talked while they sewed, but they also spent entire afternoons in comfortable silence, not needing to force words or topics into the empty spaces. Hope didn't care for handcrafts—Grace was much better at it than she was—but the companionship was worth any amount of sewing.

The boys made a point of eating less noisily.

"We did our chores, all of them, and when we had time, we worked on handcrafts. That's all," Hope said at last. "We might have enough to set up a table at the Farmer's Market next month." Papa had let them do that a couple of times.

"What exactly are your chores?" It had been a while since Papa had to oversee the girls' chore list. At some point he stopped checking in with Hope, who was capable of managing it on her own. She went through it from memory, identifying what she and Grace had done that day and explaining how they rotated certain tasks to keep everything manageable.

"Would you say Grace has learned what she needs to know in order to be a helpmeet?"

"Mostly, Papa." Hope's cheeks flushed. "She can cook and clean and sew and everything, but she doesn't have much experience with babies or children. Just watching them after church on Sunday. And I never let her help with homeschooling. She wasn't far enough ahead of Benjamin." A woman's greatest value was in raising children, and that was the one thing Hope hadn't prepared Grace to do. The weight of her failure threatened to crush her in her seat. "I'm sorry, Papa."

Papa, however, was surprisingly sanguine about the subject. "It's not your fault, Hope. It would have been inappropriate for Grace to teach Benjamin. But we do need to get her some experience taking care of children in the home."

Grace looked first at her sister, then at her father. "How are we going to do that, Papa? Megan doesn't need my help with Christina and Cassandra, and Faith can manage Brady in her sleep." Faith had given birth to a son the previous July, and her position in the church had improved considerably as a result.

Papa took another bite of food and considered as he chewed. "I'll ask Pastor Kinsley if there's anyone at church who could use a little help."

A week later, Grace caught a ride with Papa and Benjamin when they left for work. Kevin and Courtney Lanzara had joined the church two years earlier. God had blessed them with a son, a daughter, and a set of twins in quick succession, and Hope wasn't the only one who had noticed how overwhelmed Courtney was with her brood. Grace was going to help them on weekdays and sit with them at church on Sunday mornings as a kind of surrogate eldest daughter. Mr. Lanzara couldn't afford to pay her, but Papa told him that wasn't a concern. This was about Grace earning experience, not money.

Paul and Timothy left at the same time, and Hope realized with a start that this was the first time she'd ever been alone in her own home. For most of her life the house had been full of people, but even in recent years she'd always had at least Grace there with her. Now there was no one. The lack of accountability gave her a heady, dangerous feeling, and she pushed it down, determined not to fail Papa again.

The breakfast dishes were done, and the chore schedule identified that day's tasks as deep cleaning the bathrooms. That wouldn't take her long at all.

As expected, she finished before lunch. She heated up some leftover soup and ate it in the eerie silence, wondering what to do next. The only sound was the humming of the refrigerator. Normally she and Grace would sit near the wood stove—unlit, this time of year—and stitch, but Hope had no interest in working on her sorry patchwork quilt alone.

She wandered from room to room, then decided to do the next day's cleaning as well. By the time she began preparing supper, she'd scrubbed the entire house spotless.

Hope did it all again the next day. And the next.

Every day that week, Hope cleaned the house from top to bottom, just for something to do. Timothy and Paul were home at different times during the week, neither of them having a regular nine-to-five schedule, but they stayed in their room and out of her way. She'd never had the kind of relationship with them that she had with Grace. Hope cleaned their room, did their laundry, and told them when their meals were ready, but other than that she had nothing to say to them. For their part, they hardly noticed she was there. Grace was home for supper each night, but Papa didn't allow for much chit-chat at the table and cleaning up didn't take very long.

Grace laughed on Saturday when Hope told her the chores were done except for the grocery shopping. "You didn't have to do everything!" Grace chided her sister.

"What else was I supposed to do?"

While stitching, Grace told Hope about her week at the Lanzara home. "Mrs. Lanzara really needs the help. She's younger than you and never had to take care of her siblings growing up. Adam's four, and he's a real handful! Phoebe's two, and really sweet. But she's determined to do everything her brother can do. They knew me from watching them after church on Sunday mornings. Leah and Rachel are so adorable! But when they're awake, they're a lot of work. Mrs. Lanzara was barely keeping everyone fed and in clean clothes, and Adam and Phoebe were into everything!"

Hope was gladdened by her sister's excitement. "What did she want you to do?"

Grace giggled. "I thought she'd want me to start by cleaning the house, and I offered, but what she really wanted was a break from the kids. She didn't put it that way, though. She asked me to take everyone out for a walk so she could clean, and when I came back an hour later the house was still a mess, and she was sound asleep in her bed." Grace laughed at the memory.

Hope smiled wanly. She remembered that kind of exhaustion.

"I hope you let her sleep."

"Of course I did! I shut her bedroom door and kept the kids on the other side of the house. I did a little cleaning, gave everyone lunch, and kept them as quiet as I could for the rest of the afternoon, but I woke Mrs. Lanzara up when it was time to start getting supper ready. I felt bad, but I didn't know what to cook." She giggled again. "She was really embarrassed. But she said she felt better, and she was really happy with what I did. The twins keep her up all night, so she said she'd like to take a nap every morning when I get there, but I should wake her up so she can prepare lunch for Adam and Phoebe. We've started to get into a routine now. I take care of the kids until lunch, we work together to get everyone fed—that's an adventure, because of course the twins wake up and need to be fed at the same time as the toddlers, so Mrs. Lanzara and I are each feeding an infant with one hand while helping one of the toddlers with the other!" Grace paused to take a breath. "After lunch Mrs. Lanzara plays with Adam and Phoebe while I clean, but I help her whenever the twins need attention. Then I take over the kids while she gets supper ready. Next week I'm going to start teaching Adam the alphabet in the morning. He's a little young to homeschool, but I can start him on that, at least."

Hope smirked. "So, what you're telling me is you hate your job."

"I love it! It's so much fun!"

Hope could think of many words to describe what she thought about Grace's activities at the Lanzaras', but 'fun' wasn't one of them. It had been a long time since she'd had to juggle a bunch of little kids while keeping the house, and she didn't miss those days at all. As lonely as she'd been without Grace at home, Hope still preferred solitude to the chaos and noise that seemed to energize her sister. "I'm getting tired just listening to you."

"It's hard, but it's important. And I know God created me to do this." She lowered her voice. "I'm glad Papa got me this opportunity. I wasn't sure if I was ready to have a family of my own, but now I think I can do it. I'm actually excited to think that I might be doing this in my own home with my own kids soon."

Sadness replaced the amusement Hope had felt as her sister recited the events of her week. At least now she could see Grace every morning and every evening, and she got to spend all weekend with her. Once she married, Hope would only see her at church, and then only if Grace married someone local.

"Let's not rush things," Hope said. "It's only been a week, and you're still only seventeen."

They stitched on through the afternoon, with Grace chattering on about the Lanzaras and Hope listening patiently. Mr. Lanzara was nice, too, according to Grace. He worked from home most days and had his "office" down in the basement with the washer and dryer. He hugged his children and was sweet to his wife. He was friendly to Grace when their paths crossed, asking her things about herself, what she liked and whatnot. As long as he wasn't in a Zoom meeting, he didn't mind when she came down into his office to do the laundry.

Grace insisted on cooking supper that night since Hope had done it all week. They continued to chat as Grace bustled around the kitchen and Hope sat in her seat at the table, feeling useless. On Sunday she missed having her sister next to her but had to admit that the girl handled the young Lanzaras with expert care. Hope wondered if Grace learned how to care for children because of her example or in spite of it. She suspected the latter but was contented by the knowledge that, no matter how it happened, Grace was blossoming into a truly virtuous woman.

When Hope was younger she'd yearned for time alone, time to fill however she chose. But now that she had it, she had no idea what to do with it. Timothy spent a lot of his free time on the computer, but that wasn't a lot of use to Hope. Years ago, she'd learned how to type a document and look things up on the internet, but there was nothing Hope needed to type and she couldn't think of anything she wanted to look up. Her duties to her family never allowed her time to develop and explore interests of her own. But Hope didn't have as many duties as she used to, and she didn't want to do handcrafts unless Grace was doing them with her. Hope thought about her first experience with leisure time, when Jennifer took over her household duties, and tried to remember what she did back then. She recalled making decorations and quilts for her future home with Joel. No point in doing that now. Thinking of Joel still brought sadness, and she hoped he was well and happy in Seattle. Joel's family never did find out Beth had left Oregon, and Hope had kept that secret for him. It was the least she could do.

Putting Joel out of her mind, Hope tried to remember what else she did with her spare time back then. She'd read her Bible more. With a pang of guilt, Hope realized she hadn't opened her personal Bible outside of church in months. She prayed the same prayer out of habit every night after family devotions, but she didn't do her personal devotional time the way Papa expected her to. Come to think of it, Papa hadn't asked or reminded Hope and her siblings about their personal devotions in some time. Perhaps with all the boys working, Papa had loosened his expectations.

Hope dismissed the thought as soon as it formed. Papa might have loosened his expectations for his working sons, but she had no excuse. It was yet another way in which she'd failed God. She committed to spending more time reading her Bible, not that it mattered.

Jennifer had encouraged her to read, so Hope wandered into the schoolroom to see what was there. She'd already purged all the old, half-completed workbooks and finished assignments. A coffee can of broken crayons sat next to a stack of coloring books and blank paper. Cassandra and Christina used them when they came over to visit sometimes, but they were the only ones who used this room anymore. The *Elsie Dinsmore* books lined one shelf, with the *Little House on the Prairie* series on the shelf beneath. Their few Jane Austens sat next to the *Little House* books, along with the McGuffey Readers, and that was the extent of their book collection.

Except for the McGuffeys, Hope had read everything several times already. *Elsie* and *Little House* were for children and held no interest for her. The Jane Austens were better, but how many times was she supposed to read the same three books? Idly she picked up the first McGuffey Reader. Mama had used it to teach her how to read, and Hope used it to teach her younger siblings. She flipped through the worn pages of the slim volume, the trite and antiquated stories dredging up memories of different people who wore the familiar faces of her family. They'd all been different back then. She put the book back on the shelf and turned away.

The walls of her house, once so protective, were closing in on Hope. The faded needlepoint hanging above her bed describing the deeds of a virtuous woman mocked her. Sure, she could garden and do handcrafts, but the passage was mostly about how a woman cared for her husband and children. Hope would never be a wife or mother, so how could she be virtuous? She had nothing to do, nothing to see, no one to care for. Hope had to get out, even though there were no errands to run.

Hope got behind the wheel of the much smaller and easier to drive minivan and guided it to Faith's house. It felt wrong to go for a visit in the middle of a weekday, but Hope convinced herself she wasn't being a gadabout. Faith was her sister, and they hadn't had a chance to talk in a while. Jimmy wasn't an elder and didn't like to converse with the men after church, so Jimmy and Faith usually left right after the service ended. Feeling like she was getting away with something, Hope parked in the unpaved driveway and walked up to the front door.

"What are you doing here?" Faith's reception heightened Hope's feeling of wrongdoing. The younger woman stood a few feet from the screen door, her face in shadow.

"I thought I'd visit." Hope's voice was small, the voice of an intruder caught sneaking around.

"Why?"

Hope's cheeks flushed crimson. She'd come because she was bored. It had never occurred to her that she should visit her sister before this. "I miss you." The moment she said it she realized it was true. She and Faith were sort of close once. Not as close as she was with Grace, but they'd gotten along well and sometimes enjoyed each other's company. But that was before Faith ran away. Hope wanted to be close again. She tried not to think about her selfish reasons why.

Faith didn't move. "I miss you, too, Hope, but now's not a good time."

"How come?"

"It just isn't."

From deeper inside the house, Brady began to wail.

Faith turned to look, and the light from the living room lamp illuminated her features.

Hope gasped. "What happened to your face?"

Faith's left cheek bore an ugly purple bruise. Her hand flew up to cover it and she laughed weakly. "Oh, this. I fell. You know how clumsy I am."

"Faith, you've never been clumsy. Did this happen today? You didn't have it at church."

Brady continued to cry.

Faith stood, torn between her sister and her son. Finally, she stepped all the way back. "Come in if you want, but just for a little bit."

Hope followed her sister into the house. Jimmy had been able to scrape together the down payment for a property charitably listed as a 'handyman special.' Jimmy himself lacked the skills to bring the house up to livable standards, but Papa and Joshua did a lot of work on it as a wedding present. It had been in such poor repair that 'livable' was all they could accomplish by the time the couple was ready to move in. Hope could see that Jimmy had done nothing since then to improve it. Faith had tried to mask the peeling wallpaper with quilted wall hangings, but masking could only accomplish so much. The ragged carpet was stained in some places and completely worn through in others, and heavy grey duct tape sealed the many large cracks in the windows.

Brady was in a large plastic contraption with brightly colored buttons, levers, and baubles surrounding a fabric baby seat. Faith picked him up and cuddled him, and his wailing ceased. "He's such a good baby. He loves this play station and falls asleep in it all the time, but he hates waking up and finding I'm not there."

Hope wouldn't be distracted from her sister's cheek. "Faith, please tell me what happened."

Faith placed the uninjured side of her face against Brady's soft skin and refused to meet her sister's eye. "I told you. I fell. It was a few days ago. I wear a little make-up over it at church because there's no point in worrying anyone."

"I see." Hope's words were low and controlled, just like Papa's when he was about to explode. "Do you fall often?"

"Sometimes." Faith still wouldn't look at her sister. "Like I said, I'm clumsy."

"Does Papa know?"

The false friendliness disappeared from Faith's face. "There's nothing for Papa to know. I fell. It happens. Now I think it's time for you to leave."

Hope clutched her hands in front of her. "I don't want to fight, Faith. If you don't want me to tell Papa, I won't. Just please don't lie to me, okay?"

Faith's features softened, and she sank onto the sagging couch, still cradling a contented Brady in her arms. "Jimmy is under a lot of pressure at work. His boss keeps giving him lousy assignments an hour or more away and dangles the promise of a promotion in front of him whenever he complains. But the promotion never happens, and Jimmy gets frustrated."

"He hits you?"

Faith's gaze slid away from her sister. "It's not like that. I'm not sensitive enough to his moods and I provoke him. He doesn't want to hit me, but I make him do it. He's always really sorry afterwards."

Hope had heard this before from a few other women in the church. It was never the man's fault. And she'd always believed they'd provoked their husbands to violence, just like she'd provoked Papa the night she'd tried to reject his authority and marry Joel without his permission. Even Morgan Reed, Faith's mother-in-law, had convinced Hope and the other women that Al was only 'correcting' her when necessary. Morgan did everything she was asked, hardly ever spoke, and never disagreed with anyone, but Hope had believed she deserved to be corrected with disturbing regularity.

But this was Faith, and Hope knew Faith. She'd been raised to be submissive and attentive to her husband's needs, and Hope doubted she'd done anything to deserve that mark on her face. She said as much to her sister.

Sadness and regret radiated off Faith. "No, I've done plenty. I made some bad choices, and this is the consequence. This is what I deserve. It's God's plan. Maybe if I can help Jimmy be a better Christian, I'll atone for my sins and God won't punish me anymore." She smiled at Brady. "Anyway, it's not all bad. God has blessed me in some ways. Brady's wonderful. And don't tell anyone yet, but I'm expecting another one."

Hope forced a smile onto her face. "I'm happy for you."

"I was hoping for a girl, but Jimmy wants another son. He's probably right. A brother for Brady would be better. So now I'm hoping it's a boy."

Hope didn't want to be there anymore. She couldn't bear to see her sister like this. But Faith was just warming up to the idea of this visit, so Hope made herself stay and pretend everything was okay. She had a lot of experience with that.

The conversation moved to other topics while Faith nursed Brady and rocked him back to sleep. She never offered to let Hope hold him, and Hope didn't ask. They talked about Grace's new position and Faith began speculating about who might make a good husband for her. Hope didn't want to talk about that either, but Faith enjoyed the game. For all that Faith had initially tried to send Hope away, she seemed delighted to have someone to talk to. But Hope wished she'd stayed home and cleaned the house again. The bruise on her sister's cheek demanded to be seen no matter how hard Hope tried to ignore it. Faith's dress was ill-fitting and second-hand, and Hope could see the places where her sister had repaired it with patches. The house, though spotless, was dingy and run-down. Hope couldn't imagine living in such a dismal place.

"Do you sew anymore?" Hope asked.

"We can't afford a sewing machine, and fabric's expensive anyway. We make do with what we can find at the thrift store, and I hand-sew quilts out of clothes when they get too worn out."

Hope couldn't take it anymore. She stood to leave. "Well, I think I need to get back. I still have some chores to do before starting supper."

Faith stood, too.

Brady was back in his play station, happily chewing on a soft rubber key that dangled before him.

"I'm so glad you came, Hope. I really have missed you. You will come again?"

"Sure," Hope said without enthusiasm. "Maybe I'll come on a Saturday so Grace can come, too."

A shadow crossed Faith's features. "Call first. Sometimes Jimmy works on Saturdays, but not always. He doesn't like having visitors."

Hope nodded. She had no desire to visit when her brother-in-law was present. "I'll do that."

They embraced and Hope walked back to the minivan, feeling like she was abandoning Faith.

~

Hope returned to the McGuffeys and picked up the fifth-level reader. Rather than manufactured morality tales, this one contained excerpts of historical essays and novels. Surely, she could find something worth checking out of the library.

An hour later she had a list of several titles.

She'd never been a fast reader, but she'd also never had so much time to lose herself in a book before. The first thing she read was Louisa May Alcott's *An Old Fashioned Girl*, one of Jennifer's favorites and one Hope had read before. The last time she'd been struck by the independence the young ladies of the story enjoyed. This time she was astonished to discover that individuals with distinct and obvious flaws could still be good and honorable people, and as someone changed over time, their relationships changed as well. A single mistake, or even a series of them, didn't necessarily define a person for the rest of their life.

Hope shared her insights with Grace on Saturday as they sat and stitched, her words coming in a torrent like the one Grace had unleashed the week before when she talked about her work at the Lanzaras. Grace listened, but Hope could tell the younger girl had no idea why she was so enthused by a story about pretend people someone made up over a hundred and fifty years ago.

For Hope, these people had become as real as anyone she knew. She was fascinated by how the characters changed and grew over time and how others responded to those changes. Hope wondered what it would be like to remake herself in such a profound way. But what would she remake herself into? What did she want? It was a question she hadn't dared ask herself since Papa ended her courtship, and merely entertaining the question felt subversive.

And subversive felt good.

~

Michael walked up the front porch steps, his work boots making footprints in the yellow pollen that coated everything this time of year. The smell of spring was heavy in the air, the trees once again displaying their greenery, annuals and weeds shooting up from the ground. The strip of grassless soil that separated the porch from the lawn had more of the latter than the former. Michael was used to seeing it filled with fragrant blooms, but Libby must have stopped tending it. It had been a while since he last visited. Years, actually.

His sister opened the door. "What do you want?" Her frostiness toward him and his family had not thawed.

"Can I come in?"

Libby hesitated, then stepped back so he could open the screen door. "Be quiet. Nick's resting."

Michael closed the door carefully behind him and followed Libby into the kitchen. "How's he doing?"

Libby shrugged as she took a seat at the table. "He has his good days, and he has his bad days. I care for him the best I can and leave the rest up to God."

"Any idea what's wrong with him?"

"We don't waste money on shyster doctors like *some* people. God's will is God's will, and if it's His will to bring Nick home to his reward, then we'll accept that."

Annoyance flared in Michael, but he worked to keep his voice calm. "I never gave Joshua my approval to bring Megan to the hospital, and God will hold him accountable for his actions. He's already cursed Megan with barrenness because of their sin. Anyway, that was years ago. You've avoided my house for the last four Christmases, even though I know you didn't go to Jake's this year, and you've barely spoken to any of us at church. Isn't it time to let this go?"

"Nick wasn't feeling up to much this year, not even going to your house. And it's not just that Joshua took Megan to the hospital. He didn't even tell me she was sick. I could have helped if I'd known, but he never gave me that chance."

"He should have, Libby. I agree. But it's done now, and there's no use dwelling on it."

Libby slumped in her seat. "What are you doing here, Michael? What do you want?"

Michael got right to it. "I want you to teach Hope how to be a midwife."

Libby laughed. "Again? After all this time? Why?"

"She needs something to keep her busy." Something besides all those books she'd been getting from the library. "Most of the children are gone. Timothy and Paul are both working full-time and will probably move out on their own in two or three years. Benjamin's apprenticing with Joshua full time, and Grace will be courting soon. She spends most of her time working for the Lanzaras, getting more experience with babies. Hope's alone most of the time, and she needs something to keep her occupied."

"What about a courtship of her own?"

Michael shook his head. "It's too late for that. She's almost thirty—"

"She's thirty-one."

"Really?" He'd never been good at remembering his children's ages or birthdays. "There you go then. Nobody wants a woman that old. She only has a few childbearing years left to her. And besides, Benjamin at least will be home for a few more years, and I need someone to keep house and cook meals. Even after Benjamin leaves, I'll still need Hope for that."

Libby studied her brother. "Would you like a cup of coffee?"

"Coffee would be good."

Libby leaned back in her chair and smiled, raising one thin arm to gesture toward the counter. "Coffee pot's over there. It works just like yours. Make enough for me, too, if you would."

Michael gaped at his sister.

"Don't you know how to make a pot of coffee?" she asked.

"I've never had to."

Libby sat up straight. "Then I suggest you learn. Learn to make coffee. Learn to cook. Learn to clean. Learn to take care of yourself! Hope isn't your wife, and you have no right to keep her from having a family of her own."

Michael sat in stunned disbelief as his sister's words hung in the air between them. She didn't let go of his gaze until Jared wandered into the kitchen carrying a piece of paper with a crudely drawn picture on it. "Look, Mom, look what I made for you!" He grinned as he pointed to different elements of the drawing. "That's me, and that's you, and that's Dad, and that's our house! I put Dad's bed outside so he can be in the sun. Do you like it?"

Libby gushed over her son's drawing, the two of them acting for all the world like a young mother with her six-year-old child. But Michael remembered Jared being a young boy at his wedding—the first one—so he was at least a few years older than Hope. His graying hair and expanding belly made him look older than his years. Except for his eyes. They were wrinkled at the corners, but they were still the eyes of a six-year-old, full of the wonder of childhood and delighted by the world around him.

"Can I go show Dad?" Jared asked his mother.

"Peek in his room. If his eyes are open and he's sitting up, you can go in and show him. But if he's lying down, let him rest. And make sure you're very quiet when you peek."

"I will, Mom." Jared crept out of the kitchen on tiptoes,

trying to be silent. Libby's smile as she watched him go was fond but sad.

"He's going to be lost without us," she murmured.

Michael tensed. "That's not a worry yet, is it?"

Libby's features had softened when speaking to her son, but they hardened back into the rigid exterior she was so well known for. "I'm seventy-one years old, Michael. Nick doesn't have much longer in this world, and I probably won't have a whole lot of time after that. At least not where I'll be well enough to take care of Jared." Her eyes moved around the kitchen. They'd lived in this house ever since following Pastor Kinsley here to plant Church of the Covenant. "Nick wants to die here, and I'll honor his wishes. But once he's gone, Jared and I are going to live with Matt."

"Matt? Isn't he in North Dakota?"

"South Dakota. Custer. He's got a good job with the National Park Service."

"Why not Jake? He's closer, and you've been to see him more. When's the last time Jared even saw Matt?"

"He sees him on Zoom two or three times a month. Jake, too. But Jake doesn't have the space, and Marilyn—" she made a face and spat her daughter-in-law's name. "Marilyn doesn't have much patience when it comes to Jared. Matt and Kelly will take much better care of him. Kelly has a cousin with Down's Syndrome, so she understands."

Michael pondered this. He hadn't realized his sister was past seventy—his failure to remember dates and ages extended well beyond his own children—but now he saw that not a strand of brown remained in her hair. It was thinner than it used to be, pulled into a small, white bun. Wrinkled skin hung from her face and neck, and she looked tired.

Then again, there was no pepper left in his hair, either. It was iron grey. His face had always been lined, but now many of those lines came from age and not his years working outside in the sun and wind. He was fifty-six—he knew his own age, at least—and other than the work he'd done on Jimmy's house he hadn't wielded a hammer outside his workshop in over three years. He got winded easily, sometimes a little lightheaded, and had to rest after only a few minutes of exertion. Four years earlier he'd turned management of his company over to Joshua. Now Michael spent most of his working hours ensuring their contracts conformed to an ever-growing number of government regulations and thinking about retirement. He'd believed his thoughts about retirement had more to do with wanting to quit the bureaucratic quagmire the construction industry had become than with accommodating his aging body, but the truth was he and Libby were both getting older. More than that, they were getting old.

"I'll be sorry to see you go," Michael said.

"Me too. But I won't be around forever, and I need to make sure Jared's taken care of after I'm gone. And you need to do the same. That's why you need to find a husband for Hope."

The conversation's sudden change in direction confused Michael. "What?"

"Let's say things go as you said. Timothy and Paul move out, Grace marries, and Hope stays to take care of you and Benjamin. And then Benjamin moves out. Then it's just you and Hope. She takes care of your house and your meals until you die. Then who takes care of her?"

Michael hadn't thought about his own death, let alone beyond it. "One of her brothers..."

"Maybe. But maybe not. Hope's not much older than Joshua or John, and they're probably the only ones who will have the means to take her in. Maybe Samuel, too, but she's not much older than him, either. Their wives won't appreciate another woman their age hanging around the house. She'll have no place there."

"The younger ones," Michael began, but Libby cut him off.

"Amos? That boy's got problems. He's probably never getting married, and anyway, he's living with Samuel and Jodi. Another reason why they couldn't take Hope in. Timothy? He's a wage slave retail worker. He'll barely be able to support his own family once he has one. Same with Paul. Grease monkeys don't earn much, either."

Michael winced at the harsh description of his two younger sons, but he couldn't argue. Despite his best efforts, neither of them had chosen a career path that gave them freedom and independence.

"That leaves Benjamin," Libby continued. "Do you really want to trust Hope's future to him? He's a good boy, but is it fair to saddle him with the care of his sister for the rest of his life?"

This conversation was giving Michael a headache. "It's a difficult situation," he agreed. "I trust God will provide."

Libby threw up her hands. "You're her authority, Michael! God provides for her through you. So, provide for her! Find her a husband who will take care of her. Maybe someone new to the faith. Maybe a widower. Thirty-one's not that old. She can still have children. Maybe even a proper quiverfull if you don't wait too long."

"What about me?" Michael hated the note of petulance he heard in his own voice. "Who's going to care for me as I get older?" His heart ached with loss. Sixteen years of living without her hadn't healed the gaping hole Lucy's death had torn in his soul.

Libby smiled, and her face softened again as it had when she was talking to Jared. "It's not that difficult to make your own coffee. Or cook your own meals. And there might be a place for you in one of your children's homes. A father-in-law is a lot less threatening to a woman's sense of place than a sister-in-law."

"I'll think about it," Michael promised, just to end the conversation. "But I can't handle two daughters courting at once. Grace first."

"Don't wait too long on Hope. Talk to Pastor Kinsley about it. Maybe he'll have some ideas."

Michael wasn't looking forward to that conversation. Pastor Kinsley and the elders seemed to enjoy reminding Michael that his place was now beneath them. But as long as he approached them with humility, they did try to ensure his home and life were ordered in a way that was pleasing to God.

"And you'll teach Hope about midwifery?"

Libby shook her head. "I don't do that anymore, Michael. I can't leave Nick. I trained Shannon Murphy to take my place a few years ago, and she's doing just fine. Her six are grown, and she can certainly use the money with the way that husband of hers squanders his paycheck. She's the one who caught Brady."

Michael smiled in spite of himself, thinking of his only local grandson. John had three boys and a girl down in Tennessee, but he never saw them. "I didn't know that was Shannon. I assumed it was you."

"It's been Shannon alone for a little over a year now. Forget about Hope being a midwife. If that's what God had intended, she would have been one long ago. He has other plans for her. Find her a husband. That's what she really needs. Now, not later. Not after Grace is married or Benjamin is grown. Those two have time. Keep Grace with you for a few more years. Five more years. It won't be hard for her to find a husband at twenty-two, and Benjamin will be able to look after himself by then." Her smile widened into a grin. "And so will you."

Michael rose from the table. "I'll think about it," he

repeated, knowing the words were a lie. Grace was turning out beautifully, and he wanted at least one daughter to fulfill her calling as helpmeet without drama or scandal. The sooner the better. He'd think about having a conversation with Pastor Kinsley and the elders about Hope after Grace was settled. Maybe. "And thanks for the coffee," he added dryly.

Libby laughed. "The pot was right there on the counter. You could have made some any time you wanted."

Chapter Twenty-Three

ope paused at the top of the staircase. The house was
usually silent when she rose to prepare breakfast, the
sun just beginning to peek between the trees populating their
property, but this morning she heard something. A muffled sob.
Coming from Grace's room.

Hope knocked softly. "Grace? Are you okay?"

"I'm fine," said a shaky voice. "Go away."

Hope opened the door and stepped into the room. The
window was a pale rectangle in the wall, the early morning sun
filtering through the curtains and bathing the room in rosy
shadows. The night had cooled the room only slightly, the late
summer air a hot soup. Despite the heat, Grace was curled up
under her covers, shaking with the effort of silencing her sobs.
Hope sat on the edge of her bed and put a hand on her sister's
shoulder.

"Grace, what's wrong? Please tell me."

Grace pulled the covers over her head, knocking Hope's
hand away. "I can't. I can't go to work today. Tell Papa I'm sick.
Ask him to call the Lanzaras for me."

"What is it, a headache?"

"Just tell him, please? And leave me alone."

Grace had never shut Hope out like this before, and black dread filled her. But Papa and her brothers were still home, and they expected their breakfast to be on the table when they came down.

"I'll tell him," Hope promised. "And then I'll come back and check on you when everyone's gone."

The lump on the bed didn't answer, and Hope left, closing the door gently behind her.

Papa wasn't pleased when Hope relayed Grace's message and demanded to know exactly what was wrong with her.

"I don't know, Papa. She seems really bad off. It looks like she might be coming down with the flu." Hope didn't like lying to her father, but the need to protect her sister, even if she didn't know why, was greater than her discomfort with lying. How far she'd fallen from the immediate, unquestioned obedience of her youth.

"It's the first week of September. That's too early for flu."

"It's not usual, but it does happen."

Papa shoveled a mouthful of scrambled eggs into his mouth, chewed, and swallowed. "When Grace has her own family, she won't be able to call in sick. I think she needs to learn how to work through this. Go tell your sister to get up and get ready. We're leaving in thirty minutes."

Hope began shuffling out of the kitchen but paused in the doorway. "When Grace has her own family, she'll do what she has to do. But I'd hate to see her give the flu to the Lanzara children. It could be dangerous to the babies."

Papa glared at his plate. Hope could see the struggle on his face. He hated it when he had to change a pronouncement once he'd made it. "Tell Grace to stay in bed. I'll call Kevin and tell him she won't be over today."

Hope shuffled back to the stove, hiding her relieved sigh.

An hour later, Hope and Grace were alone in the house. When Hope went up to check on her, Grace was still huddled under her covers. The room was brighter than before, the cotton curtains unable to do more than mute the morning sun, which was now above the treetops and shining directly on the house. The heat was rising to an almost unbearable level.

"I saved some biscuits and eggs for you."

"I'm not hungry."

Hope crossed to her sister's bed and hesitated, not knowing if she was welcome to sit or if she should give Grace some space. She compromised by kneeling on the hardwood floor and resting her arms on the mattress.

"I told Papa you have the flu. He called Mr. Lanzara and told him you're staying home today."

Grace pulled the covers up to her chin. "Good. That'll give me a few days to figure this out." Her eyes began to leak again.

Hope couldn't imagine how her sister wasn't roasting under those covers. Her body was curled up beneath her quilt, wrapped in a tight ball as she wept. "Figure what out? Grace, please tell me what's going on."

Grace's sobs increased and she scrunched herself up tighter.

Hope leaned forward and pulled the seventeen-year-old's trembling body into a gentle hug. "Whatever it is, I'm sure it's not that bad," Hope murmured into Grace's tangled hair. "Tell me, and I'll help you."

"You can't help me," Grace choked. "I'm pregnant."

Hope's breath exited her lungs in a whoosh, and she wasn't sure if she was going to faint or throw up. She let go of Grace and slid back to the floor in case either happened. Grace's sobs resumed but Hope didn't hear them; the ringing in her ears deafened her to all other sounds. The humid air was making her lightheaded.

Pregnant?

After a while Hope managed to get a hold of herself and turned back to her sister. Grace had rolled over to face the wall, her body curled, and her head covered with the quilt again.

"I don't understand, Grace. How did this happen? Who's the father?"

Grace mumbled something. Hope couldn't make out the words, so she asked again.

This time Grace's muffled voice came through the quilt. "Mr. Lanzara."

Hope felt as though she'd been hit again. "You committed adultery with a married man?"

The curled figure on the bed hunched even further. "I guess so."

Hope tried to make sense of this revelation but couldn't. This wasn't the Grace she knew. Her own eyes stung with shocked tears and her heart beat rapidly in her chest. She willed herself to breathe in, then out again, until she'd regained some semblance of composure. She climbed off the floor and crawled under the covers of her sister's narrow bed, not caring about the oppressive heat.

Grace tensed, then scooted closer to the wall.

Hope didn't know if she was making room or trying to get away. She put a hand on her sister's sweat-soaked shoulder. "I love you, Grace. This doesn't change that. Nothing can change that."

Grace didn't respond.

Hope stayed where she was, murmuring affirmations.

Finally, the younger girl wiggled and shifted until she was facing her sister. Her face was blotchy and swollen, her eyes filled with tears. Tendrils of escaped hair were plastered to her forehead and cheeks. "My life is ruined." She shuddered and gave in to her anguished cries.

Hope wrapped her arms around the girl and held her close, but she didn't try to contradict her sister's words. She couldn't.

By the time Grace had cried herself out and was able to go downstairs, the eggs and biscuits were cold and unappealing. Hope brewed half a pot of coffee for herself and began to boil water for Grace's tea.

"Does he know?" There was no need to specify who 'he' was.

Grace shook her head and looked down at her lap in shame. "I wasn't sure myself until last night. I was late by a few days, so I stole a pregnancy test from Mrs. Lanzara. She has a whole bunch of them under the sink in her bathroom. I used it last night after everyone went to bed, and that's how I found out."

"Where is the test now?" If Grace left it in the trashcan in the bathroom, Hope would retrieve it and dispose of it some other way. She didn't want to imagine what would happen if Papa or one of her brothers found it.

Grace gave her a wan smile. "I'm not stupid, Hope. I wrapped it in duct tape until you couldn't tell what it was anymore, then I buried it in the woods."

Hope smiled back. No, Grace wasn't stupid. She just managed to get herself pregnant with a married man's baby. Her smile faded.

"How did it start?"

"How did what start?"

"You know. The affair."

The teakettle whistled, and Hope got up to remove it from the burner. As she poured the boiling water over a tea bag, she sneaked a look back. Grace was resting her elbows on the table, her face buried in her hands.

Bringing the hot mug of tea to the table along with a spoon and the sugar bowl, Hope sat back down and waited.

Eventually Grace raised her head. Her unbound hair hung limply down her back. "Ever since the pandemic started, Mr. Lanzara has been working from home most of the time. I told you about his little office nook in the basement near the washer and dryer? I do laundry in the afternoon as part of my cleaning, when Mrs. Lanzara's with the kids. There's always laundry to do. He schedules all his Zoom meetings in the morning when it's quieter." Grace paused to spoon some sugar into her tea. "I tried to be quiet and not interrupt him, but he always wanted to talk when I was down there."

"What did you talk about?"

Grace blushed. "Me, mostly. He wanted to know all about me. What my family was like, how I liked church, what I did in my spare time, things like that. He was nice. After a month or so he asked me if I had a boyfriend. I told him Papa was thinking about finding someone to court me, but it hadn't happened yet. He told me how beautiful I was, and that any man would be lucky to wake up next to me every morning." She looked at Hope and winced, and Hope tried to moderate her shocked expression. "That's what he said," she said defensively.

Hope closed her gaping mouth. "Sorry. Go on."

Grace blew on her tea and took a tiny sip. "I didn't like it when he said things like that, so I didn't say anything back and finished the laundry as quickly as I could. Before I went back upstairs, he asked if he'd made me uncomfortable, and I said yes."

"What did he say to that?"

"He said I shouldn't be uncomfortable, because he was only speaking the truth in love."

The coffee pot had stopped brewing, and Hope rose to

pour herself a cup. She was glad to note that her hand had stopped shaking.

Grace continued. "The next time I went down to the laundry room, he got up from his desk and stood right in front of me. Like, really close. He told me again how beautiful I was, and then he began touching me." Her voice grew soft, and Hope had to lean forward to hear her. "First my face, then my neck, then my..." she glanced down at her chest.

Hope felt the color rising in her own cheeks. "What did you do?"

"I told him I didn't think he should do that, but he kept doing it anyway. He told me Papa had sent me to him so he could prepare me for courtship and teach me how to be with a husband, and that's all he was doing."

Hope closed her eyes. "And you believed him?"

Grace began to cry again. "Why wouldn't I? He's the man of the house and my employer. When I'm there I'm under his authority. That's what Papa told me!"

Hope opened her eyes and took her sister's trembling hand. "I'm sorry. You're right."

A few minutes passed before Grace calmed down enough to continue her story. "He only touched me and kissed me that day, but the next day he was waiting for me in the laundry room. As soon as I walked in, he grabbed me and shut the door. He pulled a dirty sheet from the basket and put it on the floor. Then he pulled me down." Tears filled her eyes again. "He was touching me all over and kissing me and telling me if I screamed and brought Mrs. Lanzara down, he'd say I seduced him. I didn't know what to do, so I didn't do anything. I just lay there as he undressed me and got on top of me." She covered her face with her hands. "I let him have what I was supposed to save for my husband."

Hope got up and knelt beside her sister's chair, hugging her. "You didn't let him have it, Grace. He took it."

"I didn't stop him, Hope. I didn't even try!"

Something broke inside Hope, and she was flooded with years—*decades*—of suppressed frustration and rage. From earliest girlhood she and her sisters had been taught to obey their husbands and fathers and brothers and pastors and any other man in a position of authority over them. They'd been taught that instant and joyful obedience was the only godly response to any command or request, and to reject a man's authority was to reject God's authority. This was God's will, and it was how godly men protected them from the world. Worldly men raped and abused their women; godly men didn't do such things.

"You didn't know you could!" Hope fumed, frightening both of them. She lowered her voice. "You did what you were told, just like you were taught." Hope wanted to say more, but her angry sobs swallowed her words. Her kind and trusting sister had been violated not only by Mr. Lanzara, but by the very faith in which they'd been raised. She'd never thought about it in those terms before, hadn't allowed herself to doubt or even think critically about her faith since that horrible night when Papa had beaten her to unconsciousness. She'd believed the questions Joel had encouraged her to explore had caused her suffering, but now she realized that Joel had come very close to saving her. His ideas weren't poison; Papa's were.

Papa's beliefs had caused Mama to die in childbirth. Papa's beliefs had separated Hope from a man who loved her and wanted to partner with her and build a life together with her. Papa's beliefs had driven Joy into exile. Papa's beliefs dictated that Faith live her life with a man who beat her. Papa's beliefs had caused sweet, innocent Grace to be raped and believe she was to blame for it.

Hope got herself under control. The rage helped. She was through with Papa's beliefs. If his God was real then He was an evil child abuser, and Hope wanted nothing to do with Him, His church, or His people.

Grace continued to sob into a tissue Hope had given her. "It's been going on since the beginning of August. He waits for me in the laundry room nearly every day. I didn't want to keep going over there, but I'd have to give Papa a reason, and I couldn't think of one he'd accept." She blew her nose. "He'd never believe the truth. Mr. Lanzara acts like nothing's going on in front of Mrs. Lanzara, and she's so busy with the kids she doesn't notice how I spend my afternoons, as long as the laundry's done and parts of the house are cleaner. And he told me if I told anyone, he'd name me a harlot and say I led him astray." She shook her head, berating herself. "And I believed him."

"On that one you were right to. He would have blamed you, and the church would have agreed with him. It's always the woman's fault." Hadn't Hope jumped to that same conclusion?

Grace took another sip of her tea, trying to compose herself, but fresh tears slid down her cheeks. "But now everyone's going to know. I can't hide a baby, and people are going to ask where it came from." She got up and put her mug in the sink. "My life is over." It wasn't a lament. It was a fact.

Hope dumped the rest of her coffee down the drain and began washing out the coffee pot. "We'll figure this out, Grace. You're not alone. We will find a way to get through this."

But she had absolutely no idea how they were going to do that.

～

Hope helped Grace fake the flu that evening when Papa came home from work. It wasn't difficult. She told him Grace was still in bed sick, served everyone chicken soup for supper, and watched Papa retreat to his workshop until it was time for family devotions. Her brothers didn't want to get sick, and they kept their distance even from Hope, who had presumably been exposed to the illness all day. She even thought to fake a few coughs of her own.

They continued the ruse the next day, and then it was Saturday. After Hope returned from the week's grocery shopping, she spent the day in Grace's room. As usual, Papa spent the day in his workshop. Timothy had to work, but Paul and Benjamin kept themselves occupied away from their sisters. Grace was despondent and couldn't be diverted from the scandal her pregnancy would cause. All the family's previous scandals—Papa's divorce, Megan's sterility, Joy and Faith running away—all that paled in comparison to this. Grace was convinced she'd be kicked out of the house and shunned by everyone she knew, and she felt horrible about the shame this would bring not only to Papa's household, but to Joshua's and Faith's as well. Samuel and Amos would probably suffer too, somehow. She'd be a liability for John's ministry.

Hope couldn't honestly contradict any of it.

Telling Grace it wasn't her fault brought the girl no comfort. They both knew that didn't matter in the eyes of the church. The only thing Hope could think of that might spare her sister was an abortion, but Grace responded to the idea with such a look of horror that Hope dropped it. She would have been horrified herself not long ago. But Hope had changed, and now she was willing to consider possibilities that had been unthinkable when she'd accepted Papa's beliefs as truth. But Grace was not willing to consider those possibilities.

Hope imagined them running away together. She'd get a

job and support Grace and the baby. But what would she do? What *could* she do? She'd never worked a day in her life. She had no education, not even a high school diploma. She didn't know where to look for a job, let alone how to apply for one. Or how to find an apartment. Or open a bank account. Or manage household finances. All she'd ever been taught was how to keep within a grocery budget. Her tears of frustration matched Grace's tears of despair.

Maybe Faith could help. She'd once gotten a job. She and Joy had found and kept their own apartment. She must still know how to do these things. There were too many ears at church for Hope to talk to her there, and Faith and Jimmy never stayed after the service anyway, so Hope resolved to visit on Monday and ask her.

Grace listened dispassionately to Hope's plan. "You never give up, Hope. That's something I've always admired about you." She didn't seem optimistic, but it was all Hope had. She spent the rest of the day thinking of questions to ask Faith on Monday.

But first they had to get through Sunday. Papa thought Grace must be over her illness by now and should go to church with the family. Hope convinced him that Grace was too weak, and she might still be contagious. She fabricated a fever of 102 degrees that had plagued Grace the day before, generated a few phlegm-filled coughs into her own sleeve, and Papa relented.

"But she is going to work tomorrow," he said. "You tell her that. Kevin Lanzara was very upset that Grace wasn't there Thursday and Friday. His wife depends on her."

Hope struggled to keep her face impassive. She just bet Kevin Lanzara missed Grace. Hope didn't mention that part when she conveyed Papa's words.

"I can't go back there, Hope! I can't!" Grace's voice was shrill with fear.

"You won't have to," Hope promised. "I'll think of something." She almost prayed for an idea before she remembered that she had no God.

At church Hope couldn't stop glaring at the Lanzaras, but they were too busy keeping their children quiet to notice. During Pastor Kinsley's sermon, she tried to think of something she could say that would persuade Papa to let Grace quit.

She came up with nothing.

Ignoring the chattering women in the kitchen after the service, Hope mentally counted the money she and Grace had earned from selling their crafts at the farmer's market. She thought they had about two hundred dollars saved up. Was that enough to get an apartment? Probably not. Maybe a hotel room for a couple of days. There was one she'd seen on the highway with an electronic sign that advertised a rate of $79.99 per night. But what would they do once the money was spent?

She was still pondering such questions when Courtney Lanzara planted herself in front of Hope and pulled her attention back to the present.

"How's Grace feeling?"

"She's in rough shape," Hope said through gritted teeth.

Courtney's face showed genuine concern. "I'm so sorry to hear that. She's such a good girl and a hard worker. My children adore her, and I don't know what I'd do without her."

"I imagine you'd have to do your own laundry."

"What? Well, of course I'd do my own laundry," Courtney said, confused.

Hope couldn't bear this conversation another moment. "Excuse me. I have to talk to Carolyn." She pushed past the bewildered woman and headed toward the other side of the kitchen.

"Tell Grace I hope she feels better!"

Hope ignored her and joined Carolyn. The two friends

hadn't had a real conversation in quite some time, as Carolyn was always immersed in conversations about pregnancy, child-rearing, homeschooling, and all those other things that dominated the lives of the church women but didn't apply to Hope. When Hope reached Carolyn she was discussing morning sickness remedies with Robin McAndrew. Their rounded bellies almost brushed each other as they talked. This was Robin's first and Carolyn's seventh.

"Hi Hope. What's up?" Carolyn's smile, usually infectious, couldn't penetrate Hope's foul mood.

"Just thought I'd come over and say hi."

"Hope and I have known each other since we were little," Carolyn explained to Robin, who had just married into the church a few months ago. The younger woman, who couldn't be much older than Grace, nodded in greeting.

Hope tuned out as Carolyn expounded on the efficacy of fresh ginger root and the blessings of pregnancy, childbirth, and child-rearing. Her friend was the model of a godly woman, fulfilled by producing arrows for her husband's quiver. Everything about her suggested she was happy with her life, and Hope wondered what it would have been like if Carolyn's parents had never come to Church of the Covenant. Would Carolyn have been better off if she'd been raised in the world, without all those siblings her mother never wanted and with all the options worldly girls had? Hope didn't know. Carolyn was so well-suited for this life.

But so was Grace. And it wasn't working out for her nearly as well as it was for Carolyn.

Hope was grateful when Papa signaled it was time to leave. She still had no answers, but she hated being away from her sister for so long.

Papa didn't bother going into the house when they arrived home, choosing instead to spend the rest of the day in his workshop. Timothy, Paul, and Benjamin began gathering wood for the woodpile. Late summers often meant colder winters, and Papa wanted plenty of fuel for the wood stove before winter arrived.

The house was quiet when Hope entered. She was supposed to get lunch ready, but she wanted to check on Grace first.

At the top of the stairs, Hope noticed Grace's bedroom door was open, and one of the bathroom doors was closed. She didn't hear any water running, so she waited a minute for her sister to finish her business and come out.

But the toilet never flushed. Hope's concern turned to fear as she knocked on the closed door.

"Grace, are you okay?" There was no answer. "Grace? I'm coming in."

She expected the door to be locked, but the knob turned easily in Hope's shaking hand. Her stomach was tied in knots as she pushed the door open, and then her ragged breathing caught in her throat.

"Oh, Grace!" she whispered, tears stinging her eyes.

Grace lay in the bathtub, fully dressed, submerged in red water. Her head was turned slightly toward the door as though to greet the intruder, her eyes half-closed, her face pale with death. A kitchen knife lay on the bathmat next to the tub, along with a few drops of blood that trickled from her wrist as she'd dropped the blade.

Underneath the pounding in her ears, Hope could hear a much younger Grace cry out *Papa! Hope's got blood! Papa help! Hope's got a lot of blood!* Only Hope never had this much blood. Grace was there to save her, but Hope couldn't save Grace. She was already gone.

Chapter Twenty-Four

Eggs cooked on the stove and biscuits baked in the oven, and the warmth of the kitchen was a welcome relief from the frigid air of the bedrooms. The wood stove took the edge off the chill in the living room, but Michael was beginning to rethink his policy of keeping the thermostat set to 58 in the wintertime. He felt the cold much more now than he had when he was younger.

He dismissed these thoughts as he poured his first cup of coffee. What did it matter what the temperature was? The world was cold and empty.

Not a word was spoken during breakfast; no one had anything to say. Hope cleared the table in silence, Paul and Timothy left for work without saying goodbye, and Benjamin wordlessly put on his coat and waited for his father to fill his thermos before climbing into the truck.

It was a normal day.

Michael didn't acknowledge his youngest child's presence next to him as he drove to work. He rarely spoke at all anymore.

Even Joshua restricted his conversation to necessary work-related topics. Michael couldn't muster the energy to berate Hope for her haphazard cleaning or uninspired meals. He didn't question why Timothy and Paul left the house every morning even when they didn't have shifts scheduled. He already knew. Didn't he only go into the house for meals and sleep? He spent the rest of his time at work or in his workshop.

Benjamin had turned sixteen a week after Grace's funeral, but Hope hadn't marked the occasion with pancakes or a present. He was pretty sure either Paul or Timothy had had a birthday since then, as well, which also passed without comment. For the first time in thirty years, Michael had not hosted Christmas dinner. The creche stayed in its box, and on Christmas Day they ate at Joshua and Megan's house. Even Christina and Cassandra, with their playfulness and their fussing over Brady, couldn't penetrate the cloud that hung over the adults.

Michael tried to understand. How could he not have noticed his daughter struggling with demons? What had he done to allow them to enter his house and his family once again? He saw blame in Hope's eyes every time she looked at him, and he didn't try to defend himself from it. How could he? This fact more than anything ate away at him.

Despite the amount of time he spent in his workshop, Michael hadn't made much progress on his furniture projects. His cold and numb fingers were clumsy no matter how hot he ran the propane heater. He prayed instead of working, wrestling with God. But God was not inclined to provide him answers, comfort, or absolution, and Michael could only follow Pastor Kinsley's advice and examine his soul.

But after five months of examining his soul, he'd found nothing. And he was tired.

So tired.

Michael dropped Benjamin off at the house he'd been working on with Joshua, then drove to the office. A blizzard was forecast to arrive in two days, and they wanted to finish this basement remodel before it hit. These small interior jobs were the best they could hope for in the depths of winter. At least there had been a lot of them, with so many people working from home now.

At his desk, Michael stared uncomprehendingly at the pile of paperwork before him. Not for the first time, a wave of despair washed over him and he covered his face with shaking hands. How did he come to this? He hated the dull, empty existence his family had settled into, but he could see no way out of it. It was his responsibility to lead them in the ways of the Lord, but how could he do that when he wasn't sure he was on the right path himself? Michael had always tried to be faithful, but between his divorce, his runaways, and Grace's suicide, he could only conclude that he'd failed God as well as his family.

How could he expect his children to follow a failure?

Two days later Michael sat in the living room, huddling near the wood stove along with Hope and his three youngest sons. The power had been out since early morning. The whiteout was so severe that the electronics store where Timothy worked and the garage that employed Paul were both closed for the duration of the blizzard. The four vehicles parked in the driveway were snow-covered lumps, and Michael couldn't get to his workshop without digging a path. They were all stuck inside until Michael sent his boys out with shovels, and there was no point in doing that until the snow stopped.

He had a generator that ran the kitchen appliances and the well, but it would be hours before Hope began supper. She sat wrapped in a quilt Michael recognized as one Grace had made, her Bible open on her lap but her eyes staring at the orange glow of the wood stove. Michael had instructed his children to use this time to study the Bible and pray, but while his sons were obeying his command, Hope made only the barest pretense of compliance. Michael knew Grace's death had hit her hard, and he'd tried to help her find comfort in God's Word, but his assurances of the Lord's mercy fell on deaf ears. She stared at the floor during evening devotions, glared at the cross during Sunday worship, and only said 'Amen' after table grace because he'd insisted that no one would eat until she did.

It was as though she was responding to the emptiness he felt when he reached out to the Lord, as though she knew he wasn't really getting guidance from God, despite his pretensions. He was losing her, but he didn't know how to get her back. The more he tried to direct her according to the wisdom he'd always known and depended upon, the more closed off she became. He didn't want to fail her the way he'd failed his other daughters. At a loss, he left her to her own thoughts and closed his eyes in prayer, hoping God would reveal His will. Or at least His presence, so Michael wouldn't feel so alone.

He started when he felt someone shaking his arm. He'd fallen asleep.

"Papa, John's on the phone," Timothy said.

"John? What time is it?" The snow outside was still falling, but not as hard as before, and Michael could see the shadowy trees that surrounded the house through the windows.

Timothy checked his watch. "It's almost three-thirty." He smirked. "It's a good thing you didn't let me talk you into switching to VoIP. We would have lost the phone along with the power."

"Progress in technology isn't always progress," Michael muttered as he pulled himself out of his chair.

The telephone was the same one that had sat on his desk since the day he'd finished building his home office. An antique now. Panting slightly from the short walk, Michael settled behind his desk and picked up the heavy black receiver. His skin already prickled from the cold. The wood stove in the living room didn't do much for his office.

"Papa, I heard about the blizzard up there. Are you okay?"

Michael's brow furrowed. Blizzards weren't exactly rare in Massachusetts, and John had never called him because of a storm before. "We're fine. We lost power, but the generator's working and we've got the wood stove."

"That's good."

There was an awkward silence. "Is that what you called for?"

"No, Papa. There's something else." Michael could hear John taking a deep breath. "I've been talking to Joshua and, um, we're worried about you."

Michael's voice hardened. "You've been talking to Joshua about me?"

"Not disrespectfully, Papa. We've been talking every week since...since September."

Michael closed his eyes. Since Grace's funeral. John and Ashley had come to it, though they'd left their children with Ashley's parents.

"And?" Michael prodded.

"We think you should come down to Tennessee and live with Ashley and me."

Michael tried to put cold fury into his voice, but he only succeeded in sounding hollow. "And why do you think that?"

"Come on, Papa. You've done your duty for the Lord. You've supported and raised your children, and now it's time to let us take care of you."

"I still have children at home."

"Timothy and Paul have jobs and are old enough to take care of themselves. Benjamin can live with Joshua and Megan and continue his apprenticeship, and Hope can come down here too and live with us until she gets married."

Michael barked a laugh. "I've already had this conversation with your Aunt Libby. Hope's too old to get married. She's my responsibility until..." He thought about the rest of that conversation with Libby. Until he died. Libby and Jared had moved to South Dakota in November, a few weeks after Nick had finally succumbed to his illness. "She's my responsibility."

"Papa, my congregation's big. Bigger than Church of the Covenant. We've got a few older single men, most of them divorced from unbelievers or widowed, and I'm sure one of them would be a good match for Hope. I've already got someone in mind. And you could oversee the whole thing if you're both down here." John paused, and Michael heard the wind howling outside. "Papa, I'm your son, and I'll honor you no matter what. But I'm also a man called by God, and I know this is what He wants. You've served the Lord faithfully your whole life, and your service will continue, but in a different way that He'll reveal in His own good time. As you think about this, be careful not to be wise in your own eyes. You've done good work for the Lord, but don't let pride be your folly. 'A man's pride shall bring him low: but honor shall uphold the humble in spirit.'"

The light outside was fading, and the gloom of Michael's office made it feel colder than it was. Part of him was indignant that his sons had discussed and planned his future as though he were senseless. But part of him was proud that Joshua and John had stepped up as men.

"Think about it, Papa, that's all I ask. And when you do, also think about the fact that it's fifty-one degrees here right now, and we've had less than two inches of snow all winter."

Michael chuckled. The sound was foreign to his ears, and he stopped. Laughter had no place in his life. "You're selling this pretty hard, aren't you?"

"Yes, I am, Papa. Joshua's told me how difficult it's been for you these last few months."

"John, I appreciate this. I really do. But this is my home. I built this house for your mother, for all of you." His voice choked up. "I've spent the happiest years of my life here."

John's voice was gentle. He probably made a very good pastor. "Are those memories sustaining you now, Papa? When you're in that house, do you think of Mama and the happy times you had together?"

Michael couldn't speak. His chest felt tight, and his head pounded. His house didn't echo with the happiness of his earlier life. It was haunted by the ghosts of those who died or had left. Lucy haunted his bedroom. Grace haunted the bathroom. Jennifer haunted the living room where her shrewish mother overpowered him with the law, along with a tiny, quilt-wrapped bundle he couldn't quite visualize. Joy haunted the chicken coop he'd sent her out to clean so often, and Samuel and Amos haunted the expanded garden that had grown nothing but weeds for years. Hope haunted the kitchen, living flesh and blood, but a ghost nonetheless.

"I'll think about it," Michael said when he could speak without his voice cracking.

"I'm glad, Papa. Should I talk to Duane about Hope?"

"Duane?"

"The gentleman I'm thinking might be a good husband for her. He's a widower with four children. His wife died in a car accident two years ago, along with their youngest. You'd like him, Papa. He's a lot like you. He's an electrician, and he's around forty, so he's not too much older than Hope. I think they'd be good together."

"Go ahead," Michael conceded. Even if he decided to stay in Massachusetts, perhaps it would be good for Hope to have a husband and family of her own to focus on. Maybe it wasn't too late for him to give her that. He'd figure out what to do about his own housekeeping later.

That evening Michael didn't have much of an appetite. Hope served a thick pea soup that sat heavily in his stomach. His head still pounded, and the tightness in his chest had worsened. He got up from the table before everyone else was finished and tasked Timothy with leading the evening devotions.

He piled his bed high with quilts, most of them old with batting sticking out of bare places. Lucy had made them, and Michael still enjoyed being enveloped by something that came from her hands.

His conversation with John had brought back some of those old, happy memories. Rather than dwell on her death, Michael imagined himself being caressed by the same hands that expertly stitched the fabric into its complex design. He remembered when they discovered the true meaning of intimacy, how they had been so careful and gentle with each other on their honeymoon. Images of another honeymoon tried to intrude, and he pushed them away. Lucy had always been his wife, and that other was only a temptress who led him astray for a time. He'd atoned for that by now, he was sure.

The tightness in his chest became a squeezing, and pain radiated down his left arm. Michael barely noticed. He was immersed in memory, and he could almost feel Lucy's presence with him. Her love infused the room, and Michael felt at peace for the first time in ages.

His face was still peaceful the next morning when Hope went into his room and found that he would never wake again.

~

Hope sat motionless in her usual place on the couch near the wood stove, trying to absorb what her brother had just said. Nine of Michael and Lucy's ten surviving children were gathered there, along with Ashley, Jimmy, and Samuel's wife Jodi. Megan had stayed at her own home to watch everyone's children.

Ashley still wore her winter coat and sat as close to the wood stove as she could without burning herself. Even though Michael had been buried next to his wife and daughter the day before, no one thought to raise the thermostat to a more congenial temperature. John sat by her side, his eyes on Hope. Faith, her belly large, sat next to her sister on the couch, clutching her hand as though she were a child again. Jimmy was on Faith's other side, legs spread wide and taking up as much space as Hope and Faith combined. Joshua sat in Michael's chair, and the rest were scattered about the living room.

"Why can't I stay here?" Hope asked, her voice shaking.

Joshua leaned forward. "Papa stopped paying into his life insurance policy when the construction industry collapsed, and he had to use a lot of his savings to get by during those years. Even with the snowplowing he did in the winter, the recovery was weak enough that he was never able to put it back. We have to sell the house, Hope. There's nothing to pay property taxes, utilities, or maintenance."

"Then I'll take my share of the proceeds and set myself up in an apartment somewhere."

Joshua looked uncomfortable. He glanced at John, who nodded encouragement. "You're not going to get any proceeds, Hope. Papa didn't want to keep updating his will every time something changed with one of us, so he left everything to me. He told me to be a good steward and use my judgment on how best to take care of the family. Well, you know how much Papa hated debt. The business took on a few loans during the pandemic, and I need to pay those off first." He grimaced. "I still owe over a hundred thousand dollars in medical bills for Megan. Medevac helicopters, emergency surgeries, and long stays in the ICU aren't cheap when you don't have health insurance, and I refuse to go into bankruptcy." His voice hardened. "Papa taught me to avoid debt when I can and pay it off when I can't, and that's what I intend to do."

John, Samuel, and Amos nodded in agreement. Jimmy looked uncomfortable but said nothing. Joshua shifted his gaze to him.

"We should get enough for this house that we'll be able to pay off your mortgage, Jimmy. I know things are tight, especially with another baby on the way." He smiled at his younger sister. "That should take some of the pressure off and give you a little more breathing room."

Faith smiled back and glanced at her husband. Jimmy looked like he'd just won the lottery as he put his arm around his wife's shoulders. She snuggled against him, judging his mood to be good.

"Thank you, Joshua. I don't know what to say."

"Just take care of my sister."

Jimmy nodded and kissed the top of Faith's head. "I will."

Hope felt sick. Faith had told her Jimmy wasn't always violent, that he tried to be a good man, but Hope only saw hypocrisy and injustice. Jimmy beat her sister and was getting a free house for it, while she...she...

"If you're supposed to be a good steward and take care of everyone, then how come I'm not getting any help for my expenses after you sell my home out from under me?"

John cut in. "You are getting help, Hope. You'll stay with Ashley and me for a while, and I'll arrange a courtship. I've already spoken to someone I know, and he'd like to meet you." He smiled encouragingly. "You'll finally have a husband and children of your own."

Hot fury coursed through Hope's body, and she struggled to keep her voice calm. "I don't want a husband and children of my own. I don't want to move to Tennessee. I want to stay here and live my own life."

Faith squeezed her hand. "Your life has never been your own, Hope. You belonged to Papa, and now you'll belong to a husband. That's the way it's supposed to be." Ashley nodded in agreement, along with John.

"And Papa and I talked about this, Hope, just before he died. He gave me the go-ahead to talk to Duane about you. It's what he wanted."

Hope yanked her hand free of her traitorous sister's grip. She'd expected Faith to be on her side, at least, but only Jodi and, to Hope's surprise, Amos looked sympathetic. She pleaded with them. "No one ever asked me if it's what I wanted. I'm thirty-two years old. I've lived my whole life taking care of someone else's children. I don't want to go to a strange place and live with a strange man and start all that again. I don't!"

Benjamin spoke from his spot on the floor, his eyes full of hurt. "Is that all we are to you? Someone else's children?" Paul and Timothy wore similar expressions.

Hope remembered Grace saying Hope was the only mother she had ever known. Grace wasn't the only one to have no memory of their actual mother. Her fury began to ebb.

"No, Benjamin. I loved you. I still love you all. But I was never supposed to be your mother." She hated the tears that filled her eyes. "I was only a child myself. Joshua, John, you two grew up faster than you should have, too. But you got to choose your own paths. I was given a household to run and eight children to raise when I was only fifteen years old. How many more do I have to raise?"

Her words hung in the chilly air. Benjamin, Paul, and Timothy still looked hurt. Jodi took Samuel's hand, and he avoided meeting Hope's eye. Amos sat tight-lipped next to them, his eyes full of understanding, and he gave her an almost imperceptible nod.

John spoke into the silence. "As many as God gives you, Hope. You've been blessed, don't you see that? You get to raise many more children for the Lord than most women. You've already served this family, and now He's sending you another one. Duane's got four children already, and you'll be able to give him a few more. You can raise his children, and you'll finally have children of your own. Just like you've always wanted."

Hope shook her head and let the tears fall. "I wanted that once, but not now. Not anymore." She pleaded with Joshua. "Don't make me leave, please?"

Joshua sat in Papa's chair, with Papa's children around him, and said the words Papa would have said. "I'm sorry, Hope. This is the way it has to be. Pray that God will change your heart, and with His help you'll find joy in your new family."

"Ashley and I are staying until the end of the week to help tie up Papa's affairs," John said. "You'll ride back to Tennessee with us then."

The matter settled, Joshua turned to the boys on the floor. "Timothy and Paul, you're going to need three months' rent for an apartment: first, last, and security. Find a place to share, and I'll give that to you and a little more to get you started. Take whatever furniture you want from the house." He shifted his gaze to Samuel and Amos. "I don't know how much will be left after that, but whatever there is can go to expanding your farm."

The conversation continued, weighing needs against wants and trying to estimate how much the house and land were worth in the current housing market. Hope stopped listening. Something Joshua said had given her an idea, and she was working on a plan.

She was going to find Joy.

Chapter Twenty-Five

Hope had never driven anyplace more than thirty minutes away, and Worcester seemed terribly far. She was fine on the highway, but once she had to maneuver the minivan onto the narrow, unfamiliar city streets she felt as though she'd never been behind the wheel before. Giant, dirt-encrusted snowbanks left over from the blizzard made the streets virtually impassable. Twice she caught herself just before turning the wrong way down a one-way street, and once she was nearly sideswiped by a bus pulling away from its stop.

She almost wept with relief when she found Damien's Restaurant. Hope pulled into a parking spot near the door and tried to calm her breathing. When she'd turned on Papa's computer that morning, Hope had a purpose. Finding the address of the restaurant where Joy worked after she ran away hadn't been difficult, but now Hope was frazzled from the drive and nervous about what she planned to do. Part of her wanted to put the minivan in reverse, maneuver it back onto the high-way, and go home.

But in a week, it wouldn't be home anymore. In a week

she'd be riding in the backseat of John's minivan, on her way to Tennessee to marry some man who needed a wife to clean his house, cook his meals, and take care of his kids.

She pulled the key out of the ignition and went inside.

It was eleven-thirty, and the lunch rush hadn't begun yet. No one stood at the hostess station, and Hope waited in front of it awkwardly, looking around.

Papa and the rest of the church always spoke of Faith and Joy's time in Worcester with disgust, as though everything about it was sordid and shameful. Faith contributed to that impression, treating her months away as a traumatizing experience she wished she could forget. Hope had expected a seedy diner with unwashed bikers sitting at a long counter drinking coffee and beer, slapping the waitresses' behinds as the harried women bustled about in their miniskirts and aprons carrying trays laden with pungent, deep-fried food.

Instead, she saw a tastefully decorated restaurant and sports bar. The bar dominated the middle of the large dining room, a massive rectangle surrounded by tall stools with black leather seats and wooden backs stained the same dark mahogany as the bar itself. A large flat screen TV hung above each side of the bar, all tuned to the same sports news network. More flat screens were scattered throughout the dining room, ensuring that every patron could see one from wherever they sat. The tables and chairs were made of the same dark wood as the bar, but large windows and champagne-colored walls kept the restaurant's interior light and welcoming. Two elderly women sat at a table by the front window, and one middle-aged man in khakis and a polo shirt sat alone at the bar, a cup of coffee in front of him, his gaze glued to the television screen.

A young woman in black pants and a white shirt was putting silverware wrapped in linen napkins on the tables nearby, and she hurried over to Hope, smiling. A nametag pinned to her blouse read 'Chelsea.' "Table for one?" she asked.

Hope's heart pounded. This was it. "Um, no. I'm uh, looking for someone."

Chelsea nodded and glanced around the dining room. "Well, you must be the first of your party to arrive." She indicated a small alcove with benches. "Would you like to wait for them here or at your table?"

Hope's cheeks flared. "No, uh, that's not what I meant." She paused, trying to figure out what she wanted to say. "I'm looking for—someone—who works here. Or used to work here, uh, about five years ago."

The waitress cocked her head to the side and looked at Hope curiously.

Hope was suddenly conscious of her oversized wool coat with its frayed sleeves and missing button. There wasn't a spare big enough in her button box, or she would have fixed it. Her worn denim skirt hung down to her mid-calves, revealing black knee socks and brown winter boots. Without realizing she was doing it, Hope put a hand to her head, checking her bun for loose tendrils of hair.

"Who are you looking for?" Chelsea asked.

"Joy Wagner."

"I'm sorry, I don't know anyone with that name."

Hope's heart sank and her eyes began to burn. This was her whole plan. If she couldn't find Joy here, she didn't know where else to look.

Chelsea's expression became concerned, and she hurried to add, "But I've only been here for a few months. Let me ask my manager. He's been here forever."

Hope blinked, trying to keep her tears back. "Thank you."

The waitress scurried through a door marked "Employees

Only," and Hope waited. She used her sleeve to scrub at her eyes.

A minute later the door opened again, and Chelsea followed a squat Black man with a round belly and grey in his hair. He wore a blue shirt with 'Damien's' stitched on the breast, and a tie. The lower half of his face was covered by a surgical mask. Not as many people wore those anymore, but they weren't an uncommon sight, either.

"I'm Chris Edwards, the manager," he said in a deep, rumbling voice. What Hope could see of his face was lined but friendly. "Can I help you?"

"I'm looking for someone who used to work here. Joy Wagner?" Hope held her breath.

Mr. Edwards nodded. "Why are you looking for Joy?"

Hope gasped. "You know her?"

"I do. Why are you looking for her?"

"She's my sister."

Mr. Edwards studied Hope for a moment. "If she's your sister, why don't you know how to reach her directly?"

This last barrier was too much for Hope after the fear and grief of the last few days, and she lost the battle with her tears. She tried to speak, but all that came out was a gasping sob. Mr. Edwards murmured something to Chelsea, who ran back through the door while he guided Hope to the alcove and sat next to her on one of the padded benches. Hope was too upset to be bothered by his proximity. He pulled a clean handkerchief from his pants pocket and handed it to her. The overhead light reflected off his gold wedding band.

"I'm not trying to upset you, Ma'am. I just don't give out personal information about my employees to anyone who walks through the door. You understand, don't you?"

Hope nodded and dabbed her eyes with the handkerchief.

Chelsea returned with a glass of ice water and handed it to Hope.

"Chelsea, why don't you go back and finish getting those place settings ready?"

Chelsea nodded. "Sure, Chris." She looked at Hope, her eyes full of sympathy. "Good luck," she said, then walked back to her pile of napkin-wrapped silverware.

Mr. Edwards turned back to Hope and looked at her expectantly.

Hope tried to sort out how much she should tell this man. She decided the less said the better. "We had a falling out, and I want to try to make things right."

Mr. Edwards was silent for a long moment, waiting for more.

Hope shifted on the bench, inching away from him, and avoided his eyes by looking around the dining room.

"What's your name?"

"Hope."

"Well, Hope, Joy told me a little bit about her family. Just a little bit, but enough. She's got a good life now, and she doesn't need anyone coming and trying to mess it up for her."

"I'm not trying to mess up her life. I'm not trying to bring her back. I want to see if..." Hope trailed off, uncertain.

"See if what?"

She had been going to say, "See if she can help me," but she decided that would lead to more questions she didn't want to answer. "I want to see if we can be friends again."

Hope glanced at him and looked away when she saw him peering at her. Her hands twisted the damp handkerchief in her lap.

Finally, Mr. Edwards chuckled. "Families," he muttered. "Okay, Hope, I believe you're not telling me everything, but I also believe you don't mean your sister any harm. I'll tell you a few things you could probably find for yourself on the internet, but I'll save you some time. First, she's not Joy Wagner anymore. She's Joy Bellows."

Hope's head snapped up. "She's married?"

"Uh huh. I lost my best waitress to my best cook." His smile widened when he saw Hope's confusion. "Dan was a cook here for years, and he was building his own catering business on the side. Well, it began to take off. He was a good guy and he left on good terms, so sometimes if he had a wedding or something, I let him borrow some of my waitstaff to help out, if I hadn't already scheduled them. He began asking me not to schedule Joy on days he had an event, and like a fool I did it." He shook his head ruefully. "I had no idea they had a thing going. Anyway, long story short, they got married and she went to help him build up his catering business full time."

"Is she still there?" Hope asked. "Where can I find her?"

"Slow down, Hope. That's only the beginning of the story." His eyes crinkled with amusement. "I never saw such a hard worker as your sister. She was going to school at night, some massage program, while working here and helping Dan grow his business. The lockdown slowed them both down a bit, like it did for everyone, but they turned it around and made it work for them. Now he's back in business and she recently opened up her own. A day spa sort of thing. Dan recommends her to all the brides who hire him. She spends most of her time there now, but she also does the books and keeps the calendar for Dan. That girl is something else!"

Hope had trouble reconciling the person Mr. Edwards described with the sister who always gave her a hard time and hated doing her chores. "Please, Mr. Edwards, where can I find her?"

"'Chris' will do just fine."

Hope had never called a grown man by his first name before. But if it would get her to Joy... "Chris, then. Please?"

"Her place is called Tranquil Oasis. Hold on here, and I'll get you one of her cards." His eyes crinkled again, more than suggesting a wide smile beneath that mask. Hope wished she could see it. The rest of his face was kind and friendly. She smiled back. "Joy and Dan recommend this place for rehearsal dinners, and I return the favor. We don't cater here, so I'm happy to send anyone who comes asking to Dan. We've got a baker and a florist in the loop, too. I'll be right back."

He returned a minute or two later and handed Hope a cream-colored business card with Joy's information written in plum script.

"I hope you're able to work things out with your sister, Hope. Joy's come a long way since I first knew her. Be good to her." He looked Hope up and down. Hope cringed under the scrutiny, though she detected no malice. "And be good to yourself," he added.

"I'm trying," Hope said before she could stop herself. She stood and held out the sodden handkerchief. "Thanks for this. Sorry if I ruined it."

"You didn't ruin it. It just needs to be washed. And you keep it. I've got a supply in my office." He laughed. "You'd be surprised at how dramatic the restaurant business can be!"

Hope thanked him again and exited the restaurant. She was still nervous about seeing her sister after all these years, but she was relieved that Joy seemed to be in a position to help her.

Hope pulled the tattered road atlas out of the minivan door's pocket and mapped her route to the address on the card. Her stomach rumbled, but she was too anxious to eat. She just wanted to find her sister.

∽

Tranquil Oasis was in an old Victorian home that had adapted to the increasing commercialization of the neighborhood over the years. A wheelchair ramp stretched along the side of the building and turned back again, ending on the front porch. A sign hanging on the door read, "We're open. Please walk in." Hope gathered her courage and did what the sign instructed.

Soft music like chimes playing near a waterfall filled the lavender foyer. A large desk had been built against one wall, and behind it sat a young woman with straight black hair and light brown skin. Not Joy.

"Good morning," she said to Hope, then glanced at the clock hanging on the back wall. She laughed sheepishly. "I mean, good afternoon."

"Hi," Hope said, walking over to the desk and trying hard not to stare at the woman's pierced nose. "Um, I'm here to see Joy?"

The young woman typed a key on her keyboard and looked at her computer screen. "Do you have an appointment?"

"No, I'm her sister."

The receptionist looked up in surprise. "Her sister?"

"Yes, I'd like to see her, please."

The woman reached for the phone on her desk, glanced at Hope standing right there, and left the phone alone. She rose. "Wait here a moment."

Hope unbuttoned her coat and looked around while the young woman climbed the stairs to the second floor. Three women were having their nails polished in a large, sunny room to Hope's left. A small parlor served as a waiting room to her right. The foyer opened to a few other rooms deeper in the house, but Hope couldn't see what was in them. The dark antique wood gleamed, and a few vases of jaunty flowers brightened the hall. A stained-glass window at the landing bathed the staircase in red, yellow, green, and blue sunbeams.

A few moments later the receptionist descended the stairs, followed by a woman who stopped and peered at Hope as soon as she came into view. Joy was slim and tall as Hope remembered, but everything else had changed. Her tight brown bun had been replaced by a short, layered mass of red-gold hair. Light from the stained glass window bounced off her large hoop earrings and chunky necklace. She wore a purple v-neck t-shirt over tight black, stretchy pants, and comfortable-looking black flats carried her the rest of the way down the stairs. As Joy got closer Hope saw that her eyes hadn't changed at all. They were still brown, of course, and accented by a little make-up, but they were narrowed and cautious, just as they'd always been.

And then Joy smiled.

Hope walked past the receptionist's desk and met Joy at the bottom of the stairs, an uncertain smile slanting her own mouth. The two sisters stopped a few feet away from each other.

"Hope," Joy said, a little breathless. "I wasn't expecting to see you here."

Hope shrugged, not knowing how to respond. Despite Joy's smile, the caution remained in her eyes.

"Hi Joy." They stood in awkward silence for a moment, until Hope finally added, "You look good."

Joy grinned and twirled, showing off her figure under the tight t-shirt and pants. "Thanks." She looked at Hope's open wool coat, her oversized black sweater, and her denim jumper. "You haven't changed a bit."

Hope's cheeks grew warm, but she said nothing.

"What are you doing here, Hope? I mean, I'm glad to see you and everything, but this is...unexpected."

Now that she'd been invited to say what she needed to say, Hope was unsure of how to say it. Where should she begin?

"Papa's dead," she blurted. "He died last week."

Joy's lips formed a grim line. "How?"

The front door opened, and Hope turned to see a man a few years older than Papa walk in. He was mostly bald and walked with a slight limp, and his winter coat strained to contain his girth.

"Hey, Joy!" he called across the foyer. "I'm here for my twelve-thirty!"

Joy smiled at him. "Hi Frank. Check in with Navya and then go ahead upstairs. Room four. I'll be there in a minute." She pulled Hope away from the stairway to the other side of the foyer. "I have a client, but I do want to talk with you. Can you wait? It'll be an hour."

Frank nodded to the two women as he slowly limped his way up the stairs.

"Sure you don't want room one?" Joy asked him.

"No thanks," he replied without pausing. "Doctor says I need more exercise and I should take the stairs whenever I can. Sadistic bastard." The last part was muttered under his breath, but his booming voice carried it across the hall.

"Well, take it easy. I'll be right up." She walked to the reception desk, Hope following in her wake. "Navya, when's my next appointment after Frank?"

Navya typed a few keys and looked at her screen. "Three-thirty."

"Block out my time until then." Joy took Hope's arm and led her to the side parlor Hope had noticed earlier. "Wait here for me, okay? There's coffee on the sideboard. Help yourself. I'll be down as soon as I'm done with my client."

Hope wasn't used to being ordered around by her younger sister, but she acknowledged to herself that this was Joy's territory. She let the younger woman take the lead, although she was surprised by how easily Joy slipped into that role. "Sure, I'll wait."

"Thanks." Joy smiled at her again and disappeared up the stairs after Frank.

Hope shrugged out of her heavy coat and hung it on one of the coat racks by the doorway. She could use a good cup of coffee.

She located the sideboard at once, and her heart sank as she studied the items it held. Rather than a regular coffee pot, Hope saw a machine with the word 'Keurig' emblazoned on the front. Next to it sat several boxes filled with tiny sealed white cups. One was labeled "Breakfast Blend,' and another 'Breakfast Blend Decaf.' 'Hazelnut,' 'Caramel Vanilla Cream,' and 'French Vanilla Decaf' were also options. At the end were a variety of tea flavors, also in those little cups.

Hope had no idea what to do. She was too embarrassed to ask Navya for help. Instead, she picked up a pitcher filled with ice water and lemon slices and poured herself a glass of that. Her stomach was churning with nerves and hunger, and Hope reasoned that coffee would probably make it worse anyway.

She sat on one of the white couches and noticed a dish of candy on a large square coffee table, along with a variety of magazines. She helped herself to a piece of chocolate, then another. She should have eaten lunch. Hope had seen a few restaurants and convenience stores nearby, but she hadn't thought to bring any money. Papa gave her the cash she needed for the grocery store or the fabric store, and Hope kept that in her pocket and then returned the change to him. She wasn't in the habit of carrying a purse or wallet. Her driver's license lived in the glove compartment of the minivan. As she took her third piece of candy, she realized that was a habit she'd have to change. Hope wondered what else she'd have to change. The magnitude of what she was doing threatened to crush her.

An hour later Joy returned and brought Hope up the stairs to her office. It was a small room with a desk, some shelves, and a loveseat. Joy beckoned Hope to the loveseat as she settled herself in her desk chair.

"How did he die?" she asked.

Hope shrugged. "In his sleep. I don't know from what. He didn't come down for breakfast the day after the blizzard, so I went up to get him, and I found him."

Joy nodded. "He still didn't believe in doctors, right?"

"Right."

"That's another death that didn't have to happen." Joy's eyes narrowed at Hope's expression. "What is it?"

Hope took a shaking breath. She'd never had to tell anyone about Grace. Papa did all the notifying. "There's something you should know."

Joy's face tightened in worry. "Is Faith okay?"

Hope shook her head, then realized how Joy would interpret that. "No, it's not about Faith. She's—" Hope couldn't honestly say she was okay. "It's Grace. She—she died in September."

Joy closed her eyes. "Another illness? Was it Covid?"

Hope wanted to lie, but she felt Joy should know the truth. Some of it, anyway. "No. Suicide."

Joy's eyes popped open. "Suicide! Why?"

Hope pursed her lips. Grace chose death over the shame of having her secret revealed, and Hope had to respect that. She gave Joy the same answer she'd given her father, her brothers, Pastor Kinsley, and all the other people at church who'd asked her that question.

"I don't know."

Joy didn't believe her any more than anyone else had, but Hope stuck to her answer and refused to say more.

"Fine," Joy said, slumping back in her chair. "Anything else I should know? I assume Faith made it home okay?"

Hope nodded, not much happier to be talking about Faith

than she had been talking about Grace. "What happened between you two, anyway? I know you had a fight, but Faith would never say what it was about."

Joy's smile was cold and angry. "I don't know."

Hope took a deep breath, trying to calm herself. This wasn't going how she'd wanted. In some ways Joy hadn't changed at all. She was still the vindictive, sarcastic little girl Hope remembered.

But Hope needed her help. She looked around the office, trying to find a way to move the conversation back to safer topics. "The manager at Damien's said you opened your own business. This is your massage parlor? You don't just work here?"

Joy's eyes flashed and she took on the deadly calm of Papa's voice when he was furious. "It's not a massage parlor, it's a day spa. I'm a licensed massage therapist. And yes, it's mine."

Hope felt her own anger rising. She thought of Frank and her sister's hands running all over his naked body. Massage parlor, day spa, what was the difference? She bit her tongue, though, and tried to find some last, hidden store of patience.

"He also said you were married," Hope said.

"I am." Joy's voice was still too low and controlled.

Hope looked at the fourth finger of her sister's left hand. It was bare. "Where's your wedding ring?"

"I don't wear it at work because of the massage oils."

"And your husband allows that?" Hope couldn't imagine any of the men she knew allowing their wives to take off their wedding rings because of a job.

"Dan doesn't have any say in what I wear or don't wear. It's my ring, my fingers, my body, my job. It doesn't bother him, though, if that's what you mean."

Hope shrank away from the vitriol in her sister's voice. "Joy, I didn't mean—"

Joy stood and cut her off. "Thanks for dropping by, Hope. I think it's time you left."

Panic seized Hope. "No! Joy, I came because I need your help!"

Joy lowered herself to her chair slowly, her body stiff with tension. "Help with what?"

Hope looked away from her sister's gaze. She didn't want Joy to see the naked fear in her eyes. "Joshua and John are trying to marry me off to someone in John's congregation. In Tennessee! I don't want to go. Help me."

Joy closed her eyes, took a deep breath, and shook her head. "I'm sorry, Hope. I can't."

The room lurched, and Hope thought she might throw up the candy she'd eaten all over Joy's loveseat. "What?"

"I can't. I've worked too hard to put all that baggage behind me, and just talking to you for ten minutes has brought it all back. My therapist is going to have her hands full with this as it is. You trigger me, and I need to avoid triggers." Her tone changed, becoming surprisingly gentle and sympathetic. "I don't mean to abandon you, and I hope you can find a way to get what you want. But for my own mental health, I have to ask you to leave and not contact me again."

"Joy, please!"

Joy stood. Her voice was steady, but her eyes sparkled. "I'm sorry, Hope. Please go."

Hope stood on shaky legs. She had worried that Joy might be unable to help, but it never occurred to her that she might be unwilling. "What should I do?"

"If you really want to get out, then get your GED and get a job. You won't make much money at first, so you'll probably have to live with roommates. Craigslist is a good place to look for that." She opened the door to the hallway. "That's the best I can do for you, Hope. Good luck."

Hope's feet were rooted to the floor. GED? Timothy and Paul had GEDs, but Hope had no idea how to go about getting one, and she doubted her brothers would tell her. And who in the world was Craig?

Joy was still standing by the door. "Good luck, and goodbye."

Head down, Hope shuffled past her sister and down the stairs. Once she was behind the wheel of the minivan, the reality of her situation overwhelmed her, and she gasped for air. John and Ashley were leaving for Tennessee on Friday. What was she going to do?

Chapter Twenty-Six

The professor looked at her watch. "Okay, that was a good discussion. Let's wrap it up for today. For our next class, I want you ready to talk about the relationship between the Seventh-Day Adventist Church and the Branch Davidians. Thank you."

As she gathered her notes one of her students approached her. "Professor, I'm not sure I understand why the FLDS is considered a splinter group and the Church of Jesus Christ of Latter-day Saints is the legitimate modern embodiment of Mormonism. It seems like the FLDS is more faithful to the original teachings than the LDS is."

The professor smiled. "That's a good observation, Ryan. But there are important divergences between the FLDS and historical Mormonism, based primarily on which doctrines the FLDS choose to emphasize and which ones they ignore. I have a book in my office you can borrow, if you'd like to read up on the subject in more depth." Her blue eyes twinkled. "Maybe this could be the topic of your final paper?"

Ryan looked horrified. "But I don't understand it!"

"That's exactly why it should be your topic. By the time you finish writing your paper, you will understand it."

Ryan shook his head ruefully. "I'll start with borrowing the book, Professor, and go from there."

"It's a deal. Do you have time to go to my office now?"

"Sure. Wednesday's my light day. Just Pauline Theology at nine-thirty and you at one."

All her notes tucked away in a manila folder, the professor led Ryan out of the classroom door and toward the staircase at the end of the hall. Faculty offices were on the top floor.

"How are you doing with all of this, Ryan?" she asked as they walked.

"With all of what?"

"Graduate level theology. I know a lot of students of faith find an academic approach to their beliefs challenging."

"You are making me question a lot of things I always took for granted. Not just you, I mean. The program. I wonder if anything I believe is real, and that scares me a little."

The professor nodded in understanding. "Challenging our assumptions can be uncomfortable, but it can also be free-ing. A lot of our assumptions need to be challenged. Studying theology at the graduate and doctorate level actually gave me my faith back. I'd lost it because I'd been shown a very limited vision of what God is. But I learned that God isn't limited by our beliefs, and just because we believe something doesn't make it true. The only danger here is if you believe in your own understanding of God more than you believe in God."

They reached the top of the stairs and turned down the hallway.

A young woman sat on the floor across from the professor's office, arms wrapped around her legs and rocking slightly, her head resting on her knees. She looked vaguely familiar, but the professor couldn't place her right away. A former student, maybe?

As she and Ryan walked closer, the woman raised her head.

The professor stopped.

Ryan continued for another step or two, then stopped as well. "Professor?" he asked, turning back to her.

The young woman got to her feet, her hands wiping the dust from the floor off her long green polka-dotted skirt. The light-green sweater she wore looked hand knitted. Her frightened eyes stared at them.

The professor wasn't sure if the young woman was about to bolt or faint.

The professor wasn't sure if *she* was about to bolt or faint.

"Professor," Ryan repeated. "Are you okay?"

She shook her head to clear it. Her fear was irrational. "I'm fine, Ryan." She took one step forward, and found the second one was easier.

Ryan looked at the young woman with open curiosity as they approached.

When they reached the professor's office door, the three stood in awkward silence.

Finally, the professor spoke. "Hello Hope."

Relief softened the young woman's features, though her terror remained. "You remember me."

"Of course I do. Let me get a book for my student, then we can talk."

Hope nodded, and the professor pulled her keys out of her pocket. She was proud that she was able to keep her hands from shaking as she unlocked her office door. Once inside, she found the book for Ryan and handed it to him. "The bibliography in this will be helpful, if you want to research further."

Ryan accepted the book with a rueful grin. "You're not going to let up on this, are you?"

She smiled back. "No, I'm not. I think this is an excellent topic for you to explore."

"I'll think about it," Ryan said, walking to the door. He cast one last curious glance at Hope. "Thanks, Dr. Levine."

"You're welcome," she said, and closed the door behind him. She turned to the young woman standing in front of her desk. "I must say, I'm very surprised to see you here, Hope."

Hope took a shaking breath. "It's been a long time, Jennifer."

Hope couldn't take her eyes off the woman in front of her. It had been almost thirteen years since her stepmother left the family. In some ways she was merely an older version of the woman Hope remembered, with a few changes in her style: her blonde hair was cut to her shoulders and hung loose, and her blue eyes were accented with a touch of make-up. A few shallow lines spread out from the corners of those eyes. She wore a white silk blouse beneath a royal blue blazer, and black dress pants. She held herself with the same confidence Hope had seen the day she'd arrived at Church of the Covenant, alone and uninvited but certain of her place there. But her place there had cost her that confidence. Now it was back. Her eyes flashed in a way that told Hope no one could push this woman around. Given what she was here to do, Hope didn't know if she was encouraged or frightened by that.

Jennifer strode to her desk and sat herself in her chair. "Nobody calls me Jennifer anymore," she said, indicating that Hope should sit in the guest chair next to her. "Call me Jenny."

"I thought you hated that name." Hope sat awkwardly at Jennifer's side. She'd be more comfortable with the desk between them, but this was where Jennifer told her to sit.

"Let's just say it grew on me." She studied Hope.

Hope looked away, afraid Jennifer would see her desperation. She couldn't mess this encounter up the way she did with Joy. She had to get it right.

"Jenny, then," Hope mumbled.

The two were silent for a moment, each waiting for the other to begin. Hope was sure her former stepmother could hear her pounding heart. Her gaze darted around the office, occasionally landing on Jennifer but quickly flitting away.

Jennifer's scrutiny was intense and relentless.

"How did you find me here?" Jennifer asked.

"I remembered you went to Smith, so I called there. The alumni office told me you were teaching at the Boston University School of Theology, so I came here."

"I see. Very resourceful of you. Why did you want to find me, Hope?"

As much as she wanted to, Hope couldn't say the words she needed to say. She'd gotten along well with Jennifer, but this woman was a stranger to her.

But she was also Hope's last chance.

Hope scanned the room, looking for courage or inspiration. She spotted a framed photograph on Jennifer's desk. "Is that Mercy?" she exclaimed, looking at the gangly, smiling girl wearing a navy-blue swimsuit with the words *Brookline Recreation* emblazoned in red. Her blonde hair was tied back in a ponytail. "She's grown up so much!"

"No."

Hope jumped at the sharpness of Jennifer's voice.

"That is my daughter Alexandra. She prefers to be called Alex. I never named her Mercy."

Hope shrank back in her chair and fixed her gaze on the ground, blinking away the tears that stung her eyes. Why did she keep saying the wrong thing?

Jennifer leaned forward. "Look at me, Hope," she said, her voice still firm but no longer sharp.

Hope glanced up, then down.

Jennifer exhaled. "Look at me."

Hope tried, she really did, but she couldn't keep her eyes on the stern, searching face before her.

"I don't know what you're doing here. I don't know if this is some ploy of your father's to reassert control over me or my daughter. But I will not let him or anyone else in your family near her, do you understand? She is strong and intelligent and independent, and I will not let anyone try and tell her she can't be that way because she happens to have a vagina!"

Jennifer's fury struck Hope like a physical blow. No longer able to stop the tears, she tried to lurch to her feet. But before she could get out of her chair, Jennifer grabbed both of Hope's wrists, held her in place, and leaned in. Hope tried to look away, but Jennifer put her own face mere inches from hers, filling Hope's vision just as Jennifer's mother had done in Pastor Kinsley's office the day of the wedding. Defeated, Hope gave up and submitted to the older woman's penetrating scrutiny.

Hope didn't know how long she sat there with Jennifer immobilizing her and gazing into her soul. She only knew she couldn't hide anymore. All the fear, anger, sorrow, shame, and disappointment she'd tried to bury over the years burst to the surface and presented themselves as hot tears and gasping breaths. Her entire body shook, and her face contorted in anguish as she filled the office with keening. She couldn't stop, and she didn't try. What did it matter? It was too late. Jennifer could see what a worthless person she was and would soon throw her out on the street. By next week Hope would be in Tennessee, being courted by some man named Duane, praying he wouldn't find out what she really was, wishing she believed in the one she was praying to. At this point it was the best she could hope for.

Suddenly Jennifer pulled Hope into a firm embrace. Hope bawled into the white silk, soaking it with tears, snot, and drool as Jennifer held her tightly and rocked her back and forth. Jennifer never told her to shush, never told her to calm down, just held her and rocked her and waited.

Eons later, when Hope's wails had tapered off, Jennifer loosened her hold and Hope pulled back. To her surprise, Jennifer's face was red and wet with her own tears. This time Hope didn't look away.

"Oh, Hope," Jennifer breathed. "Look what they've done to you. What can I do?"

Hope's throat tightened again, but before a second wave of hysteria overtook her, she croaked, "Help me! I don't want to go back. Please don't make me go back!"

Jennifer pulled her into another embrace.

Hope held on for dear life.

"You don't have to go back," Jenny murmured. "I'll help you, Hope. I'll help you."

Epilogue

One Year Later

Hope sat on her bed, her back resting against a propped-up pillow, her laptop balanced on her blue-jean clad thighs. Next to her lay a pile of syllabi. She smiled as she typed the assignment schedule for her last class into her calendar. She'd learned the hard way the previous semester that assignments had a way of sneaking up on her, and she didn't want to pull any more all-nighters.

Her calendar complete, Hope checked her email. Lots of spam and a few from UMass Boston, mostly from the administrators' offices or professors. She read through them, proud that she wouldn't have to ask Jenny for help figuring out what they wanted. For months Hope had been entirely dependent on her stepmother to navigate her through getting her GED, applying to UMass, and applying for financial aid. But that hadn't been nearly as embarrassing as those times when Jenny hadn't had time to help her, and Alex had been her guide instead. Hope's half-sister was only one month shy of fourteen, but her knowledge and skill never ceased to amaze Hope. If there was something Alex didn't know, she knew how to find the answer in a matter of minutes.

Alex was equally amazed by Hope's level of cluelessness. Despite all her mother had told her about Hope's family and upbringing, Alex still had trouble comprehending how Hope could have made it into her thirties without ever having watched TV, or gone to a movie, or gone to the mall, or even worn a bathing suit.

And there were other things Alex did without thought that baffled Hope. Like navigating Boston's public transportation service, for instance. Alex could go virtually anywhere in eastern Massachusetts on the MBTA, or the T as it was called by the locals, and did. Hope knew how to get from home to school and back again, but heaven help her if she needed to go someplace else. It hurt her brain trying to figure out whether she was going inbound or outbound, not helped by the fact that her inbound train would suddenly become outbound if she rode it past a certain station. She could never remember which station because it changed depending on the color of the train.

Dorchester, where the UMass Boston campus was located, was too far from Brookline to walk, but Hope preferred walking everywhere else, even if there was a train or a bus that could take her there. The life and vibrancy of the city, while frightening at first, now energized her. She loved to stroll down the street and watch people. She could sit in a cafe for hours, observing the interactions of those around her. Hope remembered how she was once fascinated by the dynamic lives of characters in books, and now she got to see those dynamics in real life. Better yet, the combination of her undergraduate psychology program and her regular visits with her therapist was giving her the language and the tools to interpret what she saw. And she was beginning to experience a dynamic life of her own.

Joy still wouldn't see her, but she emailed occasionally, and those emails were becoming less guarded. Hope had Alex to thank for that. Alex had wanted to know her other half-siblings, so Hope helped her reach out to them. Unfortunately, most of them wanted nothing to do with her. Or with Hope. Joshua and John insisted they had no sister named Alex, and unless she repented of her sins, they had no sister named Hope either. Joshua prevented Hope from contacting Benjamin at all. Faith didn't want to know Alex, and she told Hope she would regret it if she didn't come home and submit to her brothers and her future husband. The last time Hope saw her, Faith was holding her infant daughter in her left arm because her right arm was in a sling. She said she tripped.

Timothy and Paul were sharing an apartment twenty miles away from their childhood home, close to both their jobs, and they rarely attended Church of the Covenant anymore. They weren't cold to Hope, but they weren't friendly, either. They were strangers who were unwilling to become acquainted with their newfound half-sister, or with this new version of their old sister.

Samuel could accept Hope wanting to stay in Massachusetts and could even accept her going to college and becoming independent. His wife Jodi had a college degree and had worked as a nurse in an assisted living facility before her marriage. But Samuel couldn't forgive Hope for going to Jennifer. As far as he was concerned, Jennifer destroyed their family when she forced Papa into a divorce and took Mercy away. Hope could be independent if she wanted, but how could she associate with that woman? In his mind Mercy died the day Jennifer took her, and Alex was a stranger he had no reason to know.

Amos never said a word to contradict his brother, but he did quietly ask Hope for her phone number and address before she left. Since then, she'd spoken to him on the phone a few times, and he even came to Brookline once to visit. He'd been polite to Jenny and friendly to Alex, though a little awkward, and seemed envious of Hope's new life. But when she'd asked if he wanted to move to the city as well, he vehemently denied any such desire. "I love farming," he'd said. "And choices have consequences. The truth doesn't always set you free."

Hope hadn't known what he was talking about, but Jenny had nodded in understanding and told him he was always welcome. He'd mailed them a Christmas card in December. In early January Hope received another card addressed only to her, wishing her a happy thirty-third birthday. Somehow, he'd found out. That card was taped to her bedroom mirror, a reminder that old relationships could change and grow.

Joy was the only one who responded enthusiastically to Alex's overtures. In Alex she had a sister who didn't have all the baggage of their childhood, who was lively and normal and everything Joy had wanted to be when she was young. It was Alex who'd encouraged Joy to give Hope another chance. Alex had gone from being an only child to having two sisters in her life, and she desperately wanted her new sisters to get along with each other. Hope was willing, but she was also patient. With the help of her therapist, she now understood some of the ways she triggered Joy. And some of the ways Joy triggered her. But they were working through it. Their emails allowed them to say what they needed to say without interruption, and gave them time to think through how they wanted to respond. They were considering meeting for coffee in a month or so. Joy said she was doing it mostly for Alex, who would also be there. Hope accepted that, and took comfort in the fact that if it was *mostly* for Alex, then it was a little bit for her, too.

Hope closed her laptop and wandered downstairs.

Jenny was in her office preparing for her next day's classes but came into the kitchen when she heard Hope pulling out pots and pans. "Is it that late already?"

"Yeah. I was just about to get supper started."

"Well, Alex went to youth group right after swim practice, so it's just you and me tonight." She cocked her head to the side. "Do you really want to cook?"

Hope looked at the skillet in her hand. "Not really." A part of her cried out that she was being lazy and selfish. Hope put the skillet away with more force than was necessary. "No," she said. "I don't."

Jenny grinned. "Me neither. Reverend Nicole is ordering the kids pizza. Want to do the same, or would you rather have Chinese?"

Hope grinned back. "I was kind of hoping for Indian."

"Indian? Again? But they don't deliver."

"I'll go get it. It's only a ten-minute walk."

"It's February."

"I'll wear a coat."

"The food will get cold."

Hope rolled her eyes. "We have a microwave."

Jenny threw up her hands in defeat. "Fine, you win. Indian it is."

They walked into Jenny's office to look up the menu online, even though Hope already knew what she was getting.

The lamb vindaloo was delicious.

For the latest news and offers go to
www.AnnGoltz.com and subscribe to my newsletter!

Also, reviews really help authors like me, so please leave a line
or two telling what you thought at Goodreads or Amazon.
Thanks!

Author's Note

In some ways, I feel like this book wasn't mine to write. I did not grow up in a Quiverfull home or join the movement as an adult. My knowledge comes from years of research, but no personal experience.

And yet, when I stumbled across the existence of Quiverfull, I knew I had to write this book.

My career as a parish pastor had just gone down in flames, in part because the congregation and the church hierarchy had forced me to choose between my ministry and my family. I chose my family and decided to put my focus entirely on that. After the toxicity of my last call, I wanted my home to be a haven of peace for myself, my husband, our toddler son, and our infant daughter. But I'm the classic GenX latchkey kid, an only child raised by a divorced single mother, and I had no idea how happy, two-parent households with multiple children and a stay-at-home-mom were supposed to function. So I turned to the internet and googled "how to be a good wife and mother." That's how I discovered the Quiverfull movement.

Dozens (if not hundreds) of women were blogging about exactly this topic. Many didn't use the word Quiverfull, but I began to see the pattern. All these women were religious (not a problem for me, as I'd lost my career but not my faith), and all promised that dedicating yourself fully to the roles of wife and mother would result in a close, happy family. Children were blessings from God, and to be cherished. I'd never felt that growing up, and I wanted it for my own children. I considered talking to my husband about having more kids—a lot more—and I liked the idea of devoting my life to raising them and showing them that they were loved and valued. I dismissed the parts about women being submissive to men because neither my husband nor I had any interest in that type of a family structure. My seminary training gave me a solid understanding of the socio-historical context of the Bible, and the appeals to scripture as mandating such a system didn't convince me. The promises of a happy, loving home, however, did. I felt pulled to this simple, family-focused life filled with love and happiness. According to these blogs, it was mine for the making.

But as I continued to read these blogs and look for more, I began to find testimonies of women who had left the movement. They had very different stories to tell about those simple, family-focused households with traditional gender roles and lots of children. Stories of abuse, control, neglect, and isolation. I realized that something very dark hides behind the promises of Quiverfull: men have all the power, whether they use it wisely or not, and they insist that being a wife and mother is the *only* option for women. Women who are unable or unwilling to accept that life are shamed and scorned, or worse.

I began to reflect on what it means to be a woman. Specifically, I wanted to explore what traits are valued and celebrated in womanhood, what traits are demonized, and who gets to decide.

This brought me back to the last congregation I'd served. I'm sure some of the problems I experienced there stemmed from the fact that I was the first woman pastor they'd ever called, and that gave me less authority in their eyes than they'd afforded my male predecessors. Before that, in my first call, I'd been the only woman pastor on staff along with two men, and I was definitely seen as "less" than my male counterparts. When

I compared the treatment I received in my mainline, liberal denomination with the expectations of women in more conservative and unapologetically patriarchal branches of Christianity, I couldn't ignore the overlap. I couldn't stop thinking about how often women are defined by the men around them, even within a belief system that professes equality between the sexes. It's the men who decide how much power a woman can have, and how she can exercise that power. At least, that's the assumption, whether it's articulated or not.

I began to imagine what it would be like for a girl growing up in a Quiverfull household where that assumption was clearly stated and enforced. I imagined her completely sheltered from the world and unaware of any options beyond what her father dictated. I also imagined what it would be like for a modern woman to choose that life, as I'd been tempted to do, only to discover too late that Quiverfull doesn't always deliver on the promises it makes to women.

And I was imagining all this as the rights of women were being eroded in American society. Hulu's adaptation of *The Handmaid's Tale* has taken off, and protesters regularly chant "Make Margaret Atwood fiction again!" Over the last decade, the specter of Christian theocracy in America has become embedded in the public's imagination. But as I discovered, for many women this is not a potential dystopian future; it's their present reality.

In the end, *Virtuous Women* is an exploration of what makes a woman virtuous, and a celebration of some of the different ways women define virtue for themselves. It also explores the dark reality of contemporary patriarchal Christianity and the high price paid by women who have no choice but to be that version of virtuous. Even without a Quiverfull background, that's a book I am qualified to write. I hope you enjoyed it.

Acknowledgments

There are so many people who helped me get to this point. I'd like to send a special thank you to my early beta readers: Leslie Poitras, Marti Robbins, and Kelsey Gallant. Your feedback helped me find the story hidden behind all those words. Leslie, your medical expertise allowed me to make a few scenes far more realistic than they would have been otherwise. Dick and Ferol Groves, your insights were incredibly helpful during that critical midpoint. Beth Kurth, Nicole Manni, and John Hopkins, thank you so much for feedback on my later versions. I'd also like to thank Heather Doney for her advice on what language and behaviors are believable within Quiverfull communities. Many thanks to Suanne Schafer for her early editorial feedback, and to my developmental editor, Erin Bartels. Erin, thank you for helping me with tightening the prose and cutting out the bits that didn't need to be there. Also, a big thank you to D.S. Davis at Nightbloomer Publishing Solutions for his proofreading and copyediting services. I disagreed with him on a few things, so any errors that remain in the manuscript are mine, not his.

I'm also grateful to the monks of Glastonbury Abbey in Hingham, Massachusetts for their hospitality every time I needed to spend a few days writing in a peaceful environment away from my usual distractions and obligations. Their witness and the Liturgy of the Hours helped to keep me grounded in my faith as I wrote about how religion can be used to inflict such terrible harm on others.

Of course, writing a book is very different from publishing one. I'd like to thank the Women's Fiction Writers Association and the New Hampshire Writers' Project for their resources and guidance on how to get this book into the hands of readers. And I'd especially like to thank Lainey Cameron and her 12 Weeks to Book Launch Success program. I was honored to be part of the founders' round of this great course, and I learned so much from Lainey and the other participants. Thank you for breaking it down into pieces and helping me to make order from the chaos of a book launch.

Finally, I'd like to thank my children for putting up with their 'sibling.' I worked on this book throughout most of their childhoods, and they knew it was as much a part of me as they were. I'd especially like to thank my daughter, Naomi, for finally telling me, "Stop editing and publish the damn book, already!" I did, honey. I did.